Bid Whist at Midnight

Marva Washington

Bid Whist at Midnight

This is a work of fiction. All of the characters, names, incidents, organizations, and dialogue in this novel are either the products of the author's imagination or are used fictitiously.

iUniverse books may be ordered through booksellers or by contacting:

iUniverse
1663 Liberty Drive
Bloomington, IN 47403
www.iuniverse.com
844-349-9409

ISBN: 978-1-4502-7670-2 (sc)
ISBN: 978-1-4502-7671-9 (hc)
ISBN: 978-1-4502-7672-6 (e)

Library of Congress Control Number: 2010918108

Print information available on the last page.

iUniverse rev. date: 09/19/2024

Acknowledgments

A special thank you to my first draft readers: Myra Washington, who with her red pen served as my first unofficial editor; Karen Vereen, for providing insight from a sociological viewpoint; Veronica Vereen, for bridging the generational gap; and Delores for giving it a try.

Thanks to Howard L. Vereen Jr. for his willingness to serve briefly as my intern, and recognition to my Australian editor, Geoff Whyte, for helping me to organize the manuscript.

Dedication

To my late parents, Margaret Ophelia and James Lee Washington, who knew the value of higher education and ensured that their four daughters obtained college degrees.

BOOK I—DAYS OF INNOCENCE

Preface

Where should this story begin? It could begin in the 1950s; things were simpler then. There was a place for everything, and everyone knew their place. Black or colored did not mix with white or beige. Red and other related colors were secured on reservations, while yellow hid in alcoves separated by cultures and traditions. Colors did not run together. Those who would eventually become friends had no way of knowing each other yet, even though they were virtually neighbors, living only a mile or two apart, because the colors were never allowed to blend. For all they knew, they might as well have lived on different planets. The story could begin in the 1960s, when they first became friends, but it would have to end on February 8, 1968. Or perhaps it could begin on that day, but then, how could you begin the story on the day that was to bring an end to the innocence and the fun and the bid whist?

February 1988

"The game is postponed until *what* time?" asked Dorcus in disbelief. Mrs. Fontain was dying—again! She sighed gently. *I am surprised she is still with us,* thought Dorcus. *I could handle starting this game at 6:00 PM when it was originally planned, but midnight? Well, I need to take a nap.*

Grace was the first to arrive. As she approached the door, she pulled out her reading glasses and held her wristwatch up to catch the faint glow from the nearest street light. "Eleven forty-five PM," she whispered to herself. "I haven't been up this late in ages." Her hand moved toward the bell and then froze. She wondered how she would appear to the others, who were probably already inside. She was forty years old and hadn't seen these women since they'd been in their early twenties. "I still look a lot like my old self," she reasoned, patting her face and thighs while still gathering the courage to announce her presence, "but I'm no longer the same Grace X they knew in those days."

She was Grace Pinckney again. The road back had been a long and difficult one. Her once dark-brown, full-blown afro was now permed and spotted with flecks of gray, and the stylish African garb that had once adorned her sleek physique had been replaced long ago, in fact four pregnancies ago, with a loose-fitting dress, or frock, as her mother had used to refer to them, that covered a now rather full frame. "No age spots, thank goodness," she chuckled to herself. Women as dark as her didn't develop age spots, and her face was also relatively wrinkle-free; just a few worry lines here and there. "Let's get this show on the road," she sighed, finally summoning the courage to press the bell.

The chime disturbed the tranquility of this neighborhood of small but well-tended houses, but only momentarily. Nothing rustled; nothing moved. There was no constant traffic like in New York. In fact, there was no traffic at all, and no dogs barked, unlike the neighborhoods where she had lived in Washington DC. The nearby street sign, which was difficult to read, having faded over the years, confirmed this was the intersection of Logan and Beaufain Streets. In the city of Charleston, South Carolina, especially in the historic district, nothing changed without an act of Congress, in a manner of speaking, or at least the consent of the local historic—or hysteric, depending on your point of view—society. If it had been there prior to the war, either Revolutionary or Civil, it was staying put. If it had arrived after the war, it was still staying put. South Carolina took pride in being one of the original colonies in the United States and Charleston in being one of its oldest cities. This was a colored neighborhood, one that, once upon a time, Grace could not have contemplated entering, let alone living in. It was indeed literally colored, because the people who lived there were neither black nor white. They were in that no-man's land of being colored; it was one of those color separation things—black from beige.

Hesitantly, the door opened, and Grace immediately recognized the welcoming smile of her old college friend and card partner, Sardis. "You look just the same," said Grace, wrapping her arms around the slender Sardis and hugging her. "The years sure have treated you right."

Sardis silently motioned for Grace to follow her inside. The white house, with its green-trimmed doors and shutters, was typical of most structures in the low country. It wasn't called low in jest, either. The streets had a tendency to flood during the rainy season, so many of the houses were built well off the ground, on high foundations. A lot of them appeared to have three stories when, in reality, most were only two stories, with a large side porch attached to both upstairs and downstairs.

Houses were separated into functional areas, with the upstairs used for sleeping. There was normally a large bedroom at the front where the parents slept, and then three or four smaller children's bedrooms toward the rear. Downstairs, there was a separate parlor, located directly under the parents' bedroom. This was a large, formal area, reserved for receiving and entertaining guests. Despite being fully furnished, with numerous overstuffed chairs and small tables, it mostly remained unused and was off-limits to children, unless they were sent in to dust the furniture, a frequent task, as there is something about unused furniture that seems to make it attractive to dust. Sardis liked this task as a child, for with her active imagination, one particularly regal-looking high-backed chair had become her throne, from where she would hold court as the queen of her imaginary empire. Sometimes she would dance with her imaginary prince of the House of Logan.

The rest of the downstairs area contained a formal dining room, used for Sunday dinner and for guests, a large kitchen with an informal table and chairs that were used for everyday meals, and in many cases, a small back porch where many family activities were held. The large side porches were rarely used, being too exposed to the streets, allowing for little privacy. The back porch, however, faced the yard area, where there were no prying eyes. Since most of these structures had been constructed prior to the introduction of indoor plumbing, many had outhouses. However, all over the neighborhood one could see where the washhouses had been torn down and bathrooms added. Some were professional jobs, while others looked like hasty afterthoughts, unsuited to the style of the existing structure. Sardis's house had a well-constructed addition, and the entire house had been well maintained.

As Sardis led the way on tiptoe through the downstairs area to the rear, Grace had a chance to take in a lifetime of treasures and secrets the house held. The large dining room table could easily seat six to eight people, which was more than enough for Sardis's immediate family. Grace recalled there were only Sardis, her older brother, her mother, and her father. The rest of the chairs must have been for when they had company. Most of the space that was not taken up by the table was occupied by a very large and imposing china cabinet. Grace guessed this was the good china, for special occasions only, because it looked new, and as far as she could see, not one piece had a chip. It looked as though it had never moved. The third piece of furniture in the room was a cabinet, on which was displayed a fireman's helmet surrounded by prayer candles and pictures of a very handsome man.

Grace had a thousand questions to ask about this shrine, but Sardis motioned for her to follow through the kitchen and into a back room, which had obviously once been a small back porch but was now a converted den. A stairway leading from the kitchen had been added to make access to the rear of the house easier, with doors top and bottom to hide its existence, although the lower door was wide open. Sardis went over to it and gently pushed it almost all the way closed. Finally, she felt able to talk freely. "Mom is very ill. The doctor has been with her all day, and now she's asleep. The doctor said it would be best to put her in a room directly above us, in case she moves or needs help, so I set things up back here so I can listen out for her." Grace nodded.

"How have you been?" asked Sardis, hugging Grace again. Now that both were in full light, Grace noticed that Sardis seemed much smaller than she remembered. She'd always been slightly built, but her thin arms and pale complexion made her look skeletal. Grace feared for her old friend's health. She hadn't contacted Sardis over the years but heard about her mother's constant illness from mutual friends. Sardis's mother had to be at least eighty by now, and since she'd lost her son, and then her husband, Sardis had been her life. The strain of caring for her mother all these years had clearly taken its toll on Sardis. "Bring me up to date while I get the sandwiches," said Sardis as she turned and headed toward the kitchen.

Grace glanced around the room, which was warm and comfortable. The card table had been placed in the middle of the floor, and four chairs were set out around it. Space was tight because, like the rest of the house, the room was stuffed with furniture. A large beige leather couch was pushed back against one wall, while a matching chair sat against an adjoining wall. Grace could see that the couch had only been moved recently, probably to make more room for the card table, because there were indents in the rust-colored carpet where it usually sat. There was a bookcase squeezed into a corner behind a black easy chair that sat facing a television set, and a whatnot stand was squeezed into the corner opposite.

"Your best actress award!" exclaimed Grace as she scanned the whatnot stand. "I heard about this at State." With a hint of regret in her voice, she added, "I'm sorry I missed it."

Sardis reentered the room just as Grace picked up the statuette depicting the masked faces representing comedy and tragedy and held it up to the track light as if admiring a Tony or an Emmy. At first, Sardis's face showed no emotion. She hadn't thought about all that for a long time now. It was just another memento among the other odds and ends of her life that sat collecting dust. The pain of a long-suppressed memory, and of a career that should have been, began to surface, and tears began to well in her eyes. Just then, the bell rang again. Sardis turned away quickly, giving silent thanks for the distraction as she went to welcome her other guest. She had grave misgivings about hosting this game, but the joy of sharing company with her old friends overshadowed her doubts. Her mother's condition flaring up as it had fed her fears, but she'd resolved that she wasn't going to let Mom ruin this for her. She headed quickly to the door before her visitor rang the bell again. She didn't want to wake her mother now.

Dorcus was, well, Dorcus. When she came through the kitchen, she practically bounded into the room where Grace was waiting, engulfed Grace in a warm embrace, and then turned back to Sardis and held her tightly again, just as she'd done when Sardis opened the front door. It was as if they'd last been together just three days ago instead of twenty years ago. Time had been good to Dorcus, who had added very few pounds to her petite frame. Her thick-lens glasses probably weighed more than she did.

"Girl, who are you kidding? Those are not reading glasses," Grace teased after Dorcus tried to tell them that she didn't really need to wear the spectacles. "Those things are so thick you'd probably walk into a door if you took them off."

Dorcus's eyes had paid the price for years of teaching at a private school. It hadn't been her plan to remain in the classroom all those years, but life does not always turn out as you imagine. They all had to face that fact, especially now, as they sat down to play and silently acknowledged the empty chair, for although there were four chairs set out around the table, they knew that Taletha would not be joining them this evening.

II

February 1968—The Protest

As the voiceover used to say at the beginning of the old television series *Dragnet*, it was a Thursday. The city was Orangeburg, South Carolina, a sleepy college town where two college campuses existed side by side. Both were schools for Negro or colored students, terms subsequently replaced by Afro American and then black. South Carolina State, as the name implied, was a state-supported institution that had grown out of Claflin College. Founded in 1869, Claflin was the state's oldest black school, having been set up by the United Methodists to help prepare freed slaves to become full American citizens.

The campus at SC State College had been unusually quiet all day. However, the city of Orangeburg, South Carolina, had not. This was the third day of demonstrations by students from both colleges who were determined to obtain their rights. As in many cities across the South, students were leading the way toward changing the segregationist policies that were in place. The targets in most cities had been segregated lunch counters, located primarily in cheap five and dime establishments. Colored people could shop in the stores for their shoddy merchandise, but seating at lunch counters was reserved for white patrons only. On this day, however, and on the preceding two days, the students had targeted All Star Bowling Alley, an establishment whose management was in the habit of locking their doors whenever they saw black faces approaching and refusing them entry.

❧

Taletha came bounding through the front door of the senior dorm and flew up the stairs to the second floor two at a time, no mean feat for a woman of her size. When she reached the top of the stairs, the others could hear her huffing and puffing all the way down the long hallway. The hall was usually teeming with life this late in the day, but this evening, because of what was going on in town, it was quiet. The strains of Otis Redding's "Try a Little Tenderness," a song that black women really connected with, could be heard from one room, and reading lamps burned brightly in other rooms here and there, but Taletha knew that her girls would have a game going. That was how they always coped with stress. Lately, they'd been playing a lot. "I know y'all didn't start the game without me!" she yelled down the half-empty hall.

"We could have," came a voice in reply. "The way you play, you should be the dummy hand all the time."

"I'll ignore that," she replied as she dashed past their room mumbling something about having to go real bad. Taletha hoped the bathroom on their dorm hall was not already full with other women who, like her, were returning from the protest. She didn't have to ask who made that snide remark about her playing skills. It had to be Grace mouthing off again; Dorcus and Sardis were too polite to make a remark like that. Besides, Dorcus had Anton on her mind, as she often did these days with graduation drawing ever closer. She was hoping for a special gift from him. And Sardis was probably mentally rehearsing for the next student production. She amazed everyone with her ability to focus on so many things at once. Taletha was relieved to find the bathroom practically empty; she wasn't sure she could have made it to an adjoining floor.

The dorm was a relic, one of several classical brick structures built in the 1890s when SC State had been conceived as a land grant school for Negro students. Most of the buildings bore the names of some long-deceased black person, names like Miller, Bradham, Manning, and Bethea and along with the student center and cafeteria, formed a square that was the hub of student life. It was campus central.

The school was still necessary so that the segregated school system could remain intact. However, the design did little for the comfort or convenience of its students. The halls were long, drab firetraps, with each floor containing one bathroom to service anywhere from thirty to forty women. Dorms that had been built to house white students in other colleges, even those erected around the same era, were designed as suites for the most part, with four students sharing a connecting bathroom between their adjoining rooms.

The only thing four students shared at State was living space. Many of the rooms, which had originally been designed for two students, now contained one or two extra beds to accommodate the expanding student body. Juggling schedules and reading and study times was a real challenge.

And of course, fate could be relied on to bring the wrong roommates together. If one or more of them were morning people, there would be at least one who was a night person. If one was quiet and neat, the others would be boisterous and incapable of finding the dirty clothes hamper to save their lives. Coupled with the fact that no two roomies ever had the same class schedules, dorm life was something to be tolerated rather than enjoyed. The dorms were divided according to seniority, with the freshmen girls living in one dorm, the sophomore girls in another, and so on. The senior dorm, where our quartet was now congregated for their game, was the only dorm where the rooms contained no more than two beds; call it seniors' privilege. And by the fourth year, friendships or alliances had generally been well and truly formed, so students could request a particular roommate. The rooms were still small, however, which meant that two of the players had to sit on the twin beds, facing each other, while the other two occupied chairs. Taletha entered the room and sank into the chair just inside the door, filling the entire space.

The bid whist game board was a makeshift item discovered during their freshman year. It was made from a piece of lightweight plywood that a summer construction crew discarded near a dorm and balanced perfectly on the legs of the two players who happened to be sitting on the beds. As long as no one breathed hard or sneezed, they could play comfortably, and on weekends, their games were lengthy affairs, often continuing long into the night.

Sardis was appointed the official keeper of the board and undertook her job with the seriousness the others had intended, keeping it tucked safely under her bed whenever they weren't using it. She always had problems lugging it home on the Greyhound bus for summer break at the end of each year. Even though she checked it as baggage, she had to find a good excuse for carrying a piece of wood home, and she also had to come up with a convincing explanation for the neighbor who collected her from the bus station.

"It's for an art project," she remembered telling the guy at the bus station. "I'm taking art appreciation, so I have to paint a picture over the summer and take it back next year." It worked like a charm. Her mother hadn't even batted an eye when she arrived home with the board, so she decided to follow through on the art project story. First, she found some bright yellow paint and covered the board with it. Then, she painted squiggly lines all over it in different colors. She had a lot of fun, and it gave the board a modern, abstract look. Different friends transported her to and from the bus station each year, and they all accepted her story about it being an art project. She only had to modify it once for a friend who had retrieved her from the station once before. "My teacher thinks I have great potential as an artist, so he hangs it in the student gallery each year as an example to the new students," she told the driver, whose look questioned why she was struggling with the same piece of board as he'd seen the previous year. His puzzled countenance immediately changed to an expression of pride when she mentioned the gallery.

I've got to remember to share this with the girls, she thought, smiling at the driver. They howled with laughter the first time she produced the "object d'art," as they dubbed it, and when she told them about her driver friend, it produced even more laughter. And so, like their games, the board became a treasured tradition.

"Well, I'm here, let's get this game going," said Taletha. She was sitting opposite Sardis, who was her partner this evening. Usually, Dorcus and Sardis liked being partners because there was a psychic connection between them, even though their personalities differed. Dorcus was outgoing, while Sardis was quiet and reserved. Sardis the actress, however, was an entirely different entity when on stage. Taletha was covered in sweat, even though the weather was still a little cool. She was wearing her usual "uniform," a tent-sized dress, and she was breathing hard when she arrived. During the two years of mandatory physical education classes, she managed to lose ten pounds, but since those days, now two years hence, she'd regained those ten and added another ten on top of that.

"I didn't expect to see you this evening. How did things go at the bowling alley today?" asked Dorcus, concern showing in her voice. Taletha was the only one of their group who'd decided to join the demonstration, the first major one in Orangeburg to be fronted primarily by students. It hadn't been planned that way; it had just evolved. As the Civil Rights movement had taken root, business owners began to see the writing on the wall and in many cities, quietly opened their doors to people of color and removed those dreaded "colored only" and "white only" signs. Orangeburg was no exception, and so a group of students assumed they would be welcomed at All Star Bowling Alley. They were wrong. They hadn't planned to enter a civil rights fray, but they couldn't tolerate discrimination. Why would this business owner refuse them service? What did he fear? The students? Losing his white clientele? Losing his standing in the community? The answer may never be known, but the one thing known is that his fears quickly turned into his worst nightmare, and what he should have feared was the shameful mark he left on history.

Although SC State College and Claflin College were located in Orangeburg, they were not really a part of Orangeburg. State students spent most of their days on campus, immersed in academic life. It kept them out of trouble and the administration out of hot water. But there was a new breed of student entering the school. Many had already been exposed to and participated in marches and demonstrations before entering State. They came from a climate of activism, and thus it made sense to them to continue their activities.

Taletha had marched in a peaceful demonstration when her church had gotten involved, demanding that more municipal jobs be opened to colored workers, and she refused to ride on city buses until the segregation barriers were lifted. "Man, all that walking my dogs used to kill me," she said, glancing down at her sore feet, "but it helped my figure. I was a little bitty thing then," she added. The other players, viewing her massive girth, exchanged knowing glances as if to say that the walking should not have ended. When the student leaders called for demonstrators to return to the bowling alley, Taletha was ready and eager to go. She tried to encourage two of the others to join her, but they declined. Neither of them had experienced that type of exposure before, and each harbored her own personal fear about what might happen, either then or in the future.

Dorcus was concerned about the possibility of being arrested. She dreamed of a life as a military spouse and didn't want anything standing in the way. She feared that she wouldn't be able to become the wife of an army officer if she had a criminal record. It would hurt Anton's career, she reasoned. She did everything with Anton in mind. Well, almost everything. "Besides, demonstrating is just not my thing," she told Taletha, not wanting to admit her real concerns. Dorcus didn't like the changes she was seeing in Taletha, so she wasn't willing to do what Taletha was suggesting.

Indeed, ever since Dorcus had returned to the campus from her six weeks of directed student teaching in Beaufort, South Carolina, she felt she didn't even know Taletha anymore. Taletha had become more distant and had grown more militant in her views. Now she went around espousing something called Black Nationalist philosophy: "Power to the people" and "Black is beautiful." Colored people spent half a lifetime trying *not* to be black, and here she was referring to herself and everyone else as black people. The most startling change was in her appearance. She'd discarded the wigs she previously wore religiously and began to wear her own short, damaged hair naturally.

She called it an Afro. Even though she was almost bald from years of covering her head beneath the wigs, she insisted it was the new black beauty. Dorcus shrugged it off as a phase, one she hoped would pass quickly. She, along with the majority of State women, still stuck with the medieval torture known as the press and curl, a system of hair processing. Although it had long been accepted as a method for hair straightening, it could easily have fitted into the category of cruel and unusual punishment. From the time they were young girls, colored women had subjected themselves to this "beauty torment."

Slavery in the United States had left black women with such deep psychological scars and with such a false sense of beauty that this heat treatment system became accepted as normal. It was designed to make hair look straight, long, and silky, just like the glamour magazines, movies, and television commercials said it should. Ironically, these straightening devices had originally been used primarily by white women, until the turn of the century, when they were adapted for black use. The twin metal devices, a straightening comb and a curling iron, could be heated to temperatures rivaled by the old western branding iron. An open fire wasn't normally used but frequently served as a substitute when the little stove specifically designed to heat the implements was not available. After the comb was heated to the point where it was red hot and smoking, the hair was sectioned off a little at a time. Each section was then slathered with a ton of grease, or other oils designed for the process. Then, the comb was placed as close to the scalp or the nape of the neck, often referred to as the "kitchen," as possible, and pulled until the hair became stiff and straight. If the person flinched, or if the practitioner had a less than steady hand or a sadistic streak, the results were often painful and ugly. The finished hair was stiff and usually weighed down by a ton of oil.

The curling iron was the final torture. During the heyday of the Shirley Temple curl, every young colored girl sported stiff, spiral curls for special occasions, having been tricked into submission with the promise that she would look just as cute and lovable as her blond movie star counterpart. In the hands of trained, licensed beauty practitioners, undergoing the process was tolerable, but in most college dorms, where it was done by amateurs under less than ideal conditions, the iron comb and curler became objects of mutilation, both of oneself and one's "sisters." On weekends, the dorm hallways were frequently filled with the mixed scent of perfume, frying hair tonic, and burnt hair and flesh. The old dorms' wiring systems were so fragile that only a hot plate was allowed for heating the devices. These could never quite generate the same heat as the little iron stoves, which may have been a blessing in disguise. The hair was never permanently altered, and so every week or so, the process had to be repeated. It didn't handle rain or sweat at all, but colored women wouldn't dream of letting their hair get "nappy," so they continued to submit to this draconian process week in and week out. After noting Dorcus's shock upon seeing her wearing her hair natural in public for the first time, Taletha proudly pronounced, "You should try it. It frees me from a fake beauty standard and is a statement of who I am as a black woman." By the end of the school year, a few more women had joined her in the hair revolution, including Grace.

Grace thought briefly about joining the demonstrators but had too much to lose. She was on a work scholarship, and if she left her job at the cafeteria to join the demonstration, she would jeopardize her only means of support and wouldn't be able to continue. She was torn, however, because she, too, was becoming more sensitive to civil rights activity. Her long time steady, Willie, had begun to enlighten her about the Black Power and Black Panther movements and other activism going on in New York, where he now lived. She was astounded to hear about activism in northern cities that she always thought of as being open to equality. All her life, she heard about the North. There were no "colored only" and "white only" signs in the North. Everybody worked side by side in the North, and colored people were paid the same as white people. The North was a mysterious paradise, a place where every southern person of color aspired to go. Now, Willie wrote her letters about strife and conflict even in the North. She had no problems identifying what they were fighting and marching for in the South, but was this the same fight in the North? Was the fight for equality the same all over, or was the southern fight different from the northern fight?

She also thought about her mother's efforts to get her into school. The administration was not happy with students becoming involved in the local unrest. They had an obligation to the parents, and to the state, to keep things orderly, and they were determined to meet it. They did not wish to bite the hands that fed their coffers, so they made it very clear that work study students would not remain employed if they joined the demonstrations. Grace did *not* want to have to explain to her mother why she would not be graduating. It was only February, but her mother already had a new dress and shoes on layaway for the May event. "I can't go, Taletha. It would break my mother's heart if I don't finish school," she said when Taletha cornered her while she was working in the cafeteria one day.

"You have to stand up for your rights sometime," Taletha replied, somewhat miffed at being turned down by the second person she'd counted on for support. "Just explain to her that when one black person gets equality, we all get equality. She should ..."

"Taletha, I'm sorry. I can't do it." Knowing the futility of starting a volatile argument over rights and wrongs in the middle of the evening meal, Grace returned quietly to her task, leaving Taletha to continue her exposition with another student. All the same, she hoped that the marchers would enjoy success.

Taletha did not invite Sardis. Despite all her bravado and posturing about rights and equality, she did not, could not, and would not give Sardis an opportunity to be a part of the struggle. Even though Taletha had finally accepted Sardis as a card game partner, although not by choice, she still had a hard time warming to her. If Dorcus hadn't insisted on letting Sardis play, Taletha would have continued to shun Sardis, just as all the other girls had done. Sardis would have joined the demonstration if she'd been asked. She had to show that she belonged. She needed to fit in, something she'd never been able to do in her home town. She thought she would fit into the culture at school, but she hadn't been accepted there either, until by chance she got into a bid whist clique.

Bid whist was an extremely popular card game that the entire student body played at one time or another. Playing cards was a natural pastime on weekends, especially following the weeks of mid-term and final exams. It was down time, and students from out of state, or those who simply had no desire to leave the campus, could be found huddled together in clusters here and there over any object remotely resembling a card table. State harbored a family atmosphere, and one or two of the dorms remained open throughout the school year to accommodate the few foreign students who lacked the financial means to travel back and forth to their homelands and had no family members to assist them while they were in the United States. Most of the students had no means of personal transportation to leave the campus. Having a car was a privilege for those seniors who could afford it, but very few could, and so, during down times, they had to find ways to entertain themselves. Card games fit the bill, and bid whist was the game of choice.

No one knew where the bid whist tradition had come from, or why it was preferred over, say, poker or blackjack. Was it because of the skill involved? Or was it, as some had suggested, the closest thing to gambling without actually gambling, which of course was strictly forbidden? Students played virtually everywhere. The student center usually had two or three tables of games going, with new players dealing in periodically. Co-ed games were allowed in the student center and in some common dorm areas, and romantic alliances were formed over a deck of cards. Certain dorm rooms on each floor hosted card games that continued until all hours of the night, as long as the players held out. The freshmen and sophomore dorms had strict lights-out rules, which meant the games were supposed to finish by 10:00 PM, but there was always a means of getting around every rule, and those who were determined to play until late into the night knew how to stuff door cracks so tightly that flashlight beams would not betray any activity to hall monitors. Floor monitors, however, were invariably wise to their actions, but left them alone, knowing that those involved would pay a heavy enough price the next day as they fought to stay awake in classes. Dorms even had tournaments, with floor pitted against floor, or one dorm challenging another. No money was involved—just bragging rights. The strongest players were almost as well known as the best football players, and since the game was played in pairs, good players sought each other out as potential partners. The right pairing could potentially rule the campus for all four years of their residence, but like the fastest gun in the West, they had to accept all challengers.

The student center was usually the place for the challenge games, and all other play would be suspended for the duration of the challenge. If the winners belonged to a certain fraternal group, you could bet that organization could look forward to a strong pledge line the following semester. Just as stronger players were sought out, weaker players were shut out. It was far better to be known as a non-player than a weak player. Such was the importance of bid whist.

The Sardis–Taletha–Dorcus–Grace game was unusual because, during the four years they were at State, the group never changed. Even when one or more of them was absent for some reason or another, they dealt dummy hands in place of the missing players. They had a rocky beginning but grew to respect one another and to like each other's company. They shared each other's personal trials and growing pains, the boyfriend sagas, including the one that nearly split the team, and each one's rapidly changing philosophical views on life. They listened to each other collectively and individually and accepted changes, such as Taletha's new "do."

Grace sparked no end of conversation when, one day during their senior year, she announced out of the blue, "Henceforth, I will be known as Grace X," stopping the game dead. She liked dropping bombshells like this in the middle of the game, rather than before they started or after they had finished. She felt that it provided her with a psychological edge over her opponents, until she discovered that it also affected her partner's concentration. Nonetheless, she continued to pull these stunts, so the others simply learned how to deal with it.

"Girl, what are you talking about?" said Dorcus, laying her cards aside. "Is that what you plan to have printed on your diploma?" she continued, to the amusement of the others.

"Go ahead and laugh. I do not want to be known by that slave name of Pinckney."

"Slave name?" said Dorcus.

"Willie!" said Dorcus, Sardis, and Taletha in chorus.

"So what?" said Grace defensively, resuming play. "He's changing. He read ..." She scanned their faces before continuing. "Yes, he can read. He went to school up North, remember? His schools were far superior to ours, so he learned to read, and he knows a lot. He can get books up there by black writers that they don't even sell in SC because they don't want us to know about them. But he's been sending them, and I've been reading them too."

Again in chorus, the trio, without even glancing up from the table, responded with a very church-like, "Uh-huh!"

"He read about the teachings of Brother Malcolm and sent me the book. So now I call him Willie X, just like Brother Malcolm calls himself Malcolm X. None of us knows our true names. I know that Pinckney was a master's name. You know of any Africans with the name of Pinckney?" Then, as an afterthought, she asked, "Do you know any Africans at all?"

They all roared with laughter at the barb. While Grace was speaking, they thought of other changes that were infiltrating their world. Besides Taletha's "nappy do," as Dorcus insisted on calling her afro, people were beginning to speak of each other as brother and sister, as if somehow all black people were twins who'd been separated at birth. "We may not know any African people personally, but all of us are related, so when I say brothers and sisters, it includes all black people, worldwide," Grace droned on.

Sardis shifted in her chair, hoping that no one had noticed, not wanting to draw attention to her uneasiness. She was having a really hard time with all these new philosophies, because it placed her in the middle of a racial division that even colored or black people still hadn't sorted out for themselves. Sardis had already spent most of her twenty years just being accepted as colored. Now, the shift to black created a conundrum. Grace weighed in again. "We're all colored with something. Black expresses not only color but an attitude. I name myself. Nobody had to tell me about me."

"Willie," the Greek chorus chimed again. However, the passage of time was to prove that Grace and Willie had their fingers on a pulsating surge that marked the beginning of an era. The changes were coming, whether they liked it or not.

For now, though, bid whist occupied their minds. Their regular games had begun in Sardis's room, which had become Sardis and Dorcus's room in the second semester of their freshman year. Since then, they'd been permanent roommates. Theirs was a special friendship. If it hadn't been for Dorcus, Sardis would never have had a second semester that year. Indeed, she may not have had a college career at all.

"Who is that white girl?" was the first comment Sardis heard when she stumbled through the doors of Bradham Hall, wondering how she was going to get her suitcases and steamer trunk up two flights of stairs. Unlike most of the newly arrived freshmen, she had no family member on hand to help her, and the taxi driver who brought her from the bus station to the dorm was now well on his way to his next fare. Eventually, some very congenial young men came to her rescue. However, their gallant efforts ignited a heated backlash from the other freshmen girls, who were consumed by jealousy. "I know she isn't coming to State," said one of them, her voice dripping with venomous derision.

When Sardis reached her dorm room, she waited anxiously to see who her roommate would be. Always a neat freak, she immediately went to work unpacking and putting everything away. She did not want to make a wrong impression on whoever would be occupying the second bed. Having lived at home with only one male sibling, she'd never had to share a room with anyone and looked forward to the new experience.

The hallway was bustling with activity, meetings, and greetings as students continued to arrive on this, the Sunday preceding freshman week. They would have an entire week to become oriented to campus life before assuming their lowly status as college freshmen. Even though Sardis was shy, she ventured out into the hallway and approached every open door with a cheerful hello. However, her greetings were met with stony stares and silence. After her fifth or sixth attempt at striking up a friendship, she retreated quietly to her room to await the arrival of her roommate. In the lonely world of the freshman, a roommate was very welcome, even if you didn't end up becoming the best of friends. She waited and waited, until the dorm director, a wise woman in her mid-fifties, finally arrived to confirm what Sardis had already begun to suspect; her roommate had asked for a reassignment. Her fellow "home girls" had met with Rommie as soon as she'd walked in the door of the dorm and issued her an ultimatum.

"You roomin' with a 'white' girl," the ringleader warned. "If you wan' friends, you better get yourself away from her. Ain' nobody gonna visit that room. We already warn people. We gon' make her go home fas'. This *our* school. She think she colored, but she gon' have to go somewhere else."

No one else dared defy the clique by moving in to Sardis's room, even though the freshman class was a large one this year and there was a shortage of bed space. The larger rooms had extra beds installed, with three girls sharing closet space designed for two people. Attrition would eventually ease the problem, but right now, things were tight. The dorm director faced a dilemma. Should she move Sardis to one of the three single-bed rooms, which were located directly under the stairway of each floor? It would free up two more beds, but after contemplating the situation, she decided against such a move. The director had detected a fragility in Sardis that told her she wouldn't be able to handle the isolation. Besides, Sardis was the victim, not the problem. Although Sardis would be alone in the room, she would stay on the main floor. The director decided that, instead, she would make the others live with their decision by putting the complainant into a room with three of her friends where they could joust with each other for space. The director hoped that either the jealousy would subside or someone would have the courage to share Sardis's room.

The dorm director was an experienced woman, now entering her thirtieth year of guiding freshman girls in their first foray into independent living, and could tell as they were moving in who would make it to their senior year and who would not. She knew the ones she had to watch, either because they were so fragile they might hurt themselves or they were so strong-minded they might hurt someone else and themselves. Every year, one freshman girl drew the ire of the others for no reason and was made a target for ridicule, either because of her failure to conform or for being too smart, popular, outgoing, or whatever reason. When Sardis walked through the door, the director immediately recognized this year's sacrificial lamb. Sardis was being shunned by her fellow freshmen because her pale skin and long, straight, sandy-colored hair looked, according to them, too "white."

Sardis was hurt by their attitude, but she was determined not to let it show. She held her head high but longed for the acceptance afforded her darker-skinned sisters. Her light skin had been both a blessing and a curse all of her life, and she hoped things would be different once she left the closed society of Charleston, but now they were worse. There, she could hide within her false, protective environment, whereas here, she was exposed. She hoped to endure, though, for while she hated all of it, she could not go home.

Marva Washington

February 1988—Mother's Room

In the dark room upstairs directly above the players, voices were seeping through into the barely conscious mind of Eartha Fontain. Dark rooms had always held not mystery but pain, and this particular room was unfamiliar to her. Was this her house, or was she somewhere else? And those voices—whose were they?

III

The old friends greeted each other warmly, but a strange atmosphere soon settled over them. They couldn't ignore the fact that a lot of time had passed. Should they catch up on each other's lives? They wanted to, but at the same time, they did not want to step into some of those dark spaces—the places where Anton and Byron and Willie resided. There was much from a lifetime ago that they did not wish to visit anymore, so the three women sat silently at the table, ready to play. Sardis left the door ajar so she could hear if her mother stirred. "How come we always end up playing at this late hour, and in Sardis's room?" said Dorcus. It broke the ice. They all looked at each other and snickered, because she always asked that question whenever they ended up in Sardis's dorm room around midnight. During their school years, midnight was when they had time to spare. What the others didn't know, however, was that if she hadn't been included in those games, Sardis would have dropped out of school at the end of her first semester. Prejudice is a difficult thing to overcome, especially among your own kind.

Sardis, Dorcus, and Grace all called Charleston home, but they lived in three very different worlds. Dorcus's house was on Duncan Street, near downtown, but not in downtown, and Sardis lived downtown, but not in the downtown area, while Grace lived in no man's land in the Alley, one of two enclaves that ran off Duncan Street. Each occupied a world that was the same, yet not the same: same race, different culture; same color, different hue; same people, different class. Sardis lived at the corner of Logan and Beaufain, in a world where, once, neither Dorcus nor Grace could ever live. She had grown up "privileged" in the minds of other colored folks in Charleston. It didn't make any difference whether your skin tone was black, brown, or tan; everyone was colored in a world that was divided into "white" and "colored" signs. However, among those of a darker hue, Sardis and her family were referred to as "high yellow." Many were direct descendants of their white slave masters and carried their features and traits. Some even crossed the color line and were able to pass for white should their circumstances dictate that they do so.

Sardis had never felt privileged, however. She'd felt as if she were an outcast, unable to enter a black world and made to feel guilty about entering a white world. She'd been forced to do that once in order to get a job, and had spent every day in fear of being discovered. All she wanted was some place where she would fit, where she belonged. She'd known that attending an all-black school like State would pose some challenges, but she hadn't realized what a nightmare it would be. As much as she wanted to break the bonds that held her in her tiny community, she wasn't prepared for what that first year out of her enclave would throw at her.

Charleston was segregated; that was a given. But this premier city, the home of Ft. Sumter, the pride of the Confederacy in a State that still flew the Stars and Bars, commemorated Confederate Memorial Day, and took pride in being the first to secede from the union to protect their rights, was also separated. The unofficial dividing line was Calhoun Street, named after a favorite son, old John C., who'd represented the state well as a congressman, senator, secretary of war, and vice president under Andrew Jackson. His statue had been placed on top of a pedestal that seemed about a mile high, and now there he stood overlooking the heart of the city, forever remembered for his determined defense of the institution of what else but slavery.

Behind him stood the fortress-like walls of the Citadel, with its yellow gravel parade grounds. The Citadel was segregated not only by race but also by sex. That institution eventually moved to a different location and opened its doors, not always willingly, to all races and to women. The old building housed federal offices for a while, until it was eventually closed for public use. Across the street was another landmark, a hotel named for Revolutionary War hero Francis Marion. The South revered its heroes, unless they were colored.

The main street over which the statue of old John C. presided was King Street, a fitting name, since the shopkeepers and merchants tended to rule and reign. In downtown, surrounding King, was the old, old town, where retail outlets were housed in stately old buildings. Their merchandise was primarily high-quality imported goods. One store might specialize in European fashions, while its sister store, often owned by the same family, sold domestic imports from New York. Many of the stores were owned by wealthy Jewish merchants who, even though they made a good living, were excluded from the cream of Charleston society because they were Jewish; hence further division. These stores catered primarily to the white upper class, the old money set along with the doctors and lawyers who occupied the large mansions facing the Cooper River along the Battery. The Cooper River and the Ashley River were the two primary waterways surrounding the Charleston peninsula.

The financial district, courts, art galleries, theaters, and the College of Charleston were all located in the old downtown district. Charleston boasts of many "first of a type" structures or "oldest surviving" and/or "longest in continuous use" facilities, and you could rest assured that the majority of black faces to be seen were those of housekeepers, nannies, chauffeurs, and butlers. Even the five and dime store boasted of its well-being, with highly polished hardwood floors. It was among the first to be targeted during the civil rights era, not only to open the lunch counter, but also to open employment opportunities. Prior to the '60s, however, the downtown merchants had no need to rely on economic input from the black population, so why change? They had no desire to hire colored clerks and thus did not do so until years later, when they were forced to comply with civil rights legislation.

Going past dear John C. to uptown, the environment on King changed dramatically. About a block or so beyond his pedestal was Amar Drugstore and Pharmacy, an intriguing, somewhat intimidating place that fired children's imaginations. The entrance was through a set of darkly colored stained glass doors, and once inside, you found yourself in a land from another time—one of fairy tales and wizardry. Its shadowy interior revealed a quaint old store with wooden floors, a throwback to the days of the old apothecary shops with their powders and mortar and pestle. It was a place where you could still buy a headache powder instead of a tablet, and small bottles and vials lined the shelves along each wall from top to bottom. It served as the landmark for the uptown stores. Beyond Amar were furniture stores with excellent layaway plans that advertised on black radio stations that they, "Don't turn nobody down!" The buildings were old, and most were weather worn. Forget stately facades; these were crude, glass-fronted structures advertising poorly constructed knockoffs of the latest styles from New York. Also present were the five and dimes with their cheap tiled floors, where a nickel purchased a bag of candy or a cone filled with soft, yummy vanilla custard. Some merchants even hired colored clerks, if they were of a lighter hue with a good education. It didn't take much imagination to realize that this was the heart of the Negro community. This was uptown Charleston, and Dorcus and Grace were very familiar with this part of the city.

To enter Sardis's world, however, you had to go downtown again, where there were colored folks who lived in the shadows of downtown, residing in their own "high yellow" commune, hidden from those deemed too dark to enter and invisible to the white community surrounding them. They were sometimes called mulatto or octoroon, depending upon the amount of white blood or white features they had. There were also a few wannabes who slipped into the mix, pretenders in light pancake makeup, conked hair, and bourgeoisie attitudes. They were shunned by whites, who were loathe to admit and accept these cousins, and were often outright despised by blacks, who thought of them as privileged, or holding "better than thou" attitudes. Some were indeed privileged to an extent, because their genetic makeup afforded them the opportunity to slip back and forth between the two worlds at will, pretending to be any race or no race at all. It also provided an economic advantage by conferring on them the luxury of upper middle-class status.

Most of them embraced the Catholic faith, which was another entity that was foreign to most people of color, whose first exposure to western religion was primarily through white Protestant missionaries sent out to evangelize Africa. During and immediately following the period of slavery, some of the Protestant sects were further transformed and redesigned into derivative denominations that fitted the emerging black American culture. The most prominent denominational offshoot was the African Methodist Episcopal Church, known collectively and nationally as the AME Church. This was the church of Dorcus and her family. "It is a proud part of our history seldom told," her dad, the preacher, thundered from the pulpit. "The first bishop, Rev. Richard Allen, would not be denied. We are a people of a great heritage." Dorcus knew this sermon by heart. Once her father got fired up on Sundays, they knew they were in for a long day.

The sect had been founded by former slaves after Bishop Allen, as he was formally known, had been denied the opportunity to worship in St. George Methodist Episcopal Church in the city of brotherly love, Philadelphia. The resulting church was the first major religious denomination in the western world whose roots were planted in social soil, rather than that of theological differences, and so Protestantism, the natural outcome of a protest movement against the Catholic Church, became a perfect fit for most people of African descent. The masters could keep the religion of kings and queens, while the descendants of slaves found their voice and strength in the congregations of the dissenters or protesters. The "high yellows" for the most part adopted the master's religion. This may have had something to do with their exposure as a result of their close proximity to their masters, or because of their interaction through a private Catholic-sponsored institution by the name of Immaculate Conception School, or ICS for short. Either way, this symbiotic relationship served both the "high yellows" and the Catholic Church well.

ICS was a strange entity, an enigma born out of necessity. It was created as a school for the colored population, while its counterpart, Bishop England, was for white students. The church's intentions were good; their desire was to provide a unilateral parochial education for everyone, both colored and white, not superior for one race and inferior for the other. However, their attempts, though noble in theory, created a further schism by inadvertently producing an internal division within the black race. The school sat on Cumming Street, right on the boundary of where uptown began, where the colored population resided, but most were too black to enter. A red brick structure, it was surrounded by a well-constructed stone wall topped by wrought iron. The gates were hardly ever opened, which, to those on the outside, made it appear sinister, mysterious, and evil, and lots of stories, mostly the products of children's vivid imaginations, circulated about the black-garbed, stern-faced nuns and their uniformly attired charges. It was Sardis's birthright that she would attend ICS.

The voices were not matching Eartha's visions. In the pitch-black room, she had no concept of time. Was this still 1988, or did it become 1918—no 1923? That's it, because she ... she could see her parents, although they could not see her, because she had secreted herself in the dark closet. Little Eartha often hid in closets. She hid because she was her mother's shame, and she hid to keep the sun away, because her mother told her to do it. She was not fair-skinned like her two elder sisters, so Mother did not want her to be seen. Therefore, the dark became her friend, and she learned to see everything and not to be seen. She also heard everything.

*"How could she **not** be admitted to ICS? Both of her sisters got in. Eartha has the same amount of intelligence. We never missed a payment to the school. I was sure they would take her." It was her mother's voice. She was not happy. Eartha wondered what she had done to displease Mother.*

"Dear, she has darker skin. You know how they are." This was her father's voice trying to appease her mother's anguish. "Now we have to figure out what to do. Maybe Avery? They have a really good academic program." Father was Eartha's friend. He always found Eartha when she hid. This made her feel special. He also made her mother treat her better, but this time her mother would not be consoled.

"This is your side of the family," she spat contemptuously. "Let's send her to Aiken. Grandmom might be able to work her magic." Her father's protests fell on deaf ears, and in the dark confines of the closet, her five-year-old mind could not comprehend what was happening. All she knew was that neither of her parents was happy with her anymore, and soon she would be going away.

IV

Sardis's parents knew she would have no problems being admitted to ICS. They had some initial concerns about her older brother when the time had come to enroll him, because he was a few shades darker than she was. However, they found that the school had relaxed many of their unwritten admission policies and secret requirements. In the past, families had been torn apart, and sibling rivalry and jealousy reached fever pitch, when one child was accepted into the school and the other was not. These practices did not bode well for an institution whose existence was predicated on promoting harmony and keeping families together, and so it came to pass that the church hierarchy determined that if one child in a family was accepted, the others would also be admitted in their turn. Even though the student body still did not reflect the general colored population, at least a few darker-hued, but still not black, children finally took their place alongside their lighter siblings. They also valued the offspring of their alumni, which paved the way for Sardis's brother's admission.

Even with these changes, however, it was not lost on the overall population that ICS's existence depended on the high yellow community. Or more to the point, the high yellow community was able to continue to exist as a separate entity because of ICS. Being admitted was a status symbol, a sign of upward mobility, that they had made it. Within this population existed a well-educated, primarily professional class of people. Most of the doctors and lawyers and civil servants in the community were products of ICS. Did the school really exist solely for their benefit? Had it helped to create this class of people? Did it perpetuate an odd form of Jim Crow within the race itself? Or had it given up on educating the masses in order to concentrate on the privileged few in order to benefit from their financial and influential status? Did the school intend to support further division, or were the populace happy to use it as a means of self-perpetuation? Finding answers to these questions would have provided ongoing job security for an army of sociologists. Much remains unknown, but what is known is that it served its purpose in the racial history of Charleston. The division made it very difficult for people of color to know, trust, and accept each other. It ignited and fueled feelings of jealousy and perpetuated self-hatred, and it made Sardis's transition into a college like State all the more difficult.

Sardis, like many of her fellow ICS alumni, was expected to eventually move on to a college located anywhere except South Carolina. Many moved to large metropolitan areas like New York, where they blended into the general population. New York and Sardis would have worked very well together, not only because of her skin color, but also because of her talents. However, she ended up attending State, the decision being made for her by circumstances beyond her control. If she'd been able to develop her natural talents, Sardis would have majored in theater and minored in acting, for she was made for Broadway. However, State did not offer a major in theater or performance. If she had a choice, she would have found a school where she could hone her craft, but by a fluke, she was granted a full scholarship to State, and so it was either that or no college at all.

State had been set up as a land grant college back in 1896, with a mission to train colored students to become teachers and farmers. The limited training was just enough to ensure that once they graduated, they would be able to perpetuate the separate and unequal Jim Crow system. It was, at best, a higher form of high school. By the time our four friends entered the institution, however, the core curriculum had grown extensively from those early days, and while most performing arts were still not offered as major study areas, subjects such as music and art appreciation had been added as mandatory electives. Eventually, music education and performance broke through to become major study areas. Other artistic study areas took a bit longer to attain higher status, because colored people had to be convinced that they were viable professions. Colored folks had a hard time recognizing that jobs in the arts, such as acting, were legitimate work. Teaching was real work. Nursing was real work. Even preaching was real work, but nobody was going to waste their time studying for unattainable jobs like acting.

Music was different, however. It had always resonated deep within the souls of black people, ever since the days of slavery, and even earlier, and therefore music was considered to be part of a heritage that had to be passed on. Music could be justified as a major, especially if it was combined with education. Gospel and spirituals spoke of where the race had been and had sustained a people for centuries, so music had to continue to be performed and taught. However, artistic talent could still remain hidden forever, for concessions had to be made. State had a large auditorium, where they held student assemblies and showed movies, and the Collegiate Chorale gave concerts and sang for other general assemblies. It wasn't long before teachers realized that there were other possibilities for the use of the space, and so a dance troupe was formed, and a little theater company named the Henderson-Davis Players was born as a result of teachers' imaginations. These pursuits could not compete with the academic environment, however, and so they became extracurricular activities, providing outlets for the pent-up muse. Sardis had plenty of pent-up angers and frustrations, and was soon dragged into the world of theater, which she quickly embraced as if she owned it.

The car had stopped moving, and Eartha's mind was trying to focus on where she was, and who the voices belonged to, but it was still too dark to tell. She was buried in the backseat, fully clothed from head to toe, with not an inch of skin showing. Her dad was with her, but her mom had stayed home, hiding behind her perpetual headache whenever she had to interact with her country in-laws or country kin, she called them. "Let Grandmom know I send my love but couldn't make the trip." Same message every time.

They were in Aiken, South Carolina, a long way from Charleston. Eartha peered through the car window to see a tall, light-skinned woman greet her dad. Grandmom Fletcher, as she was known to all of her children, was a very youthful-looking woman, in spite of her sixty years and five children. She lived on a farm that had been in the family since their white descendant turned it over to his former slaves. Colors were still segmented here, but they lived more harmoniously with each other here than they did in Charleston. Grandmom and her sister were now the only remaining direct descendants still living on the property. They had lots of descendents nearby, but none of them liked farming. Most, like Eartha's dad, had gone to college, and were now professional people.

Eartha had never met her grandmom before, so when her dad opened the car door, she retreated back into the seat as far as she could, but she could not escape, so when he lifted her out, she clung to his neck. She still didn't know why her mom, especially, wanted her to go away. She wanted to ask her Dad what she'd done to make them dislike her so, but Grandmom had already received her safely into her small farm house, and her dad's car was retreating in a cloud of dust before she'd been able to bring herself to say anything to either of them.

Grandmom scared little Eartha. She did strange things, like pinching her nose together and clamping it with a clothes pin. It didn't hurt, but Eartha couldn't understand why her grandmom was doing it. Little was she to know that her grandmom was performing her own form of plastic surgery; over time, the pin would prevent her nose from growing too broad. Eartha still spent lots of time indoors, out of the sun, and Grandmom applied oils and roots to her skin and hair. Some of it was soothing, but some of it burned and hurt her. Slowly and relentlessly, the transformation continued. The root cellar became Eartha's friend. It was cool, and dark, and no one bothered her down there. The creatures that inhabited the dark with her didn't care if she was dark or light; the dark was still her friend.

V

Dorcus's family life and social upbringing made it possible for her to accept Sardis. In the colored world, Dorcus's parents were pillars of the community. Her father was a preacher with a large, fairly well-to-do congregation. They provided the basic needs for him and his family, but in order to pay for his children's college education, he taught English in the one and only public high school for colored children, Burke High. Her mother was also well known in the education community, having taught in many elementary schools in and around Charleston. Both wanted Dorcus to follow in their footsteps, and she could have easily managed any profession, for she had compassion and empathy for the underdog and patience tempered with kindness and understanding, all good traits for either entering the ministry or to becoming an educator. There had never been any question about whether or not she would attend college, for while her parents were not considered rich, they made sacrifices to ensure that Dorcus and her four brothers received a good education.

Dorcus knew one high yellow girl at Simonton, where she attended junior high school. All the seventh- and eighth-graders had a begrudging acquaintance with her, but Dorcus became her friend for the one year the girl was her classmate. Her widowed, fair-skinned mother had remarried and moved to South Carolina to begin a new life with her dark-complexioned husband who was a native. The girl attended a public school because her mother taught in a public school, and besides, her parents thought the experience would enrich her life. Dorcus befriended the shy child because no one else would go near her. The boys pulled her long braids, and the girls threatened to cut them off. It was as if a bull's-eye had been painted on her chest, and she became the target of every cruel prank that was thought up. Dorcus stood by her, though, inviting her to her home and trying to undo the effects of some of the punishment that was being inflicted.

ICS did not want that type of controversy spilling over on their campus, so to try and have her admitted there would not have been an option. Even though both parents were black, they began to draw as much attention, ire, and animosity as if they'd been a mixed race couple. The girl's mother's family disapproved of the union and disowned her. Her new stepfather's Charleston relatives welcomed them, until they discovered hate mail in their box and shattered glass on their living room floor after someone tossed a brick through the window. By the start of the next school year, Dorcus had lost her friend. The family moved North, wanting to experience a more normal life. It was no stretch, therefore, for Dorcus to seek out Sardis during their freshman year at State, although it did not happen right away.

Grace, on the other hand, was one of the junior high school girls who had been victimizing the poor, dejected girl. Her life in the Alley made her bitter and hard, and she didn't trust anyone who looked and acted white. Her road to State had been a difficult one, and she couldn't accept anyone whose life, as she saw it, had been handed to him or her on a silver platter. She was particularly resentful that, on campus, Sardis had been singled out as one of the "hot" girls, something Grace would have given her right arm to become but knew would never happen. She simply could not make friends.

Given Dorcus's passion for lost causes, however, she somehow managed to befriend Grace. They shared the same classes from junior high through high school, but at that time a close relationship was not allowed to develop. Grace was a good student, but given her family's financial circumstances, it seemed that college was out of reach, and so Dorcus could not mask her shock when she arrived at State for orientation week and found Grace in the dorm. Dorcus's mother was equally surprised, and never being one to stifle her thoughts, or her tongue, she exclaimed, "Wonder how that little ragamuffin got in!"

Dorcus shot a telling look in her mother's direction, hoping that Grace hadn't overheard her comment. Dorcus had been warned all her life about "those Alley people." Her family knew of them, and some had even attended her father's church sporadically, but there was a dividing line, and the preacher and his family maintained a respectable distance. In their colored world, the Alley dwellers were always referred to as "those people" or as "your folks." They all knew of each other, and their children all attended school together, thanks to Jim Crow, but Dorcus's family, well meaning as they were, built walls between themselves that shut out what they considered undesirables within the community. Although they were forced to interact, and were civil when they met, the Alley people would never be guests at Dorcus's house, and once they were beyond the school walls, Dorcus and Grace were strangers within their segregated neighborhood.

"I saw that look you gave me," said Dorcus's mother, shuddering. "Alley people!" she spat contemptuously. "Remember where you came from, and where she grew up," she said with a warning look. Then she turned her attention to Grace, and continued her tirade. "She must have found some government assistance from somewhere. I heard about all of these programs. Free money. Minority benefits. They don't help decent, hard-working people like us. We still have to pay our way, not that there's anything wrong with that, but they hand out our hard-earned tax dollars to people who sit on their butts all day long not doing a thing. I heard that her father hasn't held a decent job in years. And that sister of hers ..."

Dorcus had heard this lecture before, and knew that once her mother got on her soap box, there was no stopping her. "Don't you ever let that tramp into your room. Remember, you're the product of a good, moral upbringing, not like those people. Her mother ..." The lecture droned on and on to a captive Dorcus, while the male members of the family unloaded her possessions from the car, although she was too excited to concentrate on yet another of her mother's long-winded speeches. Her mind wandered, and she thought about how easily she'd managed to catch the eye of a cute guy in the receiving area downstairs. Her imagination soared as she thought about potential conquests.

Every now and again, she would briefly tune in again. "Now remember, you're here to make us proud. The usher board sent their blessings, and Miss Julie sent some home-baked cookies." Dorcus groaned inwardly, gagging a little upon hearing that Miss Julie was gaining her final revenge with her hard, stomach-churning home-baked cookies. There should have been an ordinance passed outlawing home-baking by spinsters with no talent for cooking. She wondered if any of them had ever made the direct connection between their lack of cooking skills and their lack of a husband. "Mother Sadie knitted you a scarf," her mother continued, pulling the item from a box placed on the desk. "Are you listening to me?" she said, noting Dorcus's apparent lack of interest. Dorcus nodded in false affirmation. She'd learned a long time ago to always be ready for that question, and to always give a positive response. This pacified her mother, and her mind was then free to roam at will for at least another thirty to forty minutes.

Dorcus loved her family, but she was ready to leave. She was the youngest of five, and the only girl. Be fruitful and multiply, the Scripture said. Her parents had taken the command seriously. "Having four older, protective brothers," she related to her new roommate later in the day, after they departed, "was like having five fathers, and on top of that was my smothering mother, always hovering. I love all of them, but now I'm free!" She underscored the last word by falling back onto her bed, arms outstretched. Then she got up and grabbed the foil-wrapped plastic plate bearing Miss Julie's cookies. She removed the foil and started to toss them out the window to further celebrate her emancipation, but suddenly something made her stop. She realized how much care had gone into making them, and knew that she would miss seeing Miss Julie on Sunday mornings from now on. She looked lovingly at Mother Sadie's knitted scarf. "That woman is still as color-blind as ever. Wonder if she'll ever knit colors together that actually blend?" She smiled at the thought and then carefully placed the scarf at the very bottom of her dresser drawer. She knew that she would never wear the red, green, and black monstrosity.

Now, reality set in, and a thought dawned on her: *Will I really be able to survive with all of my support systems gone?* Suddenly, her glee vanished and was replaced by a sense of panic, which quickly evolved into sadness, and then loneliness. Just at that moment, Grace happened to wander past her open door. Seeing Dorcus, she stopped and knocked. Here was a familiar and welcome face, so in spite of her mother's admonitions, Dorcus smiled and beckoned Grace to join her. "Want a cookie?" she said, extending Miss Julie's treats to a hungry and thankful Grace. They sat and talked late into the night, and the former neighbors became friends for the first time.

With the protective walls and her controlled environment now gone, and with her homesickness vanquished and new friends in tow, Dorcus began to discover herself. Stepping out on State's campus in her freshman year ushered in an age of freedom. Before she entered State, her parents had imposed a limited dating policy that had been strictly enforced by her brothers. They were older, and so they were allowed more freedom, but as the youngest, and the only girl, Dorcus had great limitations placed on her. The family pledged that this preacher's daughter's virtue would remain intact. In addition to the intimidating presence of her four burly older brothers, prospective boyfriends had to face a barrage of questions and close scrutiny from her parents. It was an honor to date the senior pastor's daughter, but many a potential suitor had second thoughts when he suddenly realized what he faced. This limited the dating pool to a few well chosen but dull prospects, none of whom captured Dorcus's interest. She became frustrated at not being able to date whomever she wished, but she hadn't panicked at the limited local prospects, for her mother had drummed it into her mind to set her sights higher.

"You should only consider a college man. These high school fellows have no future ahead of them. You're destined for college. Make sure you finish your education, because once you have that degree, no one can take that away from you. Then, while you're there, get that college man. They know how to do things right. Educated men respect and want educated women. And if anything happens to him, you'll be able to take care of yourself and your family."

And so it was that Dorcus, in her newfound freedom, decided to experience college life to its fullest; so many boys, so little time. Deeply ingrained habits and beliefs cannot be discarded overnight, but her dorm mates helped her make the transition from demure preacher's kid to mature preacher's kid. Whenever they exchanged makeup tips and experimented with new hair styles, Dorcus soaked it all up. She wanted to have fun, to explore her new world. The social structure at State allowed her to indulge in her revelry while maintaining control at the same time. In her mind, she was free, but within their structure, she was restrained. They understood the freshman mind, and so they gave them a taste of freedom, while subtly holding their hands along the way.

Dorcus stood all of five feet tall, with an average build, and her features were typical of many black women. She had full lips, almond-shaped eyes, which had been concealed behind glasses until her junior year in high school when she discovered contact lenses, and very short hair, which she wore in a pixie-style cut. Perms were not yet in fashion, and so she continued to struggle through a weekly press and curl routine to keep it looking fresh. Dorcus was cute, no question about it. The male members of her family had always thought so, and her cuteness had always worked in her favor when she wanted to have her way at home, but this was a new playing field. Cute got the guys' attention but not a date with them. Cute had got her onto the cheerleading squad in high school but not in college. Cute got a wink and a smile, and maybe a peck on the cheek, but not a serious relationship. Cute got a friend but would not get that cherished ring by senior year. "So, what will it take? What am I doing wrong?" a frustrated Dorcus asked Grace one day, figuring that Grace was more knowledgeable about these things. "I changed my look, my hair, the way I do my makeup, yet these guys still pretend I don't exist."

Grace was amused by Dorcus's innocence. She considered Dorcus to be a work in progress, and enjoyed taking the naive girl under her wing. Although contrary to what Dorcus's mother may have thought, Grace was not as experienced or worldly as she suspected. However, the Alley had given her much more exposure to the real world than Dorcus ever had, and so she gladly stepped into the role of mentor. "The term you're looking for is 'hot,'" said Grace. "Very few girls come by it naturally. Takes a lot of work. Some grow into it, but most have to work like crazy for it. Most never make it. You're cute. You have the makings, but you need a lot of work." This was the first time Dorcus had heard about the so-called hot girl, and she was puzzled, so Grace proceeded to enlighten her.

"They are the most popular girls, the ones the boys date first. Most are extremely attractive physically, but even if they weren't, they had an air and a confidence about them that made others think they were attractive." She paused, and seeing Dorcus hanging on to her every word, she continued with an air of authority. "Many were high school homecoming, prom, and/or school queens, the majorettes with long, shapely legs, naturally straight or nearly straight hair, and brown to light skin. They are the ones destined to be elected the college queens, and to be rushed by the popular sororities on campus. Their crowning achievement will be to reign as queen over a male-dominated organization like a fraternity or a male dorm. The hot girls are singled out almost immediately by the fraternity men for relationships and are invariably the ones who have male escorts walk them back to the dorm from the Friday night dances. They are the ones selected to be on the color team and," Grace paused to emphasize her point, "they will get the rings for graduation." Dorcus got the picture.

Sardis qualified by virtue of her light skin, dainty features, and long, sandy-colored hair, and she eventually came to reign as the queen of the male junior/senior dorm, primarily because she was dating the dorm president at the time. She never saw herself as hot, and she would have been more than willing to abdicate and pass her title on to Dorcus or anyone else who coveted it. She simply wanted to fit in with the rest of the freshman girls, who continued to shut her out.

Grace would have accepted the hot title if given the chance, but she was happy being who she was, in total awe of the fact that she was now a college student. Dorcus, on the other hand, had a goal. She had to leave cute behind; somehow, she had to become a hot girl.

VI

The Protest

Orangeburg was just one of many cities that experienced civil rights protests, but because it was a relatively small city, with no national ties or leaders to attract the national media, their demonstrations were only so much fodder for the local news. Elsewhere, student activism was increasing, and by now demonstrations had taken place in at least forty cities in the South. Most were in the form of lunch-counter sit-ins, peaceful in nature. A group of people simply sat down at segregated lunch counters and demanded service, vowing not to move until they were served, and/or treated with respect. The protests in North Carolina and Mississippi attracted the most attention, because big-name civil rights leaders were involved. This protest in this small backwater town was different. It boasted of no big-name leadership.

Since Orangeburg was a college town, it had a relatively large black middle class, and a large population of educated black residents. Education was the great equalizer, so the city began yielding quietly to desegregation, especially as activism increased across the South. The bowling alley protest was sparked by impatient students who did not think changes were moving along fast enough for them. They held meetings in the Student Center, and in some of the local churches that students attended, but there was no organized protest effort. As of yet, most of the student body didn't want to create any trouble, because these were innocent, fun-filled days.

Dorcus quickly discovered Quad life. The Quad was campus central, and Dorcus determined that it was as good a place as any to begin her hot girl campaign. At first, she merely observed everything and soon surmised that the Greeks, the circle of sororities and fraternities, seemed to rule everywhere. The student body president was a member of a fraternity, Miss State was a member of a sorority, and on it went. Even the plain women stood out, walking around campus in brightly colored sorority sweaters, so she figured out which sorority would bring her the most popularity and made inquiries about joining.

Each sorority was paired with a fraternity, a concept that worked well for Dorcus, who reasoned that if she belonged to a sorority, she would automatically be noticed by their fraternal brothers. From there, it would be a shoo-in for a date, and then there would be a real possibility that she could reign as fraternity queen. She began to formulate scheme after scheme in her mind. Should she pick a sorority first, or should she decide in which fraternity she would like to reign as queen? As time went on, she discovered her precious quest would come at a price, because her pursuit of hot girl status meant that academia took a backseat.

It was early fall, and the weather was cooling slightly as the stifling summer heat began to loosen its grip. However the dorm rooms were still a little warm, which made hanging around outside more inviting. The bug population had settled down considerably, and now the streets surrounding the Quad sprang to life as the rest of the student body returned to join the freshmen, who had completed their orientation week. On one side of the Quad was the student center, a good co-ed meeting place, as was the cafeteria. In these "dark ages" before the proliferation of fast food outlets, the cafeteria was the only game in town. Everyone ate there, and Grace was one of many students who worked the cafeteria line.

With the exception of the few students who were locals, a student's entire life revolved around the campus. Freshmen were confined to grounds and could only leave with the permission of their parents and/or the administration. The vast majority of students lived on campus, studied on campus, and apart from the occasional African student who stayed on campus, having nowhere else to go, only left during semester breaks. A few seniors enjoyed the privilege of owning a car, but for most, limited mobility meant limited options.

Most students liked to hang out for a while after the evening meal, milling around in the Quad before hunkering down to their studies. Gradually, the Quad would empty until it resembled a ghost town, with only a few students seen walking to and from the library. Study could be done in the student center, but everyone knew that it was more of a place to see and be seen, and concentration was limited by the incessant small talk, coupling, and card games.

Two of the female dorms and all the male dorms bordered the Quad, which was famous for hosting the bi-annual fraternity and sorority initiations known as Hell Week. It also played host to each incoming Greek pledge line twice a year, when the new pledges were introduced. The sororities and fraternities were strictly governed by a representative group known as the Pan-Hellenic Council. Each sorority and fraternity had a representative member on the council, which was responsible for devising the rules and guidelines by which the organizations governed themselves. State had no dedicated sorority or fraternity houses. Individual members generally tried to room with fellow members, but it was not unusual to find a dorm room with one half decorated to the hilt in fraternal colors and symbols and the other side sporting posters of the Supremes or Marvin Gaye.

Council rules dictated that one week of each semester was designated for initiation rituals. After six weeks of being "on line," learning the histories and contributions made by their respective organizations, the pledges were then put through a week of mild, very controlled hazing. Their antics during this time provided a source of entertainment for the rest of the student body. The groups were very competitive, though they denied it. Historically, black fraternities and sororities devoted themselves to community service and racial equality, so there tended to be a greater spirit of cooperation, with less emphasis on the social aspects. Each line would dress alike in his or her organizational colors; Alpha women, pink and green; Alpha men, black and gold; Delta women and Kappa men, red and white; Omega men, purple and gold; Sigma men and Zeta women, blue and white; and on it went. Even the drama fraternity would get involved and dress up in theatrical costumes, but they never performed on the Quad. Some of the men even went to the extent of carving their fraternal symbol in their hair.

The big drawing card was to see who had the best song or choreographed routine. The men usually broke out into a quasi drill standard called stepping, while the women tended to sing original songs, although at times they would also get into stepping or perform some of the latest dances. It was a great recruiting tool for the next pledge line, and the strongest act invariably drew the most spectators and attracted the most new members. One year, one fraternity managed to recruit a lot of new members from the ROTC drill team. That line in turn proceeded to pass their new routines down to each successive pledge line, and that fraternity ruled the campus unchallenged until the original group eventually graduated. Once a line "went over," a new line would be introduced. This happened at the end of each semester because, again, unlike many traditional Greek organizations, the ability to pledge and to become a member depended upon grade point averages. If a potential candidate did not have good grades, he or she could not pledge. Also, if a pledge's grade point average dropped below the mandated requirements, he or she could not become a full member, so it was not unusual to have freshmen and seniors on the same pledge line, or to see someone on a fledgling pledge line but never see him or her in sorority or fraternity colors. Very few active members fell below the required grade point average, as members provided each other with mutual support to ensure that they held to the required standards. Dorcus learned the lesson about grade point averages the hard way. In mid-semester, her evolution to hot girl status hit a major snag when her grades suddenly began to plummet.

The Quad also hosted the ROTC parade. On this campus full of rituals, the Friday afternoon ROTC parade was a real crowd pleaser. It may not have been fun for the men involved, but the women loved it. Military service had always been a viable career option for colored men, for job opportunities were scarce, and meaningful career paths were frequently closed in the civilian world, so after high school, men often signed up or were drafted into the enlisted ranks. The judicial system often used the military as a means of solving disciplinary problems, and it was not uncommon for a judge to offer a defendant a choice of three years in the military or five years in jail. Military service provided the structure and the discipline many men lacked in their lives, and in return, society was benefited by the return of a more mature and potentially productive member of the community.

Few colored men were given the opportunity to become officers so, along with providing a college education, State played its part in preparing men of color to take their place in the ranks of the military officer corps. By hosting the ROTC program, the college opened doors to another career path for educated men. The Reserve Officers Training Corps was, at that time, practically the only means by which men of color could enter the officer ranks. Other avenues were through either an extremely rare direct battlefield commission or military academies and institutions like Charleston's segregated Citadel, which kept the officer corps primarily white.

Freshmen and sophomore men became members of the corps of cadets, because for them, ROTC was mandatory. Many remained in the program through their junior and senior years, becoming the student commanders. If they completed the entire four-year program and finished regular basic training in an active duty military unit prior to graduation, these men were then commissioned as Second Lieutenants during their graduation ceremony. Parents burst with pride when their sons received those hard-earned yellow bars and returned their first salute to the enlisted men who, until minutes earlier, had been their trainers.

Freshmen and sophomore women did not have the option of taking ROTC, which caused no end of consternation for some. Instead, the women were subjected to two years of physical education. Learning to play field hockey and tennis fell a long way short of preparing for a long-term career. Being entirely separate and unequal rankled even more when the women discovered that the men received a salary as enlisted active armed forces members during their senior year. Some protested the policy to the Dean of Students, but no changes were forthcoming.

The parades were a big hit, however. A band made up of cadets who in their daily lives were regular members of State's Marching 101 provided music as the cadets trooped from their staging area near the ROTC building around the perimeter, through campus center and back again. The women lined the parade route and cheered as they passed by. As soon as the last cadet marched past, anyone who had not yet eaten would break into a run for the cafeteria, because they knew that as soon as the parade ended, the famished men would make a beeline to the facility, and it was not uncommon for the cafeteria to run short of the daily special toward the end of the day, especially at the Friday evening meal. They also ran short of the Sunday morning special of pancakes and sausage.

For Dorcus, campus life was fast becoming a three-ring circus, and she longed to perform in each ring. She wanted to experience sorority life to the hilt. She wanted to sing in the choir, as she had done for so many years in her father's church, and she wanted to learn the latest dance moves, but most of all she wanted to capture the heart of a college man. Meanwhile, her studies fell further and further behind. *I've always managed to get good grades before without breaking my back,* she reasoned to herself, *so I can do it now.* Wise faculty staff had seen it all before and knew the inner workings of the freshman mind, so at State, they placed a lot of restrictions on the newly emancipated, incoming college students during their freshman year. This put a damper on some of Dorcus's ambitions, but she merely braced herself and maneuvered her way around the obstacles.

The freshmen girls and freshmen boys were housed in separate dorms, and only limited visiting was permitted between the two entities. Socializing was only allowed in the first-floor lounge, and the only time a man was allowed into the dorm itself was for specific tasks,

50

such as making repairs or assisting with moving heavy objects. Even these had to be accomplished during daylight hours with permission from the dorm director. A man had to have an escort with him at all times who had the responsibility of issuing a warning in a very loud voice of "man on the hall," which was generally met by cat calls and whistles. The ratio of males to females in the freshman year was generally fairly even, but attrition meant that the ratio of women to men gradually increased until it was closer to two women for each man. By the time the class entered their junior year, the upper-class men could generally be housed in one junior/senior dorm, while the upper-class women remained housed within their individual class years. State also adhered to the philosophy that all work and no play made for some really dull and frustrated students, so it promoted controlled play time. Every Friday, and frequently on Saturday nights as well, dances were held in the gymnasium.

Dorcus, along with many of her dorm mates, looked forward to these social events, which provided access to sophomore, junior, and senior men, in addition to the freshmen. The upper-class men generally stopped attending after a week or so. Many of them just went to check out the new blood on campus, to see who was hot and who was definitely not. These were days when there was a new dance craze every month, and Dorcus made sure she knew them all. The hot girls had the best moves and danced all night, but most importantly, they got escorted back to the dorm. Dorcus had had very little opportunity to dance at home. A holy shout or shuffle was allowed every now and then, but there was no "butt shaking" or "jive timing" allowed, so now that she could let it all hang out, she was determined not to end up a wallflower along with the other girls who were either too shy, couldn't dance at all, or didn't know the latest steps. Her dance moves failed, however, to win her that all-important escort back to the dorm, which did not sit well with her.

Besides the weekly meet and greet on the dance floor, there was a formal ritual that involved the freshmen class. "Are you telling us that we have to go to the football games?" squealed the girls, thinking this was too good to be true. The dorm director loved teasing them during orientation when she announced this mandated requirement.

"It's true," she said and smiled sweetly. The excitement gradually abated, however, as she revealed more details and it began to dawn on them that if something sounds too good to be true, it usually is. "You have to dress in the school colors of garnet and blue." No problem there, they decided. "And all of you have to sit together as a group." As expected, this drew a few moans and groans, especially from the hot girls who already had dates. "And you have to wear these." The director reached into a large box behind her and pulled out a white hat with a blue brim and the school's logo and their graduation year printed on the front. She braced herself for the barrage of protest that was sure to follow, and as in past years, she wasn't disappointed. Being the experienced guardian of customs that she was, she waited patiently until the venting was over before launching into her annual discourse about carrying on school customs and traditions, and about how it was now their turn to take their appointed place in history. By the end of her speech, she usually had them believing that this entire scheme had been their idea.

Many, especially the dateless ones, grudgingly admitted that this custom had some advantages. After all, they had reserved seats, and they were very close to all the action. Since they were a part of the extended rooting section, they sat near the band, directly in front of the cheer squad, almost on the fifty-yard line. By the first game, most had resigned themselves to making the sacrifice. The silly-looking hat remained an issue, but it was a tradition, and part of what being a freshman was all about. The men were spared the humiliation of the hats. They attended in ROTC uniforms and sat together, a few rows behind the women.

The school also made sure it attended to its neophytes' souls. Since most of the students came out of a strong black church tradition, and since most black schools themselves had histories planted in religious foundations, State attended to those spiritual roots. Different denominations, such as the Methodists, the Lutherans, and the AMEs, sponsored campus clubs. Because most of the students had no means of transportation, every Sunday morning some of the neighboring black churches were allowed to shuttle those who wished to participate to their respective denominational services. The school also assumed responsibility for spiritual guidance by holding a Vesper service in the main auditorium each Sunday afternoon, which all freshmen were required to attend. These nondenominational services were more about heritage than about religion.

The Collegiate Chorale, or one of their two male or female ensemble offshoots, presented music derived from the literature of the black church. In addition to these spirituals, they entertained with popular show tunes or classical selections, such as the choruses from Porgy and Bess. It was all designed to educate and motivate students to do their best, live their best, and strive to achieve.

The school also sponsored movie nights, which were very popular social events. Admission was free for students and faculty, while guests paid a minimal fee. In addition to the football games, this was one of the few in-house activities open to the local community, but few outsiders attended, other than relatives of students or visiting boyfriends or girlfriends. The movies were classified for general exhibition, and were very tame. The *Flint* movies, starring James Coburn, were popular, and every now and then they would show a mystery or a borderline horror flick such as Alfred Hitchcock's *The Birds*. The freshmen women soon learned not to sit on the last row of seats bordering the main aisle.

One woman with a very strong pair of lungs provided the lesson during the first horror movie of the year. The auditorium was completely still, and all eyes were glued to the screen, where the main character was about to be devoured by some unearthly creature. The screen grew dark, and music swelled toward a climax when suddenly there was an ear-piercing scream, not from the screen, but from the middle of the auditorium, followed by howls of side-splitting laughter from the experienced upper-class men who knew the routine and had been waiting in anticipation. The movie projector came to a halt, and the lights were turned up. "That always kills the movie," said a young man sitting near Dorcus and Grace. "I wish those guys wouldn't do that. One of these days they're going to pick someone with a weak heart. It won't be so funny then," he continued to the perplexed friends.

"They had an incident about a year ago and … let's just say, the poor girl lost control of her bowels and had to make an extremely undignified exit. People complained, but it obviously fell on deaf ears." Noting the freshmen's continuing confusion, he explained what had happened. Someone, usually a guy, had reached across the aisle during the scary scene and either touched an unsuspecting girl on her neck or dropped an object down her back. "They look forward to the first suspense movie every year so that someone can pull it off. It only works once and on that row with the open aisle. So don't ever sit there," he admonished. "With no one sitting directly behind you, who would expect a hand to reach out and touch you? The women wised up to it after that. Last year, one woman even managed to turn around and smack her intended assailant before he had a chance to attack and return anonymously to his seat. Now that was funny," said the upper-class man, smiling with satisfaction at the memory. Once the poor, traumatized girl had calmed down, the lights were dimmed again and the movie resumed, but as their unknown adviser had predicted, it killed the movie. The mood had been ruined, and all sense of drama and suspense was now gone. No fake movie scream could ever match the timbre, pitch, and volume of the one they just experienced from the mid-row.

Given all the social opportunities that were available, it was inevitable that pairings were formed. Some women went to State not only to get their MS or MA degrees but also to obtain that special designation of "Mrs." Dorcus, recalling her mother's advice to get herself a good, college-educated man, was among those who had that goal in mind. However, her hot girl campaign was not going well. Grace had warned her that some women had it, whatever "it" was, while others didn't. Still, Dorcus was determined to become popular. She needed to hang out with the right people in order to find the right guy. Then it struck her that the right people were always hanging out together playing this bid whist game. Having grown up as a preacher's kid, however, she'd never even touched cards. "The Devil's tool," her dad had called them when he found a deck of cards that one of her brothers had sneaked into the house. Her brother paid dearly for his transgression.

The children falsely assumed it was their father's convictions against card playing that brought down the wrath of God upon them, but in reality, their mother had a secret about why the preacher took the heavy-handed measures to discourage card games. Her po-ke-no parties had once become an addiction that almost cost them their marriage, so she couldn't go anywhere near a deck of cards, and her husband, in his overly protective manner, made sure it never happened. But Dorcus was out of her father's house now, so she decided she would have to learn that game if she was to achieve her goal.

Grace became her first teacher, until Dorcus's ineptitude drove Grace to distraction. She then sat and observed game after game until she thought she had acquired a working knowledge of how the game should be played. She got herself into a game but quickly learned that knowledge was nothing without the experience needed to "read" the cards. She also learned another, damaging, lesson. Bid whist players were very impatient with rank amateurs and made sure they spread the word about who could and could not play, so instead of attaining instant popularity, Dorcus became a pariah, a total outcast. She was one very depressed person.

Eartha adjusted well to the country life. Grandmom Fletcher was not very giving or loving, but she left Eartha to her thoughts and games and didn't question her need to spend time alone in the dark comfort of that root cellar. She'd raised five children of her own and did not particularly care to take on the burden of a five-year-old Eartha, but her son had told her, untruthfully, that Eartha had serious health problems and needed to move to a different environment. How could she resist one of her own?

But having the child around brought out her long-dormant maternal instincts, and she discovered she liked having the unobtrusive child with her. She never saw, however, any evidence of her alleged health problem other than the fact that she was darker than her sisters. She suspected that her uppity daughter-in-law just didn't want the shame of raising a dark child, even though she was by no means black, and so she used her knowledge of country medicine, applying salves and creams every day until eventually she achieved the desired results. Eartha became a few shades lighter, as long as she stayed out of the sun.

Eartha coped well in this new environment, but just after she turned fourteen, Grandmom Fletcher died suddenly, and her world changed again. She returned to Charleston to a place she did not know, a strange and unwelcoming world that was dominated by two older, very light siblings and a mother who wished that Eartha was still in Aiken. She hadn't seen these people in nine years, and now she had to adjust to their world. Her sisters had near-white complexions but lacked white features, both of them having broad noses. Grandmom hadn't gotten a chance to fix that, Eartha thought. Clothespins and gentle pinches would have done the job. Bee-stung lips were not in fashion in those days either or else they would have fit right in. Eartha had inherited her grandmom's long, thick, wavy hair, which produced no end of consternation for her sisters, whose manes were sadly lacking in length, grade, and luster. Eartha had been transformed into a beautiful young woman, albeit still a shade darker than her siblings.

"Do you think ICS would take her now?" she overheard her mother whispering curtly to her father shortly after her return.

"We can try," he responded, not wishing a repeat of nine years earlier, "but keep in mind, dear, there's nowhere we can send her this time."

"We have the summer to lighten her up," said her mother. "I won't be embarrassed again."

For Eartha, this meant staying indoors during the hottest and brightest hours of the day so that the sun could not make her any darker. Grandmom's potions were gone, but there were beauty creams on the market, most notably Artra skin cream with bleaching agents designed to lighten pigmentation. Her mother made it her mission to see to it that Eartha practically bathed in creams and lotions each day. By fall, she was convinced it had worked, but to make sure, on the day of enrollment, her mother touched up her natural golden beauty with some carefully placed light face powder and prayed that the faculty and staff members had short memories. It worked, and she was granted the long-coveted admission.

VII

"I know you're not going to play that card." Sardis looked into Dorcus's still-girlish face as she spoke.

Dorcus paused and took a good look at the cards on the table before placing the card she intended to play back in her hand. "How do you do that?" she asked incredulously. "I can never figure out how you know what card I plan to play before I put it down!"

Sardis always knew; she just knew. Her calculating mind could follow what cards had been played, and she read faces, so she could tell who had good trump cards and who didn't. She was able to deduce what her partner and their opponents had in their hands. Their pained faces gave them away when they were beset with a poor hand, and a blank stare, bordering on happy, let her know when their hand was good. This uncanny sense created a bond between Dorcus and Sardis that saved Sardis's college career.

VIII

Dorcus was never one to walk away from a fight, and this exasperating game became a formidable opponent. She became obsessed with learning bid whist. It was a quest. It continued to elude her, but that didn't stop her from busting in on games at every opportunity. On a small campus like State, it didn't take long for word to get around that she was a poor player, and being continually thrown out of games was depressing. "This isn't helping my image," she mumbled rather loudly to herself as she slunk down the empty dorm hall following her latest defeat. "How can I learn to play bid whist?"

"I ... I can ... teach you," stuttered a shaky voice, barely above a whisper. It was the first time Dorcus had noticed the lonely, dejected figure in the room directly across the hall from hers. In fact, it was the first time Dorcus noticed anyone other than herself since setting foot on campus. It was mid-semester, so it was strange seeing half-packed bags lying all over the room.

"Are you a-going or are you a-coming?" said Dorcus jokingly.

This made Sardis smile. "My father, my brother, and I loved playing bid whist and other card games." Her face brightened at the memory of those hot summer nights out on the back porch with that single dim bulb overhead. "Mom wasn't much of a player, but she would watch from her corner. We always dealt her in, but after a while, her hand became the dummy."

"Dummy?" said Dorcus, bewildered.

"A player whose place is there, but who's missing. The other three players take turns playing as if the person was there." This was a foreign concept at State, of course, since there were always people lined up to play a hand.

"But ..." Sardis paused and stared at Dorcus. Like a wounded animal, she waited for the rejection she felt sure would follow. Dorcus stared back at Sardis, waiting for her to continue, but now the pain that Sardis had been suppressing for weeks surfaced as she realized that someone was talking to her, actually listening to her, and the tears began to flow. She grabbed a box of tissues, pulled out a handful, and tried to stem the torrential flow, but to no avail. For almost six weeks, she had endured a living hell, holding her head high when they called her "yellow" and "whitey" and other names she never even heard before. She determined that she would *not* let them get to her, get the better of her, even when they pulled her hair, dared her to fight, and threatened to beat her up and "break that pretty nose and kick that flat butt." She had prevailed and walked away, but now she felt like a cornered cat with no claws left. Would this person stroke her gently to calm her down, or would she pull her tail and kill off the last of her nine lives?

Dorcus entered Sardis's room and quietly closed the door behind her. "Want to talk about this?" The old Dorcus had returned, the gentle, caring, and compassionate pastor's kid.

"Why are they treating me like this? What have I done to them? If they speak to me at all, they just call me names. The sons and daughters of slaves stooping lower than the masters!" she spat. "I am also cut from the same cloth, even though I may not look like it. Why can't they accept me?" Dorcus listened for hours while Sardis cried, vented, and paced the room, and by the end of the evening, a friendship was formed.

IX

The Protest

Everyone's eyes were glued to the red and black playing cards in front of them: kings vs. aces, diamonds vs. spades. The games were a great distraction from boyfriend troubles, and from tests and grades, but life-changing events were about to displace the cards; trumps and tricks were about to be superseded by guns and bullets. State was about to occupy a unique place in history and then be denied that place in history. Many college campuses were becoming hotbeds for upheaval. Student protests were not new; entire European governments had been overthrown as a result of student activism, and now the Vietnam conflict was producing challenges on many white campuses, but State's student cause was far more personal. While white students protested a war that was being waged on foreign soil, black students protested the inequality that was rife in their own backyards. They were to spend three nights demanding equal and fair treatment, three nights after centuries of denial.

"No, no, no," was the response Dorcus received whenever she tried to start her own bid whist game. People had long memories when it came to poor players. However, Sardis was an excellent, and very patient, teacher, and Dorcus's skills gradually improved until eventually she was welcomed into some of the ongoing games around campus. Sardis remained an outcast, however, although Dorcus boldly began sitting with her during their meals. Then, other girls began to join them, but there was still an influential clique of bullies who seemed determined to drive her off "their" campus. Dorcus accepted another mission to change those stubborn attitudes and hearts.

One evening, Dorcus managed to get a game together with her roommate, Taletha, and with Grace. At one time, Dorcus and Taletha planned to join the same sorority, but Dorcus's poor grades had killed those plans. Nonetheless, there was still a close friendship between the roommates. Grace joined them for the game, so the three women sat down, and Dorcus began to deal the cards.

"Who's the fourth?" asked Grace, a note of suspicion in her voice. Dorcus pretended not to hear her question and went on dealing. Just as she finished, Sardis entered the room. Grace shot a severe look toward Sardis and then Dorcus as she rose from their makeshift playing table. "What you mean inviting this white girl into our game?" she demanded, throwing her cards down and turning to the door to make a fast exit. Grace had never been one for tact or discretion. Whatever it was that had to be said, they could count on Grace to let it all out.

"It's the right thing to do," said Dorcus, gently but firmly. "Besides, she *is* one of *us*. The poor girl was in her room alone. Lighten up, Grace. She's never done a thing to you." The tension hung heavily in the air for a few minutes, and no one moved, until Sardis quietly sat down in her dignified manner and picked up her cards. Taletha looked at Grace, searching for a sign as to whether she should join her in walking out or not. Dorcus sat still, but her face pleaded with Grace to sit down and join them. Finally, Grace relented, sat down again and picked up her hand. The foursome was now complete and was to become permanent. Dorcus breathed a sigh of relief, and their first game began.

X

Grace didn't really hate Sardis. She hated what, from her perspective, Sardis represented—prosperity, privilege, and pampering. She also hated life itself. Grace grew up in an Alley, Michele Alley, in fact. Along with Despotes Court, these were two inlets within Duncan Street where a lot of people resided in close quarters. It was reminiscent of Porgy and Bess, but without the glamour. No one knew the history of those housing tracts, if indeed "tracts" was the right term. Some surmised that they were what was left over from the plantation system, from property that had been subdivided and then transformed as streets grew up around them. Their structure, placement, and location fitted that theory. The Alley consisted of two front houses that faced each other, abutting the street. Three more houses existed side by side on each side of similar style facing each other. The median was a dirt walkway that terminated in a dead end at a back wall. Vehicles were unable to enter, because the pathway was too narrow, and the houses were so tightly spaced that very little sunshine got through, even on the brightest of summer days.

In terms of architectural style, they were duplicates of the house in which Sardis lived, but these had seen better days. Many now appeared to be so fragile and unstable that it was hard to believe people still occupied them. Unlike Sardis's well-tended abode, the staircases linking the bottom porch with the upper porch were external, which meant that the houses became duplexes, with one family renting the upper half and another family living below. Each flat had been redesigned and reduced by one or two bedrooms, one of which had become a kitchen. Bathrooms had been installed in later years. The houses had once been painted white, but bare boards had long since replaced the paint. Hurricane-force winds acting as natural sandpaper had reduced the once well-maintained exteriors to a dingy gray color, and the only reminder of the once-grand splendor were flecks of white paint that still clung to columns of staircases. Rusted ceiling hooks were all that remained of porch swings that disappeared from all but the two downstairs front units.

The Alley, unlike the court, was not fenced in, which, because the houses were so close, gave the place a sinister appearance. During summer months, it served as a hangout for assorted characters of dubious and nefarious natures. The air was stifling, since there was such poor circulation. The residents spent most of the hot days hanging out on large porches in the Alley itself or on Duncan. This gave a particular meaning to the line from the song, "Summertime, and the livin' is easy," but it wasn't really all that easy. Apart from the heat and the bugs, mosquitoes and monstrous cockroaches called cicadas, tempers often flared. Somebody was always in somebody else's business or with somebody else's husband or wife. With structures built that close together, it wasn't hard to mix, mingle, and cohabit, and so common-law relationships abounded in the Alley. It wasn't unusual for one flat to contain several members of an extended family, or for cousins and uncles and grandparents to occupy a single housing unit, and while they might have been related, that didn't necessarily mean they got along with one another.

No matter what happened in the Alley, the people had a way of taking care of matters themselves, legally or otherwise. They had to; phones were scarce, and party lines put everybody's business out into the street. Even when they really needed help, no one wanted to call the two overworked, colored police officers who had been assigned to handle the colored community, for they had a way of making a bad situation worse, so the Alley took care of the Alley. Whenever the police turned up, they were usually looking for moonshine runners. The Alley was famous for that, too. Everybody knew who it was, but no one wanted the supply to end. Early every Thursday morning, before sunrise, a car would pull up on Duncan Street, mindful of the fact that the Alley could not accommodate a vehicle. The driver always made sure never to stop directly in front of the entrance to the Alley. A shadowy figure would scurry to the car, grab a box from the trunk, and then disappear just as quickly. With the weekend supply of hooch delivered, the trunk would close almost as if by magic, and the car would vanish into the gray pre-dawn like a ghost. Since few Alley residents could afford a car in those days, whenever one appeared, everybody knew that it had to be either the police or the supplier. No one ever knew anything, saw anything, or said anything to either entity about the other.

Despotes Court was different. Located three houses away, it really could have been slave quarters. Like the Alley, there was a big two-story mustard-colored house at the front, but this house fronted a large fenced courtyard, which contained four smaller one-story structures. All had been painted in the same mustard-colored tint and resembled houses that had been built on the prairie, with one main bedroom, a dining area, and a kitchen that had been added later on. These were primitive structures, for at the very back of the yard stood an outdoor privy, next to a hand-cranked well that was used to draw water. Large tin tubs were still used for bathing. The Court residents were far quieter and more reserved than the Alley people. The fence afforded them some privacy, but it also hid a lot of secrets.

Grace entered the Alley world on a very cold January morning, in a barely heated house. Time stood still for the family momentarily, but then the hands of the clock moved backward after her father lost his job at the cigar factory. They moved further back when her mother could no longer make the long walk to her housekeeping job with the doctor on downtown's Society Street and they took another giant leap backward when her sister got pregnant, dropped out of school, and introduced her common-law husband into the household.

XI

The Protest

The students who went off campus each day were warned that they risked expulsion if they participated in the demonstrations. Many had not been involved in the Civil Rights movement at all. As with so many revolutionary and social changes around the world, the indigenous population was initially somewhat placid, but over time, a few "rebel" leaders arose from within the student ranks and fired up the young, impressionable minds, urging them to take action. The powers, city fathers along with law enforcement, who were white, of course, were obliged to respond and, as was to be expected, they were hell-bent on maintaining the status quo at any cost, so they weighed in with heavy-handed force in an effort to keep their colored students in their place. They grabbed their guns and bully clubs and employed all the scare tactics and threats that had been effective in the past, causing colored students to cringe and become compliant. Negro students grew up with a healthy respect for authority. They even feared it to some extent; it kept them from getting hurt, arrested, or lynched. But times were changing rapidly now, and what the powers-that-be didn't realize was that these colored students were on their way to becoming black. Black students had dreams, black students challenged the status quo, black students didn't back away from the badge, and black students were determined to obtain their rights.

❧

"Will you please get your mind back on the game? You just cost us a trick," said Grace to Dorcus. She was even more distracted this evening than usual, and Grace knew the source of her distraction, which had been happening all too frequently recently. Dorcus had made a good playing partner in the past, but not anymore. It reminded Grace of when they first met, and Dorcus couldn't play bid whist at all. The four of them tried not to play with the same partner for each game, an arrangement that, in normal circumstances, had helped to sharpen their playing skills, but Grace had been dreading having to partner Dorcus this evening.

"I'm sorry," said Dorcus. "I haven't heard a word from Anton in months. I'm concerned about him."

"Dork," said Grace. Dorcus recoiled, and the others rolled their eyes, knowing what was coming next. Grace only called her that when she was getting ready to level some unwanted and unasked-for advice. She made no bones about the fact that she didn't like Lieutenant Anton Baylor, and thought that Dorcus should move on. "Anton is not worth your time. If you ask me ..."

"I didn't," replied Dorcus curtly.

"If you ask me," Grace continued, undeterred, "Charlie is a much better choice. At least his head is on straight. He knows what's what. And he really likes you." Charlie was Sergeant Charles Jordan. Dorcus had no interest in him. Anton was who she wanted, and she'd worked hard to get him.

Dorcus first saw Anton at a football game during her freshman year. She couldn't miss him, because he was on the team. The school had a winning team that year, in spite of the fact that very few of the players, including Anton, had a prayer or enough bulk to make it beyond college football and into the professional leagues. Knowing this, the coaches always placed emphasis on academic success if a player was to remain on the team, and Anton became their key player that day after another team member sat it out on academic probation. The day she first saw him was homecoming day, and the team was expected to win. In fact, in order to ensure a win, they often played their weakest opponent of the season on this day. State never lost a homecoming game.

Homecoming was a major event on the school's calendar, when they welcomed back alumni, crowned the homecoming queen, and held a parade, the route for which extended off campus onto the surrounding streets and then back. There was a float-building competition, with each sorority and fraternity decorating a float and engaging in good-natured rivalry, competing for bragging rights. Their reigning queens were always the centerpiece of their floats. Dorcus, full of envy, watched all those "hot" girls, with their gleaming crowns and gorgeous gowns, waving to the crowds. All she could do was sit in the stands and sway along with the band together with the rest of her classmates, wearing their beanies and dressed in their school colors. The Ray Charles hits "I'm Busted" and "Hit the Road, Jack" were two of the band's favorites that resonated with the students, who knew all the words and sang along with gusto.

The evening highlight, following the ensured big victory in the game, was the gala ball. Students, alumni, and a handful of faculty all trooped over to the gym for the festivities, where the football team and each organization's queen were introduced with great pageantry. While the spectators sat on the surrounding bleachers, each team member and their hot girl escort, sometimes an assigned date and sometimes their real date, promenaded around the open court. Anton was paired with his dorm queen, but it was obvious that they weren't a real couple. He was what Grace called a pretty boy, and indeed he was, with his sleek black hair, green eyes, and smooth, dark chocolate skin. He was on the smallish side and would need to gain twenty or more pounds of muscle to survive on a pro field, but he was fast, so on the local team, he was one of the heroes. He sported a well-trimmed mustache that gave him a debonair, sophisticated look, and yet, in spite of his good looks, he seemed somewhat shy with the ladies. *It's all an act,* Grace surmised. *Every good-looking guy I ever knew always saw themselves as God's gift to women, and this guy is shy? What is with that? I don't buy it.*

If it was an act, it worked well for Anton, for the ladies loved that quality. Dorcus fell hard but feared acting on her emotions. Her hot girl campaign was failing miserably, and so her self-esteem and self-confidence had taken a battering.

After the presentations, the five-piece combo switched from marches to dance music, and the bleachers suddenly emptied as most of the alumni and faculty headed for the nearest exit, leaving the current student body to party until midnight. Dorcus decided to push her way toward where she'd last seen Anton, but then she stopped short and thought to herself, *Why bother? I should get him out of my system,* after she saw the crowd of women surrounding him on the dance floor. It was like trying to get an autograph from a celebrity. She'd had a long day and was tired. Her world was closing in around her. Her hot girl ambitions were failing, her grades were failing, and she felt she couldn't risk another failure, so she slipped silently out the nearest exit. The walk back to the dorm was long, dreary, and silent. With most of the student body still back at the gym, she had the dorm all to herself. As she climbed the stairs, her footsteps echoed through the empty corridors. Her heart was heavy. She missed the encouragement and the love of her parents, her brothers, and her church. She heaved a heavy sigh as she opened the door to her dorm room. She entered the room and sat down on the bed with her face in her hands. Then the tears began to fall.

"Want to talk about it?" said a concerned, consoling voice. Dorcus, who was startled, having thought she was all alone, looked toward the doorway and saw Sardis's cheerful face. "You look terrible," she teased, noting Dorcus's tear-stained face, now terribly smudged with the heavy makeup that she was wearing.

Sardis decided to skip the dance, even though she'd begun to flourish and bloom like a spring flower, thanks to Dorcus. Now she became the lighthouse that Dorcus needed to get her through this terrible, stormy night. Dorcus managed a slight smile at Sardis's comment. The two women, neither of whom had sisters, had formed a special sibling-like bond. Tonight, it was Dorcus's turn to lean on Sardis, who was glad that her friend trusted her enough to share her pain. They talked for a long time, and Dorcus knew that she had to turn things around. The two women agreed to become study partners, for Sardis's private school education had prepared her to become an excellent college student. Girls being girls, however, they also talked extensively about boys. Sardis had no particular interest yet, but Dorcus still had Anton on her mind, and in her system.

Because the freshman schedule was so regimented, they had little interaction on a daily basis with upper-class men, except in the common areas like the library, the cafeteria, or the student center. Dorcus was anxious to get Sardis's approval of this guy, but during the week following the game, she didn't spot him once on campus. It was as if he had disappeared, until suddenly, on the Friday, two full weeks later, she saw him.

"There he is!" she shouted excitedly, pointing to the disciplined figure that was marching by them. "He's a Corp Commander!" she squealed. "Isn't he all that I said he is? Isn't he?" she said to a puzzled Sardis, while continuing to point at him. Sardis tried to follow her finger as the ROTC parade passed in review, but there were too many men, and although she hated to admit it, in uniform, they all looked alike to her.

Anton cut a dashing figure in his full dress military uniform, and just seeing him again made Dorcus's heart beat wildly. She wondered how she could have missed him before, but then she remembered that the football players were excused from certain optional activities during their practice season. Anton had never marched before, but now that the season had ended, he could resume his place in the corps of cadets. As a junior, he'd risen through the ranks to a leadership position and was now barking orders as he marched in front of a company, exuding strength and confidence. His sense of leadership made him very attractive, not only to Dorcus, but also to a host of women who were standing nearby. In her exuberance and anxiety to point him out to Sardis, Dorcus ruffled feathers. The other women sensed competition, and a chill crept into the air as battle lines were drawn. No less than five women had set their sights on the prize.

Dorcus didn't know how she would get him, but she knew this was the man she wanted, so she sized up the competition and enlisted

Sardis's help. At that moment, her hot girl campaign officially ended, and "Operation Anton" began. This was one skirmish she was determined to win. She asked Sardis to do a little research to appease Grace, who kept asking, "How come he managed to get all the way to his junior year without some girl latching on to him? With his looks and everything going for him, he should have a harem. There is something wrong with this picture."

"Flunked out?" laughed Dorcus when Sardis reported the results of her research. "So he is free!" said Dorcus, spinning gleefully in Grace's room following the revelation. Grace merely smiled politely as Dorcus danced back out of the room and down the hall. Grace had already heard the rumors about Anton's girlfriend, with one slight variation. The girl was pregnant. She hoped that Dorcus wasn't getting in over her head.

"It appears that Anton's girl studied Anton more than she studied the books," said Dorcus, still giddy after racing to tell Grace the news, which prompted Sardis to provide a gentle reminder of her own precarious grade situation.

"You have to get serious, or history will repeat itself," said Sardis, referring to her friend's academic future. Secretly, she hoped the other part of that particular history would not be repeated either, for she too knew the other variation of the rumor. Out of concern for her friend's happiness, however, she kept the knowledge to herself. Rumors come, rumors go; Sardis was sure that all would be revealed in time. Perhaps, by then, Dorcus's infatuation with Anton Baylor would have run its course. She hoped so.

Dorcus took Sardis's advice to heart, but nonetheless, they agreed to strategize. During the weeks that followed, Sardis served as a lookout. If there was an Anton sighting anywhere on campus, she let Dorcus know, reporting where he'd been seen and more importantly, who was with him. Dorcus became obsessed with Anton. She ate, dreamed, and studied Anton. Somehow, she had to get his attention. She sat in her classes writing his name next to hers, and her name next to his, and various combinations thereof. She waited, at times half-starving, for him to enter the cafeteria for his meals so she could magically appear in the line behind him. The first time she pulled that stunt, it almost resulted in a fight with another girl who was obviously using the same strategy. A few times, she managed to sit directly across the table from him, but on each occasion, she had to share him with at least two other women. "This is getting me nowhere," she conceded to Sardis during one of their study sessions. "He speaks to me every now and then, and he knows my name, but I may as well just be a face in the crowd. What to do? What to do?" she mused.

Sardis, ever the sage, took their anatomy text, and pressing it to Dorcus's forehead, mimicked her lament, saying "Study the skeletal system. Study the skeletal system. It's on tomorrow's test."

"Study! That's it. I'll study the competition from a distance. Figure out their strengths and weaknesses. See how I can exploit them. See which ones he tends to favor; let them eliminate themselves, and then pull a sneak attack." Sardis threw up her hands in despair and hoped that one day soon, her friend would become equally diligent with her studies. The library became a hunting ground. Whenever he entered the stacks, she mysteriously appeared. The library had individual study cubicles, so when he chose to use one of those desks, she always sat nearby, and actually got some study done. At times, she found him in the Student Center playing bid whist. Her now-advanced skills at the game got her dealt into some of his games, which she played with great proficiency. Sometimes, she just sat and watched, silently assessing his skill level. This helped her to take a dive and lose if she found herself playing against him, and to ensure that they won when she played as his partner. "You inspire me," she told him one day as they celebrated a victory. "You're a born leader. You bring out hidden talents and skills I never knew I had. We'd make a formidable team, you and me."

His warm smile told her that her comments were massaging all the right places. She discovered years ago that a little flattery carried a lot of weight when dealing with the male ego; her brothers had taught her that. Unbeknownst to them, they now reinforced the lesson during their weekly calls from home. She wouldn't go into specifics about her crush, but gave them just enough information for them to volunteer their advice, which she told them was "for a friend." She even helped him to cheat a few times. Once, he was in a very tight match and she managed to maneuver herself into a position where she could peek at his main opponent's hand. She then caught his eye and signaled for him to play a diamond, which won the final trick and the game.

Every Sunday, she entered the Vesper service at the very last minute. Many upper-class men were present each Sunday out of force of habit, but Anton only attended sporadically. As a junior, he was free to please himself, so she kept a careful watch on the entrance, and if he made an appearance, she was ready. She, as a freshman, couldn't sit with him, but she watched where he sat, and if one of her competitors was sitting nearby, she would sprint and latch on to his arm before the final amen had even been spoken, and being the gentleman he was, he would escort her back to the dorm, which raised her hopes while giving her warm, fuzzy feelings.

She learned his class schedule and made use of this knowledge by "accidentally" running into him as he left classes. This was not always practical, because his classes were usually across the campus from where she was located most of the day, so she had to time these "coincidental" meetings around her free periods. There was only one boundary in this hunt; the men's dorm, which was naturally off limits. She needed to find a way around that, so once again, she solicited Sardis's help.

"Here he comes," whispered Sardis. They were standing near the entrance to the cafeteria. "The wispy little guy. That's his roommate. You can take it from here," she called as she disappeared into the building.

"Oh, excuse me," said Dorcus after deliberately bumping into Charles Jordan. Once she flashed her trademark smile at Charlie, he was ready to forgive her for anything. The two roommates could not have been more dissimilar. Whereas Anton was outgoing and popular, Charlie was introverted and unassuming. He had a slight build and a narrow face that was almost completely concealed behind a pair of oversized black-framed glasses. He was also in his junior year and had been a permanent fixture on the dean's list for outstanding academic achievement since his freshman year. Most of the time, he barely spoke above a whisper, and his mama had taught him well; his manners, and his respect for women, were beyond reproach. Despite all this, however, he didn't have a steady girlfriend. He was a living, breathing example of the old adage that nice guys finish last. "I feel so terrible about bumping into you like that," Dorcus continued as they joined the line inside the cafeteria. She knew that Anton had already eaten and left, but then she always knew where Anton was and what he was doing, so this was a good time to corner Charlie. At first, he responded to her apology with a brief, mumbled acceptance, and then countered with an apology of his own for not looking where he'd been walking. Then, when Dorcus began to use flattery on him, he warmed up.

"Would you care to join me for dinner?" he asked, finally venturing out of his shell, although in a way, he hadn't had much of a choice, because Dorcus had talked nonstop since they joined the serving line. Now she guided him to a table far away from the middle of the cafeteria where Anton usually liked to dine. Once they settled in to their seats, Charlie began to open up a little more, and she soon discovered that beneath that mousy exterior was a very warm, intelligent man with a great sense of humor.

"I could really like him, if it weren't for Anton," she told Sardis when she returned to the dorm, "but Anton has my heart, and Charlie will help me to capture his heart." With her full attention focused on Anton, Dorcus's grades began to suffer again, and one evening she found herself in Sardis's room cramming for an exam she hadn't realized she had the following day. Sardis agreed to help her again, on one major condition. "You will not be permitted to utter the name 'Anton' at any time during this study session," she said frowning.

Dorcus agreed, reluctantly, but was unable to prevent her imagination from taking over, and the dorm room soon faded, to be replaced by a recurring daydream. In it, she was sitting by the pool of her gorgeous home, one befitting a national football league player. In spite of the fact that Anton did not have the speed, heft, or skills needed to play professional football, Dorcus's dreams led her into stadium after stadium following her NFL husband, their children in tow.

"Dorcus," chided Sardis, after a question she posed had been met with complete silence, accompanied by a faraway stare. The sound of her name snapped Dorcus back into the present moment. She pulled out her class notebook and discovered to her horror that it contained nothing but a bunch of gibberish. She couldn't follow what she'd written because the pages were full of cryptic scribbles. Some were the names of foreign lands where she imagined she would travel with Anton if he ever decided to ditch the NFL for the military. She'd never traveled beyond the state of South Carolina before, so the thought of traveling around the world, as the wife of an army officer no less, fascinated her. She was thankful that Sardis had a clear mind and took good notes, because neither one of them could decipher what Dorcus had written down. "You're hopeless," sighed Sardis. "Just remember, one girl has already had a sudden career change after, as you said, studying Anton and not the books."

That comment jolted Dorcus back to reality, and she managed to pass the test by a single point. Convinced, at last, that she did not want to share the fate of his former girlfriend, Dorcus finally managed to balance her focus on Anton with her academic work. To her surprise, she found herself beginning to make progress at both. She felt sure that getting to know Charlie had played a big part in her Anton campaign. During their next cafeteria meal together, Anton lingered a little longer and engaged her in conversation, and after the Vesper service the following Sunday, he sought her out. That was something he hadn't done before, and now just holding on to his muscled arm on their brief stroll to the dorm sent wave after wave of chills up and down Dorcus's spine.

Along with gaining Anton's attention, however, she noticed something else. Charlie really liked her, even though she was careful not to lead him on. After their first "accidental" meeting, they met several other times. Charlie was wise and caring, but he wasn't naive. He knew she had no interest in him, but he enjoyed being around her. She didn't make him feel awkward or insecure, like most women did. She listened to him and encouraged him to open up about himself, even though the conversation always returned to Anton. Being a level-headed realist, Charlie quickly realized that she had an ulterior motive for being kind to him. She wasn't the first woman to cozy up to him in the hope of getting to Anton, but she was the first one he liked. He enjoyed her sparkle and her smile, and he liked her caring attitude, which shined through even though her attention was directed at someone besides him, so he decided to help.

Unbeknown to most people, Anton and Charlie were cousins, and they watched out for each other. Charlie was the smart one, and Anton was, well, Anton. Charlie figured things out, while Anton had things figured out for him. If Charlie had told Anton the sky was lavender, Anton would have asked what shade of lavender. They were closer than brothers in many ways; alike, yet opposites. Charlie, the scholar, pushed and pulled Anton, the jock, throughout their entire academic careers. What Charlie suggested, Anton usually did, and now Charlie liked Dorcus, and therefore Anton was also going to like Dorcus.

One afternoon, Dorcus burst into the dorm, tore through the lobby, took the stairway three steps at a time, and came to a screeching halt in the middle of Sardis's room, where a startled Sardis looked up from her desk as Dorcus struggled to get the words out. "He asked me to the dance on Friday!" Then, reality suddenly began to dawn. Dorcus felt a knot in her stomach, and then the room began to spin and fade to black. Her last memory was the face of her obviously frightened friend, and those of others who had gathered around her and were encouraging her to inhale deeply.

The dating relationship was rocky from the start. Anton, for his part, enjoyed the attention Dorcus gave him, but remained aloof, while Dorcus's competitors, realizing their loss, turned their attentions elsewhere, so Dorcus was able to enjoy her conquest. If she couldn't be a hot girl, having a hot boyfriend afforded almost as many benefits. She enjoyed being Anton's queen.

Charlie hoped he had done the right thing by bringing them together. He retained a glimmer of hope that this would be a short infatuation; he knew his cousin's track record for short-term relationships. If things progressed as he surmised, in six months or a year's time, maybe he would have a chance with Dorcus himself. He was torn, because while he wanted them to be happy, and to remain together, he was well aware that he could benefit from a different outcome. He decided that he would simply watch as events unfolded. His greatest fear was that Dorcus might suffer the same fate as Anton's former flame who, he'd heard, had given birth to a baby boy.

Grace doubted the relationship would work, while Sardis hoped, for the sake of her friend, that it would. Dorcus knew in her heart that, with time, they would bond into the perfect couple who would spend an eternity together.

Eartha didn't like ICS, right from her first day as an eighth grader on campus. She looked stunning in her new uniform, but her sisters, now in their junior and senior years respectively, made her life a living nightmare with their rumors and snippy comments. Father was still her friend, which made Mother angry for some reason, so in order to stay out of the line of fire, she retreated to her dark room yet again. It was safe and cool and comforting in there, but she always heard their voices.

"I told you I would help you raise the child, but I never said I would love her." It was Mother's voice again.

"You could try a little more. She's a sweet child, and has developed into a beautiful young woman," said her father.

"Don't talk to me about love, Walter ..." Now the voices trailed off, leaving Eartha to wonder if it was she who caused Mother to rant so much. It seemed she could never please Mother. She wondered what she'd done wrong this time. My grades are good, and I'm staying out of the sun, *she reflected.*

XII

Sardis cocked her ear toward the open door and raised her hand for the others to be quiet. "I thought I heard Mom. Did you hear anything?" The other two shook their heads, their eyes focused on the cards in front of them. Sardis rose and went into the kitchen to refresh their snacks, and to listen secretly with extra care. Watching her go, Grace felt a tinge of jealousy, thinking how life had been very good to Sardis, who had changed very little since their college days. Was that a good thing or bad thing? Grace pondered silently.

Sardis still had her childhood home, with all its mementos and memories, but Grace's history was all gone, swept away by desegregation and urban renewal. Her elementary schools, Simonton, Buist, and Henry P. Archer, had either been condemned, transformed, or abandoned. They'd been good enough for colored children to attend, but as soon as the order came down to integrate, they'd been declared substandard and "poof," her history was erased. At least her high school, dear old Burke, with its renowned high-stepping band, still existed, but it was still as segregated as ever.

Childhood friends scattered after her home became part of an urban renewal project and was "renewed" out of existence. Despite Charleston's desire to maintain its antiquity, apparently there were some things that were just too antiquated to retain. Her Alley had been the ghetto of its time, and the houses were on their last legs even then, so, antiquated or not, any attempts to save them would have been futile; they had to go.

She wondered what happened to some of the other Alley people, especially the strange character everyone called "the Judge." Given the right timing and the right circumstances, along with a hefty dose of equal opportunity, he probably could have become the colored J. P. Morgan or Rockefeller of his day. He had an entrepreneurial spirit and a willingness to be a successful businessman, but he was unable to overcome the lack of means, lack of education, lack of connections, and wrong racial hue. Instead, he did what he could with what he had. He lived directly across the Alley from Grace's family, and during the summer months, he did a thriving business selling snow cones and ice cream from an old freezer he kept on his porch. The board of health would probably have frowned on this set-up and shut him down for unsanitary serving and storage conditions, but the kids loved the cool, refreshing treats. As to how he got the name the Judge, like everything else in Michele Alley, the story was shrouded in mystery, and Grace, along with everyone else, never learned his given name. He was, simply, the Judge.

Rumor had it he acquired his moniker after he served as an intermediary in a dispute between two Alley families. Someone told him he was like Moses from the Bible, who served as the first judge for his people. Back then, colored people were a disenfranchised people, just like those wilderness dwellers. They could demand neither attention nor respect from the Jim Crow legal system, and the only time they faced a judge was as a defendant, so disputes frequently had to be settled within the neighborhood.

The Judge might have been one of those unofficial magistrates. He was held in high esteem by most folks, had the bearing to demand judicial respect, and possessed a lot of wisdom and common sense, all traits that carried a lot of weight with the Alley people. There was, however, a dark side. He was a toothless, totally bald old man, with leathery, blue-tinged black skin. "You wouldn't want him sneaking up on you on a dark, moonless night," Dorcus's mother was prone to say. "You'd never be able to see him, the man is so black."

Dorcus's family knew of the Judge even though they did not live in the Alley. They knew the role he played in the residents' lives, and they didn't like him. Besides being known by the Alley people, he must have attracted the attention of the local detectives, who had to have known about the other "refreshments" he sold to adults every weekend, but they did nothing about it. Dorcus's mother was right about not being able to see him on a dark night, and he used his natural camouflage to the utmost during his Thursday morning runs to the mystery vehicle carrying bottles of white lightning. Then, from late Thursday night all the way through until before daybreak on Sunday morning, people could be seen coming and going to and from his house at all hours of the day and night. At dawn on Sundays, however, all activity stopped. "My soul is not going down ta Hell for desecratin' the Lord's Day," he would tell his relieved wife. At the stroke of midnight, however, heralding Monday morning, and with his soul now safe again, he went back to business. Sales would dwindle as the working week unfolded and his supply ran low, but early on Thursday morning, the car would bring a fresh supply, and the cycle would begin all over again.

The kids' treats were a cover for his real trade, and most of the time he never even charged for the snow cones. He was especially generous toward the little ones whose parents were out of work, or with those folks who had more month than they had money. He liked having people around, and with all ages coming and going, things looked legitimate, all cozy and warm. He made sure that everyone kept a cool head, ensuring that his business continued to run smoothly, and didn't attract any unwanted attention. He had a monopoly on the trade and didn't want anyone cutting in on his action. "Young fools," he called potential troublemakers. "Get dat white lightnin' in 'em an' deys crazy. Crazy, I tell you. Got to make sur dey don' mess things up fo' everybody, 'specially me," he often confided to his patient wife. He made it his business to know who the potential troublemakers were and kept a close eye on them. Mysteriously, those he couldn't control invariably ended up in the hands of the law. "Make things nice fo' da po-lice. Don' wan' no trouble here wit dem. No suh." By giving up a few hotheads and sharing a few inconsequential secrets, he managed to make things really nice for the police. They got an arrest every now and then, and the Judge stayed in business. The universe was in balance.

Grace was twelve years old when she developed a big interest in the Judge's house, not in relation to his snow cones, but involving another "sugary treat." Willie was two years older than her and from New York. Her eyes nearly jumped out of her head the first time she saw this lanky kid swagger out through the Judge's front door and take a seat on the porch swing, right in front of her eyes, large as life.

"Who you?" she called from across the way. The Alley never had strangers. He smiled at her forwardness, not used to such openness, and introduced himself. Grace was beside herself when she heard that New York accent. "Boy, you talk so proper," she said, with the emphasis on "proper." That drew a big laugh out of Willie, as he sauntered across the Alley's dusty dirt road to get a close look at his inquisitor.

Grace saw that he was tall, with very delicate features, different from most of the Southern boys she knew, who tended to be more husky and stocky. Many of them played football, or worked on family farms during the summer, so they developed more muscle. He also had the neatest and straightest white teeth she'd ever seen, and his close-cropped dark-brown hair had natural waves. His dark eyes seemed to dance against his golden tanned skin, and he did indeed talk "proper," as Grace had observed. She was as much in love as a twelve-year-old could be, and she wanted to know as much as she could about this fourteen-year-old nephew of the Judge's wife. It was his first trip "down South," but it wasn't to be his last. He visited with his aunt and uncle all that summer and for the next three summers as well. He was a good kid, but his family was coming apart, so he, along with his two siblings, was temporarily farmed out to other family members to get them away from the fighting. Many hoped that the situation would improve between his parents, but it didn't. People from "up North" held a special fascination for those who lived in the South, and Grace glued herself to Willie. Never having ventured far beyond the Alley, she wanted to know what New York was like. She bombarded him with questions, the answers to which generated even more questions. She was like a sponge, soaking it all in. They sat on the Judge's porch swing every afternoon until late in the evening, just talking and swinging.

Willie would not admit it to himself at first, but Grace held a special fascination for him, too. She possessed a refreshing innocence that was delightfully different from the other girls he knew, and she was not afraid to show her zeal. She began to dote on him and made no attempt to mask her feelings. With her encouragement, it didn't take long for him to open up about his feelings for her, and so they both began to look forward to his summer visits, the northern boy with street smarts and the southern country girl.

After Willie graduated from high school in Brooklyn, New York, he decided to move in with his aunt and uncle in Charleston. His home life had now fallen apart, and his parents were trying to rebuild their lives. His mother's new boyfriend did not take kindly to male competition or distractions, even if it was her own, almost-adult, son. Grace was thrilled, but her mother was not. Ever since Willie appeared, Hatta Mae began having nightmares. She didn't want Grace to follow in the footsteps of her older sister, nor the extra responsibility of another baby in the house and another out-of-work "husband" to aid. Besides, they didn't have room in their crowded flat. Things were already tight, with two families living in a space not even adequate for one. From the time Willie first appeared, Grace's mother watched them like a hawk. She warned Grace that she was never to set one foot inside the Judge's house with that boy; the porch swing was the only place she could meet with him. Grace knew better than to raise the ire of her mother, so she followed her instructions to the letter. Hatta Mae was living with a lot of guilt, feeling like she'd failed with Grace's older sister, and she was determined she wasn't going to fail with Grace. She hated Michele Alley and its loose-living residents, but her contempt was directed at the Judge in particular. While most folk saw a kindly, generous old man trying to survive life, Hatta Mae did not. "That old devil," she would practically hiss whenever he was anywhere around. "Got everybody else fooled, but not me."

Things were always breaking down, and no one could be found to fix them. Leaky roofs, broken pipes, and broken windows stayed that way. People had to tread lightly over wobbly stairs when they climbed to their second-floor flats, and one family had to stop using the rickety steps all together. A widow had to use her meager savings to buy a ladder so that she and the rest of her family could reach their second-story dwelling. She registered complaint after complaint to the landlord Judge, who offered soothing words of comfort and promises of compliance, but no action, and so the ladder became a permanent fixture.

The bug infestation was unreal. If someone went into the kitchen at night, they had to turn on a light; otherwise every step was accompanied by a crunching sound underfoot. The light would reveal hundreds of roaches scampering for the holes in the walls. No amount of insect spray or floor scrubbing could get rid of the creatures, and tenants had no one they could hold responsible. The Judge collected the rent every month and sent it off to who knows where. Grace's mother always held a sneaking suspicion that the Judge was indeed the owner, in spite of his protests to the contrary. "I just collects, Miss Hatta, I just collects. The mister who takes it is unbeknownst to me. He just t'anks me fo' doin' a good job." She complained every month and always got the same answer: "Jus' thank goodness that youse even got a place ta stay, with yo' man not workin' an' all. You don' have ta go on the county. A leaky roof better'n no roof 'tall." His false words of encouragement fell on deaf ears, however. She knew he was just protecting his moonshine business. He had to keep the peace and keep everyone in line. He didn't want any questions, and he didn't want anything to change.

Grace's dad was a good man, until he lost the ability to take care of his family anymore. Then, he found old, generous Judge, who showed him a way to ease his pain every weekend. The first few samples were free, out of sympathy for his plight, but he soon found a way to pay for his weekend binges. Hatta Mae pretended not to notice the money that was missing from her purse, but she knew where it went. She also knew he "borrowed" money from his older daughter whenever she got paid for her housekeeping job. The Judge was cleaning up from his trapped tenants. "My chil' is gonna git out this Alley. No place to grow up or raise no more chil'ren." Hatta Mae had the determination and the drive; what she didn't have was the resources. She continued to work long, arduous days until her feet betrayed her, the corns, bunions, and calluses causing no end of pain. Cheap uptown shoe stores that sold shoes with no support, coupled with the long walk downtown over cobblestone streets, was starting to take its toll.

No one noticed that Eartha was missing, and she preferred it that way. She stole away to her room, where she could still hear the music and the voices clearly. It was the graduation gala for sister number two, who was leaving the nest to follow sister number one northward. Mother did not like the idea. "Why do you have to live so far away?" she had asked both of them. New York got into their blood, and no amount of pleading could change their minds. Eartha hummed and twirled to the sound of the music below, fascinated by the idea of being the only child at home. "Since I'll be the only one left, will Mom finally like me?" Eartha wondered. At least her world would be a bit happier without her nagging, annoying sisters around, but as she was to discover, life with Mother changed very little.

Mother got letters every now and then, which made her cry. Dad, just being Dad, hid some of the letters, because he hated to see Mother cry. Finally, the letters stopped. "Now I've lost both of them," Eartha heard her say one day.

"It's as if I am not even here," Eartha moaned, submitting to her solitary existence. But in the foggy haze of her subconscious mind, she could have sworn she heard laughter. Laughter was nice; laughter meant fun. Had her sisters returned? Was someone having a party; another party where she was not welcome?

XIII

Sardis was in the kitchen preparing more drinks when suddenly she stopped dead in her tracks, sure that she'd heard humming coming from upstairs. Excusing herself, she climbed the stairs silently to her mother's room, pushed the door open, and peered inside. It took a few moments before her eyes adjusted to the gloom, the only light coming from the dim nightlight on the stand next to her mother's bed, but in the faint glow, it looked for all the world as if her mother was … smiling!

Sardis's eyes widened. It had been years since she'd seen even a glimmer of a smile on her mother's face. She turned on another low light, just to make sure of what she had seen. Looking at her now, Sardis did not remember her mother being that frail. Her olive complexion, which she usually camouflaged with clownish, white face powder that was far too light and made her features appear leathery, and the hair that was always pressed straight down to the roots now revealed its coarseness as it lay draped over the pillows.

People always remarked about how much Sardis's brother looked like his mom. Now Sardis saw it clearly. His ruddy complexion had given him his robust good looks, but in their world, lighter skin was prized, retaining a certain purity that the high yellows valued. However, he was the son of a physician, so it hadn't mattered as much if he didn't have the very fair complexion that had been shared by Sardis and her father. The girls loved him, and many families had considered him a good match for their daughters. Sardis smiled at the memory of two families whose daughters were in competition for his attention during his high school senior year. He didn't choose either of them as his prom date, and their families didn't speak to each other, nor to Sardis's family, for almost a year. Sardis liked the girl he'd chosen as his date and hoped they would eventually marry, because she looked forward to having a "big sister" to share things with, and nieces and nephews and ... but just like that, suddenly he was gone, taking all those dreams and hopes with him.

His loss was a tragedy the family never overcame. Their father's demise followed shortly afterward, and there was little doubt that it resulted from losing his son too soon. There'd been tension between them, ostensibly because her brother had rejected their father's profession, among other things that neither of them talked about openly. Both had said harsh and bitter things to each other, words that, once spoken, could never be recalled. Regrets could not be righted from the grave, and so her dad's spirit died along with his only son. Shortly thereafter, his body followed.

Eartha withdrew from life and sat hiding in her dark room for hours on end. Sardis wondered if her mother knew that the world was continuing on. She wouldn't let Sardis into her world, and she did not enter into Sardis's teenage world. There was constant bickering between them. Sardis, being a typical teen, needed and wanted to get on with life, while her mother remained somber. Her mood, like the house, never brightened.

Sardis's friends still longed to visit, because her house had been the "in" place for her friends to gather. It was no secret the girls all had a big crush on her brother. His tragic demise had only served to magnify the angst in their teenage hearts. Now, they longed to be near the house of tragedy, to share their memories and listen to his favorite music.

Her brother had loved the mellow sounds of Johnnie Mathis. "He is sooooo romantic," one admirer swooned, although Sardis never knew if she meant the singer or her brother, who, when he'd been alive, enjoyed the gaggle of giggles he evoked simply by appearing at the right moment. Now the visits and the giggles died, and Eartha's spirit continued to darken. Sardis encouraged her friends to continue their visits, until one ugly incident changed everything.

"We must have played *Chances Are* once too often," Sardis confided during one late-night game in their dorm. She still hesitated to share information about herself, but her memory had been triggered when the strains of her brother's favorite music, which was being played somewhere in the dorm, reached their ears. "Mom threw a major fit. Called them ICS lackeys and a whole lot more; she said a lot of strange things that day. Even said they were no better than her sisters, who'd never wanted her around. Until then, I'd thought my mom was an only child, so what she was saying didn't make sense. My friends stumbled over themselves trying to get out of the house, and they never came back. Neither did anyone else. I couldn't blame them. In that closed community, we were known as the strange house." In a robotic voice, she said, "Warning, warning. Crazy lady and her odd daughter. Keep clear." Reverting to her own voice, she added, "We didn't need a quarantine sign. The closed shutters were sufficient to keep everyone away."

"What about boyfriends?" asked Dorcus.

"Boyfriends? You're kidding, right? Who wanted to know the odd girl with the loony mother?"

This exchange, during their freshman year, gave the card-playing group their first look into Sardis's so-called privileged life. Until tragedy struck their house, she'd been a bit of a free spirit, but her mother soon became a millstone around her neck, gradually suffocating the life out of her. As her mother's mood darkened, Sardis knew she had to get out of that house. But how, and at what cost?

She took on more of the household duties, doing the cooking, laundry, and cleaning. Mother and daughter had effectively changed places. Isolation and loneliness became Sardis's constant companions. In the afternoons, with Eartha locked in her bedroom, not to mention the prison of her own mind, Sardis often took long walks through downtown. She would look at the fashions she could no longer afford and sigh. With her dad being a physician, they'd previously been in a position to patronize downtown. "Uptown is off limits," her mother had told her in no uncertain terms. *"We* do not shop uptown. The products are so poorly made they'll fall apart while you're putting them on. Besides, it makes you common. We are not common. We can afford downtown." So downtown it was. But now her dad was gone, and he'd left very little behind for them to live on. Insurance for colored people, no matter how fair-skinned, had been limited, to a large extent, to small burial policies. He had some savings, and so they managed to survive, but not like before. Now, Sardis just wandered and looked and looked some more. One day, she varied from her usual route along King Street.

Spring had arrived early and brought with it a warm, gentle breeze. The days were getting longer, and since she loathed returning to that sad, lifeless house, she decided to stroll in a different direction. She just wanted to keep walking, preferably right out of her present life and into someone else's; anyone's. *Mother won't even realize I'm gone until later when she wants her warm milk to help her sleep,* she thought as she turned down Queen Street. *King and Queen. That's cute,* she mused as she strolled along. When she reached Church Street, she thought about going to the Battery. She loved that strip of land bordering the calming river. Even though they lived close by, she hadn't been there since she was a little girl. Her proud dad would drive that route on one of those rare days when he took his children to Roper Hospital for a private show and tell with his staff. Now, just thinking about him caused a catch in her throat. He'd been gone a year, and she still had a hard time thinking about him without crying.

If I walk all the way down there, it might get too dark before I can make it home, and besides, I might linger too long and ... Suddenly, she paused mid-thought. Something caught her attention. She found herself standing in front of a beautiful old structure with a wrought-iron balcony. "Dock Street Theater," the sign said. Sardis had never been to a theater in her life, either to watch a live performance or to see a movie on the screen. Charleston had several movie houses, the Lincoln, the Magnolia, and the Riviera, all located on King Street, but like everything else, they were segregated. Downstairs was reserved for white patrons, while the stuffy, overcrowded balcony upstairs was for colored people. Their family did not go; could not go. "Something to do with the Church," she'd told Dorcus during one of their many discussions about the Catholics versus the Protestants.

"Tools of the devil, if not the devil itself, right?" replied Dorcus, laughing, as they discovered another commonly held tenet of both faiths.

Unlike the movie houses, the Dock Street Theater did not welcome people of color at all. The old building's history said it all. It had once been a hotel where Southern planters stayed on their visits to acquire plantation labor. It provided easy access to the slave market, which was only a mile or so away on Meeting Street. The market still remained as a grim reminder of the not so distant past. Now, however, merchants hawked postcards, T-shirts, and unique woven goods made from Carolina sweet grass. Many were fashioned right before tourists' eyes by descendants of the market's original commodity.

"You need a ticket?" A voice came from behind her as she stood transfixed by the façade. She turned abruptly and found herself staring into the most handsome face she had ever seen. His luxuriant dark hair and striking green eyes caused her knees to buckle, and she was at a loss as to how to respond. He was partially shaded initially, but now he stepped out into the light and she could see that he was very well dressed.

He shops way downtown, she thought and smiled inwardly.

"Do you need a ticket?" he repeated, and then smiled, revealing a set of gorgeous, even, white teeth. His flirtatious glances made her realize that he must have mistaken her for a white woman. She was momentarily gripped by fear but managed to compose herself. "I'm in the play," he said, strutting around as if he owned the place. "I love to surprise people, especially one as charming as you, my dear, with a free ticket. Here. No strings attached. It's for tomorrow night's performance."

91

She smiled as she accepted the gift. "Thank you," she said, her voice barely above a whisper. She was reluctant to say any more, out of fear that he might discover her secret. He continued to make small talk for a few minutes, telling her all about the production. Sardis was so excited. The sound of her heart beating all but drowned out whatever else the man was saying until eventually she heard him say, "My name is Steve. There's my picture." He motioned toward a poster on the wall of the building. "When you show up tomorrow, come backstage and I'll sign your program." She thanked him again, and then he vanished just as mysteriously as he had appeared, leaving her dazed and bedazzled. Life had suddenly returned.

Tomorrow couldn't come fast enough. The school day crawled, and dinner dragged on interminably. Mother even seemed to take her time retreating to her room, but she finally locked herself in for the night. Sardis didn't have anything elegant to wear, for she was in high school and wasn't expected to look elegant, so she grabbed some church clothes. Of more immediate concern, however, was her fear that her color would be discovered. *Flour,* she thought. Even though her skin was very fair, she dusted herself all over with baking flour, which lent her a somewhat ghostly appearance. Still, she was satisfied that no one would ask any questions about her race. Previously, passing for white had never entered her mind, but now the thought of pulling it off thrilled her. She'd lived on the periphery of both the black and white worlds all of her life, but like her darker-skinned sisters and brothers, had never had any interaction with the white race. By law, those identified as colored never crossed that invisible line, no matter how fair their skin.

She practically ran all the way to the theater. *Can't sweat,* she kept telling herself. *I'll look like an under-baked cake if I do.* Not knowing the decorum at a theater, she made a quick study of the crowd, watching to see what the other patrons were doing, and then fell in line. She remained calm when she handed her ticket to the usher, even though he seemed to hesitate before taking it. At that moment, she knew that he'd seen right through her. She never thought of herself as being attractive, but her smile was always her best defense, so now she flashed her pearly whites at the usher. Like many black residents of Charleston, Sardis did not speak with a natural southern drawl, but now she took a deep breath and heard a strange voice say, "Mighty fine uniform y'all wearin'." To her relief, it worked, and the usher fell all over himself escorting her personally to her seat. She smiled at the success of the deception and so, found herself sitting with bated breath waiting for the commencement of her first ever stage production, Tennessee Williams's *Summer and Smoke.*

As the house lights dimmed, Sardis relaxed. She was delighted with herself for pulling it off. She'd stepped out of her skin and become someone else, just like the actors who were, at that very moment, entering the stage. Soon, she was drawn in by this make-believe world of contrived plots and characters. She found herself inhabiting the soul of the lovesick Miss Alma and felt her every pain, and she quickly fell in love with the costumes, the makeup, and the theatre life. Closing her eyes, she envisioned herself in the spotlight, up in front of the audience, who gave her the love that she no longer received from anyone close to her. She drank it all in and decided that she didn't want this feeling to leave, ever.

*"You did what?" Eartha heard Mother's voice. Somehow, though, it sounded different. She sounded excited—happy even! "That's **wonderful,**" Mother continued. "Then she can leave for her own house right after her graduation. Just get her out of mine." Eartha knew that Mother wasn't talking about her sisters. Their letters were now fewer and fewer, and when they did arrive, Mother would withdraw for weeks. For a while, Father had often responded with large checks, but then he stopped, and so the letters stopped coming.*

"They're a good, solid family. The boy has been out of school for a while now, and has set up his own practice as a doctor. He's been living with the family until he could get on his feet, but he'll do just fine," Father was explaining.

"Wonder what's really wrong with him?" mused Mother.

"What do you mean, dear?" replied Father, with a tone of slight irritation.

"You know what I mean, Walter. A single, colored doctor—how old; thirty—living in his parents' house. Even if he is setting up his practice, some girl should have snatched him up long ago."

*"I don't know, dear. But I do know that his folks were very happy when I mentioned my daughter. **Very** happy."*

"Well, it doesn't matter. All I know is ..."

Eartha didn't need to hear the rest. She could tell by the voices that Father was resigned, Mother was very happy, and she was leaving again. For the last time.

Now she found herself lying here, listening to those strange voices.

XIV

Sardis left the theater floating on air. *This is it. This is what I want to do,* she thought as she walked home. For the next few days, she went back to the theater every evening hoping that someone would offer her another chance to see a play. *Summer and Smoke* had completed its season the night she saw it, and with the resulting cast changes, there was no chance of running into Steve again. She needed to find another patron to get back into the theater. *If I managed to get in once, I can do it again,* she reasoned, determinedly.

Fate stepped in and lent her a great hand. One evening she noticed a "Help Wanted" sign posted at the theatre entrance. *They need ushers,* she thought. *And I could use a job. It's a perfect match.* Prior to applying for the job, she took great precautions with her appearance. Rather than taking a chance with baking flour, this time she managed to swipe some of her mother's light face powder to even out her complexion. When she arrived at the theater, she once again flashed her megawatt smile at the same usher who took her ticket the evening she attended the play. "Why y'all are back again. Come to see our new production?" he asked, dripping with sugary hospitality.

Summoning up her fake Southern drawl, Sardis inquired about the job. "Y'all come to the right person. I recall y'all vera' well, pretty lady. Y'all had a guest pass, so y'all must know somebody heauh."

So that's why he stared at my ticket, she thought, relaxing into her role. If there's one thing about a southern gentleman, it's once he's been charmed, he lays the world at a southern lady's feet. The next thing Sardis knew, she was standing at the theater door handing out programs. She knew she had to exercise great discretion. Living two lives was tricky, and dangerous, but Sardis did it very skillfully. She was soon able to talk her way into a position inside the theater, thus avoiding having to stand at the front door as a ticket-taker, even though that was where the new ushers were traditionally stationed. She didn't want to risk the possibility of being recognized by a neighbor, or perhaps a fellow church member, who might happen to wander by. Every night, she stepped into a role and was convincing, so convincing that she soon became lost in the part, although she encountered an uncanny phenomenon that has always existed with colored people.

"One night, a chauffeur saw right through me. I still don't know how," she confided to the dorm players.

"Girl, didn't you know we always know each other?" said Taletha.

"He was hanging around behind the theater, waiting for one of the actors. I always used the back exit, so I literally walked right into him. He looked me up and down, then he smiled and whispered, 'I ain' gonna give 'way yo' secret, missy.'

"I started to deny everything, and was about to ask him what he meant, but there was something about his eyes—call it pride—that made me trust him, so I nodded in assent.

"'I understands the unwritten code,' he went on to say. 'We don' give nobody up. Your success is all our success. Anyway, who gon' believe a colored driver? Enjoy yo' job, missy, enjoy yo' job.'

"I was sweating so hard, the face powder started to run, so I got out of there as fast as I could. That was my closest call," she told them.

Sardis worked every evening there was a show and met her objectives: she was able to view each one. She even managed to meet some of the performers and was fascinated by their nightly transformations from ordinary people into fictional personas. She felt at ease with them, not only because most of them weren't from the South, but she found she was able to develop the sort of kinship that performers have with other performers.

She learned as much as she dared about acting, but given the limitations under which she was working in this little theater, there was only so much she could absorb. One actor who noticed her hunger for knowledge developed a professional and clearly personal interest in her. He was the first person to mention that magical place called Broadway, and even offered to take her there, but despite her naivety, she knew this ploy was a pipedream.

Summer vacation eventually rolled around, and now Sardis lived the life of an acrobat balancing on a high wire without a safety net. She had to measure every conversation she had at the theater carefully in order to protect her secret, and became quite adept at sidestepping probing questions from the head usher, who had become infatuated. She never uttered a word to her mother about the job, and definitely nothing about her passing for white. How would she have been able to explain it? Eartha was so withdrawn into the shadows of her mind by now that most of the time, she wasn't even aware of Sardis. As long as she didn't bring any strange friends into the house, Mother was happy with her explanation that she was taking long walks. As long as she managed to return in time to heat up a cup of milk before bedtime, her mother cared little about her activities.

Sardis managed to stay on the taut wire, and learned to walk it with great skill and precision. She actually liked the many facets that were involved, and the intrigue of leading a complex life. It kept life interesting and made it exciting, if somewhat dangerous, but she knew things would eventually collapse at some point. She didn't know when or how or what she would do for an encore. Her high school days were rapidly coming to an end, which meant she would have to let her mother know of her decision to pursue an acting career. *Mother wants me to remain enslaved and in servitude to her forever, but I have to live my own life,* she thought one day, while gathering the nerve to broach the subject. *I have to let her know I'm leaving. Just be direct. You can do it, girl.* Graduation approached, and still she said nothing. She was in a dilemma about how she would share her dreams with a mother who had long ago forgotten what it was like to dream.

XV

More and more student demonstrators began to return to campus. This was their third night of protests, and the status remained the same. There was unease in the air, and rather than returning to their dorms, they milled about on the Quad. This attracted the attention of many students who hadn't been demonstrating, and now the dorms began to empty. As the crowd grew, it became harder to concentrate and study, which only served to entice more people to abandon their books. Now the mood began to turn ugly, and many hoped that it would play itself out without incident.

"How come your folks let you come here to State?" Grace asked Sardis. Her frosty disposition toward Sardis had melted by the end of their freshman year, especially after she saw Sardis's skill at bid whist. She'd also grown to admire her sense of humor and her thespian skills. "You went to ICS, lived in 'Browntown,'" Grace continued, "never knew Dorcus or me, even though we lived within a stone's throw of your school and your house, and then you ended up here with us in a colored school. From what I remember, we never even used to see you High …" Grace caught herself before she could say the word "Yellows." She'd stopped using that epithet in Sardis's presence after Dorcus convinced her that it was insulting. To reinforce the message, Dorcus threw her a look that said, "Shut up already." If Sardis caught a drift of the discord around her, she never let on, so Grace continued with her musings. "I remember we hardly ever saw any light-skinned people. Folks used to say that all

99

of you would move up North and blend in. About the only time I even went to your part of town was to see a doctor every now and then. I remember you all had some nice houses. Never knew colored people lived in them. All them doctors and a couple of people working for the government. All had nice jobs."

Sardis smiled and took a deep breath as she thought back to those days. Meanwhile, Dorcus moved to intervene. Ever since they cemented their friendship, she'd been protective of her light sister. Sardis, however, sensing her concern, met her eyes and let her know that she was comfortable with Grace's questions and observations. Painful though the memories were, she continued her narrative, picking it up again near the beginning of summer, at the end of her senior year of high school, although she still couldn't bring herself to share the details of the prior tragedies that had altered her world forever.

"I knew I would have to face my mother at some point about my newfound interest. What I could never have anticipated, though, was that telling her about my job, and sharing my plans to move to New York once I finished at ICS, would conjure up the muse of tragedy itself," said Sardis. She chose graduation day as disclosure day. It was the first time in over a year that their house had sprung to life. They bought punch and cookies, to have on hand just in case anyone dropped by the house, and she opened up the fancy front room to air it, then dusted everything a second and a third time, because the flecks kept settling and resetting.

Friends from their parish, including their often reclusive priest, stopped by and joined in the celebration. Sardis was surprised and very pleased when her father's old hospital staff appeared, bearing a large financial gift. She counted the cash discretely and then stored it in her room, knowing that the more she had to take with her, the better off she would be. She'd compiled a rough estimate of what she needed for food and rent until she was able to find work. She knew from talking with the actors at the Dock Street Theater she would have to pay her dues, just as they had done, so she began to prepare herself for some tough times ahead. Unfortunately, her plans failed to include preparing for her departure from home.

Eartha fixed her face, white powder in place, although Sardis had to help her with her hair, which had gone a little gray and coarse. Eartha found her straightening comb and curling irons, and guided Sardis while she heated it to the right temperature to pull her hair straight. Since Sardis had naturally straight hair, she didn't know how to use these strange devices. Eartha pulled her best hat from the closet and set it on top of her curls, at just the right angle to cover the gray. Thus, she was now ready to face the world. Sardis was happy to see the light shining in her eyes again. She was also very happy to learn people actually remembered where they lived. Guests came and went all afternoon, congratulating Sardis and asking her about her future plans, and she gave each one an evasive answer. They would all find out in due course. Finally, the last guest departed, and they settled into the nightly routine. Eartha had been pleasant to everyone; indeed, she had actually been quite charming. The guests must have restored some of her lost passion for company, because she lingered in the kitchen, instead of heading right up to her room. Sardis took this as a sign and thought it would be a good time to talk.

"Mother, I am going to move to New York," she said, as casually as she could while running water in the sink to clean the few serving dishes. For a few minutes, there was total silence. Even the air grew still.

"You are not going to New York," came the icy reply. Sardis turned to face her mother and was met with a stone-cold stare. She could have sworn that the surrounding air retained a visible frost. The temperature outside was at least eighty-five degrees, but in the house, it had fallen to thirty below zero. Hell had begun to freeze over.

Sardis stiffened momentarily, caught her breath, and inhaled deeply. All of her life, she'd been obedient and compliant, never talking back, but now, mustering up all courage, she carefully prepared her arguments, as if she were a prosecutor summing up a case, and commenced her rebuttal.

"I had hoped that you would be happy that I made a good decision. I guess this is sudden, and maybe I should have prepared you for it," she began, as soothingly as she could. "If you're concerned about my welfare and survival, I can manage," she continued. "I know how to work. I earned some money here in Charleston, and I can support myself until ..."

"How?" screeched Eartha. "How did *you* earn money?"

Sardis quickly explained her clever ruse that had enabled her to get the job at the theater, making light of her fears, and adding a touch of humor. Then, while she had the floor, she told of her heartfelt passion for acting, and of her love for the theater.

Instead of calming Eartha's fears, and soothing her mother, Sardis's words had the opposite effect. The old dragon flew into a storming rage, and the icy frost was quickly transformed into a fiery hell. Eartha's white face powder couldn't mask her blind fury. She wasn't buying any of it and flew into a frenzy. Now that her ferocity had been unleashed, she inadvertently revealed some of her hitherto closely guarded, innermost secrets to Sardis. Her mind slipped, and she went into overdrive. Dark shadows came to the forefront, and long-suppressed memories surfaced. The mere words "New York" unleashed her pent-up rage toward her sisters. "They hated me all of their lives! They left! Went to your New York! Used some of your clever ruses themselves. Changed their names, changed their lives, and broke their mother's heart. Didn't even return for her funeral." Sardis gasped at the revelation that she had two aunts she'd never known about. In the meantime, the tirade continued. "I was blamed for everything! My father's indiscretions! My husband's drinking problem! My son's death!" She paused for air. Breathing hard, she noticed her stunned daughter. "Everybody's gone," she concluded, defeated. "They left me to bear their guilt! Now you're blaming me too, aren't you?" she hissed through clenched teeth.

Sardis was afraid to respond. She stood perfectly still transfixed by shock by a mother she realized she didn't know. Now she finally understood why her mother embraced the dark as her friend. Those whom she trusted and loved the most had all disappeared from her life. She felt abandoned, and Sardis was all that was left, but Sardis knew that even if she stayed, she could never repair the damage.

"New York!" Eartha spat on the floor as she uttered the name of what, for her, had become a contemptible place. "Your place is right here. Who put you up to this? My sisters? New York! It's not going to happen, and just in case you got any ideas of sneaking away, bring me that ill-gotten money you earned whoring at that job *and* everything you took to your room today. I know that people gave you envelopes. Bring all of it here—*now!*"

Sardis felt lower than dirt. Just like that, her new life was ending rather than beginning. She'd stored the money in a small chest where she also kept special pieces of jewelry, like the charm bracelet with the pennies dangling from it. It was a gift from her brother, who always offered her a penny for her thoughts. She set the chest on the kitchen table in front of her mother and started to open it, but before she could raise the lid, her mother snatched it from her hands and headed toward the stairs, intent on retreating to her room. "And you are not to go back to that … that place to work anymore," she said, not even bothering to glance back at her now totally demoralized and defeated daughter. "It's evil, and it has turned you evil." With that, she disappeared up the stairs into the gloom, and Sardis heard the bedroom door slammed more forcefully than she ever heard before. At the sound of her freedom disappearing, Sardis began to sob uncontrollably crumpling to the floor. What had been a day of joyful celebration and hope ended in a night of silent despair. It was a different type of silence than that which had prevailed previously, with Eartha in her darkened room, brooding over her misspent life, and Sardis now more determined than ever to leave and follow her dreams. She understood her mother a little more now, but it still didn't excuse her actions.

I am not about to become her prisoner, thought Sardis, as she began to plan her escape. Over the next few weeks, they spoke only when necessary. With her mother's newfound knowledge about her money-making activities, Sardis couldn't leave the house without Mother knowing where she was going. She was tethered by an invisible leash, one she felt was partially of her own making but nevertheless, one from which she had to break free. But how? Finding a way out was beginning to weigh heavily on Sardis, to the point where people who knew her began to comment on how much weight she'd lost. She had always been slender, but now she was becoming skeletal. She was toying with the idea of seeing whether the priest could help her in any way when suddenly a solution arrived in the form of a large brown envelope.

"I'm going to college!" she announced joyfully to her still-suspicious mother while holding up the letter. Sardis was inwardly insane with glee, but the actress in her played it cool. If this were a chess game, she would have shouted checkmate, for she knew her mother would not deny her a college education. When her father was alive, both parents planted the seeds of desire for a college degree in both Sardis and her brother.

"Nothing less is expected for the son and daughter of Dr. and Mrs. Fontain. I don't want either of you to forget that. Keep your grades up, and you can walk in the door of any college," Father had intoned, like a mantra. Sardis took his words to heart, but her brother was an independent thinker, an adventurer who placed more emphasis on his appearance and on being popular than on being a good student. He liked to party.

"Got your blood. Has too much of a taste for scotch and bourbon," Eartha whined to her husband on the day they discovered Junior's poor grades might never win him a cherished place in the freshman class of a good school. He'd been "Junior," even though he stood a full head taller than his dad. He had a muscular build, while his father was slender, bordering on frail, but father took real pride in his handsome son and was determined that one day Junior would follow him into the medical profession, grades or no grades.

"I have a few favors I can call in to get that boy into a decent school, and then into medical school," he assured his wife. "Just see to it that you put the fear of God into him about his grades." Junior's independent streak and impulsive actions took over, however. Sardis remembered the day vividly when he burst into the house and announced he'd broken the color lines to become the very first colored fireman in Charleston. His pride was met with their shame. Their mother burst into tears. Her son would not become a college man. Their father, the doctor, broke into a new bottle of scotch. His son would not follow the family profession. Sardis secretly cheered. She was always in his corner and loved his defiant spirit.

Breaking racial barriers in a city that was resistant to change, even when forced, was not easy, by any stretch of the imagination. He had to run faster, climb higher, and be braver than anyone else on the force. He couldn't fail, even though he was set up to fail many times. He couldn't let anyone say that colored men couldn't be firemen, because if he didn't make it, he knew it would close the door for a long time to come. And so he endured. Through all of it, his partying ways stopped, and he grew to become the man his parents always wanted him to become, but in their continued disappointment, they withheld acceptance. By the time graduation day from firefighting school came around, they absolutely refused to acknowledge his chosen profession. However, after he made headlines in the *Post and Courier Newspaper* for his heroism, their father began to warm to Junior's decision. Then the accident happened that took him away. There'd been no reconciliation, just a grudging acceptance, and then, suddenly, he was gone.

Now, because of him, Sardis received her get out of jail card. His death as an active-duty firefighter provided his next of kin with a full scholarship to any South Carolina state-supported school. Even though Sardis could have crossed the color line and made a selection from several state-supported schools, too many officials were aware of her olive-skinned brother. Thus, State College became her only possible choice, a welcomed choice. It was a life raft for a drowning woman. The chess game was not over just yet, however. Mother's queen was still on the board. "Go," said her mother reluctantly. "Get your education. But when you finish, you come right back here. Your father and I made sure you would always have a place to live. This is a good neighborhood to raise a family. This is your home."

Not if I've got anything to do with it, Sardis said to herself. Fall arrived, and she boarded the bus for freedom and adventure.

XVI

The Protest

The four players tried to keep the game going, but their concentration was disrupted by the din on the Quad. They heard a lot of shouting and swearing, and someone rushed past their dorm room yelling something about a brush fire or about a building being on fire. After three nights of activity, they become somewhat complacent and tried to drown out the distractions, but the sound of breaking glass caught their attention, and as if that wasn't enough, it was followed by a scream. Things were different. Taletha shifted in her chair, while Dorcus and Sardis stared wide-eyed at one another. Grace sat unmoved, a stoic. She knew the sound of trouble, and this was it; but on their beloved Quad?

"You all hear that crowd out there? Maybe we should go see what's happening," said Grace, craning her neck to look out the window. There was also an ulterior motive to her sudden interest in what was happening outside. She had gotten so caught up in Sardis's story that she miscalculated several card plays. Now, she and Dorcus, whose mind had never been in the game anyhow, couldn't possibly win. This was a good way to end the game with their dignity intact. A decision was soon forced upon them when the sound of more breaking glass, followed by another scream, caused them all to jump to their feet. The playing board went flying, with cards landing everywhere. At first, they cowered in a corner, all huddled together. "I'm going to see what's going on," said Grace, heading toward the door. Taletha was right on her heels. The two of them dashed out the door and down the stairs to the Quad, while Dorcus and Sardis stayed behind. Neither of them liked any form of conflict, so they preferred to watch the ongoing activity from the relative safety of the dorm window. They could see crowds of people milling about like leaderless sheep, and small fires had flared up here and there.

When she reached the Quad, Grace felt a surge of excitement as she joined forces with what seemed like the entire student body, although she was still torn about getting involved. On the one hand, she knew she had a duty to stand up for her rights, but on the other hand, she knew that, by rights, she shouldn't even have been attending college.

"Willie is a good man, Mama. He'll be able to take care of me. You'll see. Just trust us. We're in love, and we want to get married," pleaded Grace, desperately trying to convince and win over her skeptical mother. Hatta Mae knew she was going to have trouble with Grace once Willie returned from up North. At least Grace appeared to want to do things the right way, but Hatta Mae wanted bigger and better things for her younger daughter than marriage. Secretly, she wanted her to get an education, the same thing she wanted for her older daughter until she suddenly complicated her life with a baby and a common law husband.

This conversation was taking place on the eve of Grace's senior year at C. A. Brown, the second high school that opened in Charleston for colored children. Hatta Mae sat on the edge of her bed, listening patiently as Grace laid out her plans following graduation. They had a good relationship, and Hatta Mae was glad Grace would share things with her, but she was concerned about this marriage talk. Grace was still too young, she thought. She needed to get her out of Michele Alley so that she could become open to other options, but she didn't know how. As was her habit when receiving unpleasant news, Hatta Mae sat with her wire thin, frail arms folded across her chest, rocking back and forth in her invisible rocker. She was deep in thought, but pretended to listen while Grace, who was sitting on the floor on crossed legs, dreamily continued to plan her future.

"He has great ideas," Grace continued, exuding pride. "For one thing, he plans to open a restaurant and serve colored people's food. He said they call it Soul Food in New York. He'll open a small place at first. Decorate it with African colors and items. And he won't charge set prices." Hatta Mae shifted on her bed, taking care not to spill the warm water and Epsom salts in which she was soaking her tired, callused, corn-ridden feet. Now her sharp mind snapped back to reality. Hatta Mae had little formal education, but she had lots of what people called horse sense; practical wisdom and knowledge.

The chil' don' gon' out her head, she thought. "No prices?" she said suspiciously.

"That's the beauty of it," Grace enthused. "He said everybody could eat that way, 'cause people who can afford to pay will pay a lot for this kind of cookin' and those who can't afford to pay a lot will jes' pay a little less. He already has the menu in his head. He won't fix that heavy, greasy fried food. Just good seafood: shrimp, Devil Crab, She Crab Soup. Good southern cooking." Grace could almost taste the food as she excitedly laid out Willie's socialist concept.

"How's the fool gon' pay bills?" said Hatta Mae.

"It'll work out. You'll see. In some places up North, Willie said some churches and them are doing that, and people come from all over to eat."

Hatta Mae was still not convinced and shook her head, more worried now than ever. As Grace prattled on about Willie and the fairytale life she intended to lead, Hatta Mae was taking a good hard look around her roach-infested, poorly furnished flat for anything that might give her a glimmer of an idea or of hope. She didn't even have any jewelry or valuables worth selling that would give her enough money to send Grace away; anywhere. She had to find a way to get this man out of Grace's system without doing anything to push them closer together, like her mama had inadvertently done with her. Hatta

Mae was no expert on human behavior, but she knew that if she told Grace she couldn't see this man anymore, it would drive her right into his arms. At fifteen years of age, Hatta Mae told her distraught mama she was grown-up enough to make her own decisions. *Bin livin' wit dat mistake a lon' time,* she thought as she plotted. *My baby ain' gon' do the same.* Hatta Mae's concerns were not without justification. Willie may have had dreams and desires to open his own restaurant, but in-between having the dream and bringing the dream to reality stood a gigantic chasm called capital. Willie had none, and lacked the means of getting any. In fact, he was having major problems just getting regular work.

In the two years since he moved to the South, he encountered no end of problems trying to find steady employment. One major obstacle that he hadn't expected to encounter could be termed regional prejudice. He was not from the South, and in a time when most people of color moved up North to find work, he moved South. This generated no end of suspicion and speculation.

"Must be runnin' from the law," was the most prevalent rumor being spread in the Alley. "Musta got some gal in trouble an' de Pa or some man is looking for 'im," was another. "He kilt somebody; shot 'em/stabbed 'em/beat 'em up." The hearsay never ended.

Willie lived with the Judge and his wife, but since the Judge was not a blood relative, he didn't intervene. He didn't want to place his business at risk by getting involved. In the twisted Alley world, the rumors about Willie actually helped the Judge's enterprise to grow, for he was a curio people came to see. His presence also drew its share of fast-living women, and even though the Judge's partying days were behind him now, much to the relief of his no-nonsense wife, he still loved to ogle and flirt. He was even toying with the idea of opening a little juke joint. The women would draw more men, and the Judge would be ready with the liquid refreshments.

As for Willie, his heart belonged to Grace, and he wanted to do right by her, even though he had to contend with Hatta Mae, who watched his every move like a hawk. "I know your Mama mustn't think much of me right now, because I'm not working," he confided to Grace during one of their long afternoon swing sessions. "Just you make sure you let her know that I got dreams, big dreams, and I'm trying awful hard to get work, but nobody wants to hire colored men to do decent jobs. I just don't want to settle for driving some rich white lady around, or digging ditches for sewers. I got a high school education. I can use my mind and do the same things a white man can do. All I need is a chance."

Willie had good reason to be discouraged. Jobs for colored men were hard to obtain, and the fear surrounding the social issues of the day only added to the stress. Environmental issues were also beginning to make an impact. Factories were told to either clean up their act or close down, so companies like the cigar factory where Grace's father had once worked, which belched harsh chemicals and toxic smoke into the atmosphere, were closing down. The jobs were often dangerous and dirty, but they provided a living.

Some color lines were being broken within the federal, state, and municipal civil service arenas, but that didn't mean the positions were any easier to obtain. Getting an entry-level slot was almost impossible. "I thought I had a good shot at becoming a firefighter after that guy made it in," Willie told Grace after yet another failed job application. "I'm young and strong, and I passed all the tests. Then when word got out that they wanted to form a whole new brigade of men at the Cumming Street station, right in our neighborhood, I just knew my time had come. I didn't think white men would want to stay at the same station with all these colored men in a colored area, but when I got to the station house for my interview, I saw all these light-skinned guys in there and I knew for sure they weren't going to be letting me in," he said, the disappointment clear in his voice as he handed Grace the rejection letter. "Had that one pegged right." His voice caught a little, and he quickly retreated indoors so she couldn't see his moist eyes, but he couldn't hide his pain from her. Grace wept silently at this latest disappointment and failure. Their future together was being compromised by forces over which they had no control. As she sat alone on the swing, she started to understand why women like her mother had to work so hard.

Racism didn't oppress colored women the same way it affected colored men. Colored women were able to find work. Then having become the breadwinner, the woman became the head of the house. The man, robbed of the dignity of his natural place as the provider, became little more than a superfluous sperm donor for their children.

Grace determined she did not want to be the head of her household. She saw the toll her father's chronic unemployment took on her own family, and now her sister and her man weren't doing very well either, and so, without her mother's prompting, she began to think about other options besides marriage.

Charleston was a big military city, with its air force base and naval shipyard, affectionately known as "'The Yard." Both offered the best and most stable federal positions, and colored men dreamed of getting a job at The Yard. Even though the jobs were labor intensive, and often the most dangerous around, the hours were good, the work was steady, and because it was a federal position, the pay was equal.

The testing system was culturally biased, however, and favored the High Yellows, many of whom found work at The Yard. Once they were in the system, though, they soon found that nepotism and favoritism kept many blacks out of management positions, and they were stuck in entry-level jobs with little or no opportunity for career advancement. Even in the federal system, a colored man wasn't allowed to manage or supervise a white person; it just didn't happen. No one dared complain, however, for they considered themselves too blessed to complain, so the system never changed.

Municipal jobs were just as scarce. Not only were colored people not allowed to sit at the front of the bus, but they were also denied the opportunity to drive the bus. "Ain' no colored man gon' drive no bus in dis here city," the Judge cautioned when Willie asked about applying for a driver's position. In his folksy wisdom, he concluded by saying, "The driver's gots at sit at de front, and no colored sits at de front. So how you gon' drive? From de back?"

Willie countered with some wisdom of his own. "Don't colored people pay taxes to the city? Why can't we have our fair share of the jobs that we're paying for?" At the time Willie expressed these sentiments, colored leaders, particularly among the clergy, began to proclaim the same ideas so loudly that Charleston City Council couldn't ignore them anymore. Some of the civic leaders began to sense this changing tide and grudgingly determined that it was time to toss the coloreds a few bones. Thus the doors creaked open ever so slightly, and a few were permitted to enter. These minimal actions were primarily token gestures, made in an attempt to keep major civil rights activities at bay. The entry-level jobs that were now opened up to colored applicants carried much more demanding eligibility requirements for black applicants and extracted a high price in terms of personal sacrifice. Those who managed to obtain one of these positions had to work twice as hard and put in longer hours than their white counterparts in order to keep their positions. They were under great stress to perform well, because they knew if they failed, it would reflect not only on them personally, but also on the entire race. They had to make sure that those doors remained open, so that others might also enter.

"I heard that municipal bus drivers only need a high school diploma and a driver's license to get a job," Willie told Grace when word got out that the city was finally going to open bus driver jobs to colored men. "I'm going to be first in line to put in my paperwork. If I manage to get on with the city, we'll be set for life, and then maybe your mama will see me as good enough to marry you." When applications opened, Willie was true to his word, heading a line of more than a hundred men who turned up to apply, but his hopes, along with those of the other young colored high school grads, were soon dashed. When he went to submit his application, he discovered that, under newly minted guidelines, potential candidates now had to have a college degree. In the end, they hired just one colored person.

He discovered there were a lot of openings for black men with the sanitation department, but with one major limitation—he could only apply to collect garbage. To become a driver/supervisor, which paid more and which he would have preferred, required at least two years of college. Prior to these jobs being opened to colored applicants, high school completion had been sufficient, and white applicants were still being hired under the "old" guidelines. Truth be known, job advertisements, just like the putrid public bathrooms that dotted the city, should have been labeled "white applicants" and "colored applicants," but of course no sane personnel director would ever admit that the standards differed. People knew, however.

Swallowing his pride, Willie turned to the domestic arena and soon discovered he didn't qualify for work as a domestic. He wasn't overly disappointed by this surprising turn of events, because he still resisted doing that type of work; too many stereotypes came to mind, and he knew he could never support a family entirely on the earnings from such work. Fortunately for him, or unfortunately, depending on your viewpoint, a little-known Southern tradition intervened. At each interview, Willie was invariably asked about his "wife," and whether she could be hired to work as well. A negative response met with a quick dismissal, which mystified him until a long-time friend of the Judge provided enlightenment one day. "Boy, they ain't gon' let you have no job in a house when you ain't got no woman around," the old domestic confided. "You young, single, and they don' trus' their womenfolk. You a good-lookin' boy, too. Even if you as innocent as Joseph was with Potiphar's wife in the Bible, if they scream 'rape,' or even less than that, you as good as dead." Willie thanked his mentor and stopped looking for work as a domestic.

Trade jobs were largely unionized, and black men were excluded from the unions. Some professions tolerated separate unions, but jobs for coloreds were limited to specific areas. Janitorial work was always available, but it wasn't steady. The armed forces would have been a viable alternative, but there were rumblings of a skirmish in a place called Vietnam, which was then in its infancy. Even though, when he moved from New York, he never notified the draft board of his new address in South Carolina, Willie feared he might still be drafted. Given a choice, he would rather stay out of the military. Gracie, as he called her, had a lot to do with this desire. After almost two years of trying to find work, failure, defeat, degradation, and self-pity were becoming his constant companions. He thought about moving back to New York, but he wasn't going without Grace. They talked about getting married, but she was still in school, and her mama wasn't about to let her go anywhere. He felt hopelessly stuck.

Hatta Mae, in the meantime, had begun a campaign of her own. The crafty old fox began planting seeds of discontent. While she may not have been aware of the military strategy known as "divide and conquer," she certainly knew how to play mind games, and now she went to work. First, she became skillful in influencing her daughter. With every opportunity that presented itself, she planted seeds of discord and doubt—about Willie's ideas, about his abilities, and about his willingness to find work. She understood the problems, and she knew deep within herself that he was doing all he could to become gainfully employed, but nevertheless, she continued with her campaign of subterfuge. It was so subtle and so gradual that over time, Grace began to lose patience with Willie's constant failure to find work and his excuses. Simultaneously, Hatta Mae managed to influence Grace to strive for high academic achievement, convincing her that college awaited, even though neither of them knew where she was going to get the finances to make it happen. While she was working on her daughter, Hatta Mae also managed to plant seeds of confusion and self-doubt in Willie's mind. As her own working days became fewer and fewer, she began to establish a rapport with him, sufficient to enable her to get into his psyche, and begin to weave her webs. "My Grace was sayin' ta me a few days ago, you had a good idea fo' a business," she said one day while Grace was in school. While Grace was absent, she would wait patiently for Willie to appear and then strike up a conversation, flattering him, getting him talking, winning his trust. "Yo' resturant is sho' a smart idea. Wish I had me some money ta give ya'll. Would so lik' ta do that." She made him think he was the smartest person in the world and then, with the cunning of a prosecuting attorney, ask question after question about how would he do this, and how would he accomplish that, knowing full well that he was unlikely to have answers.

Eventually, her constant barrage of who, what, where, why, and how began to produce the desired effect. While she appeared to be supportive and full of encouragement, ultimately their conversations would leave Willie drained, mired in self-doubt and confusion. Out of embarrassment, he never mentioned these sessions to Grace, while she, thinking her own sessions were private mother/daughter affairs, never spoke to him about her conversations with her mother. They each thought they were simply sharing their innermost dreams with a mature, caring, sensitive confidante, never for a moment suspecting that Hatta Mae had become a manipulative serpent. They sensed they were growing apart, too, but could never get to the root of the problem.

Meanwhile, Hatta Mae's concerns about Grace's education increased as Grace neared graduation. Even though Hatta Mae worked hard, she knew she could never afford to send her daughter to college. She always dreamed of both her girls graduating with good grades and becoming college girls, marrying college men who would rescue them, and her, from the Alley. Now, whenever she thought about her elder daughter, tears began to flow. "I took my eye offa her," she would grumble, laying the blame entirely on herself.

Grace held a different view. "My sister fell in love, or make that in lust," she laughingly explained to her playing partners during the session when she recounted the story of her road to State. "Got herself pregnant, and thought she had a prince, but he turned out to be a pauper real fast," she told them. "My mama was beside herself. Then they got into a common-law relationship and moved in with my folks."

Hatta Mae's meager check had to stretch further and further as time went on, but a mother's determination can overcome gigantic obstacles. Grace proved to be a good student, and thanks in large part to Hatta Mae's encouragement, she got high grades in all of her high school classes. Hatta Mae was bursting with pride, because Grace had already gone much further than her own grade school education. She also realized that a new era was dawning, and a woman needed to have something more than a man to depend upon. Grace had to be able to take care of herself. That's when the light bulb flicked on in her head. "Sadie," she said suddenly, snapping her fingers. "She got money fo' hur daughter las' year. Why did'n I think a hur befo'?" The New Society, or the Great Society, Hatta Mae couldn't remember what Sadie said it was called. All she remembered was that it was government money, and it was opening doors, so she made a quick trip to Smith Street, which was a few blocks away, to visit with her fellow church member.

Once she was armed with the information she needed, Hatta Mae returned home, got out her best Sunday dress, ironed it, and pulled out her fancy shoes, even though they tortured her feet. She knew in her mind she had to look good. She had to do exactly what Sadie told her to do, and so, bright and early the next morning, she set out on the long, laborious walk to Meeting Street. She was going to C. A. Brown School, to plead for government money, "So's my baby won' have at liv' lik' me."

"My mama did it," said Grace proudly. "I was in shock when the school counselor told me my mama managed to qualify for a government tuition grant. Then the work fellowship arrived on top of that to pay for room and board. Would you believe my butt was twice this size before I worked it off?" she teased, shaking her very small rear, much to everyone's amusement, "But at least I don't owe anybody for anything. Willie's reaction surprised me. I thought he'd be happy for me—for us. Instead, he got into a funk and started talking trash. 'Baby, I don't want you to leave me—to leave here,'" she said, mocking his voice. "'I'm looking down this dark Alley where the sun never shines, and he's sayin', 'You don' need the white man's education,' sounding like a fool!" she said in disgust. "Even asked me to run away with him, have his baby, but knowing what my mama had gone through to get that money, and seeing what my sister had done, and how she was living, I told him, 'No thanks.'"

"But don't you two still date?" said Dorcus, completely puzzled.

"Oh, I couldn't stay mad at him. We made up even before the end of freshman year. He wrote me the sweetest letter," Grace replied, smiling broadly. "I really like him. Easy on the eyes, with his New York self. And he has changed. A lot."

Willie had to change. He was a man staggering from a sucker punch when Grace told him about her plans to attend State, and he felt betrayed. He made a lot of sacrifices for her, and suffered a lot of humiliation, being rejected time and time again in his quest for a good job. He thought she understood and would stand by him and marry him after she finished school. Now, she was leaving him stranded, defeated, and dejected. The first time he saw Hatta Mae after he received Grace's news finally opened his eyes to the role she had played. She was beside herself with glee at how well things had turned out. She sat on the front stoop celebrating with a glass of whiskey from her husband's hidden but not so secret stash. He couldn't remember ever seeing her so happy and contented before as she raised her glass in a silent toast to his impending departure.

There was a look in her eyes when she saw him that said, "*I won. I won my baby's freedom from a doomed relationship; I won my baby's future with a better man; I won my baby's success. You no longer matter; you can take your slick New York self home. 'An don come bak, neither. Now Grace kin git a college man.*" She smiled broadly, raising her jelly glass high again. "*Take care of her mama in the future.*". The added thought made her chuckle as she leaned back on her bony elbows in triumph.

She played me for a fool, and probably Grace, too, he thought. *All the time I thought she was trying to help us get together, she was working to keep us apart.* He was livid, but he knew better than to try to discredit Hatta Mae or to redirect their destinies from their current course. For now, however, he was a man who had lost everything, and he didn't know what to do next. He and Grace spent their last summer together, but by now they had become strangers. He tried to sway her into sticking with their original plan; they would get married as soon as she finished high school, and then … but he had no way of filling in the next step. He was supposed to have found work by now, so they could begin a life and a family together.

As a result of Mama's constant reminders, Grace began to see her future in a different light. She could hardly wait to begin college, and Willie didn't look as good anymore. Fall came, and Grace left for Orangeburg. Willie had no reason to stay in Charleston, so he left for

New York. The Judge's wife gave him a little cash, along with his bus
ticket, and he let her know that, as far as he was concerned, it was
just a temporary loan. After all, he still had his pride.

XVII

Willie didn't stand much of a chance of returning to the same life he'd been escaping when he left New York. He tried living in the Bronx with one, then the other, of his estranged parents, but things didn't work out. Finally, he found one of his brothers in a small walk-up apartment near Harlem, so he moved in with him. It wasn't a good solution, but it was the only one he had for now. Work wise, things didn't change for Willie now that he was back in New York. The city had changed in his absence, at least that's how it felt to him, and he didn't fit in anymore. He lost that sense of rhythm and timing that people get into after they've been living in a city for a while. Charleston was slower paced and far more mellow. It made New York seem frantic and rushed. Further, during the two years he spent in the South, many of his homeboy running buddies had been drafted and were now serving in the military. Uncle Sam was probably looking for him, too. The "greetings" letter was probably sent to his parents' old address; it never caught up with him in the Carolinas.

After drifting for about six months, he finally resigned to drafting himself, even without the letter. His money had just about run out, and his brother, who was barely supporting himself with a delivery job, was starting to run out of patience. He stood gloomily looking at the posters with soldiers and sailors wearing fake smiles enticing America's youth to sign up, and his unsteady hand was just about to grasp the door handle when suddenly, a voice came out of nowhere. "Little brother, you need to come with me." Willie turned abruptly, startled because he hadn't heard anyone approaching. The man who was addressing him was slightly older and had a full beard topped by a wild mane of long, untamed hair. He was wearing a dashiki, an African garment just beginning to appear in the United States. Willie wondered why this stranger was addressing him as "brother." "You look like so many of our lost young brothers. Can you use some direction, and a job, and a way out of your aimlessness?"

Willie's forlorn expression conveyed his mood, that and the fact he was standing outside a recruiting station, still debating whether or not he should go inside. Time froze as he stood rooted to the spot pondering his options. While there was something inviting about the stranger, Willie wondered if he could trust someone he just met. What did he really want? Generally, people didn't just materialize out of the blue with legitimate offers. Before he could back away or flee, however, the stranger got right into his face and in a barely audible voice, said, "You can make your own destiny, you know. We don't need any more of our black brothers killing our yellow brothers in that war. And we don't want our yellow brothers killing any more of our black brothers. The only thing that's benefiting is the white man's green economy. Come with me, and I can show you another way."

Willie's eyes grew as big as saucers. He took a step backward, reclaiming his personal space, and looked intently at the man with the strange ideas but intriguing ideas. Who was this guy? Then, he said something about blacks empowering other blacks, which was enough to convince Willie that he might as well find out what this man had to say. Soon, Willie found himself being ushered into what had once been a lodge hall of some kind, where he was greeted warmly and welcomed into a new, underground world. The walls were lined with pictures of black scholars, the most prominent of which were posters of the founder of this movement, a man named Malcolm, who had replaced his last name with an "X."

Willie had a sharp mind—Grace told him so when she tried unsuccessfully to convince him to go to college—and he learned quickly. He quickly absorbed different ideas, and embraced new thinking. He liked being black and not colored, he liked the way his hair was naturally long and soft, and he adapted easily to the dress code, but most of all, he readily inhaled the black history that was such an important part of the group's purpose. He found a part of himself that had been missing for so long. He picked up and devoured books by contemporary black authors, and read *The Fire Next Time* and *Go Tell It on the Mountain* by James Baldwin several times. Since these books were set in his native New York, he was able to relate to them easily. He learned all he could about the author and in so doing, found a kindred spirit. Other books he came across included Richard Wright's *Native Son* and Eldridge Cleaver's *Soul on Ice*. These books gave him a new perspective on race, politics, and his inner manhood and served to restore what Hatta Mae had previously taken away.

As his knowledge increased, Willie found himself thinking of Grace. Her presence was always with him, and now he could think of no better person to share his new life with than his beloved Gracie. They'd had no communication since they parted, and so he feared she wouldn't answer his letter. Indeed, he wasn't even sure where to send the letter, but he wasn't about to ask Hatta Mae or any of the other Alley dwellers. Finally, he took a chance and addressed the envelope to South Carolina State College. It reached its intended destination, and when Grace responded, he felt complete again. He opened his heart and shared his rapidly changing world with her. His mind was expanding quickly, and he had evolved so much that, at times, Grace wondered which one of them was getting the college degree. Willie had already discovered what black colleges had not yet embraced— black literature, black history, and black philosophy—an entire Black Studies curriculum. While Grace was getting an education, Willie was getting a life.

There were those strange voices again. They were disturbing, because everyone was gone now. They had all died, first Mother, then Father, three years later. She never heard their voices again, nor those of her nagging sisters. They were so buried into their alternate universe, they never returned, not even for the funerals. They were afraid of being recognized, that someone would see them and learn their secrets.

She had nothing to hide. Father made sure she would have security. He matched her up with a proper husband from a proper family. "My husband," she groaned as the nightmare played itself out again. "My husband." Was she trying to convince herself that she was actually married ... to this ... person ... she didn't know?

"You will grow to love him over time," was the advice her father offered when Eartha complained about the alcohol and the neglect and the rape. Did she say rape? She was married ... to this ... person.

"It is a wife's duty to please her husband," was the answer she got as the back of her husband's hand struck her cheek. It taught her not to complain or to resist. The two children were a joy, but she was married ... to this ... drunken person ... she never came to know ... or love.

XVIII

"What happened to Byron and what was the other guy's name?" Grace finally asked.

Dorcus remained silent, while Sardis, inhaling deeply, seemed to suck the air out of the tiny room. Both were hoping beyond hope that no one would delve into that territory—old boyfriends and past loves—but there went Grace. Sardis didn't mind talking about Byron too much; it was the memory of the other guy that still hurt. A dreamlike haze descended dragging them unwillingly back to the '60s.

After Dorcus convinced the rest of the freshmen girls that Sardis wasn't the monster they thought she was, they began to embrace her. Her personality and flair for the dramatic began to show, and she became popular. Not everyone liked her, of course, but she made enough friends to convince her that she should finally unpack her bags and stay. "The last thing I wanted to do was to return to my mother's house," she confided to Dorcus, "but I couldn't continue to exist, frozen out of everyone's lives."

Her mother maintained control of the money she earned from the job and received by way of graduation gifts and doled it out a little at a time for necessary school items. They achieved reconciliation, but the camaraderie between them had been destroyed forever. Eartha could not get over the fact that Sardis held a secret job and was passing herself off as white. She wondered what else Sardis was hiding—too many secrets.

For her part, Sardis discovered her mom had two sisters; she had two aunts she'd never even known existed. What else was her mom hiding? Nothing more was ever spoken by either of them about their respective secrets. Both retired to their own world, with Sardis's mother still controlling the pieces on the chessboard.

"You mean your mama didn't let you have your own money? That's what you're telling us?" Grace asked one day. She found Sardis a curious entity. Having had very limited exposure to lighter-skinned blacks, she grabbed every opportunity to ask Sardis questions about her life, even at the risk of embarrassment. This habit irked Dorcus, but Sardis, sensing a hunger for knowledge, answered most of Grace's questions stoically, even though she sometimes wished Grace wouldn't probe so much. Questions about her father and brother, however, were off limits. She refused to answer those. Whenever Grace tried to broach the subject, Sardis could depend upon Dorcus to remind her that she'd gone too far. A pinch on the rump, if she was sitting by Dorcus, or a sharp kick under the table, caused Grace to change the topic immediately.

When Sardis met Byron, however, she opened up more than ever before. Now, she wanted to talk, needed to talk. He was her first love, which brought a strange, new dimension to her life, one she never expected to experience. "Is my stomach supposed to get upset like this?" she gleefully asked her fellow bid whist players right after she met him. "He walks into a room and that smile ... my knees ... I just ..."

"Girl, do you realize that you haven't finished a sentence all night?" laughed Dorcus.

"She hasn't finished a trick all night, either," Taletha chimed in. She had drawn Sardis as her partner this evening, and would have gladly traded her for one of the others. Sardis was all aglow. What a difference a month could make. She discovered Byron Knob in her speech class one day, or they discovered each other, which wasn't hard to do, since they both stood out with their light complexions.

Fortunately for him, the other men were totally indifferent to Byron's light skin, blue-gray eyes, and sandy hair, which was already thinning and receding, even though he was only twenty. He was two years older than Sardis but possessed a maturity far greater than hers. He grew up in the North and later in Washington DC and hadn't been subjected to the type of isolation she experienced.

Government jobs, always a mainstay for people of color, were opening up in DC. Residual effects from the Great Society Era started to put federal funding to work for black society, as Hatta Mae had discovered. Beyond that, however, many of the programs that put black employees on the government payroll also put many black people on the dole.

Byron's father worked in a senator's office, and his mother was a nurse, but Byron himself represented a new breed. He was of mixed race from an intact home, with parents who still loved each other. That made him an even greater oddity than Sardis. The South still operated under Jim Crow racial laws, with statutes on their books forbidding interracial mingling and marriages. However, Sardis, together with her fair-skinned parents and their racially mixed parents before them, served as evidence that those laws had frequently been broken. The perpetrators invariably carried their secrets to their graves.

Here was Byron, however, the product of a new age. Initially, he mistakenly thought Sardis shared the same Zebra parentage he did, so she gave him a quick lesson in Southern history. Their friendship blossomed as a result, and soon grew into a dating relationship. They shared each other's interests, and both loved the theater. Unlike Sardis, Byron's parents purposely exposed him and his younger siblings to the arts, thus his knowledge was able to fill in gaps that were missing in her life. She loved hearing about the life he led, and about the movies and the music and the ballet. He told her about concerts he attended and about productions that were sung entirely in Italian. "Opera," he called them, before delighting her with pompous imitations of famous tenors. She hung on every word as he described the grand costumes and sets, and sat wide-eyed and astounded that such worlds existed beyond the realm of her meager knowledge. "An awful lot of people must be in Hell," he commented after she explained what the priests and nuns told her about acting, and she was absolutely flabbergasted when he told her religious plays existed. This served to strengthen her resolve to eventually enter this world.

Sometimes, in the vast expanse of the universe, the stars align themselves to form arrangements that have never previously existed. During Sardis and Byron's freshman year, the stars not only brought two potentially outstanding actors to State, but also brought a dynamic speech and drama teacher by the name of Cyrus Bloom. Speech was a core class that every student had to take, either in their freshman or their sophomore year, but for the previous two years, the school had no speech teacher. This meant some students who were now juniors and seniors had not taken speech. They, of course, hoped the requirement would be waived, but once the new teacher was hired, an edict was issued whereby no one would be allowed to graduate without having taken the course. The juniors and seniors were stuck and annoyed.

The lack of a speech teacher had a greater impact. Teachers were assigned extra duties as advisors for extra-curricular student activities. Whether by tradition or default, an English teacher was invariably handed the task of advising the drama club known as the Henderson-Davis Players, but once again the stars aligned themselves and that particular advisory position became vacant. Cyrus Bloom quickly let the administration know about his passion for the theater, and faster than they could write his name, he was appointed to the post.

Bloom was a short, portly, balding, fortyish man with a Napoleonic complex. He loved his work as a speech teacher but craved acting. He would never be able to win a role as a leading man, but no one could convince him otherwise. His grammar and syntax were impeccable, and he spoke distinctly, as if playing to the balcony. His vowels were all in place, and his final consonants were enunciated with finesse, with facial expressions and hand gestures to match.

Some of his fellow teachers took strange detours and ducked into open doorways in order to avoid an encounter with him, and several made him the endless source of good-natured faculty humor. One of the science professors did such an amusing parody at the annual faculty luncheon that he stole the show. None of this bothered Bloom, however, for he craved and loved the attention. It made up for the adulation he might have received had he not been forced to defer his sought-after acting career. Besides being a faculty novelty, he also became a favorite among the students, except for the upperclassmen who, thinking they were on the grad track, now found themselves in his class.

Rumors abounded that, when he attempted to pursue acting as a full-time profession, the Great White Way, living up to its name, had shut him out. At that time, there was only one fledgling black production, *A Raisin in the Sun* by Lorraine Hansberry, coming into its own on Broadway. One day, he told his students, "I just happened to come along at the same time as Sidney." He was, of course, referring to Sidney Poitier. "The world can only deal with one colored man at a time," he lamented. He never had the ghost of a chance in that production, but the rationalization gave him resolve, while helping him to save face. Thus he sought a day job whereby he determined to dedicate his life to teaching and preparing a new generation of black students for what he was convinced would be an emerging vocation. Working with young, fresh, eager performers also gave him the chance to indulge his second great love, directing. He also had a play in mind he wanted to write and produce, but that would have to wait for another day. In the meantime, he needed to earn a living, and so when he found out about the job opening for a speech instructor at State, he jumped at the opportunity. He was hired even though he was still one semester's worth of credits shy of obtaining his PhD. Educational requirements for black teachers in black schools still didn't match the standards set for white institutions. That was all to change with integration.

Once he learned the speech position was his, he had no idea he would end up directing the drama club as well, but when those stars aligned, he looked forward to being able to assist the aspiring young actors. He assumed everyone shared the same passion for the arts as he did. However, no sooner had he stepped into the director's chair than he discovered why his predecessor had gladly relinquished this assignment.

No one cared about what was happening. After years of parental objection and religious indoctrination, pushing the line that acting was not a legitimate profession, not a real job like teaching, the drama club was largely ignored, and treated with contempt. He looked at the schedule of past productions and saw another problem. All the productions had been meaningless. Some musicals had been performed, along with numerous allegory plays that were only slightly above the level of Sunday school productions; appeasement pieces. Things had to change. He had a lifetime of prejudice against the theater and against actors to overcome, and so he reasoned that the logical place to start would be with the department chairman. The first idea he presented received an immediate response. *"No!"* Bloom leaned back in his chair as the hurricane-force response flew past his head. He thought he had made a reasonable request by asking if the school could implement a curriculum whereby drama was offered as a major.

"Acting and speech go hand in hand. If they become major study areas, the students will become motivated to take the classes. We must make it worth something to them," he persisted. The chairman, however, would not budge, until Bloom added, "At the very least, let me exchange credit." At this, the chairman sat up and asked for more information. He had just been trounced for his failure to offer the speech elective for two years. Some juniors and seniors held sit-ins outside his office once they discovered they now had to complete the speech requirement. Bloom, well aware of the chairman's dilemma, knew he had some leverage, so if plan A was unsuccessful, he suspected plan B might just work. Thus, when Bloom suggested State should give students credit for the speech requirement if they worked on one production, the chairman suddenly became very interested.

After winning his concession, Bloom excitedly explained to the class, "You don't have to act. Just help out working behind the scenes, and you can earn a passing grade." The strategy worked, and Bloom was on his way to making drama a hot commodity. He also had a plan to secure an audience. It became mandatory for those who declined to work in the productions and remain in speech class to attend two productions. This proved to be a productive and agreeable compromise for everyone. The chairman was off the hook with the students, it gave the Henderson-Davis Players more credibility than they ever had before, and it gave Cyrus Bloom his first dynasty to build. Sardis and Byron had both been ready before the deal was struck and now, together, they became part of the empire. The honeymoon was to be short-lived, however.

"Cyrus, what is this play that you are producing?" Bloom shifted uneasily in his chair as he once again faced the department chair. It had been a little over a week since his triumphant compromise, and now he knew what was coming from the manner in which the chair spoke his name. He felt like a little kid feels when his mother calls him by all of his given names. Trouble was brewing. Bloom argued with all the conviction he could muster that his production company would become world renowned, even if it was located on the campus of a small black school. The rumors about his previous attempts at an acting career were not without foundation, and he actually knew people, people who could make things happen, if not for him, for the kids, but he also knew that it would not happen with musicals and simplified, safe, sanctioned plays. His motive was not entirely altruistic, however, for he was desperate to get back into the acting world himself, and so there was a well thought out method in his madness in terms of play selection. While living in New York, he had the good fortune to meet a Southern playwright by the name of Tennessee Williams, and loved his dramas, in particular his way of bringing out the soul of his tortured women. The first play of the new season was to be a Williams play by the name of *Summer and Smoke*.

Sardis wept at the news. "I have to get the lead," she told Byron. He couldn't understand why she was so adamant, but was greatly moved by her passion.

"Let's get both leads. I'll be your Dr. John and you can be my Miss Alma."

Cyrus Bloom still had obstacles to overcome, since *Summer and Smoke* did not exactly fit the strict definition of an allegory or morality play, but he stood his ground. He convinced the chairman, but would he be able to win over the parents, entrenched in tradition, or the angry students or a skeptical faculty, all of whom thought acting was a waste of time? Contrary to dire predictions, the play was a major success, and the drama club became the toast of the campus.

XIX

The Protest

The mood on the Quad was hard to describe, a cross between a homecoming pep rally and a mob on the verge of rioting. The students didn't want any real trouble, and most were still inspired by the recent successes achieved by Martin Luther King Jr. in Birmingham, Alabama, and throughout the South. Up until now, they pursued the concept of passive resistance, with boycotts and marches being their only weapons, but it wasn't possible to boycott a business that refused to even let a colored face in the door, so now activism was initiated. Tensions were escalating. Two days of protest had produced intolerant attitudes on the part of law enforcement agencies, and white patrolmen reverted to plantation days, when heavy-handed whippings were used to keep the "darkies" in their place. Now batons and bully clubs replaced the whip. Predictably, their actions produced anger and frustration—anger at being treated as second-class citizens, anger at Jim Crow laws enforcing segregation policies, anger for not having the power and ability to move from hopelessness to hope for the future and frustration with life. All this anger and frustration reached flashpoint, and state policemen and national guard troops were on their way to light the fuse.

131

In spite of the government grant and the work fellowship, money was extremely tight for Grace. Indeed, it was so tight she had to work year round to make ends meet. State offered an on-campus summer school, during which they had to keep the cafeteria operational, so rather than returning to Charleston, Grace stayed on campus and worked. This meant that, on occasion, she ran into Dorcus's mother, who was completing her education through summer sessions. Dorcus's mother had been a teacher for many years, working in the Charleston public school system. She hadn't attended college but had gone instead to a school designed to teach colored women how to teach. Along the way, she managed to pick up two years worth of college credits, which served her well until the school system was eventually forced to cease being separate but equal. Suddenly, she and her colleagues, many of whom shared the same or similar backgrounds, were faced with a fight to keep their jobs. They now had to become degreed, licensed professionals.

"After years of teaching colored children in colored schools, suddenly I'm no longer good enough!" she lamented to her family, crumpling a letter she received on that fateful day that amounted to a pink slip. She, along with many others in the community, resolved not to take this turn of events lying down. After a barrage of statewide protests, the school board's response was to qualify and license colored teachers by administering a teacher's examination. As with most standardized tests, however, the examination was culturally biased, and most, if not all, of the colored teachers failed. This was expected, the board figuring it would get them off the hook and the colored teachers out of the schools, the general consensus being that they were only good enough to teach colored, not white, students.

Board members patted themselves on the back crowing about how fair they thought they were. The president even issued a statement confirming they had given all teachers "equal opportunity," which effectively turned the concept around like a slap in black teachers' faces. Ultimately, their ploy did not work. Most of these teachers had been in the field all their lives, slaving away under a Jim Crow system in schools that were often poorly equipped and poorly heated, using inadequate copies of out-of-date textbooks, making the best out of near-impossible situations. Nonetheless, they taught their students, but now the colored schools were being closed, condemned as being substandard, and the teachers were being shut out of jobs. They were unwilling to accept the situation. Thus, after some wrangling and continued protests, a second compromise was reached. The teachers would be granted permanent licenses if they obtained a bachelor's degree and sixteen units toward their master's degree in education. As long as they worked toward these requirements, they would be allowed to keep their jobs; hence the summer program for professional development was instituted by State, allowing the teachers to work toward degree completion and certification. Since the requirements were statewide, summer school at State was almost as busy as their regular year sessions.

There were a few undergraduate students studying during the summer, and some were recruited as cafeteria workers for summer sessions, including Grace, who was very happy to get work. In addition to the much-needed income, teaching was a field that she was considering as a future career, and she enjoyed the interaction with the experienced, mature women. It helped the summer months pass quickly, even though her "home girls" weren't around, and she missed the personal interaction with the people in Charleston who meant the most to her. She didn't get to see her mother all summer, but tried, in her regular letters home, to convey how much she had grown. Unfortunately, however, Hatta Mae was not totally literate, and while she could read some, Grace knew to keep things simple. Hatta Mae's writing skills were even poorer than her reading skills, so she never answered Grace's letters. Once, her sister sent a letter to let her know that another baby was on the way, but there was nothing else.

"Sure wish they could afford a phone," Grace lamented to Dorcus one day. "You're so lucky. You can talk to your people a lot." Dorcus thought about asking her family to share one of their weekly calls with Hatta Mae, since she didn't live that far away from them, but then thought it might be better not to get her mother's dander up about the Alley people again, considering she never quite got around to telling her that she and Grace had become friends at State.

"That's all right," said Grace, when Dorcus apologized for not making the necessary arrangements. "The Judge has a phone. If we ever need to contact each other in a hurry, we all got his number." With Willie, however, it was a different matter. He was so excited about his new life in the Liberation Front, as he called it, where he was learning new work skills and had been appointed to a position as a temple guard, he simply had to share it with Grace.

"It may not sound like much," he reported to her, "but I have a place to stay, and learn, and TLF is starting a school, so I might become a teacher for the little ones. We're teaching them all about our people. You won't get that in that college. You have to join me here. Come out and live the life, Gracie. You'll love it here."

Grace was torn, but memories of her mother's sacrifice and determination made her realize she had to stick it out in college, so she sent letters to Charleston and letters to New York, making extremely sure the two never crossed. She never mentioned either party in the other's letters. However, all the caution in the world could not keep some things a secret, especially when not everyone knew that they were supposed to be secrets. Hatta Mae's blood boiled when she learned through a chance conversation with her beloved landlord, the Judge, that Willie was still in touch with Grace. Now, however, she was too far away from either of them to have any impact. All she could do was fume and cuss, which sent her blood pressure through the roof. Most of her tirades were aimed at Willie, but she took some solace in the fact that they were separated by several states. *He can't git hur pregnant from da Noth, so maybe I kin still sav' ma baby,* she reasoned. She determined to keep a remote eye on the situation, and enlisted the Judge as her unwitting ally and "Willie detector."

Meanwhile, Dorcus's parents were equally unhappy when they discovered that their daughter had begun to major in boys, one boy in particular, and had almost flunked out of school. This information wasn't revealed by Dorcus, but by the staff, who had such a vested interest in seeing that colored students succeeded they often took extra steps and went the extra mile for their charges. Freshman progress was closely monitored, and those who were underachieving were frequently counseled in an effort to resolve academic and other problems. The faculty knew that if they could successfully guide these gentle souls through their first year out of the nest, the subsequent years would take care of themselves. Dorcus was eventually assigned to a counselor, who quickly assessed the situation. It wasn't hard to diagnose the problem. Here was a bright young woman who was failing primarily as a result of love sickness. The cure, however, was painful, as Dorcus was placed on academic probation.

"Dorcus, we received a call we didn't enjoy," her mother said through clenched teeth over the telephone one day. It was an uncomfortable conversation, and the next day, her parents arrived unannounced at State. As she sat between them in the dorm lobby, Dorcus wished she could fade directly into the flowery slip cover they were sitting on. Her mother, as usual, did all the talking, while her father sat quietly with his hands in his lap, staring straight ahead. She tried to catch his eye a few times, to send a signal to make the torture stop. In the past, if he was feeling her pain, he would quickly intervene as an advocate, but this time, he let his little girl carry the full weight as her mother brutally unloaded. She, meaning they, threatened to stop financial support unless Dorcus improved her grades. Ultimatum followed ultimatum, and she was reduced to a quivering mass. She fled to her room in tears as her parents' car pulled slowly out of the parking lot. If she could have seen her father's face at that moment, she would have known that he shared her pain, but he had to force himself to follow his wife's "no interference" edict. He also had to face the realization that his little girl was now a woman who had to face things for herself. Dorcus also had to face the reality that if she wanted to survive until graduation, she had to make both her parents and herself happy. It wasn't going to be easy.

XX

"So, here we are. Senior year at last. I never thought I'd never see this day," crowed Dorcus to Sardis as they settled in for their last year as roommates.

"Neither did I," came the response from her delighted roommate as she slipped the bid whist board under her bed. "I'm glad you're here. The foursome would never have survived without you." By now, Dorcus had forgotten about her unsuccessful quest to achieve hot girl status. The closest she came to reigning as queen over anything was in a hotly contended contest for her dorm, but she lost. She was in a sorority, one that shared her interest and met her needs, although it was not *the* sorority on campus. She was pulling a solid B average in her field of elementary education, and she was still dating newly promoted First Lieutenant Anton Baylor. With graduation day looming on the horizon, Dorcus prayed that Anton would present her with the ultimate graduation gift; an engagement ring. She thought she was going to snag it two years earlier, when he received his diploma from State. "I'm going to meet my future in-laws," she shrieked when the formal invitation to his graduation ceremony arrived.

"Ain't got no ring yet," was Grace's in-your-face reply. There were times when Dorcus wondered how she remained friends with that Alley woman, but Grace was right, and the term "depression" couldn't begin to describe Dorcus's dark mood when it failed to materialize. She had dropped hints as large as Mt. Everest, and lobbied hard through Charlie, who, as always, served as her advocate, but in the end, she had to settle for a bouquet of flowers instead.

Charlie was an ally and supporter until the day he and Anton left college. Secretly, he pined for her attention, but he knew his only hope for success was to feed off her interest in Anton. They shared dinner practically every Friday while Anton was busy with ROTC, and they ate Sunday morning breakfasts in a near-empty cafeteria. Those times were precious for Charlie, especially the rare occasions when they weren't focused entirely on Anton. In his heart, he thought he was making progress, thought she might see him for himself and drop her interest in his cousin, thought he might be successful in winning her heart. Then, she began lobbying him to press Anton for a ring, and his heart sank. As much as he willed himself, he found himself unable to approach Anton with that suggestion.

The two years following Anton and Charlie's graduation were difficult for Dorcus. Not only had she lost Anton's presence on campus, but she also missed Charlie, even though she had no romantic interest in him. He served as her rock, her sounding board. She confided in him, just as she had done with her brothers back home. Now, they exchanged letters and he remained her chief liaison with Anton, especially after she discovered the two men were related. She was so proud of Anton when he received his Second Lieutenant bars at graduation. She liked his family, and they seemed to like her. Anton shared his mother's disposition, a bit distant and cool, but Dorcus's perkiness won instant favor with his father.

After receiving his degree and military commission, Anton went directly into active duty as an army officer, and four long, empty months passed before Dorcus heard from him. One day, however, in the middle of summer, a special invitation arrived at her home, and from that point on, Dorcus's feet never touched the ground. Anton asked her to be his escort for the formal dinner dance and ceremony to recognize his graduation from Officer Training School at Ft. Gordon, Georgia, and she accepted in a heartbeat. Her eyes glazed over, and her constant humming nearly drove the family insane. Her imagination kept running away from her, over and over again. As the big event approached, she visualized what her ring would look like as she mentally planned her wedding. Sardis would make a fantastic maid of honor, and her sorority sisters, even Grace, would be her bridesmaids.

Anton was one of twelve officers from State who received assignments at Gordon, and when Dorcus saw him in his formal dress blue uniform for the first time, her knees buckled. He was in peak physical form after weeks of conditioning and training and possessed a new type of maturity and self-assurance befitting a newly minted Second Lieutenant. Soon, he would assume the unenvied position as the lowest ranking officer, albeit with the greatest responsibilities, somewhere in the military. He would be tried, tested, and allowed to fail, and his inflated ego would become battered, bruised, and scarred by lower-ranking enlisted men with far more experience, but for now, on this humid summer night in Georgia, he had the world at his feet as he escorted an excited Dorcus to the most unforgettable event of her life.

Who wants to be a campus queen? she asked herself blissfully as they entered the lavishly decorated officer's club. *I'll take this any time.* As uplifting as the formal ball was, it paled in comparison to the wild after-party later that night, hosted by the twelve State graduates and the five other black officers in their class. Motown music blared from loud speakers as the women, in their evening gowns, and the officers, minus their hot and heavy uniform coats, got real and got with it. Dorcus had traveled and was sharing hotel arrangements with a girl she knew at State. She also recognized four other women who had attended State, but the rest of the men and their sweethearts were strangers. However, as the champagne and Cold Duck, its fruity-flavored cousin, which Dorcus favored, began to flow, everyone became fast friends. Around midnight when the party was at fever pitch, the mood suddenly changed when one of the men appeared with a white woman on his arm. The instant the couple entered the dance hall, the tension was palpable. Dorcus, and others with Southern roots, had never encountered this type of situation before and didn't know how to react, until one woman took it upon herself to ask the rhetorical question that was on many of their minds. "Why did he have to bring her? This is *our* party."

Times were changing rapidly, and black people had to face and resolve internal racial issues and conflicts. Until now, integration had been a one-way street; whites had to accept change and let coloreds in. Social integration was a separate dimension. It raised a lot of hackles, particularly among black women, who were still trying to discover their own identities as the women's movement gained momentum. White men were also impacted as they saw themselves as potentially being displaced by both black men and liberated women. Many were not prepared to deal with either. After giving the couple a few intense stares, Dorcus and the other women decided to ignore them for the time being and party on. They would deal with it later.

XXI

With Sardis in college and gone for her fourth year, her mother was deeply depressed. Her social circle were aware of her frustration, and whispered about it, but offered no help, other than talking her into getting a part-time domestic to fill the gap that had been left by Sardis. With little else to keep her occupied, she watched hours upon hours of television, while waiting in anticipation for her only family to return home. They exchanged letters once a month, and Sardis kept her abreast of her academic achievements. Eartha was proud of her daughter's good grades. Once, Sardis mentioned her friend Byron, but she shared very little else with her mother, who never knew that by her senior year, Sardis reigned, albeit reluctantly, as the queen of Ben E. Mays Residential Hall. She was selected primarily because Byron was dorm president, and she had no competition. Even more significantly, her mother could never share in the triumphs of Sardis's thespian accomplishments. By now, she ruled the stage. Cyrus Bloom had an eye for great talent and was prepared to break ranks with his predecessors, who had only put seniors into leading roles. The old-school way of thinking was to make the new players pay their dues and work their way up to the major parts. This was supposed to give the students the incentive to stay with the troupe for their entire school tenure, but the practice did not sit well with him.

Several disgruntled seniors took it upon themselves to enlighten their guileless instructor. "It's a reflection of real life. Nobody goes to New York and waltzes straight into a leading role right away."

He understood and sympathized, but none of the seniors' talents could match those of freshman Sardis, and he had no intention of letting her sit in the background for three years before being cast in a leading role. So he gave the seniors another lesson in the realities of life. All auditioned, but none succeeded, and so the Sardis/Byron dynasty was born. The duo managed to convince the student body that acting was a legitimate endeavor, and theater attendances increased four-fold to the point where, when they performed their second Williams play, all the auditorium seats were filled. Of course, mandatory attendance by speech students didn't hurt, but by now the productions had even become popular with the local community. The local media sent critics, and several of the plays received good reviews.

For Sardis, the summer months, when she was forced to reenter her isolated world, were long, dreary affairs. Even though she knew Dorcus, and realized they were neighbors, they had no contact during the summer months. Like a clock suddenly running in reverse, tradition and history served to separate them each time they landed in Charleston. The only positive reaction she got from her depressed mother was when she provided more details about Byron, who met with her approval after Sardis provided a complete description of him, from the soles of his light feet to his sandy-colored hair. She assured her mother that he would blend right into their downtown world if she ever decided to return to it.

Sardis wanted nothing more than to maintain the peace, but she chaffed at the thought of her mother holding a tight rein on the purse strings, and thus on her life, and welcomed each August, when she was able to escape to her alternate reality. She couldn't wait to see Byron again, and everyone who saw them together was sure that they would eventually get married and ride off into the sunset of stage production together. During her senior year, however, Sardis's world was tilted right off its axis when J. B. Story landed on State's campus.

"The first name is actu'ly Jeb, mon," he told his fellow juniors on his first day. "But hey, do I look like a Jeb to you? So take out the e and now you got da nom. Dat las' nom. Don' try, so Story it become."

He was new, he was different, and the Jamaican lilt drove the girls wild and Mr. Bloom crazy.

"Boy, we are going to have to work on getting you to speak the king's English." Thus Cyrus set to work on J. B.'s elocution as soon as he stepped into Speech 101. J. B. became very popular on campus. He didn't try to be popular; he just was. His velvet skin, which shone in the sun like a black light poster, was as smooth as a satin pillow, and when he spoke, his eyes flashed and his smile revealed two even rows of pearl-bright teeth. He had naturally wavy hair, or what used to be called "good" hair that didn't need processing. He was tall, had broad shoulders, and was older and more mature than the average student.

"He's a military veteran," Taletha enlightened the group during their first game of the last year. She met him in an economics class and literally fell head over heels by tumbling out of her chair when he sat by her. He smiled and introduced himself to the love-struck girl, and he immediately became her black Adonis. "He's from Louisiana. That's where his parents moved after they left Jamaica. He's a living doll," she drooled. Like many other women, she fell under his spell, and everyone expected a real slugfest to see who would eventually end up by his side. The others listened attentively to Taletha's game plan after game plan, night after night, as she droned on about J. B. Story. They shared a private concern with each other, one that brought sadness to them, because they knew in their hearts that their obese, very plain friend didn't have a sliver of a chance with the much desired J. B. Even Grace refrained from her usual outspokenness and let Taletha continue to live in her dream world.

J. B. could have been a real player, but surprisingly, he wasn't. He treated women with respect and didn't lead them on, qualities that only made him more attractive and desirable. His popularity won him his dorm's presidency, and he might have become president of the student body if not for the fact that, by tradition, the president was chosen during the last semester of the previous school term. This provided continuity and precluded situations like this where you could potentially have a student without prior history coming in and running the show. His election as president of an upperclassmen dorm was precedent enough, highly unusual for someone in their first year on campus who did not have any fraternal ties, however everyone accepted him and recognized his organizational and leadership abilities.

Two-year colleges were still foreign in South Carolina. J. B. took college courses on military bases where he was stationed, thus earning enough credits for an associate's degree. Once he left the military, he decided to follow his father's advice and finish his college education. State provided the most credit for the courses he had completed, so it was a natural fit. The one freshman requirement he had to complete, however, was speech, which was how he and his accent ran head-on into Cyrus Bloom.

J. B. had lived in his native Jamaica until he was sixteen years old, and by then, his accent had become second nature. He then moved to a southern state with a history of and a tolerance for accented speech, so now it was flavored with a touch of southern twang and Creole. He never thought much about it but found it was a great way to break the ice with the ladies, and now he wasn't sure he wanted to speak plain English. But he knew he had to pass this class, so for now, the accent had to go.

Even though Cyrus would have preferred for J. B. to take speech class, he made the same offer he made every year. Students could opt out of the class if they put in their hours with the Henderson-Davis Players. J. B. had no interest in theater, and little enthusiasm for acting or actors. However, for some reason, he decided to take the theater option. His mother had done a little regional theater, so performing might have been a recessive gene. "So, what do you think of him?" Taletha asked Sardis a month into the semester.

"Of whom?" said Sardis, who had been paying little attention to the conversation.

Grace and Dorcus's snickers made her look up just in time to catch the incredulous look that Taletha shot her way.

"Whom? Did you really ask of whom? He's been working around the theater for a whole month and you ask *whom?* I was thinking

seriously about joining the theater group until I saw Julia Jackson there. I don' want a thing to do with her. She *thinks* she got her hooks in him, but I'm gonna show her ..."

Sardis tuned out and redirected her attention to her card combination, which was terrible. She was curious to learn more about the mystery man who had gotten under her card partner's skin. It didn't take her long to find him. The following day, just as the rehearsal was about to begin, Sardis and J. B. rushed into the theater from different directions, rounded a blind corner backstage, and collided. The impact was like a wire-frame bicycle crashing into a bobtail truck. It sent Sardis flying backward over some props, sending them noisily onto the floor.

J. B. leapt to Sardis's side as she lay sprawled among the scattered debris and gingerly picked her up. She was stunned, and a bit shaken, but his protective instincts took over, and he cradled her in his strong arms like a small child, giving her a sense of security and comfort she never felt before. This was new and different, she thought. J. B.'s thoughts echoed hers. Less than a minute had passed, but to them, it seemed like an eternity. He set her gently down on a prop couch, as one would place a sleeping infant into bed, and began to stammer an apology. Cyrus Bloom had already begun to make an impact on his speech patterns, smoothing out the lilting, sing-song Jamaican dialect, but J. B. was so flustered all the progress he had made was lost. He wasn't sure she could understand anything he was saying; indeed, he wasn't even sure if *he* could understand anything he was saying. He studied her face, the blue-green eyes, the smooth, milky skin, and the blushing cheeks. He needn't have worried about his apology, because Sardis hadn't heard a word; she couldn't take her eyes off his sultry face and felt so sheltered in his arms. She and Byron sometimes embraced, but this ... she did not ever want him to release her.

Cyrus Bloom witnessed the collision and was on the verge of intervening when he stopped short. He saw the imminent birth of a star. He possessed an innate ability to spot chemistry between people, which explained why his productions were so good, something he proved during his first year at the helm. There is nothing like success to spark envy, and so, after one semester of good attendances and reviews, the original director made it known to the Speech/English chairman that he wanted to reassume his role as advisor to the drama club. Against his better judgment, and because the original director had more tenure, the department chair reinstated Bloom's predecessor. It took only one play before everyone recognized Bloom's talent, however, and the chair immediately reversed his decision. Bloom now knew his position was secure.

Ever since Sardis's freshman year, Bloom wanted to cast a lead actor worthy of her talents. Byron was good, and they worked well together. However, for the play he wanted to produce, it would take a different type of person, someone with a raw sensuality. Now was the time, he told himself. He could finally dust off another Williams play. He finally discovered his Stanley for *A Streetcar Named Desire*.

For the first time since her freshman year, Cyrus did not cast Sardis in the lead role. He had an incoming freshman prodigy, and knowing that Sardis would soon graduate, he had to groom someone else. More than anything else, however, he sensed a combustion and a chemistry between Sardis and J. B., and so rather than casting her as Blanche, he gave her the supporting, albeit pivotal, role of Stella. "Trust me on this one," he said soothingly to an upset Sardis. "You already know you have the talent to go to great heights. A great actress can play any role. Just trust my judgment." He had anticipated her reaction. She was good, exceptional in fact, but he had the eye of a theatrical producer/director, and as much as he hated to admit it, he was having a personal crisis of his own at the prospect of Sardis leaving State at the end of the year. He considered her the first of what he hoped to be a new breed of performer, molded by his hand, ready to step onto the world stage. With the advent of the Black Power and civil rights movements, things were now beginning to open up for coloreds in the world of the performing arts. Bloom lived for the theater, and his heart yearned to have his creations accepted.

J. B. had never acted before and had to overcome the usual prejudicial beliefs about the theater. However, once he got up on stage, he quickly discovered that another being lived within him. A suppressed personality emerged, one that had been so deeply hidden he would never have discovered its existence otherwise. He had raw thespian talent, which Cyrus Bloom was able to shape, and he also had charisma, magnetism, a great stage voice, and unbelievable stage presence. The dormant gene sprang to life.

Now that she was in her element, J. B. discovered the real Sardis. Ever since their backstage collision, he felt different. He needed to be in her presence, and whenever he sensed the merest hint of her presence, he felt deep stirrings. The man was in love, but there was Byron to consider. He wondered what she could possibly see in the little weasel. J. B. was jealous, which was a new sensation for him, and he doubted his ability to compete. It would have been easier if, like the other women, she displayed some interest, but it seemed that he was not registering with her. He longed for the daily rehearsals and made the most of their acting time together.

As for Sardis, J. B. had indeed registered. She relived their collision daily, from his boulder-like chest she felt when they collided to his massive hands as he quickly lifted her off the floor. She was flattered by his concern for her safety and welfare. He registered, all right—over and over again. As for Byron, she hoped he sensed her growing unease with their relationship. She was reluctant to break up with him, because she didn't want to hurt him. After all, they had been an item since their freshman year. He hovered ever-closer whenever J. B. was present and always moved quickly to her side once rehearsal was over, and she was sure he planned to present her with a ring for graduation. Once, she had longed for him to ask for her hand in marriage, but now, she wasn't sure if she would accept his proposal.

Cyrus Bloom, meanwhile, read people like he read scripts, and sensed the dynamics of the love triangle that was being played out before him. He watched with amusement and sought to exploit this energy in order to create the best production in the school's history. He sensed conflict and confusion in Sardis, and knew that while she had strong feelings for her play husband, she was holding back. For the first time since her fledgling acting attempts, she was not giving her all to her character. "Sardini," Cyrus said quietly when he caught up with her following the last dress rehearsal. She smiled warmly, because that had been his private pet name for her ever since their very first production, but she knew that he wasn't happy with her performance, because she wasn't happy with her performance. "Opening night is two days away, and I don't see the magic." Magic was another of Cyrus's pet words. He told her that she always put the audience under a spell whenever she was on stage. The combination of Sardis, the actress, and Houdini, the magician, had created Sardini, the muse, and now here was her teacher, mentor, and friend trying to pull her back into her ruling element. She had to get her priorities straight, end her confusion, and resolve her emotional conflicts.

"Bid whist, anyone?" she said when she returned to the dorm. The four friends gathered instantly, and the game began. Most of the time, playing the game cleared her head, but Taletha had chosen this evening to talk about her next futile strategy for getting J. B.'s attention.

"I plan to be at all four performances of your play. I'm going to be in the front row, so he won't miss me. Then I'm going back to the stage door when he leaves and lay a big old kiss on *my* man. I heard a lot of women talking about going to this play. They better not get in 'Letha's way."

The play opened to the biggest audience in school history, and every woman on campus attended night after night over the four-day run. J. B. did not disappoint them. Many in the local community supported the event, and a local colored newspaper gave the play a rave review, stating what was already obvious; the three leads, playing Stanley, Blanche, and Stella all had star potential. Cyrus's instincts proved to be correct, beyond a shadow of a doubt. It was his best production ever, and on the final evening, just as he hoped, the magic returned when real life intervened.

The stage was empty except for two characters. Stanley was facing a reluctant Stella, pleading with her to rekindle the fire in their love. Sardis had difficulties with the scene, but night after night she was able to fool the audiences with her masterful acting. The auditorium was dark and still. No silly pranks would disturb the moment here. Everyone sat in hushed anticipation, as if they were drawn into a secret that was about to be unwittingly exposed.

The characters' eyes met and locked on each other. They stood facing each other, saying nothing. Some in the audience wondered if they forgot their lines. Then, J. B., not Stanley, wrapped his arms around Sardis's waist, and they moved toward each other, as if some invisible magnetic force was tugging at their bodies. As he tilted her face up toward his, every woman in the audience held her breath, exhausting the air around them like a whirlpool swallowing a ship. The moment their lips met, weeks of shy smiles, coy glances, and restrained passion went off like a nuclear explosion, the detonation releasing emotional energy that enveloped the entire audience. The men cheered wildly for their conquering hero, while the women became subdued, their hearts suddenly shattered. Some sighed heavily, while others began to cry with the realization that any hope of a relationship with J. B. was now gone. The kiss was real, and everyone knew it, felt it, and would remember it. Taletha, in her front-row seat, stifled a cry. Her chest heaved, and her head dropped wearily into her hands. Byron, who was waiting in the wings for his entrance as Blanche's potential boyfriend, turned away briefly, dabbing a handkerchief to his eyes, pretending to remove excess makeup. Cyrus, standing in the wings on the other side of the stage, folded his arms, smiled, and knew that they were all destined for the Great White Way.

XXII

The Protest

The game stopped as Grace and Taletha raced from the room to join the protesters. Sardis and Dorcus remained cowering in the room, wondering what they should do. It was an eerie sight as they looked out the window to see small bonfires burning here and there. Hundreds of students were racing about seeking leadership, and there were rumors that some had gone to torch a vacant house. Dorcus and Sardis were frightened by the mood of the crowd, and they had every right to be. This mini-insurrection had increased in violence over the last three nights, and the presence of law enforcement officers had steadily increased. The previous night, several cars and shop windows in the strip mall that housed the bowling alley were damaged or destroyed. Up until now, students who hadn't wished to participate were able to stay out of harm's way, but not anymore. Trouble now arrived at their doorstep.

Fearing someone might attempt to toss a fire bomb into the dorm, Sardis and Dorcus decided to go downstairs to the lobby just in case they had to evacuate on short notice. When they reached the lobby, they found many of the other students had the same idea and were clustered together in doorways and around windows. Sardis and Dorcus peered intently into the night, trying to spot Grace and Taletha, but there were too many people milling about. They couldn't decide whether to join the growing crush of students on the quad or whether they should remain within the confines of their dorm.

Their loyalties were divided. They sympathized with the rebelling students. After all, why should their rights be denied because of their skin color? And yet they'd put in four hard years of studying, sweating, and even praying and were ready to graduate and move on, so they didn't want to make waves. They didn't want anything, not even sweet liberty, to come between them and that sheepskin saying, "You're finished. This way to the work world."

As more and more fires were lit, police officers began to move onto campus to snuff them out, which led some students to respond by throwing rocks and bottles. The police retreated, and a cheer went up from the crowd on the quad. The jubilation didn't last long, however. From their position, neither Dorcus nor Sardis could see the targets of their comrade's projectiles. Suddenly a person in uniform rushed past them as they, along with a number of other observers, stood rooted in the doorway, holding on to each other for support. Another uniform appeared, and this time, the police officer swung an object in their direction, catching Dorcus on the thigh. She crumpled to the ground, crying out in pain as everyone around them retreated. Sardis helped Dorcus to her feet, and they withdrew to the relative shelter of the dorm as other, more horrifying, events began to unfold.

Grace and Taletha had made their way to the edge of the campus, where students had lit a big bonfire, but now Grace backed away from the melee and slowly headed back toward the dorm. While she supported the cause, she didn't want to get caught in any uprising. She thought Taletha was right behind her, but found they had become separated. Panic set in. She felt like a salmon swimming upstream as a crush of students ran past her, headed in the opposite direction. Some carried incendiary devices, which they used to set an empty building alight. The fire quickly grew, and soon firefighters arrived to douse the flames, accompanied by patrolmen and National Guard troops. After three nights of unrest, local officials decided more muscle was needed to quell these uppity students. This nonsense had to stop once and for all. They had to be put in their place, taught some manners and respect.

The students, sensing the mood of the newly arrived state police and national guard, quickly determined they were not going to let them get the upper hand. Many were tired of having been pushed around all of their lives and were prepared to take a stand. They were ready to fight back. They armed themselves with rocks, bottles, and boards from the burning house. One thrown object caught a state policeman in the face. He fell to the ground, wounded and bleeding. The authorities' fear and hatred were aroused. Colored students made a white man bleed. This didn't happen in the South! Colored students had no right to hurt a white man! Now, they were going to pay! Colored students had to be punished, put back in their place so they wouldn't ever do that again! They would be stopped. *Right now!*

The sound of gunfire rent the air, sending shockwaves across the campus. At first, the students thought the patrolmen were just firing warning shots over their heads, but soon blood began to flow. The students panicked, and did the only thing panicked people know to do—they ran. Taletha became caught up in the stampede, and began to run as best she could. The sudden rush of adrenaline got her stubby legs pumping faster than they had ever gone before, but she was a large woman, and after years of inactivity, the rest of her body was unable to keep up.

Law officials, already highly agitated by the ugly turn of events, tried to control the crowd by herding everyone into a nearby open field. They were determined to restore order, no matter what it took, but tension continued to mount, and they decided the students were going to pay, one way or another, for their transgressions, and for those of their fathers, and of their entire race. Suddenly, Taletha felt a sharp pain as the baton of a state trooper slammed down on her left shoulder. She cried out and winced in pain but continued her attempt to escape. Then she felt a sharp tug on her right arm and an equally forceful pull on her left arm and realized she was now pinned between the bodies of two men who were hell-bent on doing her great harm. Unable to move, she screamed, which made them irate. "Go ahead and scream," sneered one as he leveled a blow across her back.

The terrified girl made a feeble attempt to break free, which seemed to amuse the men, who continued to jeer at her. "This is how we kept your kind in place long ago, only then, it was with a whip. If I had one now, all of you would pay." With each blow, Taletha was informed of the multitude of sins for which she was now paying. "That's for being colored, Negro, Nigra, Nigger; take your pick. That one is for being a woman; uppity; challenging the authority of a white man. That one is for thinking; trying to deny a white man of his rights. That one is for having a brain; thinking you smarter than a white man. That one is for being educated and thinking you better than us. That one is because I hate you. I hate you. I hate you."

The defenseless girl crumpled to the ground in a sorry heap, her face swollen to the point where her features all ran together as one bloodied mass. She was barely conscious, but still her mind told her, *This was not supposed to happen. We just wanted our rights.*

The two men eventually strolled away, seeking another target. Grace, who witnessed the beating from behind the safety of a fence, waited until they were gone, and moved stealthily toward her friend, who hadn't moved. Grace was horrified. She knew fear from growing up in the Alley. There was much to fear from overworked, underpaid, jealous men who being determined to demand respect, felt their only recourse was to do it at the point of a knife thrust into someone's heart. There was fear of accidentally walking into the path of a bullet headed for the body of an enraged, revengeful woman driven mad by scorn. But Grace never faced this type of fear. Snarling, enraged men set to harm her for no other reason than her skin color. As she thought of the possibility of becoming their next victim, her vision blurred as drops of sweat mingled with tears clouded her vision.

She confirmed that Taletha was still breathing but didn't know what to do. "Come on, Tee. Can you move?" she whispered, pulling urgently on Taletha's swollen arm while trying not to attract any attention not wanting to meet a similar fate. Taletha, who was obviously in great pain, began to moan, and Grace became frightened. She knew she had to help her friend but couldn't begin to lift her. "Let me help you up. I got to get you to the infirmary." With Grace's help, Taletha struggled slowly to her feet. Her eyes were swollen shut, so she couldn't see the sky light up as more shots were fired. Grace could see it, however, and she could also hear it. The shooting was close by, too close. "Tee, come on, girl!" Grace commanded urgently. Taletha, sensing the urgency of the situation, tried to ask what was going on, but her mouth filled with blood, and she began to choke.

The sound of the shooting was getting closer, and now students were running everywhere trying to find cover. A man raced past them, then suddenly turned and grabbed Taletha's other arm to help Grace, who was clearly struggling with the badly injured girl. As they moved slowly toward the infirmary, Grace looked around and saw about three hundred students who had been herded into an open field. Many were obviously wounded and in pain but weren't receiving any care. Some of them began to sing, "We Shall Overcome." Chaos ruled the night.

They eventually reached the infirmary, where they joined a host of other incoming wounded students. The facility, which until now had existed primarily to dispense aspirin, Band-Aids, and ice packs for the occasional athletic sprain, was overrun with casualties from a catastrophic situation it was woefully unprepared to handle. Wounded students were everywhere, crowded into rooms and spilling out into hallways. The floor was stained red with blood. Grace's eyes widened as she took in the sight. When her nose caught the stench of stale antiseptic and new blood, she felt sick to her stomach and retched, but nothing came up. The constant moans of the wounded added to the misery of this seemingly endless night.

Grace and her unidentified assistant set Taletha carefully down on the floor, as every chair and bed was already occupied, and Grace sat beside her, cradling her head as Taletha drifted in and out of consciousness. Grace was able to take a good look at her friend for the first time and was shocked to discover she couldn't recognize her. Her face was swollen into a mass of flesh that resembled a puffy cloud, and her body was covered with swatches of black and blue where the batons had caught her. Grace knew she needed help right away but none appeared. The infirmary operated with minimal staff, so it was no surprise that they were now overwhelmed and seriously short of help. Someone had called for an ambulance, but so far, there was no response. They needed a fleet of ambulances, but no one seemed to care about the welfare of colored students, or Negro students as the press carefully delineated when the news finally emerged.

Grace grimaced when a hand grasped her wrist, pleading for water. There was none available, and she didn't know what to do. Her face went ashen and she began to tremble when yet another student was carried in and placed on the floor right at her feet. He didn't look like the others, those who had suffered wounds to their backs as they tried to escape, or those whose feet were swollen from buckshot that had been fired at them as they lay on the ground. Some things never changed. Many of these students' slave ancestors had their feet damaged so that they couldn't run away. Now, history had found a way of repeating itself. This young man was covered in blood from wounds to his chest. His breathing was slow, shallow, and labored, and Grace stared in horror as his eyes began to roll back into his head as his life drained from him. She realized he was dying right before her eyes. She tried to scream, but her mouth was too dry, and no sound came.

That was enough for Grace. She was wedged in the middle of a bloodied mass of man's inhumanity to fellow man, and she wanted out—right then. Taletha hadn't moved for a long time, but at least she was still warm and breathing. Grace removed her sweater and placed it carefully under Taletha's head. Then she rose and fought her way to the door, stepping gingerly over crying students until at last she was able to make her way out into the night. She inhaled deeply, taking in several deep gulps of fresh air while her eyes gradually adjusted. The dorm wasn't far away, but it meant passing through an open field. She managed to move a few yards from the infirmary when suddenly she heard the sound of more gunfire. That was her last memory of that fateful night. Three students, Samuel Hammond, Delano Middleton, and Henry Smith, paid the ultimate price for freedom that night, while twenty-nine others would carry the scars for the rest of their lives.

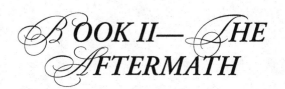

BOOK II—THE AFTERMATH

I

"Taletha! Taletha, honey!"

"Hey, Tee, wake up!" She heard the voices but couldn't respond. Her mind was foggy, and the jumble of information made concentration impossible.

"Taletha?"

Who is that calling? she wondered. She willed her mind and her eyes to do her bidding. Still nothing.

"Tee?"

That was a different person. She strained to hear more, but all became silent. *Where did they go? Where am I?* Questions swirled around and around in her brain. Mastery over time became useless, so in her mind she was back in the comfort and security of the family farm. That's it—her birthplace—where she was—Edisto Island.

Edisto reminded her of her favorite tree, a large Magnolia with numerous branches dripping with delicate, lacy Spanish moss. If you viewed it from the sky, it had one major paved road, like the trunk of a tree, which then split off into several unpaved tracks, like the branches. Every "branch" hid clusters of fruit and pods under wide leaves, the inhabitants' houses. The only way anyone would have known these houses and families existed within was by noting the clusters of mailboxes that sprouted between the weeds on the main road. Generations of families bore fruit here for decades, so Taletha was never alone. The original house where her great, great ancestors had once lived burned to the ground years ago, and now a newer, more modern house stood in its place. Along the many branches were mostly trailer or track houses, occupied by her aunts and uncles and cousins; all except for one. His branch was bare and brittle, and he hadn't produced the same abundance of fruit as the other family members. In her mind, she saw dry, broken branches falling on her; then other images took over; uniforms, helmets, and snarling, hateful faces with batons administering blow after blow. Eventually, everything faded to black.

II

"We never did complete that game, did we?" said Sardis, breaking the stillness that had filled the room.

"No, we didn't," sighed Dorcus. "Couldn't. Funny, one minute our minds were filled with boyfriends, cards, and graduation, and the next we were hiding in fear, wondering if we would live long enough to ever experience anything again." The three of them nodded in unison, their vacant stares suggesting they were all watching the same channel on an invisible television screen.

III

No U. S. college campus had ever experienced an invasion of this magnitude, and it took school officials, law enforcement officials, local and state government officials, the media, and everyone else who had a hand in creating this piece of history by surprise. How would this be recorded for posterity, people wondered, for history has its way of assigning roles of heroes and villains? Who would be assigned to those roles in this scenario? No one had answers, but no one ever wants to be assigned to the villain category. Everyone set about polishing their tarnished stars so they would shine brightest as heroes.

The federal government, with its vast experience spinning fables, fabricating situations, and formulating half-truths out of downright lies, sat on the fence for a few days to assess the situation. Three young men were dead, and many, many more were injured, some seriously. They knew someone would be blamed, but they didn't know which direction the wind would blow, or on which side of the fence they would be dislodged.

The national guard and state police justified their actions by calling what had begun as a peaceful civil rights demonstration a riot. They were right; it had been a riot. One tiny ingredient was omitted, however. They lit the fuse that caused the explosion by adding additional tension to an already volatile situation. Crowd control tactics were either unknown or had been completely ignored in their heavy-handed behavior, resulting in the utter chaos that ensued. Then, to use the analogy of a cattle drive, rather than gently turning the herd, they started firing their guns, which led to a panicked stampede. Guard troops swore they heard gunshots coming from the crowd of students, and so they returned fire. They denied that their pent-up frustration from insults, along with the rocks and bottles that students hurled at them, had anything to do with their reaction.

The state, represented by its governor, Robert McNair, grudgingly acknowledged that this unfortunate incident was a sad day for the state of South Carolina, but the state did not want to appear to be the bad guys, so he employed the age-old tactic called blame the victim. He implied the Black Panther Party was the true face of evil and had infiltrated the student body, thus instigating the riot. The militant group proved to be convenient scapegoats for the events. Their activities in Oakland, California, instilled fear in the heart of the nation as a whole. Whites feared their militancy and tactics, while blacks, who still preferred to adhere to a non-violent approach that had been effective throughout the South to date, were unable to relate to their call for freedom "by any means."

By invoking such symbolism, the governor ensured that what had begun as a civil rights protest suddenly became an insurrection with sinister overtones; it was clear the students were trying to overthrow the government, and worse. The truth was buried six feet underground, and no amount of persuasion was going to change his mind. That was the governor's story, and he was sticking to it.

The media by now had begun to grow jaded and somewhat hostile. They no longer knew how to report on all the black movements that had sprung up all over the country. Who were the good guys, and who were the bad? The civil rights movement had begun with peaceful protests headed by established organizations, like the NAACP, who had a long tradition and history in fighting for civil liberties. Now, the movement was evolving, adding new dimensions, such as protests against Vietnam and the draft. White journalists shared the same fears as the white population in general, and once the name of the dreaded Panthers was invoked, their loyalties converged. Although they were charged with the sacred obligation of reporting the truth, not one media representative actually set foot on the campus, and so the students' side of the story was never reported. One "brave" reporter, cowering behind the safety of the police-controlled perimeter, provided a phantom account of heavy gunfire being exchanged between students and police. Wire services picked up an alleged eyewitness account of another reporter who said that he had actually seen students armed with rifles and shotguns. They were works of fiction, each one, but their respective editors didn't bother to ask questions.

Balanced reporting flew out the window, and the media, acting as instruments of state propaganda, willingly perpetuated the lie that law enforcement agencies were merely trying to quell perceived acts of insurrection, rather than cries for civil liberties. In their view, civil rights demonstrations morphed into civil riots. Therefore they felt justified in reporting the incident as yet another riot. This all served to assuage the guilt of everyone involved. They felt secure textbooks would say their heroic attempts to restore law and order were justified and the loss of three black lives and the shattered ruin of twenty-nine others, while unfortunate, was necessary. History would applaud their actions. The original concept of a peaceful march by idealistic students in an attempt to integrate a bowling alley was buried under an avalanche of fabricated stories and half-truths.

In the meantime, school officials faced a major dilemma and quickly decided to close the campus and suspend all classes. Stern-faced parents swarmed the campus after receiving calls from their sons and daughters telling them of the decision. Anguish consumed those who were unable to locate their child, and many distraught parents raced to the infirmary and then to local hospitals when their child could not be found on campus. Some, after eventually locating their injured son or daughter, spirited them away to seek immediate care from hometown physicians, while others breathed huge sighs of relief after finding their children unharmed. Many were to discover over time, however, that a lot harbored invisible wounds. These took much longer to heal, because black people tend to shy away from psychological help, and the school did not provide that type of assistance.

"You have to take Sardis." Dorcus stood her ground, challenging her father, who had driven to the campus, arriving just at daybreak. "She doesn't have any other way to get to Charleston. We can't just leave her here." Dorcus's grim-faced father just wanted to quickly squire his only daughter away to safety, but he knew better than to argue.

After the gunfire died down, Dorcus ventured out into the hallway to discover the line for the telephone stretched from the front to the rear door. It was the same on each dorm floor, but after an hour, she was finally able to commandeer a phone. By then, she had a few things packed and was anxious to get going, but it took fifteen minutes of almost constant dialing to obtain a clear line and place her call. Her fear had reduced her normal, calm tones to semi-coherent babbling, and it was another twenty minutes before she was finally lucid enough to let her family know what was happening at the college.

Her parents, especially her normally docile father, didn't take the news well. As a pastor, Reverend Dupree and his church had front-line experience in many civil rights battles. The church had lost several of its beautiful stained glass windows to retaliatory actions, and on two separate occasions, obvious attempts by arsonists had greeted him when he arrived at the edifice. He withstood threats of personal danger, but news of his daughter being placed in danger, and her education disrupted, angered him to the core. He told Dorcus to sit tight, and he would be there as soon as he possibly could. As soon as he hung up the phone, he headed out the door and drove through the night, determined to remove his daughter to safety.

"I can take the bus home if you'll just take me to the station," Sardis pleaded, not wanting to be a burden. She was torn between leaving immediately and lingering long enough to learn what happened to Jeb. She hadn't been able to locate him, and he had no local relatives to check on him, so she was frantic. For all she knew, he could have been among the injured.

"No, no!" Dorcus insisted. "We will not leave you here." Sardis, sensing Dorcus's concern and her father's anxiety, relented, but she left with a heavy heart. Besides the unenviable prospect of having to deal with an overly obsessive mother when she got home, she didn't know what had happened to the love of her life. *I don't even know how to contact him*, she lamented, silently fighting back tears. Dorcus was hoping to reach Anton, who she knew would be concerned about her welfare, and let him know she survived. As they left the shattered campus, she began to think about the future. They had invested four long years in getting an education, and now this.

"Wonder what happened to Grace and Taletha," said Sardis matter-of-factly as the car pulled out of Orangeburg. The city looked like a war zone. Traffic was being carefully controlled, and there were guard troops everywhere. At least two hundred had been brought in to patrol the campus and defend the city against these chocolate-colored children and the forces of evil, and they were taking their job seriously.

Dorcus hadn't thought about Grace and Taletha until then; she was just happy and relieved to have survived relatively unscathed. The eruption of gunfire had been too close for comfort, and she was still smarting from the blow she received to her thigh. Moving her hand across the area, she discovered it was swollen and sore to touch. Now her leg began to throb, and she relived the incident in her mind, as if she were still there, but the farther they drove from the campus, the more relieved she became.

She and Sardis had raced back to their room, closed the door, turned out the lights, and huddled together in the dark. Their greatest fear, which caused them to shiver uncontrollably, was that the militia would overrun the dormitories and arrest everyone. They heard repeated gunshots, screaming students running for their lives, and someone yelling when he was hit by a bullet. Those sounds were almost drowned out and replaced by their thumping hearts beating wildly as they held each other tightly, fearing the increasing violence and anxiety encasing them would spill over into the dorm at any minute.

When the car reached the Charleston county line, Dorcus, feeling safe at last, drifted off to sleep. They had left the night of terror behind them.

IV

Grace slowly opened her eyes and looked around her. She was never so happy to see her mother's face in all of her life, but as her eyes swept the room, she was shocked to see the other familiar face looking down at her was that of the Judge. She couldn't get a bearing on her surroundings. She remembered smiling at her mother, but then the picture began to fade, and once again, everything went to black. Later, when she woke again, she had no inkling of time, or of space, for that matter. She remembered drifting in and out of sleep, as if a stage curtain was rising and then falling again before the actors could take their places or begin to speak their lines. Finally, she managed to speak a few words to her mother, accompanied by groans as her senses awakened to pain in her upper back and buttocks. She slowly became aware of her surroundings and realized she was in a medical facility of some kind. "What happened? Where am I? How did I get here?" she asked in a raspy voice that had been silent for at least three days. Her mother was clutching her hand tightly, fearing if she released it, Grace would slip away into darkness forever. The Judge left the room to look for sustenance, a daunting task in a city that was still locked down, with every black person's actions under a microscope.

City and state officials stood fast in denying their culpability, and law enforcement agencies were under strict orders to locate the phantom Black Panthers and other militants, whom they were convinced were roaming the city with bloodthirsty intention of pouncing on innocent locals and stirring up more trouble. The governor, head still firmly in the sand, like an ostrich, went on the offensive in his press conferences, managing to convince both himself and the assembled media that outsiders had disturbed the state's racial harmony, as if such harmony ever existed. In his vow to restore complete harmony, and to assure his reelection, he proudly announced that, under his orders, an arrest had been made. A solitary black man was summarily thrown in jail. Someone had seen him near the campus and reported he had ties with a militant group, and so he was made to pay for the misjudgments that had been made by the white police. He atoned for the guilt of every bullet they fired out of anger and provided justification for their unreasonable actions. In short, he paid for every sin that had been committed on that fateful night. Suddenly, the victim became the villain, shouldering the blame for everything.

Hatta Mae gave Grace a sip of water. The Judge returned. As much as she despised the Judge, Hatta Mae had to concede that sometimes, he could display a true heart of gold. Grace shifted slightly and this time feeling more pain, cried out. Her mother wished she could change places with her wounded daughter as she silently thanked the unknown stranger who found her unconscious near the infirmary. It was the first time that Hatta Mae had seen Grace in almost four years, and once she got over the shock of seeing her unprocessed hairstyle for the first time, she saw before her a mature young woman. But to her, this was still her baby lying there carefully bandaged. Education has a way of making people appear more assured and confident, and her Grace now had that look. Hatta Mae was very pleased by the way she was developing, even though she was still unhappy about her continued relationship with Willie. "I never expected to see you with the Judge," whispered Grace, her senses now returning.

"Had to," said Hatta Mae, in the gruff manner she always displayed whenever she had to make a concession that forced her to swallow her pride. The Judge was the first to learn about the incident at the school, and that Grace had been shot, since he was officially listed as her point of contact. Even though he didn't own a vehicle, he always had a driver's license and quick access to a car. "Neva kno' when da po'lice might tun on ya. Always needs to kno' I kin git when I's got ta," he had said to his wife, who never questioned his activities. If she hadn't lived like a queen, she might have turned him in herself, but she enjoyed certain privileges as a result of his various activities, so she turned a blind eye. As soon as he learned of the news, he sprang into action and offered Hatta Mae a way to get to the school. He was no dummy. He knew she was angry with him about a lot of things, everything from her husband's weekly patronage of his liquid brew supply to his nephew's involvement with her daughter, and he wanted her as an ally. Finally, he found a way to make that happen.

V

Now that the school was closed, national guard troops quickly moved in and surrounded the campus. "We have to leave," said J. B.'s roommate as he hurried to pack. When he finished, he went outside to investigate, while J. B. remained in the dorm. Neither supported the demonstrators, but now they were caught in the backlash. Soon, his roommate returned. "Don't go outside," he said. "It's ugly out there. There are cops everywhere, and they aren't wasting time asking questions. A lot of students have been shot, and a lot more are being detained." J. B.'s thoughts turned instinctively to Sardis. He desperately wanted to go to Earle Hall to find her, but the police presence and activity outside prevented him from doing so. Fear overtook him, not a cowering fear—after all, he was a combat veteran—but a nagging uneasiness about the unprecedented events that were unfolding outside his window.

J. B. had nowhere to go, as his closest relatives were in Louisiana. As more gunshots rang out, he made up his mind to race outside, prepared to brave the now-driving rain and to risk being shot to look for Sardis. His roommate restrained him and reasoned with him, convincing him not to do anything rash. Finally, he grabbed a suitcase and hurriedly threw a few items inside, with no thought as to where he would go or what he would do. Parents began to arrive, and as in the girl's dorms, chaos ensued. Rumors began to circulate about a male student being mortally wounded, and anguish gripped not only the parents but the young men themselves as they began to fear for the safety of missing roommates and friends. "Why don't you come and stay with us?" said J. B.'s roommate, who was from a small town in upstate South Carolina, when he saw the confused and worried look on J. B.'s face. He was about to accept his roommate's invitation when suddenly a welcome friendly face appeared in the doorway.

"I have been sent to ensure that all of you who were not involved in any of tonight's activities make it safely off the campus," Cyrus Bloom's voice echoed down the long hall. He and several other teachers had appointed themselves as go-betweens to ensure their students' safety. "Those trigger-happy fools are still walking around fully armed, and we don't want any more tragedies." Cyrus spotted a forlorn-looking J. B. He knew his star student was stranded, and so after escorting a handful of male students through the barricade, he returned to the dorm, collected J. B., and took him back to his rooming house. J. B. was older than most of his classmates, and Cyrus felt more of a friendship, especially since he himself was only slightly older than most of his students. Further, he knew J. B. wouldn't take advantage of his generosity or compromise his privacy.

State's unmarried instructors lived in a separate dorm on campus. However, many of them rented private quarters, mainly in boarding houses near larger cities, so they could get away on weekends to study or fish or socialize, or just for some privacy. The campus community was so small that everyone tended to know everyone else's business. "We have personal lives, after all," Cyrus explained, after extricating J. B. "The couple who owns this house are very nice, and I'm sure they won't mind you staying until we know what's going to happen." Cyrus's hideaway, as he called it, was located in Georgetown, a small farming community not far north of Charleston. This suited J. B. just fine, because he wanted to try and locate his beloved Sardis. They still knew so little about each other, and she hadn't provided many details about her home life, but he knew Charleston was her hometown.

When news about the incident broke the following day, it was confirmed that three students died, and now J. B.'s thoughts of Sardis were replaced with feelings of remorse over the deaths of his fellow schoolmates. He knew one of the three who perished, and his heart ached at the loss. Then, as he read the account of the events of the previous night, his feelings turned to outrage, which was soon replaced by anger. "Did you read this gibberish?" he ranted, tossing the paper to Cyrus. "It's all lies!" They were seated at a long table along with two other boarders. Cyrus gingerly picked up the paper, glaring at J. B., willing him to calm down, for boarding houses, most of which were in private residences, had strict rules. After Cyrus read the account, however, he was hard-pressed not to express the same degree of outrage. His mouth fell open, and he pounded the table. The news report called what began as a peaceful protest a riot and claimed it was influenced by the Black Panther Party and "other militant groups," who infiltrated the ranks of the student body. They were justifying the troops' actions by claiming they acted in self-defense.

"I guess black life is still worth nothing," said Cyrus, seething. "This is all a lie!" What was already a bleak day became even bleaker after the state governor held a press conference and added further embellishments to an already inaccurate account. A jaded press corps hung onto every word. Their account put journalistic integrity and credibility to shame. They bought into the lies and stereotypes they were being fed.

"Students fired first in a heavy exchange of gunfire," was the lie reported one rag. The stereotype, that blacks were considered violent by nature, meant this lie went unquestioned. Everyone knew that was true, so no one bothered to check the facts. Of course all of the students had guns.

"The troops had to put down a riot," was another lie touted by another news outlet. The stereotype, that blacks just didn't know how to behave, gave this credibility. This belief was further justified by the knowledge of how many black people were routinely arrested on any given day. In spite of all of the peaceful protests that had been staged in the quest for civil rights, some ideas never changed.

Finally, a truth: "Three students died, and at least twenty-nine others were wounded," but even this was a pat on the back for excellent coverage. Good job, it said. That will teach them who's in charge. Final tally: slaves, thirty-two; slave masters, zero.

"Did any of those journalists even attempt to speak to anyone from our side? Did they think to ask the students what happened?" J. B. continued ranting. "We have no voice here!"

He was pacing the floor like a country preacher as he spoke. All the others, including the owners of the house, had now read the account and understood his passion. Finally, he sat down, defeated, tears streaming from his eyes. The owner's wife hugged him gently and began to weep quietly. The others at the table, sharing their pain, bowed their heads and responded in the manner in which black people everywhere have responded for generations in order to rid themselves of pain, anger, and sorrow; they prayed.

VI

"Amen ... Amen ... Amen."

She could hear murmuring, punctuated from time to time with an amen. She recognized some of the voices, but others were strangers.

First, her mother, then her brother, and then her two great aunts and uncle. They were the last surviving siblings of a family of seventeen; seven boys, three taken while still in the womb, and ten girls. Fourteen of them had survived, but one had had an accident of some sort. People never talked about stuff like that, though. So much history lost through ignorance. *Maybe I'm home,* she thought. *That was Joe-Nathan. What's he doing in my room?* Even though her memory was a little fuzzy, she remembered the day she and Joe-Nathan met.

"What kind of name is that?" she asked. He had just come to her aid by chasing off a group of nagging kids that was teasing her about her weight. It was her first day in high school. Up until that time, her classmates had been mostly relatives. They attended school on Edisto, in a one-room building where grades one to seven were designated by desk rows. A large pot-belly stove heated the place during the winter, and in summer, they were released early, before it got too hot for field work. Once a child finished the seventh grade, *if* he finished the seventh grade, he went to a colored school in Charleston county where he was generally teased for being "countrified" because of their homemade clothing and distinctive speech patterns. The city kids weren't particularly tolerant of larger-sized kids either, and so Taletha became the butt of endless jokes and harassment.

"I think my name was supposed to be Jonathan; like David's friend in the Bible. I got a brother named Luke, and another named Mark, and one named David. Those names are simple, but my folks can't read, so when they went to name me, it came out Joe-Nathan." Taletha remembered thinking to herself that he looked just like his name. He was a really big farm boy who played football and some basketball but was too slow to be much good to either team. He was tall, however, the tallest boy in the ninth grade.

That's why he was able to scare off them kids, she remembered. He liked her and became protector, so they become an item all through school. Everybody expected them to hook up permanently once they finished, but Joe-Nathan didn't make it. During the last semester of school, he failed a class. So close, yet so far. Now, there was his voice again. *What's he saying about helping Sister Tee?*

VII

Charlie called Dorcus. The call surprised her because she never gave him her home number, but he learned a lot about her during their numerous non-date conversations about Anton. She talked about her father's church and its colorful congregates many times, and Charlie hung on every word, so he had no problem locating her through the church's listing. Even though she would have preferred to hear from Anton, Charlie was a good substitute. Charlie has always been the substitute. Dorcus had been in Charleston two days when he contacted her. She was experiencing the same dejection and outrage about everything that had happened, especially about the stories she read and heard. "Charlie," she wailed, releasing a lot of pent-up anger. "None of it is true! They made us sound like a bunch of irresponsible morons!"

This was the first time she had cried. She had a hard time reliving the fear and sharing the anguish they experienced over the last two, tension-filled days. She hadn't even spoken with her family, because she knew she wouldn't be able to hold back her tears. Her mother harbored some very strange ideas about women who shed tears. "They're a weakness, my dear, and they're also a weapon," she once advised Dorcus. "Don't let anyone ever know you're hurting, otherwise they'll control your soul, but if you ever want to instill guilt, especially in a man, turn on the waterworks full force, and watch him melt. They don't even have to be real." The strong black woman's credo was don't give people the pleasure of knowing they are inflicting pain on you, and make them suffer for hurting you, so Dorcus was unable to show her family the pain she was suffering. Left alone for the afternoon, while the others went to visit relatives, she wallowed in thoughts of self-pity and paranoia. So the familiar sound of Charlie's friendly voice brought back memories of happy days on campus, and she crumbled.

Charlie could feel her distress all the way to Columbia and wished with all his heart he could reach out and hold her. He often dreamt about having her in his arms, and at this tender moment, his heart ached because she was hurting so much. He had one of those strong, black mamas too, so he understood the significance of those tears. After graduation, he landed a job in the state's capital as the token black accountant for a legislator. He heard the governor's remarks firsthand and knew in his heart it was all a lie. "Some civil rights groups are organizing a protest march on the capital," he said. "I'm sure the truth will eventually come out." He thought briefly about inviting Dorcus to make the journey to Columbia and join him in protesting but immediately dismissed it as a bad idea. He couldn't walk the picket line with her; he was a state employee, a black man with a good job. If he wanted to remain gainfully employed, he couldn't show his partiality; and he definitely couldn't demonstrate.

Instead, he tried with all his might to provide comfort and support from afar. Dorcus poured her heart out, recounting everything that happened to her on that dreadful night. As she spoke, she rubbed her hand gingerly over the large bruised area where the butt of the trooper's gun caught her. "I'm among the walking wounded, but that's just between me and my thunder thighs; leave me out of the official tally." They both laughed at her comment, happy that she had recaptured some of her sense of humor. She then continued her account. Charlie's call provided the soothing balm she needed to speed her emotional recovery.

Their conversation lasted for an hour, and as he set the phone down in its cradle, Charlie was overwhelmed by a joyous thought: *She didn't ask about him,* he thought, breathing a gigantic sigh of relief. *She didn't say anything about dear cousin Anton. Maybe ... just maybe.* He smiled, his heart beating wildly. "Just, maybe ..." he uttered aloud, pleased at how the conversation had gone. He yearned for Dorcus and still held out hope that one day she would see him for himself, and not merely as Anton's shadow. As Anton's Cyreno, he made sure that Anton did the right thing by her, even going so far as to persuade Anton to invite her as his graduation guest for his officer basic graduation. Afterward, when the folly of this gesture dawned on him, he contacted Anton to find out how the event went, and whether he and Dorcus were still an item. Anton's responses were vague, which raised Charlie's hopes that the two of them might have decided that the romance was no longer alive. In reality, the romance never really worked, but neither of them seemed to notice. Charlie worked to keep them together, however, because it was his sole opportunity to keep Dorcus nearby.

His deception often left him wondering whether he made a good decision, and he prayed she would eventually recognize Anton for the callous, uncaring person he was, at which point he could then step in and declare his love for Dorcus. She would be so enamored by his care and concern that she would transfer her feelings and desires to him. They would get married and live happily ever after, his own fairy-tale ending. *Was I ever in a fool's fog,* he thought to himself time and again as things continued to go contrary to his beliefs. *Good guys only come out on top in the movies, I guess. All I ever managed to do was push them closer together.* Now, as he contemplated the fallacy of his earlier plan, he held out hope that things might finally be changing. He didn't bother to contact Anton about the events at the school and definitely wasn't about to tell him about his conversation with Dorcus. *The boy can read for himself,* he concluded in an attempt to assuage his rising guilt. *He can call her himself, just like I did. I'm not his keeper anymore. You're on your own, buddy,* he thought. *If she means anything to you, call her.* He hoped Dorcus would finally see things clearly, and turn her affections toward the one who always loved her.

Dorcus was smiling for the first time in days, and a calm feeling had just swept over her when suddenly she remembered. "Oh, darn!" she exclaimed, quickly retrieving the telephone from its cradle. *I forgot to ask Charlie about Anton,* she thought. She held the mouthpiece in mid-air, fingers poised to dial, when once again she cursed her memory; she also forgot to get Charlie's number. Her exuberance quickly evaporated, and she was once again gripped by despair. *Anton must have heard by now. Why hasn't he called?* she agonized as she reluctantly replaced the phone. *He'll call,* she resolved. *I just know he will.* Tears began to well in her eyes. *I know he cares. Call me, Anton. Please call me.*

VIII

Her nostrils twitched.

Someone, somewhere, was smoking a rotten pipe. The thing was made from a corn cob, and the tobacco was a homegrown herb concoction. What did that remind her of? Her great-aunt Mildred. She must be nearby. No, wait. Something had happened to her. A vision fought its way through the haze. She saw a house, more like a two-room shack. There was a front porch—or was it the back porch? Hard to tell. The place had a door on both sides, but on one side, the porch was gone. It was the original farmhouse on land that had been in the family for several generations. The story went that the land had been promised and awarded following the Great Emancipation War, as some termed the U. S. Civil War. History books generally recorded it as the War between the States, while there were those who were still in denial that a war had taken place at all. The land grant was real, however, and the property had once consisted of several acres but had gradually been depleted over the years as a result of tax auctions and family disputes. Her grandmother, along with her great aunts and uncles, had put forth massive efforts in order to keep the property from disappearing completely, splitting it among themselves and ensuring that everyone worked the land.

When the boys returned home from their various wars, they made good use of home loans and moved trailer homes onto several sectors. Later, as they gradually died, relatives took over the houses and the land. However, without deeds and wills, the right of accession became muddled. As to who held the title to what, all they knew was the taxes had to be paid so that the property would not be lost forever. Even when some of the relatives moved to large cities like Charleston, they maintained an interest in the property. "Don't ever let go of the land," one wise great-aunt admonished. "You're rich as long as you got property. The good Lord made a lot of things, but when he finished making the Earth, he didn't make no more."

The survivors appeared to have taken her advice to heart, although the property remained rather primitive. They grew basic crops, like tomatoes, sweet corn, cucumbers, and potatoes, and the roads leading to the spread remained undeveloped, barely able to sustain passage for a pedestrian, much less an automobile. One good soaking of spring rain and the worn-down ruts reverted to their natural state, overrun with a stinky weed and thick, slimy mud—not the red Georgia clay, but sticky, tar like stuff, which ruined many a good pair of Sunday shoes. Eventually, however, the county made improvements, paving a main road to provide access to the farms, allowing hand-crank outdoor wells to be replaced with running water, and electric lines went up throughout the island.

The mobile homes were gradually upgraded, but the main house remained untouched, teetering on stacks of cinderblocks, which served as the foundation. With no indoor plumbing, it came equipped with an outdoor privy and a water pump. An old wood-burning stove in the middle of an all-purpose room was used for cooking, and an open fireplace provided heat in the winter. These two fixtures ensured that the house was always full of smoke, which permeated everything, including people's skin, and left a sooty residue everywhere, even on the inoperable windows. The only relief was provided by venturing outdoors into the fresh air.

The porch was holding on by a thread, and the five wooden steps leading to it barely supported the weight of a small child, so no one used them anymore. One bright spring day, however, two young cousins who were visiting decided to explore. Boys will be boys, and these two decided to climb up the old banister. The sudden crash that ensued got everyone's attention. Not only had the stairs collapsed, but the entire porch lay in a heap on the dirt. The boys ran and hid in the high corn, as if nobody would ever find them there. As a result, there was only one way in and out of the house with one porch on the front of the house; or was that the back?

The smoke was still burning in her nostrils as yet another vision unfolded. Why did things always happen so early in the morning? Her family's trailer had been just across the road from the old house, and she remembered everyone running barefooted with pails and buckets for water, but the old place was a tinder box and was reduced to ashes before they could even prime the pump. Everyone escaped, except great-aunt Mildred.

"Look, tears!" someone nearby shouted, disrupting her dark memory. "She's still with us!"

IX

Besides inaccurate reporting, some media ignored the story completely. Editors thought they were displaying responsible journalistic ethics by not reporting the deaths of three young black men. They feared they would create martyrs to a cause that alarmed them, one they no longer understood. Many black factions were moving toward a more aggressive form of activism, which was the last thing the American press wished to encourage. Demonstrations spun out of control into riots, and there were even disturbances at sit-ins. The Civil Rights Act had been passed, and thus many editorial gatekeepers saw no further need for what they saw as civil disobedience. Secretly, they agreed that law enforcement had a duty to be as strict as possible and as brutal as necessary to quell these disturbances.

And so it was that Platoon Leader Anton Baylor, stationed at Ft. Hood, Texas, received no news about the events at his alma mater. Even when information was reported, it traveled slowly to Texas, so slowly it eventually spawned an official holiday many black people recognize and even celebrate in modern times as "Juneteenth."

In 1863, the Emancipation Proclamation was announced, freeing slaves in the United States. By tradition, it took effect in most states on the first day of January of that year. It had little immediate effect on most slaves' day-to-day lives in many states that were under Confederate control. However, it could not be ignored. Like it or not, it was the law. Texas, however, appeared to have ignored the

Proclamation entirely until the 19th of June, when Union General Gordon Granger, along with a military enforcement faction, took the order and read it officially in Galveston, Texas, and so two celebrations were born to commemorate the one event. East coast cities like Charleston began an annual tradition of holding an Emancipation Day Parade on the first day of January. The parade, which snaked through uptown King Street and surrounding areas, was largely ignored by the white population. "Juneteenth," short for June 19, became known as Freedom Day or Emancipation Day throughout the West, where many cities with large black populations held annual Juneteenth festivals, which were also largely ignored by the white population.

It was no surprise, therefore, that news from a small Negro college in South Carolina would seem insignificant to the point where the incident was either reported late or not reported at all. There was no Union general to deliver the news this time.

Anton was busy dealing with military life, and with things he hadn't learned in ROTC or in officer basic. State was a lifetime away from the hearing room where this wary lieutenant now sat. The military, particularly the army, is a microcosm of society in general, reflecting the challenges, the changes, and the ideas of a socially conscious America, and at this time, America had problems even the discipline and structure of the army could not subdue. As a platoon leader, Anton was one of four junior officers in a company of about one hundred men. Each leader worked hand-in-hand with an enlisted man or platoon sergeant. Each sergeant, most of whom were black, and officer was directly responsible for the twenty men under his control, twenty strong-headed men who, for the most part, did not want to have anything to do with the military.

The Vietnam conflict, never an officially declared war, subjected thousands upon thousands of young men to the mercy of draft boards. This conflict represented the first time black soldiers played a dominant role in a totally integrated army, where races mixed far more than they ever had in the environment they left behind. Jim Crow segregation may have ruled only in the South, but de facto segregation was still a way of life in many other places. Black soldiers had always played an essential part of the armed forces, even though their numbers were relatively low, reflecting the percentage of black people in the general population. This draft, however, proved to be different. They represented a larger proportion of the military than ever before. One reason for this phenomenon was because most could not afford to attend college and thereby take advantage of a relatively new and immensely popular education deferment option. Other deferments were also available. Those working for the government, especially in critical positions, could be deferred, as could those working in specified law enforcement positions. Practically any means that Congress could think of to defer their white sons became an avenue for exemption. There was also the unofficial exemption of crossing the border into Canada to escape. Most of these options weren't available to black men. They were forced to submit to the draft and hope they would survive. Many people secretly believed that the government was using the draft to remove a lot of the young men from the influence of what they saw as communist infiltration into the black community through influential groups such as the Black Panther Party, the Worker Union, and Students for a Democratic Society. Some of the traditional organizations, such as the NAACP and the Southern Urban League, were coming under the scrutiny of J. Edgar Hoover's FBI and other spy agencies, which saw them as tools for socialist infiltration. The idea was to get black men out of this potentially damaging environment by putting them to work for the United States as agents of war in the military.

Societal influences greatly disrupted army discipline. Black pride, in particular, was evolving rapidly, with outward expressions of that pride being displayed in the troops' manner of dress and hairstyles. The afro that Taletha had been teased about was a manifestation of that pride. Black men, along with some white men under the influence of Beatlemania also rife in that era, began wearing their hair longer and longer, but military tradition dictated otherwise. The buzz cut was still customary for basic trainees as a military, safety, and hygienic standard, and new recruits had no choice but to conform. Once they were out of basic training, however, traditions were frequently challenged. The vast majority of black troops also adopted African-influenced attire for after hours and off-post wear, and gravitated to and became active in local chapters of activist and social organizations, which many of their white officers found threatening. In typical military fashion, orders soon came down through chains of command dictating restrictions on what they could and couldn't do on their own time. The pressure of having to conform clashed constantly with the desire for self-expression, self-esteem, and self-will, all basic tenets of black pride. These new black troops were not going to take what they felt was overt oppression lying down. For them, black pride could not be suppressed, and charges of insubordination meant nothing to them. This was a new problem, one the army didn't know how to handle.

Black officer representation increased, but they were often caught in the middle. Those, like Anton, who were career-minded, had to maintain discipline and order, while trying to understand and relate to their fellow black men's needs and desires. Society had previously robbed them of a sense of pride, and now just when black nationalism was restoring it, the military appeared to be taking it away again. This posed a monumental dilemma. Anton thought he succeeded in achieving that balance until one day there was an ugly incident. During the week when the State students had been trying to desegregate the local bowling alley, Anton was in the field on a training mission, trying to get the men under his command to function as a single unit. Like all black officers, Anton had to prove himself again and again with every training cycle. Many of the "good ole boys" from the South challenged his authority, but soon learned, sometimes the hard way, that his rank was legitimate, and they had to show respect. Just as he managed to achieve a breakthrough with one group, however, their eight-week training cycle would come to an end, and the entire process would begin all over again. It was daunting, never-ending, and tiring. On the positive side, his black troops liked and respected him. They understood the need for black leaders, but as the only black officer in his company, this put him at a disadvantage in many ways, and he was tested many times by his black troops, who wanted to think of him as their "home boy," or another brother. Many of them were his peers or older, which proved challenging as he strove to establish his authority over them without alienating them. A platoon had to function as one body, and so it became incumbent upon him to exercise the right authority in the right manner at the right time. When facing the enemy, their lives would depend on it.

Anton was popular, in a manner of speaking, mainly because of his fairness and impartiality. Many of the black men bypassed their own chain of command, ignoring their white platoon leaders and taking their complaints and concerns directly to Anton, who listened even when matters were out of his hands. He was under great pressure to balance the needs of the men with the dictates of his command, and he proved successful in achieving that goal. Success brings its own rewards, but it also produces strife and envy, especially in a highly competitive environment like the officer corps. Along with coping with the enlisted men, Anton now came face-to-face with additional prejudices spawned by years of military tradition. Graduates from U. S. military colleges and academies received what was known as a permanent rank, which was fitting, since these schools were tasked with training and furnishing officers directly to the military. Those who were commissioned upon graduation considered being an officer a birthright.

Many had the "inside track" for future promotions and were frequently assigned to positions that would eventually propel them to the highest echelons. Alas, fellow officers who were commissioned through reserve training programs such as ROTC, like the preponderance of black officers, held temporary or reserve ranks and were frequently barely tolerated. The general thinking was they would serve on active military duty for a specified number of years before returning to civilian life. Some would join reserve and national guard units and continue training for promotions, while others would never wear the uniform again. These two-tiered rankings produced a caste system with built-in racial biases. Predominantly white academy grads expected to soar to the very top ranks and eventually run the military from places like the Pentagon, while the black officers were expected to eventually receive a letter thanking them for their service and a piece of paper known as a DD214, giving them access to Veterans Administration programs.

The careerists had little or no tolerance for reserve officers, especially if they were doing their jobs successfully, and a biased Officer Rating System, or OER, made black officers feel like second-class citizens. Academy graduates had to walk on water in order to remain afloat in the military system, and thus the reserve officers became their scapegoats, bearing the blame for everything that went wrong in the command. Therefore, the reservists were frequently discharged with less than stellar ratings. Black officers constantly found themselves in positions whereby they had to report to superiors who did not value their efforts and often found themselves at the mercy of superiors with lofty goals of impressing the "old boy" establishment, who failed, many times on purpose, to recognize when they were doing excellent jobs. Whereas white officers managed to obtain mentors to guide them through the system, all too often black officers ended up with the failures who couldn't help themselves, let alone provide valuable guidance for a novice officer. In spite of being set up for failure, however, some managed to survive the harsh system and reach those upper levels, where they paved the way for others who would follow in their wake.

Anton was about to experience careerist intolerance on a personal level. One of his fellow officers had just finished a military school, and whether out of jealousy or a feeling of insecurity, he accused Anton of showing favoritism toward the black troops. He knew such an accusation would get command attention, so he complained loudly to the company commander, threatening to take his complaints higher if the commander did not act. Ironically, because of the South's great military heritage and their respect for military service, a large number of the white officers, particularly the senior officers, were from the South, including the company commander, who was inclined to believe Anton's accuser. The proverbial grapevine now came alive with rumors about the accusation, and company loyalties quickly split along racial lines. Morale plummeted, and the company became a ticking time bomb.

Anton tried to encourage his fellow officers to get to know their men—all of their men—and to heal the schisms, but they took greater solace in complaining about his leadership style and began to distance themselves from him more than they had before. If it came down to a battle between a black Anton and a white academy graduate, the officers knew what the outcome would be. Many privately supported Anton and knew the accusations were false, but self-preservation and job security won out over principles. Anton never felt so alone. Meanwhile, other black junior officers were experiencing similar problems all over the post. The battalion commander, for whatever reason, had spread the black officers out among different companies, a decision that raised a lot of questions. Did he fear a conspiracy among the officer ranks? Would multiple black officers in one company intimidate the commander or undermine his authority? Or did he fear some sort of black uprising? No one really understood his logic, but it was obvious to everyone that fear was the primary motivation behind his decision.

The black officers were discouraged from congregating among themselves, but they managed to meet secretly in the Bachelor Officers Quarters, the residential area reserved primarily for junior officers from lieutenant through captain. They needed answers, for most of them felt as if they were being hung out to dry. They also needed a chance to become real again, even if just for an hour or two, and to relate to one another. To avoid arousing suspicion, they called their gatherings jam sessions, and as more and more black draftees arrived onto the post, these jam sessions became bigger and bigger.

Right from the start, music and wine were integral elements of the sessions. Alcohol could be purchased cheaply at the Class IV Store, and drinking was a way of life, with wine gradually giving way to beer and bourbon and whiskey. The sessions soon increased from twice a month to once a week, then to every day after work with whoever wasn't on an overnight field training exercise. Increasingly, Anton looked forward to the next session, eagerly furnishing his share of Class VI refreshments. It made each day more tolerable. Now all the dynamics were in place, and the pressure cooker was building up steam. When the explosion finally came, it wasn't pretty.

"The jerk had it coming, but man, I wouldn't wish that on anybody," said Anton to his fellow officers. "I just wish it had happened in someone else's company. I still got nightmares. I'm just glad it wasn't my platoon."

"But you know they gonna blame you somehow, my brotha," said a fellow session member as they lounged lazily on the floor of the BOQ.

"I don't see how. I saw it all go down, and now I just want to forget it," said Anton, taking his third, or maybe it was his fourth, drink of the session from a big jug of Thunderbird Wine that someone passed around.

"Man, who brought this cheap stuff in here?" someone teased. They all laughed. The stuff was cheap, but it gave them a big high. Anton refreshed his glass, pouring the wine on top of whatever it was he was already drinking. Taking a big gulp, he leaned back against the wall as the alcohol went to work, numbing his pain, but even though Anton wanted to forget the nightmarish vision that haunted him, he couldn't. He'd been leading a field training exercise on a live fire range, and all the usual safety precautions were in place, when suddenly there was an explosion behind him. He turned just in time to see Mr. Academy Grad, his nemesis and fellow platoon leader, blown apart. The hand grenade detonated right beneath him, leaving little doubt that he'd been murdered.

The fragging incident, as it became known, sent shockwaves through the post. From that point on, white officers and noncommissioned officers in leadership positions were put on notice. They knew order had been breached, and their lives were now on the line due to unknown enemies within the ranks. As fate would have it, Anton's fellow officer proved correct in his assessment. "I told you they'd find some way to get you involved. The dude that did it wasn't even in your platoon, *but* he was a brotha. So, they had to blame another brotha. You are the other brotha, Brotha." Anton was only half-listening as he poured himself another drink, wondering how he would weather this storm.

"They just doin' that so it can go on your record so you won't get promoted. That's all. Practically all of us in this room got low OER scores because we got somethin' on our records. Just wait, come promotion and them little white boys gon' get their captains' bars and go on ahead of us. We gon' get shown the door without so much as a thank you."

The comments did little to improve Anton's mood. The hearing summons stated that he was negligent in not following safety procedures, resulting in serious injury and a fatality. His head was swimming. He couldn't remember emptying his glass, but here he was pouring another drink. He hoped this one would make all of the pain go away.

X

"Y'all thank she kin heah us?"

"The doctor don' know. The hospital folks say to jus' talk to her."

"Hospital folks, wha' dey know."

"Mo' den you, stupid!"

"Ya all stop that!"

"Look, her eyelids move a little. I swear. I bet she kin heah us. Tee, try to let us kno' somethin'."

She felt the warm hand holding hers, but her mind held a different picture. It was another sunny day, and a nine-year-old Taletha was running and running through a field of corn. She kept slipping and getting her dress dirty, because the field was damp. It had rained, and there'd been thunder and lightning all night long. She was running from a man who wanted to tickle her. She didn't want him to catch her, because she didn't want him to tickle her. He hurt her when he tickled her, but she couldn't say anything about it, because he told her not to. Everybody thought of him as kindly, single, lonely Uncle Day. He lived near the marine base in Beaufort, and when he visited, he liked to bring sweet treats for the children and smoked meats for other family members.

"I bet I kin get you to open them eyes. Remember me, Tee?" His voice dropped to a whisper. "Remember how we used to have fun in the corn field when I would visit? Come on, Tee. Yous gotta remember."

"You wastin' yo time, Uncle Day. She can' heah ya."

Good, she thought. *Someone else is in the room,* but then they must have left, because now she could smell him nearby, the stench of stale tobacco and rotting teeth. A vision reappeared. He was almost on top of her, he had her arms pinned to her sides, and he was laughing. For him, it was all a game. He kept tickling her so she couldn't yell as he pushed her down into the mud so he could run his hands up and down her thighs and under her dress, pulling at her underwear. "You my favorite niece," he would say, his mouth covering hers. "You got the loudest laugh and the best body. I likes 'em meaty." He didn't visit them often, but whenever he was around, they always played his game. "I'm gon' tickle you. Better run." She would run, but it always ended the same way, with him on top of her, hurting her. Now, she sensed him very close to her, but this time, she couldn't even run.

XI

Sardis knew her mother's growing mental instability was becoming more and more paralyzing. She was sinking deeper into her depression and was becoming increasingly paranoid, primarily because of her isolation. She trusted very few people now, and the only outside contact she maintained was with her parish priest and the neighbors on either side. Mental health professionals were rare, and those prepared to treat black patients were even rarer.

As for Sardis, she longed to be with J. B. She didn't know where he was and was worried sick that he might have been among those who had been injured. *Oh, will things ever be as they were before?* she lamented as news accounts reached her. Her reaction mirrored everyone else's when she heard the lies.

"Two Negroes die and forty others are hurt in a gunfight at a college. It was the fourth straight night of violence on the campus of the predominantly Negro school," the newsman reported in grave tones.

"You're not going back there," said Eartha, greatly disturbed by the reports. With Sardis home temporarily, Eartha ventured out of her room, and now she was sitting directly across from her dumbfounded daughter in the den as they viewed the first incoming reports.

"That is not what happened!" Sardis protested, as much to the newsman as to her mother. She refrained from revealing details about the reason for her sudden visit, and her mother was so happy to have her back in the household she asked no questions. Sardis knew reports about the incident would eventually emerge, but she thought they would have been accurate.

Dorcus's father dropped her at her house early in the morning the day after he retrieved them from the troubled campus and had graciously offered to take her back to school once things settled down. Dorcus's family felt comfortable with Sardis, who was considered more than a roommate to their daughter, especially after they discovered that she almost single-handedly saved Dorcus's academic career. Dorcus finally confessed to them about all that had transpired during their freshman year, and now they felt they owed Sardis a debt of gratitude. The respect was mutual, for Sardis told them about the love and courage Dorcus displayed when the freshman class shunned her.

"Don't worry, little lady," the reverend assured her. "We'll get to the bottom of this, and when they reopen that school, I'll pick you up again and take you back. I want my daughter to finish, and I know you want to finish too, so the parents will get to the bottom of this nonsense; see why they're shooting up our children. It ain't right." She felt a sense of reassurance from his remarks, but the false reports coming out began to feed her mother's paranoia.

"I have to return. I have to finish. That report is a lie!"

"What?" said Eartha, turning her steely gaze on her daughter. "They don't lie on TV. Do you think you're smarter than they are? I will not lose you to that violence!"

"But the students didn't have guns. I was there," she continued to protest. "They threw rocks and cans and everything they could get their hands on, but no one had a gun. I don't understand how they could be so wrong." Tears began to stream down her face as she continued to watch the flickering screen. Eartha held her hand up to silence her daughter's protest, which meant she had stopped listening. Sardis could not tolerate any more lies, so she rose and walked out of the den, through the kitchen, and into the formal dining room that hadn't been used since her father died. She looked at her brother's picture and helmet sitting on the long cabinet and hankered for the days before that fateful afternoon.

"Why did you bring that person into this house?" she demanded of the face with the vacant half-smile that stared back at her from the dark wooden frame.

That person was Jessie. Sardis eased herself onto one of the dusty, red-striped, satin-covered seats. *I can't even remember his last name,* she thought incredulously to herself. *Did I even know his last name? It doesn't matter. He'll always be remembered as the man who changed our lives.* Her thoughts wandered back to a day she constantly tried to forget, but her subconscious memory kept throwing it up from its gigantic storage wasteland; that receptacle of times, events, and nightmares that everyone wants to purge. Sardis hadn't visited that place in a long time, and her mind could only provide snatches of details about what had happened that day, but her emotions could not purge the pain.

It was warm, bordering on hot, and she had a fairly long walk home from school, but the time passed quickly, because she and two friends made the trek together. Their parents frequently drove them back and forth, but on this day, no one was available to pick them up, so the girls had to walk home. It wasn't so bad on cool or cold days, but summer was approaching faster than usual, and the bags full of books they lugged only added to their discomfort. "I'm sweating," said Sardis to her friends, who were apparently having the same problem. "If I had known my dad was going to get tied up at the hospital and not be able to pick us up, I would have taken some plain clothes with me to change into at school. I don't want my uniform full of sweat stains. Sister Maria won't tolerate sweat stains." Then, giggling, she added, "Remember what she said to Anita when she …"

A screaming siren disrupted her thoughts. A crash wagon raced past them, followed by a police cruiser. The sounds stopped abruptly, and they wondered where the vehicles went. Their collective heartbeats accelerated, and they forgot about the heat when they realized something was happening in their normally sedate neighborhood.

They quickened their pace, and as they reached the end of Cumming Street, they spotted the two vehicles around the corner. "Sard, that looks like your house!" exclaimed one of the girls.

Sardis immediately broke into a run, her book bag flapping behind her as she went. She and two more emergency vehicles arrived at the door simultaneously, and she could see her father's car parked on the street. As she entered the hallway, she heard her mother wailing and her father's soothing tones as he tried to comfort her. This frightened Sardis. The sounds were coming from the kitchen. Strange, uniformed men pushed past her as she made her way through the house. The first thing she saw was her mother's anguished face. Her house dress was covered, as usual, by a bib apron, but both were stained bright red. The men were heading toward the back porch, and Sardis began to follow, but her father caught sight of her before she could reach the doorway. "Come with me," he said, abruptly taking her arm and pulling her along behind him.

Sardis wanted to know what was happening, but before she could ask him anything, she was deposited into the care and protective custody of a neighbor and ordered to remain inside the neighbor's house. "You don't want to see when they bring your brother out, honey," said the neighbor.

"What about my brother? Tell me what's going on?" she cried, fear now gripping her, but no one paid any attention to the weeping girl. She strained to catch snatches of conversations between the neighbors who had now gathered on the street. This was the biggest event their little neighborhood had seen since old man Ned fell down the stairs and broke his neck a few years back. She heard words like "suicide" and "gunshots" and "murder at the hands of a friend."

"They're bringing him out," she heard one neighbor saying.

I've got to see what's going on, she told herself. She remembered the upstairs porch and silently climbed the inside stairs. The door to the porch wasn't used very often, and she had to turn the dusty handle several times before the catch finally worked. She opened it slowly, so the creaky hinges wouldn't give her away. Once she was out on the porch, she crept along on all fours, staying close to the wall and low to the ground lest anyone should spot her and order her back inside the house. Eventually, she eased up directly next to the banisters, from where she had a perfect view of the street and of her own house.

After a few minutes, she saw the police emerging from the house with Jessie who, at the time, was a complete stranger to her. His hands had been placed behind his back and were bound in metal restraints. The police placed him inside their big black vehicle and then left. Next came a stretcher. Sardis leaned closer to the railing to get a better view. It was completely covered, which meant that the person on it was dead. She recognized her brother's uncovered feet. She didn't remember screaming, but the sound must have carried for miles, and within seconds her neighbors raced up the stairs and whisked her off the porch. She didn't recall much after that.

The mind is a wondrous thing. While it can recall insignificant details from birth, it can be hazy in relation to later events, and can shut down all together in order to block out pain. Several days passed before Sardis was allowed to return home, and when she did, everything had changed. Her mother refused to speak at all. "She's under sedation," her father explained. "She'll be better as soon as she's off the medication," he assured her, but her mother didn't get better, and then the arguments began. Sardis never heard her parents fight like that before.

"You let that man into this house!" Sardis heard her mother saying at one point. "I told you he was trouble. We didn't know anything about him; about his people, about his background. You should have found out. Now our son is gone because you weren't man enough to protect your own household!" It went on and on for weeks, and Sardis saw her father grow old right before her eyes. He had to deal with the funeral, and the inquest, and with going to work, and with his wife. He began to medicate himself with an ancient remedy called scotch, until eventually it became brandy with a whiskey chaser. Sardis had to cope with both of them, and with the rumors that were going around at school, rumors of a game.

"You load one bullet into a gun and then spin the chamber," one of her male classmates told her one day. "Then you put the gun to your head and pull the trigger, and hope that the bullet isn't in the firing position."

"What are you talking about?" she yelled.

"Russian roulette," he answered proudly, as if letting her in on a conspiracy. "I knew of some other guys who did it, but they didn't ..." He paused, searching for the right word.

"Die?" she offered.

"Yeah, something like that," he said, turning and skipping away, as if he didn't have a care in the world.

The sound of the television droned on and on in the den as Sardis replaced the photograph in its place of honor on the bureau. "You ... you died playing a stupid game," she whispered, her head dropping to her chest.

Her parents refused to confirm the rumors and soon stopped talking about the incident, just as they stopped talking to each other. At the inquest into Junior's death, it was determined to be an accidental shooting, not at his own hands, which allowed him to die with dignity. The fire department could retire his badge and present the family with his helmet and other honors, like her scholarship.

Jessie was released from jail, whereupon he resigned from the fire department and left Charleston for an unknown destination.

XII

Sardis was so caught up in her story, she did not realize a half an hour passed since they played their last hand. Dorcus and Grace stared at each other and then focused their gaze upon Sardis, making her aware that she had never shared this information before. In all of the dorm games, they shared every secret under the sun except for this one. The comfort and familiar setting of her own home finally allowed her the security she needed to share her most painful memory. Dorcus and Grace were becoming privy to a long-held secret. A part of them, out of compassion, wished she would stop, yet another part of them wanted her to continue, so no one broke the silence, until finally, Grace summed it up in almost reverent tones. "So your brother killed himself playing a game?" She wanted to say "stupid game" but thought better of it. Sardis, with tears streaming down her face, merely nodded. "I still don't understand why your mom blamed your dad."

Sardis took a deep breath. "She hated him. She blamed him for everything. People talk. A long-time family friend told me their marriage was arranged, and Mom, well, she never loved my dad. He was much older than she was, for one thing. Her mother, my grandmother, wanted to get her out of the house. There were even rumors questioning whether my grandmother was even my mom's real mother. My grandfather, I understand, was quite good-looking and had an eye for the ladies. I also have two aunts somewhere up

North who Mom refuses to acknowledge. They married white men and never had anything to do with her."

"This is beginning to sound like a soap opera," said Grace, rising to stretch her legs. "And now, as we look in on the Fontains today," she continued, in an exaggerated voice, "we see murder, mayhem, and intrigue." This coaxed a smile from everyone.

Dorcus wanted to hear the rest of the story. "And your dad?" she said softly. They were still again as Sardis continued her story.

"He just lost his will to live. He went to work one day and never came home. On the way back from the hospital after his shift, he drove off a bridge. There was speculation that he'd been drinking and may have fallen asleep behind the wheel. There were no skid marks where the car went over. They recovered his body from the wreck and buried him alongside my brother. Mom went into seclusion then, and she's been there ever since. She refused to have strangers in the house. Jessie was the last. The back porch was placed off-limits and was never used again. Eventually, a neighbor, our friend, talked Mom into having it torn down and redone into this den."

Grace glanced around the room, as if the shadows might expel a ghost at any minute. As she did so, her eyes fell briefly upon the wall clock, which read 2:00 AM. They hadn't realized two hours had already passed since their marathon session began. She returned to the table and started dealing the cards for another game, one, two, three, four.

XIII

Someone was holding Taletha's hand, stroking it gently.

"Tee, I don' kno' if you kin hear me. I don' kno' why you wanted ta go off ta that school. You kno' I wanted ta marry you. I waited fo' you ta come back. Never thought it would be lak this tho'." Through the haze, a conversation slowly returned. Words, hurtful words. "You fat, you ugly." Her life had been plagued with ridicule until this voice put a stop to it. It was kind and sweet, but the last time she heard it, it hadn't been so good.

Most everyone called him Joe, but just to be different, and to keep their relationship special, she called him Nathan. "Why you gon' leave, Tee? You know I loves you, baby. I got me a good job at the Piggly Wiggly, learnin' how to butcher. Will soon be a manager. I kin take care o' you and a famlee."

Their problems began during senior year in high school. Her grades were good, and one of the school's white counselors made her see for the first time that she should consider going to college. "Nobody in my family ever did that before. We're farmers," she told him, but he'd planted the seed and proceeded to obtain brochures and application forms from State.

"How you gon' pay fo' school anyway? Yo' people ain' got no money," Nathan reminded her over and over. She was not sure if he said this to build up his hopes that she would stay or to discourage her dreams to escape.

Money had always been the problem. Her mama did most of the work on their small farm, which kept the family fed, well fed, in fact, which was no mean feat, because they were all big people, but they never wanted for food. Her daddy did some carpentry. In fact, theirs had been the first trailer to have a real foundation, and they became the envy of their friends and relatives when he built screened-in decks for both the front and the back of the structure. She loved to sit outside during the hot summer days, safe from the bugs. Her daddy loved playing checkers, so he and the local men set up a big board out on the back deck. Her daddy had made all the pieces with his own hands. "Had ta make a big board wid big ole pieces, 'cause when I crowns me a king, I wants everybody ta know it," he boasted, proudly displaying his handiwork. He crowned many kings throughout the summer months, being unable to work full-time due to injuries he sustained in the war—the big war.

He received a small government check each month, which was enough to keep clothes on her back, but it wouldn't put her through four years of college. Her academic scholarship took care of that, however. When word got out that she had won it, she became an instant celebrity, and the reverend even invited her up to the pulpit during the service to shake her hand. Only very special people got a pulpit invitation during a service. At every checker game that summer, her proud daddy called for his college-bound girl to make an appearance. "She da very firs' in our famlee to grace the doo's a higher learnin'," he would boast. Amid all the celebrations and jubilation, however, she failed to notice that Nathan had slipped quietly out of the picture. Later, she wondered if he failed his classes on purpose. Joe-Nathan had a good mind and could have gotten into State or any other black college, but he kept telling himself he could never be successful, a view that was reinforced daily by his lazy friends and especially his relatives, who never tried to improve themselves. Crabs in a barrel, it was called. One would make a determined effort to claw its way to the top, but just as he was about to escape being put into boiling water, the doomed ones at the bottom of the barrel would reach up and pull him back down with them.

I would have remained true to you, even if we had gone to different schools and been separated for four years, she sighed. *Like, what was that skinny gal's name? Grace. My roommate from Charleston.* The recollection of Grace's name suddenly opened the floodgate of information that had been lurking in the farthest recesses of her shrouded mind. *Grace and Willie. They made it work. He was growing and learning and teaching in New York. That's one place I always wanted to go. She sure loved her some Willie. Turned down a lot of guys; good, solid men. Men I would have given my right arm for if they'd even glanced at me just once. Why couldn't you have been my Willie?* she lamented as her memory continued to clear. *We could have built a better life together.*

"The white man don't want us to be successful," he said. The mantra of the lost, which became his response to every challenge until she grew tired of hearing it. He stubbornly refused to assume responsibility for his own successes and failures, and so she moved on without him.

XIV

Sardis sat transfixed staring at her brother's picture, reliving that awful day. Her mother sat in the den absorbing the media lies when the ringing telephone brought her back to 1968. "Jeb," she gasped, when she heard his voice. She was the only person outside his family who called him by his given name. She quickly moved out of earshot of her nosey mother, and soon his familiar, friendly voice replaced her gloom. She breathed a major sigh of relief, knowing he was safe. He told her how Cyrus Bloom helped him to escape from campus, offered him temporary shelter, and then helped him to locate her.

This marked the first of what became daily conversations. She was glad the house had no telephone extensions; otherwise their confidential interludes would not have been possible. To keep her mother at bay, they used secret codes whenever she came within earshot and they varied the time of their calls, sometimes talking late into the night after Mother went to bed. She longed to see him, and he her, but knew that was neither wise nor possible, so they made do with their long, daily chats.

Meanwhile, Sardis's neighbor and friend, Dorcus, was having a similar experience. Charlie called her every day to check on her welfare, and she found herself beginning to look forward to his calls. She needed to rid herself of her growing anxiety and welcomed his care, concern, and attention. She yearned to hear from Anton, but there was nothing, and even though she grew increasingly angry with him, she never expressed her irritation or disappointment to Charlie. "Why should I continue to have feelings for a man who doesn't care?" she agonized as each additional day passed without any communication from him.

I could be lying in a hospital somewhere, near death, or I could have been among those who died, and he's shown no concern. I know Charlie must have contacted him. Perhaps that's why I haven't heard anything; he already knows I'm okay. But then, why won't he call me? Charlie is there for me. Charlie cares. Maybe I should say something to Charlie. Then again, maybe not. Like Hamlet, the mad Dane, Dorcus practically drove herself insane with these daily musings. During the day, in the presence of her family and during her conversations with Charlie, she appeared to be the epitome of calm, but the secret nighttime tears betrayed her agony.

Several more days passed, but still, nothing had been resolved. Newspaper accounts dwindled but continued to carry bureaucratic lies. Irate parents and students called it a bloody massacre and marched on the state capitol in Columbia, while the federal government filed a civil rights suit against the owners of the bowling alley, thereby proving they had taken decisive action. Eventually, it would amount to little more than a token gesture as the entire affair slipped quietly into the obscure annals of history. In the meantime, South Carolina state and law enforcement officials were sticking to their guns, and to their stories, about what transpired at the school. The state insisted it had been a riot, a lawless brawl. History books tended to ignore riotous acts. Mankind, as a rule, did not honor them, and martyrs were not created through riots. Heroic feats were not borne out of riots, and freedom had never been won as a result of riots. They knew what they were doing when they labeled this fight for equality a riot.

Law enforcement agencies justified their role in the affair by insisting they'd been "heroically, protectively, and loyally" safeguarding the fair citizens against the influx of militancy from socialistic factions hell-bent on overthrowing the American way of life.

They continued their heroic, protective and loyal stance by maintaining a heavy-handed approach, with a curfew remaining in effect throughout the city of Orangeburg while the guard continued its nightly patrols. No one knew when, or even if, State's campus would reopen.

XV

After two days in the regional hospital, Grace arrived back in Charleston. She was happy to return, even if it was to her cold, ramshackle abode in the Alley. Her room had been deeded to her sister's children, but now they were displaced and told to find whatever sleeping space they could. She was still in pain, and all she wanted to do was sleep, to block out the world and those hateful eyes that continued to haunt, just sleep.

At the same time, a worried Willie placed a brief telephone call to his aunt, which caused him to spring into action. She filled him in about the Judge's successful trip to Orangeburg with Grace's mother, and the day after he discovered Grace was back home, Willie was on a bus headed to Charleston. Willie was no longer the insecure person who had left town four years earlier with his tail between his legs. He was continuing to evolve. From his first, fateful encounter with the stranger he later came to know as Brother Smart, Willie had reinvented himself. Brother Smart was a true personification of his name, for he was indeed smart. Willie thought it was a chance meeting, but he soon discovered that Brother Smart was actually a recruiter, an unofficial representative of the splinter social revolutionary group the Liberation Front. According to their charismatic leader, their goal was to empower lost, hopeless young black men to become the foundation and leaders in their community. Willie's class, which consisted of six other young brothers in addition to himself, was submitted to intense indoctrination from the moment they set foot on the premises.

"Brothers, we are at war right at home in our own neighborhoods," a speaker told the new recruits at their first meeting. Willie studied the faces around him and noticed that all the young men were cookie-cutter replicas of himself, ranging in age from late teens to late twenties, he guessed. The bespectacled man who was delivering the message, however, appeared to be much older. His close-cropped afro was sprinkled with gray, his face was streaked with laugh lines, and he was neatly attired in a dark suit, white shirt, and dark tie. Later, Willie discovered that the Dashiki-clad Brother Smart used his attire to blend in with the crowds around the military recruiting stations, where he found most of his new charges. The rest of the group wore dark, preferably black, suits, white shirts, and dark ties, like their leader.

"Instead of going off to fight the yellow man, each black man needs to stay right here and join the revolution at home," railed the speaker. These ideas intrigued Willie, and apparently also captured the imagination of the others, because everyone listened with rapt attention, and not one of them made any move to leave during the hour and a half long indoctrination speech. "We revel in our blackness, brothers, and plan to build a great society without the interference of the white master." Upon hearing the word brothers, Willie's mind wandered to Grace, which made him wonder; where were the women? Now his mind generated a whole jumble of questions. What was this group really about? What where their motives? Were they legitimate, and what would joining them cost him?

Willie's queries were eventually answered over time. He discovered the organization's female cadre at the evening meal. They were impossible to miss in their flowing white garments, which were soft and feminine, covering them from head to toe. The attire was modeled on Middle Eastern culture, in the belief that a woman should be modest in dress, only allowing her husband to ever see her body, but appearances were deceiving.

One of the brothers promised them that the group would enable them to avoid military service, mentioning something about its being a priesthood. According to their interpretation of the Bible, the group considered every man to be a priest. Religion was something Willie avoided, but if it would get him out of going to war, he might be persuaded to give it a shot, he thought. He listened intently for buzzwords such as Bible, Torah, and Testaments, but the only words he heard were those affirming both his blackness and his masculinity. He liked this new religion. He wanted in.

Armed with this new-found faith, Willie entered the world of black resurgence. The members planned to create a separate society. Their utopian dream was to eventually obtain land deeded by the government to build a separate empire, but for the time being, they had to settle for a city within a city where entrance was controlled by buzzers, locks, and keys. Their model government was based upon ancient philosophy and African tribal customs, not city hall and state constitutions, and they shared a belief in male dominance, thus their women looked after all child-rearing and housekeeping duties. The men's council made the laws, and men were the undisputed leaders in each household, responsible for producing the group's shared income.

"Ever since slavery, our society has been turned inside out. The women have been taking care of us and also running the house. Brothers, we will assume our rightful place as the hunters. We will not let our women rule us." The more lectures Willie heard, the more he convinced himself that he found his calling. If only he could start his own household and share all of this with the woman he still loved.

The Liberation Front was a fairly well organized, highly motivated, and highly disciplined group that provided economic stability through self-sustaining enterprises. Everyone was assigned to a job, and they had to work hard in order to maintain their status as a member. There was no such thing as idle hands. This philosophy was the cause of frequent clashes with the outside community, for not everyone held such noble ideas or possessed such a healthy work ethic. Some were satisfied with a comfortable existence within their new-found welfare state. The Liberation Front, however, made it clear that such entitlement was not a goal but a crutch, and these were ostracized for being "uppity Negroes." The Liberation Front was eyed with suspicion by established, traditional religious groups who considered them adversaries, so they had to be self-sustaining to survive. Even the best intentions are wasted on those who refuse to hope and dream; closed minds never fertilize trees. Instead they produce dead roots. Resistance to change is something many manage to practice with ease, expertise, and aplomb.

Members occupied a multi-story residential hall that was located next door to a former church they purchased from a mainstream denomination and converted to meet the group's needs. They established a private school where children as young as three years of age were taught by the women. Men with a trade were allowed to hold jobs in the "outside" world but were forbidden to share any information about the group. All paychecks were pooled, and the funds were used to purchase food and other requirements for their survival. The former church's fellowship hall now served as the main dining room, and lectures, rather than sermons, were conducted in the former sanctuary.

The group offered refuge to many draft resisters by offering them priesthoods, thereby winning deferments based on religious grounds. Others who disappeared inside the stone walls claimed they never received their draft letters, and they conveniently forgot to submit details of their new address in the hope that Uncle Sam would never be able to find them. As in the Foreign Legion, no one asked questions. The organization had many of these shadow members. The problem with shadows, however, is that their secrets tend to compound other secrets, producing fertile ground for unwanted infiltrators, such as police informants and government agents. Traitors came in all colors and forms.

As the Vietnam skirmish escalated, so grew the group. They acquired additional real estate on the block, where they set up residential units for families, couples, and singles of each gender. They were advocates of the old adage that a disciplined mind produced a disciplined person, and so education was a mainstay. An appointed librarian scoured book stores for scarce black literature, which in turn found its way into a flourishing library, and the European history that was taught in the public schools was replaced with black literature and history. Having devoured Richard Wright's 1940 publication *Native Son*, next Willie read *Black Boy*, a 1945 work by the same author. He consumed these books, never having previously realized that black-oriented literature such as this existed. Wright was one of the first black authors to explore white treatment of black Americans.

At this time period, James Baldwin was just bursting onto the scene as the writer of choice for this new generation. Baldwin had been living in France but had now returned to the United States and was traveling around the country taking part in the civil rights struggle. He began to write about how the struggle affected those living in the South, and about black identity or lack thereof, and in 1963 he produced an explosive tome titled *The Fire Next Time*. This book also fell into Willie's eager grasp. Recalling his brief stay in the South, Willie could relate to the struggles, but at the same time, he came to recognize and appreciate subtle differences between the northern and the southern struggles. His emerging ideas fueled a major argument with Grace, who took the stance that the civil rights struggle was a Southern thing only, something to which the people "up North" could not relate. Letters flew back and forth about as fast as they could get their thoughts down on paper. "The plight of southern colored people and that of other colored people across the nation is not the same," she fired off. "Here in the South, we're fighting for such basics as getting the colored and white signs removed from buildings, restrooms, drinking fountains, theaters, and every other place. The colored side is usually broken, dirty, and just plain unusable. Why can't we have nice things, like they have on the white side? We're fighting to ride in the front of the bus, and to sit at lunch counters and be treated like human beings. We're fighting for the right to make a decent living for ourselves and our children, and for respect as human beings. Ya'll already have most of that stuff in the North. So what you got to fight for?"

Her arguments set Willie back on his heels momentarily, but after gathering his wits about him, he responded. "We're all fighting for our dignity, for the right to reverse the effects of over a hundred years of indoctrination into a foreign society that formed us into an image that did not fit us as a people. And my dear Grace, we are a proud *black* people. Those colored signs have to come off all of us."

Now, as the bus roared down the highway, he smiled silently to himself. Grace never delivered a rebuttal to that letter. He went on to explain how this indoctrination had manifested itself in such subtleties as her hairstyle and her slave name. He convinced her to free herself from the ravages of the straightening comb, and to let her natural inner beauty shine through. He shared what he was learning and encouraged her to read his books. He was on the way to share with her how proud he was of her for taking a harsh blow for the cause of liberation, but most of all, he hoped to convince her to walk beside him as his queen.

XVI

While Willie was daydreaming on his way to Charleston, Charlie arrived home to find the dreaded letter. Being the investment minded money manager that he was, he had purchased a home just outside Columbia city limits in a growing area near a number of other professional black families who were putting down roots. Four years of college managed to get him deferred from the draft, but here it was like a migraine headache. When he was in ROTC, he considered following the route that Anton took by staying in the program until graduation, but he held such a disdain for military life, with its regimentation and field exercises and weaponry, that the thought of making a career of it sickened him. "I work for the state. Wonder if I can get deferred for that," he pondered out loud. He knew that some of his colleagues had been successful, especially if they were home owners. The answer arrived quickly, and without fanfare. "Accountants can be replaced, so your position is not considered critical to the needs of the state," said the personnel director, dismissing him. "We wish you all the best as you serve our country."

"And don't let the door hit you on the way out," Charlie added sarcastically.

After submitting his resignation, Charlie left the building without speaking to anyone. Now that he no longer worked for the State, he thought briefly about joining the group of noisy demonstrators on the capitol steps. Some carried signs protesting the war, others carried signs protesting police brutality, and there were those from the college demanding justice for State students. The latter would have been his preference, but right now, his heart was too heavy. He drove blindly through the streets of Columbia, not wanting to go home just yet, but not wanting to do much of anything else, either. He had a whole forty-eight hours left as a civilian and wanted to experience freedom while it was still his to enjoy. Then an idea struck him like a rifle butt to the head. *It's a three-hour drive to Charleston. Wonder if Dorcus will marry me?* He had to pull off the road and catch his breath for even thinking such a thought. His head was swimming, and his body was emanating so much heat the car windows began to fog up. After regaining his composure, he quickly drove to his house and changed into his best suit.

XVII

Every day, Sardis waited for the telephone to ring, and every single day it did. Her mother said nothing about the calls, but Sardis could tell she was curious. Eartha wanted no strangers anywhere near the house, because strangers meant danger, but calls provoked only mild curiosity. To Sardis, however, this man was more than a mild curiosity. He was her world, and eventually, her mother would have to meet him. J. B. begged her to let him come to see her, but she didn't know how to handle a visit from him. She considered taking the bus to Georgetown and meeting him there, but Mother still controlled the purse strings, and she couldn't think of a good explanation, or even a good lie, to present in order to get the necessary funds. She considered going back to work again and knew she could get her old job back at the Dock Street Theater if she tried. Since the passage of the Civil Rights Act, the theater had opened its doors to black patronage, and she no longer had to fear being discovered. Better yet, retail stores were now hiring black staff. She knew she could walk into any of them and find work.

Downtown stores now welcomed black patrons, and rather than become targets for demonstrations and sit-ins, many of them had either shut down their lunch counters or converted them to take-out fare. What a difference a stroke of a presidential pen had made.

As always, a few die-hards remained. These were the ones who insisted the South never lost the Civil War, or that the South would rise

215

again, and found legislative loopholes that allowed them to continue their segregation practices, such as converting their establishments into private, members-only enterprises, the only qualification for membership being white skin. They had very little impact, however, and eventually the marketplace forced them either into compliance or into bankruptcy. The law's biggest impact, though, was assigning those accursed colored and white signs to the trash heap of history. Green was now the only color merchants and business owners recognized.

Sardis was a college student with a good grade point average, and she felt confident she could earn enough money for a round-trip ticket. She was wrestling with this idea, and of how she could keep her earnings out of her mother's hands, when J. B. delivered some welcome news. "School's reopening on Monday," he told her, trying to control his excitement.

"It's not official yet, but the teachers have been notified." He paused. They could almost hear each other's heartbeat. "I can't wait to see you again." A smile spread across Sardis's face that lasted for hours after their conversation ended.

"You really like that boy, I'm guessing." Her mother's voice came from behind her disrupting her euphoria. She had been so engrossed in her conversation with J. B., and giddy with the wonderful news, she hadn't heard her mother enter the kitchen. There was nothing she could do to disguise her feelings. "Remember, he must be able to fit into our community," she said, her voice trailing off as she ambled through into the den for her afternoon television session. This had become part of her daily ritual since Sardis first left for college. She would wake, rise at seven, prepare breakfast, and then eat at around eight before retreating to her room again, where she slept until noon. Then she would eat lunch, catch her favorite soap operas all afternoon, eat dinner, and then retreat to her room again. The parish priest and a next-door neighbor checked in on her once or twice a month and helped her to shop for groceries, but she refused all invitations to socialize, so people left her to herself.

Sardis immediately contacted Dorcus to relay the good news, and to make sure her dad would make good on his promise to take both of them back to the campus. Dorcus had her own great news to share with Sardis. "Charlie was here!" she uttered breathlessly, happy to be talking with her dear roommate. "He asked me to marry him! Out of the blue!" Now she was quiet. Sardis knew what was coming. Whenever Dorcus was faced with a dilemma, she went very quiet. Sardis with her intimate knowledge of her friend's history, knew that Anton was still in her heart. "What am I to do?" she said, her voice cracking as she pleaded with her friend. "You're the only person I can ask for advice. Puh-lease, tell me. My folks and my brothers all fell in love with Charlie. He's as good as in as far as they're concerned ... but ... then there's Anton ..."

Sardis was happy that Dorcus couldn't see her reaction. As soon as Dorcus mentioned Anton, Sardis's eyes rolled upward in disgust. Sardis liked Charlie and felt that Anton wasn't the right person for Dorcus, but she couldn't make her decisions for her. Back at college, she had dropped hints, and Grace, in her boldness, told her outright, but Dorcus had made her mind up. She just wanted confirmation. "I can't tell you what to do, Dork," she said, in an even tone, but her use of the nickname that her friend detested tipped Dorcus off.

"Let's talk when we get back," she said. She hadn't given Charlie an answer yet, and still hoped beyond hope that Anton would call. All he had to do was call, but ...

XVIII

Bid whist. That's the name of the game we played.

The haze lifted again, letting more sunlight into Taletha's darkened mind. She recalled more about Grace, having been her roommate, but she struggled to remember the others. *Grace was always so sure of herself. I used to ask her a lot of questions, and she always had good answers. Wish I could have been more like her. Especially as small as she was. She could eat anything and not gain a pound. Me, I'd just have to look at food and my body would blow up.* Faces came and went. A name; she wanted a name, any name, even the guy she had a crush on in her freshman year. Finally, it came to her. Robert something. *I really liked him. Grace told me to flirt. "Sit by him in class. Get in his face at the gym dance. It works," she said. He finally noticed me. Asked me to dance. We had a great time. At least, I thought so. He didn't think I knew how to dance or being a big girl, that I could move. All the girls were congratulating me in the dorm the next day; but for what?*

"I heard you really showed that jerk, Robert, up on the dance floor, girl," someone said. "He didn't think you could move like that."

"He thinks he is so hot. Likes to show off his moves to impress his friends," chimed another. "Guess you showed him. Wish I coulda seen that." *They all laughed and gave me thumbs up and high fives.*

218

He tried to use me, she remembered. *After six weeks of taking Grace's advice, I thought I was finally winning him over, but Monday's English class rolled around and he didn't say a word to me. Never spoke to me again. Went out of his way to avoid me. I shoulda seen it comin'. Getting a man to like me was going to be harder than winning a million-dollar sweepstakes. So many women wanting the same thing, and I was at the bottom of the food chain. I wasn't going to be like, oh, what is that girl's name, chasing that guy all over campus.* **But** *they did get together. Hmmm, she even managed to get another guy interested in her. Should I have tried harder? Maybe Nathan was my guy after all, but he has no ambition. He's dull, he's slow, and he accepts whatever the world hands him. He'll never be successful. I want a man who can conquer his world and fit into mine.*

XIX

Willie caught a very late bus from New York, and all the way to Charleston, two concerns nagged him. The first was Grace's well-being, and the second was Hatta Mae. Her scheme to get rid of him and turn Grace's affections against him still haunted him.

He never told Grace outright about her mama's mind games, because he didn't want to alienate himself from Grace, and he definitely didn't want to come between mother and daughter, but her mama hadn't won, as far as Willie was concerned. He determined he would never concede defeat. His letters to Grace contained lots of hints, and from the tone of her replies, he suspected she knew more about her mother's conniving than she was letting on. He remembered that, after arriving at State, she regretted the way they'd parted. Her mother had made it clear to Grace that she should find herself a college man, but Willie was far more educated in life, and in the ways of a woman's heart. The freshman boys she dated never came close to having his smarts, and her heart leapt when his first letter arrived. His thoughts rambled, and his attempts to apologize for their disagreement were spastic, but the growing stack of subsequent letters reflected a person who was growing in wisdom, knowledge, sophistication, and intelligence. As they both matured, Grace began to trust that wisdom. Willie's growing self-awareness gave her the strength and confidence to decide she wanted to be a part of his life, but for her mother's sake, she had to complete college and feign interest in someone new every year. She was the one who would have the degree, not her future husband, but they could make it work; others had.

As the bus reached the outskirts of Columbia, they made a routine stop, but not a soul got off or on. As they started up again, Willie gazed out the window, which was covered in a fine mist that gradually grew into harder rain as they neared Orangeburg. He caught sight of the troops enforcing the curfew and wished them a miserable and soggy night, before his mind returned to the problem at hand; how to placate a determined, disapproving mother.

Grace's physical wounds weren't extensive, but she was unable to shake the nightmares from her mind. Every time she closed her eyes, Taletha's face appeared, asking her over and over, "Why did you leave me here to die?" Grace knew Taletha hadn't perished, for her name wasn't among those who had been reported as dead, but she needed to find out what had become of her friend. She agonized about having left Tee alone at the infirmary, refused to forgive herself, and believed her subsequent wounds were some form of divine or cosmic punishment for running away. The guilt gnawed at her daily, but in those unenlightened days, where no grief counseling was forthcoming, her paranoia and stress had nowhere to go but back into her agonized mind.

Willie arrived late at night and attempted to see Grace immediately but ran into a disgruntled Hatta Mae. He left reluctantly and managed to control his anxieties and temper until the following morning, but his second encounter with Hatta Mae yielded the same result. "Grace is still real sick," she said, as she stood straddling the doorway, arms folded across her chest, daring him to try to get past her. "Can't see ya, and don' wanna see nobody. I'll tell hur ya aks."

Willie prided himself on being a peace-loving man, but now every muscle in his body tensed. His fingers curled, his vision clouded over, his sense of reasoning abated, and his flaming eyes locked on Hatta Mae's. He was feeling rage he never knew he possessed, an unthinking form of rage that could only lead to disaster and perhaps a long jail sentence. An image of a grieving Grace appeared in his mind, and he slowly backed away. He had to find a way to get past

Hatta Mae, and soon an opening appeared. As he sat brooding on the Judge's porch swing, he caught a glimpse of Grace's dad walking down Duncan, toward the alley. At first glance he looked sober, but as he got closer, Willie observed his glassy-eyed stare and realized he wasn't as steady on his feet as he appeared to be at first. Glancing at his watch, Willie saw it was just after noon, so he may have just been getting home from an all-night binge.

The Judge had lost Grace's father, along with a lot of his other regulars, as customers. He was still getting high, but not from the white lightning any more. "Gettin' some new stuff," the Judge warned. "I don' mess wit dat." As Grace's father got closer, Willie detected what the new stuff was; it was the same new stuff that was being dumped onto the streets of Harlem, turning productive men into nonproductive predators, from husbands and fathers into street rats who slept in doorways and on sidewalks.

It took a while for Willie to punch through the old man's foggy mind and reach his hazy memory, but eventually his eyes revealed a hint of recognition. Willie thrust a note into his hand and gave him explicit instructions. He dreaded the thought of having to depend on someone whose sole purpose in life was how to score the next high, but he was a desperate man. Anxiety overwhelmed him. He was a patient man, but patience is only a virtue if life doesn't intervene. He lowered himself gingerly on the stoop, from where he had an unobstructed view of her house.

Even though the wait seemed like a lifetime, it was not more than ten minutes when Grace came bursting through the front door, stopping dead in her tracks on the porch when she saw the stranger she hadn't seen in four years. Willie rose, and they walked slowly toward each other, measuring each step as if they were on ground so fragile it might crack under the weight of love they carried. Grace looked up into the clear, bright eyes that mirrored her image. She couldn't remember him being so tall. He folded her in his arms, and she wrapped her arms around his waist. Time stood still as they embraced. Resting her head against his chest, she felt muscles that hadn't been there the last time. His hands caressed hips that were broader than before, even though her body was still as slender as he remembered. She was greatly impressed with his physical maturity. His mental growth was evident through the many letters they exchanged, and now the entire package was that of an intelligent, well-dressed, self-assured young man.

"I see you threw away that straightening comb," he said and smiled, holding her at arm's length. She couldn't believe that he was here, standing with her in the middle of the still-unpaved alley. As they hugged again and again, he caught a glimpse of a shadowy figure watching intently from just inside the doorway of Grace's house. He didn't have to guess twice as to who it was. He couldn't see her face, but he sensed her scowl.

With Willie back in Charleston, Grace healed quickly, and they soon picked up their relationship as if time had never intervened. They spent hours in the porch swing, laughing and talking and hugging and sneaking a kiss when they were sure Hatta Mae wasn't watching. Then came the news that State was going to reopen. It was a mixed blessing, received with mixed emotions. Willie dreaded having to part with Grace again, just when they began to recapture the magic in their relationship. For her part, Grace's demons were circling. Graduation was too close now to let anything get in the way, so she told herself she would plow through. All she had to do was hit the books and envision the life that lay ahead of her with Willie in New York. "Doesn't his life with the Liberation Front sound exciting? You can't say he doesn't have a future now, Mom," she said to Hatta Mae as she packed in preparation for returning to State. Hatta Mae's silence said it all. Picking up on it, Grace moved to reassure her. "Don't worry. I'll finish my education before I join him. That way, I can get a good-paying job, and we can save and eventually buy a house and live like a king and queen in our own palace."

Willie never revealed the nature of his communal life within the Liberation Front, being sworn to abide by their code of nondisclosure. Instead, he merely painted a rosy picture of an independent life loosely connected by their shared beliefs, one he knew Grace would accept. He gambled on the fact that, in time, she would grow to love and commit to the life within the confines of their compound. Hatta Mae listened mindlessly to her daughter as she placed sandwiches into a basket. Grace's clothing, valuables, and books, like those of her schoolmates, were still in her dorm room. The irony of the situation was not lost. With the campus ringed by national guard troops, security was not a problem. When she finished her packing, Grace turned to her mother, almost as an afterthought, took her cold, skeletal hands in hers and asked, "Why don't you and everybody else join Willie and me once we settle down?"

Grace's unrestrained excitement failed to transfer to her despondent mother, however. She squeezed her daughter's hands, wishing she would never have to release them, or her, and sighed deeply at the suggestion, knowing she could never leave Charleston. Moving up North sounded exciting when she first considered it as a carefree, teenage girl with no responsibilities, but now, the idea was frightening.

From her other daughter's room came the high-pitched voices of children fighting, followed by a harsh male voice trying to tame a situation that had escalated out of control. This happened every morning for at least an hour after her wayward daughter fled to one of the few houses in the alley with a television to escape to the artificial soap opera universe called *Another World.* Hatta Mae also longed for another world, but New York wasn't it. She surmised that the whole scheme was Willie's idea and didn't want anything to do with something he suggested. Her reasoning was on the mark. Willie extended the invitation through Grace, hoping to lift the family out of poverty by instilling a sense of self-pride. He also hoped to endear himself to Hatta Mae by assuring her he had no intention of stealing Grace away from her without any consideration for her feelings, in spite of her belief to the contrary. He was concerned about what he saw as the family's deterioration and believed a different lifestyle and environment would provide stability. His group was one of many black nationalist movements springing up in inner city neighborhoods across the United States. Their goal, achievable or not, was to work toward improving poor neighborhoods by encouraging self-reliance and self-sufficiency.

Black male empowerment served as the cornerstone. Grace's father would be given a job. He would be elevated to the governing council, with direct input and decision-making authority to determine the direction his and his family's life would take. He would gain respect, something every man wants and needs, along with the ability to take care of his family. Considering his current circumstances, he needed a gigantic boost of self-worth and dignity, for he was sinking lower and lower into the quagmire of self-pity and hopelessness. His sunken eyes and incoherent speech had frightened Grace when she first saw him after an almost four-year absence, and she didn't liked the answers she got when she inquired about her father's failing health and frail appearance. At least Grace's questioning drew Hatta Mae out of her denial. "The devil weed got 'em now," she said. Hatta Mae could tolerate the drinking, but this new stuff was bad news. "It's killing him."

Willie knew what it was right away. "It's called weed, MJ, crank, hemp, and a lot of other things. It's marijuana. Lot of it's coming from Vietnam." Grace wondered if the Judge had begun a new franchise. From the time she had been a little girl, she and her friends heard the stories about his party supplies and early morning runs. "That's not his style," Willie assured her. "This new import is being dumped into our communities by a new breed. Outsiders. We're fighting it in New York, and now I see it's made its way South. My uncle doesn't even know where the stuff is coming from." With a hint of regret in his voice, Willie added, "He's losing his influence on many fronts, and it's scaring him. Despite all his faults, believe it or not, he did maintain some order and discipline around here, but times are changing. It used to be a balanced, but not perfect, society, but now it's breaking down. All the more reason for your family to get out of this place."

Hatta Mae knew how to pick her battles, and she also knew when retreat was in order. For the time being, she was forced to concede. Her daughter was old enough and educated enough now to manage her own life. If she loved this man, and wanted to be with him, she knew she'd have to let her go. She always wanted a college-educated son-in-law, but she couldn't ignore the light that shone from her daughter's eyes whenever she looked at Willie. A long time ago, that same light had shone from her own eyes. Her daughter was just like her in so many ways, but Hatta Mae knew that Grace had great prospects for a brighter future. *Maybe he'll do right by hur. Maybe he kin support hur,* she thought, before her stubborn determination ignited her musings. *No, he better do right by hur, and he better support hur!*

She hugged her daughter and her eyes grew moist, but she refused to yield to her emotions as she released her. As the Judge's borrowed car left to take Hatta Mae's precious cargo and her main nemesis to the bus station to board transports ready to whisk them to their respective destinations, a hand rose limply from the back seat in a half wave, providing some consolation for Hatta Mae. "She kin always support hurself if she gotta. I always did, but ma baby gonna hav' a degree. She be all right."

XX

"Students Not Armed," screamed several major newspaper headlines. Vindication at last! Alas, it offered little relief to the returning students, still demoralized and embittered by the episode. The mood was somber as anxious students were dropped off by equally anxious parents. As they greeted each other, there was none of the light-hearted friendliness that characterized previous returns from summer and winter breaks. Everyone was quiet and subdued. There was a science-fiction quality, as if returning from a space mission

The first order of business was a memorial service for the three slain students. Three wreaths were placed on the field where many believed they were shot. Some in the crowd provided visible reminders of what had taken place, hampered by still healing injuries. People observed a noticeable limp from tender, buckshot-riddled feet; a crutch supporting fractured limbs and joints; arms in slings. Many were missing, still mending elsewhere, while others were missing permanently, too traumatized to come back.

Residual anger lingered in the air over the manner in which students had been treated by the state government, who protected the rights of troops over the welfare of students, and over slow reaction or inaction of college administrators. Both students and parents accused them of sitting on their hands and of doing little or nothing in the midst of the drama. Some students still called for increased activism and for class boycotts in protest. Others called for an apology and for monetary compensation for the families of the dead and wounded. They were demanding recognition for their sacrifices to the civil rights cause. Still others wanted to sweep it under the rug and didn't want to hear the word protest ever again. They yearned for a return to some semblance of normalcy, but the days of innocence were gone. They couldn't return to the fun days of the past, and so almost all extracurricular activities, from fraternal initiations to weekend dances, were cancelled for the rest of the semester. The campus mood said, simply, let's finish this year, put it behind us, and get on with our lives.

Dorcus and Sardis returned to campus together, chattering all the way. The reverend, escorting them as promised, was accustomed to women shouting and singing and raising their voices in heavenly praise every Sunday morning, but their incessant prattle wore his patience thin. On his trip home, he immersed himself in the peaceful, soothing joys of gospel music from the radio. The experience inspired his next two sermons, which he titled "Taming the Tongue" and "The Silent Ride to Glory."

Charleston's continuing polarization still kept the friends in their separate worlds at home, but the campus bound their spirits as one. In their conversations during the trip back, they talked about how slavery had impacted this practice. While the colored and white signs were visible for all to see, the "house Negro" and "field Negro" signs, although invisible, remained as intact during the 1960s as they had during the 1860s.

They cursed traditions that kept them apart over the hiatus and vowed that when they next returned home, they would do something to change it. Unbeknown to them, however, it would be the last time they could call themselves neighbors, because Dorcus's family, like many other educated, upwardly mobile black families, would soon be moving into a once-segregated suburban area across the Ashley River.

Parts of Charleston were undergoing urban renewal, meaning that black families living on the fringes of downtown were being displaced to other locations. The motel concept had been conceived to accommodate the increasingly motorized public, and once the first structure, the Heart of Charleston Motel, was built, a large percentage of Duncan Street suddenly disappeared. This worked out well for the home owners, who jumped at the chance to sell their property, but for those in the Alley and the Court, it imposed a great hardship. They knew it was only a matter of time before their housing, substandard though it might be, would vanish, but none of them had the means to find adequate lodgings, and they simply could not afford to move. They were destitute and often full of despair but, like Hatta Mae, they were often too proud or too fearful to seek public assistance.

Grace's sister, now pregnant with her third child, was the first to find out about help that was available for women like her. The U. S. government provided aid to needy families since the mid-1930s, when the Social Security Act was adopted, but as with everything else under a system that was unequal, the state government made it very difficult for these funds to trickle down to black families. Stubborn pride was also a factor. Contrary to commonly held beliefs, black people attached a great stigma to accepting money or relief from the government, or the county, as it was called. The state government granted the counties the right to control funds locally, so it was assumed that the money originated with the county. To be on the county meant you had little or no self-respect, no pride. "Nobody in dis famlee ever been on de county. We always work fo' what we need. My feets may not be what dey used ta be, but I kin still git a job if I needs ta. We don' need no county help," Hatta Mae admonished her daughter when she suggested getting assistance.

Hatta Mae might have had her pride, but with another baby on the way, worry consumed her realistic daughter. The little income into the household barely covered rent and food now, and having another mouth to feed wasn't going to make things any easier. Her live-in husband had recently gotten a job doing sanitation work, but they all knew it wouldn't last much longer. The county had begun to purchase newer, more automated trucks, which eliminated the need for at least one man per truck. As a new hire, his days were clearly numbered.

Pride couldn't deny the reality of Hatta Mae's deteriorating physical health, either, especially her feet. Housekeeping was all she'd ever done, all she knew, but a housekeeper with warped feet couldn't work. She could still do light cooking, but the doctor needed her to clean. He continued to hire her out of loyalty, but the number of hours she worked amounted to little more than small change, and that went to sustain her husband's worsening drug habit. Not wanting to make an impossible situation worse by revealing her own anxiety, Hatta Mae had to privately concede that her daughter was right. She was smart enough to know it was only a matter of time before she'd have to get help from somewhere.

Now that Grace was back in school, her hopes were raised again that, in spite of her attachment to Willie and his cause, she would eventually come to her family's aid. She didn't yet know how she would manage it, but she was still determined to get Grace out of Willie's clutches, and bring her back home. *She got Charleston in her blood. First snow and cold in da North, she gon' leave dat Willie and he group and come on bak. I gots ta remin' hur who got hur school money. She owe me,* she reasoned. Hatta Mae thought and schemed, and then a smile crossed her face. She suspected that if the high school counselor helped her get Grace a scholarship, she could surely help her get Grace a job, so once again she grabbed her good dress from the back of the closet. Ever the style maven, she wished she could pay off her new layaway dress she bought for Grace's graduation, instead of having to wear the same one she'd worn four years ago. *Maybe the counselor won't remember,* she thought to herself as she smoothed the threadbare material over her hips. Then she pulled the barely worn heels out of their box, and with much tugging, managed to get them on her feet, but when she stood up, she screamed in agony. Pulling a far more comfortable pair on in their place, she resolved to keep her feet out of sight as much as possible. As she passed by the warped dresser mirror, she gave herself a final stamp of approval, and then marched out the door to find work for her daughter so she could take care of her poor old mama and keep her off the county.

XXI

Everybody! Her eyes are open! Tee's eyes are open! Praise the Lord!

Taletha awoke in the same week her classmates returned to school, having suffered great damage. On the night Grace left her slumped on the infirmary floor, she didn't receive help right away. Her injuries didn't looked life threatening, and so she was left while others were rushed to local hospitals by ambulance. The result was that she almost died from internal bleeding. In addition, she sustained several fractures, mainly in her face, and she also suffered damage to her liver and spleen, as well as a serious concussion.

"Who gon' pay for dis?" her distraught parents asked everyone when they arrived at the hospital where she was eventually taken. They were surviving just a fraction above the poverty level, so medical care was a luxury. They treated sickness the way a lot of the "country people" did, with roots, herbs, spirits, witch hazel, and Epsom salt, and it generally worked. Wounds were healed, and people recovered, but this was beyond their reach.

Since the incident was viewed as a riot started by students, under the influence of the dreaded militant Black Panther Party, medical facilities that cared for the wounded, fearing repercussions, moved to distance themselves by ridding themselves of the students as expeditiously as possible. Many were discharged before they were ready and weren't provided with follow-up care. "Take her home. We can't do any more for her. She needs to be under the care of her personal doctor," her parents were told as Taletha was placed into a wheelchair and rushed to the waiting station wagon their pastor borrowed from their church. Her mother sobbed loudly when she saw her firstborn girl, now a far cry from the happy and eager child she sent off to school at the start of every year.

"She awake, but she don' do nothin'. She don' kno' us. None us. Maybe she should git mo' care," she pleaded, as an attendant placed the lethargic girl into the car. "Can't nobody tell us what ta do?" The attendant shrugged and gave them a, "Don't ask me, I only work here" look and walked away.

XXII

Grace was welcomed back to the campus, and because of being wounded, she was celebrated as one of the heroes to the cause. Outwardly, she accepted their accolades, but her stomach-churning guilt made the praise feel hollow. Sardis and Dorcus, along with the rest of Earle Hall residents, embraced her, but life had changed. Despite years of enduring the Alley and all its hardships and challenges, she was now gripped by a fear far worse than anything she'd ever experienced. From the time she first set foot back on campus, memories of that horrible night engulfed her, and a feeling of paranoia took hold of her, paralyzing her and stubbornly refusing to release its grip. Every time she closed her eyes, she saw the faces of fallen students, heard their screams and the gunshots. Doors that slammed every time someone went in or out of the dorm were an anathema, producing cat-like reflex actions from already jangled nerves. She remembered the student who had been placed at her feet while she sat comforting Taletha, and she freaked out after learning he had was one of those who died.

Her nightmares were now consumed with his memory. She kept seeing his eyes rolling back in his head as his body grew cold and stiff. She would bolt up in bed drenched in sweat. She spent hour after sleepless hour trying to shut out memories that kept chasing her up and down falling ladders. She snuck into the lounge, hoping that the mindless drone of late-night television would cure her insomnia, but night after fearful night, sleep eluded her. *I have to get a grip on*

233

things, she told herself each time she ventured out onto the Quad, feeling like a toddler taking her first, wobbly steps. Signs of the conflict were still visible, for even though the custodial staff did a good job removing loose debris, like rocks and bottles students used as weapons, bullet holes riddled the buildings. Some students found shell casings hidden in shrubbery and kept them as morbid souvenirs.

When she entered the cafeteria on her first day back, Grace found the staff hard at work, and although they hugged her and welcomed her back, in her fragile mental state, she perceived insincerity in their greetings where none existed. She wondered if they harbored secret resentment, and blamed her for those horrible events. *If only I'd stayed in the dorm that night, Taletha would never have followed me outside and gotten hurt. If I hadn't tossed those rocks and made the patrolman angry, he wouldn't have shot anybody ... if only ... if only.* Her mind was full of "if only" scenarios playing out over and over, like a never-ending Shakespearian tragedy. *I caused those students to die. If only I'd helped that guy, said something when I saw him pass out. And Taletha. Where's Taletha? I haven't seen her. What can I do?* In her paranoia, her thoughts became one jumbled set of half truths after another as she blamed herself for acts she never even committed.

All week she tried to get back into her normal routine, but she couldn't concentrate on her work, couldn't remember where anything went. The duties she once performed with fluidly and with minimal effort now became a great strain. She was performing worse than she had on her first day on the job. "Grace, honey," the cafeteria manager said during the Friday shift. Even though she'd detected a problem on the first day, she proceeded with caution, not wanting to shatter the girl's already fragile psyche. Grace's job was to fill the salt and pepper shakers, and normally she would have breezed through this chore, but today, this hollow-eyed shell of her former self stood motionless in the middle of the floor, the shakers in her sweaty palms, staring into space. "Grace," said the manager again, gently. This time, she looked vaguely in the manager's direction, but the vacant stare made it clear that Grace was not fully conscious. The manager sized up the situation quickly and realizing that Grace was in crisis, contacted the infirmary nurse. Once again, Grace found herself back in the place where her nightmares began. She was not alone, however. Several other students, most of whom had been wounded that night, were experiencing similar reactions.

In addition to class boycotts that were initiated after students returned, administrators had another crisis to deal with. They thought that time away would have healed both physical and psychological scars, but now they realized it hadn't worked. If anything, the isolation many students felt, along with a lack of communication, only served to heighten their frustrations, either spurring them on to heightened activism or consigning them to dejected defeat.

Meanwhile, Sardis and J. B. fell in love all over again. After arriving back on campus with Cyrus Bloom, J. B. ran to his room, greeted his old friends, and exited again within a minute. His feet hit the steps of Earle Hall at almost the same time Sardis was alighting from the reverend's car. Modesty prevented them from displaying their true emotions, so they shared a respectful embrace, but she sensed the raw fervor in his eyes and caught his shallow breathing. The real reunion was forthcoming.

State, being a secular school, was not constrained by religious tradition and moral codes in terms of social interaction. However, there were myriad rules and regulations, and open displays of affection were discouraged. The only thing the rules really managed to accomplish, however, was to inspire creative ways for young, hormone-driven bodies to circumvent them without getting caught. The secrets were duly passed on to each new class, and so students were always able to remain one step ahead of their gatekeepers. Senior men with cars would drive off campus with their underclass girlfriends sequestered under blankets, either on the backseat or on the floor, while girls wearing large overcoats in sweltering ninety-degree heat sat in dark, isolated lobby corners without a stitch of clothing underneath. No one ever saw what their boyfriends' hands were doing. Forget the rules, this was young love.

J. B. and Sardis, the love of his life, the light of his world, violated all the rules. Their stage kiss had just been a prelude to the one they now shared in the middle of Earle Hall's lobby after the reverend departed. Their bodies were entwined like hot fudge syrup melting on vanilla ice cream, their passion on full display, but J. B. didn't care who was watching. When they eventually came up for air, he gazed into her eyes as if seeing her for the first time and whispered, "We will not be apart again."

XXIII

"We gots ta git some real doctor help. Miss Matilda's herbs ain't doin' nothin'."

That was Mother's voice. Taletha recognized a hint of desperation.

"Can't believe it, can't. The court let all them men shoot up our chil'en, then jes' turn dem loose wit nuttin done." Now Father was speaking.

"Unfortunately, we don't have anyone to sue. All they're concerned about is protecting each other; the federal government protecting the state, and the state protecting the federal government. They're all guilty. They've now proved that those kids didn't have any weapons, but as long as they keep stonewalling, it means no money for the victims. It's a sad day."

The reverend! The reverend is in the house. Something big must be going on. Wonder if he is here for me?

Right after Taletha was discharged from the hospital, she suffered another seizure and had a stroke. She was now a virtual prisoner in her rapidly shrinking body.

"Look. I thought I saw her move. That's a good sign, isn't it?"

"We don' know, Rev. We took her to da clinic, but des can do nuttin. We sho' need some help."

"I'll see what I can do. Don't give up hope. A lot of civil rights groups are hard at work. We've put the state on notice that they will not use live ammunition on our kids and treat them worse than animals anymore. There was a similar incident at …" The reverend's voice faded out of Taletha's hearing. *Did he leave?* She wondered. *Did the Rev leave? If … only … I … could …*

XXIV

The J. B. and Sardis "kiss" became the talk of Earle Hall. Dorcus, while happy for her roommate, sat brooding, her heart heavier than ever. Charlie had reported for basic training, and as was customary, he was now isolated from the outside world for eight torturous weeks. "I'll let you know my graduation date. I want my girl front and center with my parents." Those were his last words before entering what, for him, would be eight weeks of hell. He didn't have to travel far, since his training was at Fort Jackson, which was only a hop, skip, and jump away from his house in Columbia, South Carolina, but he would gladly have swapped what he now faced for a root canal treatment.

At one point, he thought he would fail the physical examination, for the asthma he suffered since childhood still caused breathing problems on occasion, but his lungs weren't scarred. He was slender but had good muscular structure, and while he wasn't particularly athletic, he was strong enough to carry a rifle and backpack. He was also intelligent and had a good education. In fact, he may as well have put on a stars and stripes suit, a stove top hat, and a white beard and modeled for the recruiting poster, for much to his chagrin, he was a black dead ringer for Uncle Sam. He hated the thought of his life being disrupted and reshaped into someone else's ideal. He also hated not having the freedom to come and go as he pleased, having to give up his privacy, and having to salute and respond with a respectful "sir" to people who may not have earned the right for such esteem. Tucked away in his memory was a little boy's encounter with a white store owner who insisted that the boy address him as sir. He was never so proud as when his father risked either harsh discipline or his life by standing up to that owner, letting him know that he hadn't earned the right to be called sir by his son. Charlie learned a valuable lesson, and from that time on, the only sir in his life was his dad.

Vietnam was becoming a national nightmare, and he questioned whether he wanted to serve, even though to question his sense of duty to his country was unsettling. Black men always jumped at the opportunity to prove their worth to their country by serving, but the groundswell of hatred toward the military, which was increasingly seen as a tool of the establishment, was reaching fever pitch. Amid the escalation and growing mistrust, Charlie now faced loyalty issues. However, his dad was delighted that his son was going to follow him as a second-generation army man, and his ROTC training had given him a little preparation, and might yet give him a promotional edge, so, with no legal options remaining, he bit the bullet and reported for duty.

The memory of Dorcus's smiles encouraged him. "Are you going to be a lieutenant?" she asked innocently. She wanted to add "like Anton" but stopped herself in time. He explained the ranking system to her. A second lieutenant was the lowest rank that a commissioned officer could attain, but he would be starting much further down than that.

"As a private, I'll have nowhere to go but up," he said teasingly, but from her lack of reaction, he knew his comment had fallen flat. "I just want to do my time and get out. I don't want all the responsibility officers have to deal with." He was also on the verge of adding "like Anton," but he too stifled the thought before it could slip out. He had an inkling she was still in love with his cousin, but she hadn't mentioned his name or asked about him. Even though neither of them spoke about him, Anton's spirit continued to haunt both of them to the extent that it left the question of the reality of their potential marriage unanswered.

As Charlie walked through the guard gate at the old fort, he entered into a brotherhood steeped in tradition, of Biblical proportions, of times when men went off to battle to protect their homes and loved ones, to preserve their way of life, to win the hearts of their fair maidens, and to valiantly uphold the honor of their country. All of that, however, was lost on the new recruits, whose ears rang with jody calls from one side of the fence and cries of "baby killers" from the other. "It's going to be a long hitch," he mumbled, falling in line. The transition had begun.

Meanwhile, Anton was fighting his own battles in Texas. The soldier was tried for murder and found guilty. Anton was called to testify against him, and now he found himself in the middle of yet another firestorm. He'd done something that no career-minded officer would ever do, not if he wanted to keep his career, that is; he refused to testify, not so much out of protest, but because he didn't know the accused and didn't see him commit the act. Higher ups assumed, incorrectly, that black officers knew every black troop in the company. As a result, he was charged with insubordination, resulting in actions being taken against him.

"My career is over. A field grade Article 15 won't get me promoted to captain, let alone a higher rank," Anton told his colleagues as they sat together in a particularly depressing jam session. All the black officers now began to realize they were being singled out for disciplinary actions. One shared how his commander gave him an illegal order that, as allowed by military convention, he refused to carry out. Now, he was under suspicion.

"You know what gets to me? Them white boys know I'm right. The orders changed as soon as I said something, but none of them said a thang. Ain't nobody got my back." The others all nodded in agreement, some punctuating their acknowledgment with an "amen." Their sessions moved off-post, so someone introduced even stronger substances along with Thunderbird wine to deaden their pain, thus now each of them took a hit from a joint that was being passed around while they continued with their tales of woe.

Another man, Morris, was accused of being overly friendly with black troops because he sat in the barracks with them during a late night session and let them vent. He was now facing charges of fraternization. "I kept things from blowing up, but the Old Man and I never see things eye to eye. Talk about micro-management. I got to tell him everything I do and report in and out. Everybody, even the clerk, can run errands during the day. I go to the Post Office to get a stamp, come back, and it's, 'Morris, where you been?' Man, I'm gettin' tired of it." He took a long drag on the joint while the rest of the circle provided empathy and comfort.

Even though his actions prevented a riot, the commander hadn't seen it that way. He claimed Morris hadn't sought permission to hold the unauthorized gathering, and a charge of conspiracy was being considered. White officers were given free rein to display leadership qualities, while black officers were accused of overreaching their authority or of by-passing the chain of command when they displayed the same qualities. On and on it went. Black troops were on the verge of rebellion, claiming unjust treatment, and black officers were ready to join them. Finally, just like in the old western movies, the cavalry arrived and saved the day.

The post inherited a new commander, a man with common sense and compassion. The military knew it had to deal with a new type of soldier now, one who no longer took whatever was dished out passively, but who had a new pride. Black Power and "I'm Black and I'm Proud" was sweeping the nation. Motown ruled the airwaves, presenting a new sound in black music, and there was growing recognition of and respect for black spending power. Curtis Mayfield and the Impressions recorded songs like "Keep On Pushing" that became anthems of the civil rights movement. A loud message of freedom issued from the radios in every barracks, often clashing with the country sounds of bluegrass, creating a discordant cacophony that went far beyond the music and caused many white commanders to issue edicts forbidding troops from playing any music. This wasn't good for morale, and for the sake of unity, the army was forced to institute training in human and equal rights. They had to move away from the antiquated thinking that dictated that the army only recognized one color: green. People wanted to be recognized for their ethnicity as much as for their contributions. The growing number of fragging incidents, even in the combat zone in Vietnam, led the military to recognize a growing need for change.

The new commander, after learning about the black officers' informal meetings, encouraged them to continue with their jam sessions and even took it one step further. He listened to the complaints and suggestions that emerged from the sessions. The drinking and drug use, which remained a sworn secret among the participants, began to decrease once they realized their complaints were receiving validation.

Anton provided the liaison between the commander and the sessions. Meanwhile, the number of black officers with career-ending Article 15s on their records continued to increase. The infractions were petty, but they were enough to ensure that each of them would eventually be systematically removed from active duty. Many would be denied promotions to captain, and if they hadn't been discharged by then, it would most certainly occur before the all-important jump from company grade to field grade as a major. "This is a career killer, for all of us, Sir," Anton pointed out. "Even if we're reassigned, this stigma goes wherever we go. We'll never be able to prove ourselves or make a fresh start."

With that, the commander made a bold decision. He agreed to remove the offending items from permanent records once the officer moved to another assignment. Anton felt a great sense of accomplishment once that ruling was handed down, and for the first time in months, he thought about home, and about Dorcus. His excitement was short-lived, however, for the very next day, long-anticipated orders came down. The fact that he would have to face Vietnam was inevitable but still wasn't welcome.

"Face it, my brother," said a fellow sessioner when Anton broke the news. "If you want a career in this here white man's army, you gots to pay your dues. Look at it this way; you'll get that Article 15 wiped off your record in no time." They all laughed at the irony. The mood was light even though Vietnam and the thought of going hung like a pall over their heads.

"Yeah, Vietnam will clean that record right up," said Anton, taking another swig of his rum and coke. Then he raised his glass and added, "And probably clean my butt off the face of the Earth."

"But you can't say they aren't giving you an equal opportunity to die." They were consumed with laughter that only condemned men could share.

XXV

Once again, Grace found herself on a bus. After three days of bed rest, she was discharged from the infirmary, but without proper treatment for her delusional state, she was unable to hold it together. She sobbed uncontrollably in the privacy of her room, and appeared teary-eyed throughout the day. A lot of classes were suspended due to continued student boycotts, so with no classes to attend and no study assignments, her mind became consumed with lies and distortions. She couldn't concentrate, and at work in the cafeteria her hands trembled so much the manager took her off the serving line. She retreated into corners, cowering from unseen demons that whispered only to her, telling her each student who passed through the line cast an accusatory eye at her for causing their misery. She lasted one more week and then called Willie.

"Come on up," he said. "I'll wire you enough money to buy a ticket and some food for the trip. We'll cure you. The brothers and sisters will greet you with open arms, my sweet. We'll make sure no one hurts you here." A crystal ball would have revealed how hollow that promise would eventually become. Grace left without a word or a good-bye to anyone. Her newly assigned roommate came back to their room one day and discovered Grace's side of the room empty. The concerned residential director, assuming that she returned to Charleston, immediately contacted the Judge. Grace still listed him as next of kin in order to be able to use his phone number as an emergency contact.

Hatta Mae thanked the Judge for relaying the news, and then retreated to her house.

"If deys anythin' I kin do, Miss Hatta," he called after her, "yo' let me no. I bet she wid my wife's kin. I's find out. If she wid dem, dey will tak good care o' her. Don' worry." Hatta Mae nodded and mumbled a simple word of gratitude. She had warmed to the old man lately, but not to the point of complete abandon. He had been too cordial, and she couldn't bring herself to trust him, knowing that there was always an ulterior motive for his generosity, but he provided the strength she needed by guiding her through the crisis with Grace after she was shot. He assumed responsibility after her husband, crumbling under the weight of so many trials, checked out of reality and into a foggy world of drink and drugs. He even helped make her rent payments, which were falling further and further behind. Grace's sister had moved out, taking her children and her man with her. Hatta Mae was happy to have more breathing space in their little flat, but the income they contributed, meager as it had been, was now gone. And now Grace ... she couldn't bring herself to think about it.

She slipped quietly into the darkened bedroom, where her husband lay sprawled half-clothed in a deep, drug-induced stupor. She looked at the doped-up figure stretched across the bed, then at the torn and tattered curtains covering the windows, hiding the torn and tattered events of her life from the outside world. She slumped to her knees and tried to utter a prayer, but couldn't help wondering if God had given up on her. Her chest heaved as torrential tears began to fall, tears that brought no comfort or solutions to her rapidly degenerating existence. She needed to repair this broken life, but didn't know how.

"The Section 8, and ask fa' Sister Teresa," her daughter told her that afternoon when she returned to collect her remaining items. "Mama, these programs been der fo' long time. Dey meant for people like us. I'm gettin' money for the kids, I'm gettin' vouchers to feed 'em, and I'm gettin' help with rent in a nice buildin'. This not the county. The president wants ta he'p us, so he made the gov'mint give us this. There ain' no shame."

"Wha' da presden' no 'bout me?" huffed Hatta Mae, folding her arms across her chest. Her daughter smiled. She knew her mother well enough to recognize that the gesture meant she was listening, but needed more assurance before she would feel comfortable enough to take action. Applying for anything was a painful experience for most black people, especially if benefits were involved. They were often greeted with scorn, derision, and disinterest by civil servants, even though it was their job to assist those who paid their salaries. This was all new to Hatta Mae. Federal financial assistance or welfare became a staple in the United States during the early 1930s, but true to form, the South, being the South, hid the information from those who needed it most. The slave masters still nurtured a fear that parity could develop between the races. They expressed their support for "separate but equal," but knew secretly that separate was not equal; it was a means of control. They knew it, and they fought tooth and nail to maintain the status quo.

On the playing field, he who controlled the ball determined the outcome of the game. They kept the ball out of black hands by controlling every aspect of black life they could. From contrived voting rules to impossible qualification statutes, the ball was often dribbled to the halfway line but never quite made it across the line into the black half of the court. Benefits and aid, which were easy for a white person to obtain, became an insurmountable challenge for a black person. They put restrictions in place as high as the nearest Palmetto Tree and as wide as the remote Grand Canyon, and the minutia of those who somehow managed to squeak through the qualification process were watched like hawks. Administrators loved nothing more than to pound their "benefits denied" or "disqualified for further assistance" stamps on black people's applications.

Stories abounded about surprise visits by federal workers, who took away funds for any reason they could find. Having a man in the household was a big issue. Women could not have husbands, or any men for that matter, in the household in order to receive benefits, so surprise visits were instituted. Men, no matter who they were, brothers, cousins, uncles, would be seen leaving through windows and other makeshift exits whenever the law appeared on the doorstep. Women were subjected to questions about their sex lives and were threatened with restricted benefits if there was even a hint of misconduct as defined by the law. Such vigilance kept the number of applications low, kept the playing field lopsided, and kept the slave in place without having to resort to a whip; the master's game played by the master's rules on the master's court.

Things were changing, however. The concept of the Great Society had been introduced, and new attitudes during the 1960s placed a renewed emphasis on equality. As a result of complaints by civil rights organizations, federal oversight was introduced. The masters were forced to lift local restrictions, thus ensuring that money reached those whose needs were greatest. In other words, a new referee arrived in town and made sure the game was now played full court.

Hatta Mae knew she couldn't navigate her way through the maze of qualification documents without help, so she listened intently as her daughter gave her full instructions.

"Remember, Sister Teresa. She the one the gov'mint sent to make sure we get our rights. But you ask her about the Section 8 for a house. You got that, Mama?"

Hatta Mae pulled out her best dress again, the one she'd worn when she got the scholarship money and the job Grace would not be filling. She had long since given up on dressy shoes, however. Her feet were now so damaged and painful she couldn't wear heels anymore. She found another, more comfortable pair that sort of went with the dress and left to get help. As she ambled out onto the street, she had to step around the furniture of yet another family that was moving out of the alley. This was the third or fourth family to leave in a month. Out of the corner of her eye, she saw something else. Partially hidden by the screen door, she caught the anxious, drawn face of her landlord. *Dis why he bin so hepful,* she thought to herself. His previously hidden motive was revealed. Word about the aid was spreading like wildfire, and he was losing all his tenants. As she stepped out onto Duncan, the sunshine bathed her face. Hatta Mae was leaving the Alley.

XXVI

I wonder if they miss me, Taletha mused. *They can't play bid whist without me. I guess they've all gone back to school by now. I heard the news report saying campus was open again. Sure miss it.*

Without proper therapy or care, Taletha made no improvement. Her mind worked some of the time, and her eyes were open, but they stopped letting in light, so now she became trapped in a dark world where her paranoid mind lived in the mire of what had once been a life of great promise.

Sardis and Dorcus. They were the other two. I hated Sardis for the longest time. She was so white, slender, long legs, and flat butt. Then had the nerve to call herself a black woman. And that long, straight, silky hair. Ain't nothing been colored, much less black, about her. Could have had any man on campus. Instead, she stole my man. J. B. Story could have been mine. He coulda rocked my world any time. Adonis, and so nice. When did dark men like him ever get a chance with a woman like her?

She visualized herself with the object of her desire, until reality once again reclaimed her thoughts. *Who am I kidding? I was never even a speck in his eye. But he was such a gentleman. Didn't go off like that uppity football player did when I talked to him in class. I just asked the fool if I knew him from somewhere. Wasn't even flirting, and he was all in my face. "You don't know me! Don't even try to pretend like you know me! I don't know you, and don't want to know you either, so get your pig face outta mine!" The girls wondered why I didn't bother to date. Welcome to my world. I liked the men; they didn't like me. But I sure did like J. B. Thought I'd get a great start with him, since he was so new to the campus and all; no history. But it was only natural that he'd fall for Sardis. She wasn't all that pretty, but she was a real lady. I got used to her after a while. Even liked her.*

XXVII

Dorcus was alone. Sardis was spending every waking moment with J. B., and Grace was gone. Speculation, conjecture, and gossip abounded, but no one had any news about Taletha. Either that, or they weren't talking. Plenty of rumors circulated about that, as well. She had serious head injuries and was in a coma was the most persistent one. All Dorcus knew was her friend hadn't returned. And far, far worse, she hadn't heard from either Anton or Charlie. She was suffering from near-terminal boredom, so she went to classes in spite of the boycotts, enduring some jeering and shunning from those who chose to support some vague cause. Her grades steadily improved to the point where she was receiving A's, and she didn't want to jeopardize her grade point average by risking a failing mark—the professors' weapon designed to induce compliance. Little by little, class sizes began to increase as students' anger subsided and the air escaped from the over-inflated importance of their ill-defined grievances.

Her after-hours activities ceased to exist now that the bid whist games ended with the disappearance of Grace and Taletha. Dorcus suggested beginning a new foursome, but Sardis had no interest in the game anymore. Suggestions to dorm-mates met with the same fate. Playing a card game became trivial in the minds of those concerned with what they perceived as weightier matters. Their attention remained focused on protesting, eating, and sleeping. Even though the semester was almost over, her desire for it to end was building to fever pitch.

"Telephone call for Dupree!" came the familiar yell, followed by "Dupree, you in? You got a call." Each floor had one telephone, located midway down the hall, next to the lounge. This made privacy difficult, and snatches of overheard dialogue regularly became fodder for the ever turning rumor mill at least for a day. Whoever happened to be passing by the phone when it rang would answer the call. However, the task invariably fell to those whose rooms were closest to the contraption. There was nothing like the incessant ringing of a telephone to spur the nearest residents into action, and if the pending call promised to be particularly "juicy," word spread rapidly and the lounge would fill quickly. Everyone on the floor would develop a sudden urge to watch television, play a hand of cards, or study, although curiously, the volume on the television set would suddenly decrease to a murmur, the bidding fervor would die out, and concentration would become totally disrupted.

The summons wrenched Dorcus away from her pity party, and she became overwhelmed with curiosity. She knew the call wasn't from home, because she had just finished her weekly conversation with her folks. She bolted out the door, raced down the hall, and grabbed the dangling receiver, yearning to hear just one voice. Just as she reached for the receiver, several of her dorm mates sprinted past, headed for the lounge. She knew they were placing bets on the identity of the caller. "Hello, honey," said the voice on the phone in response to her greeting. Her heart sank as soon as she heard Charlie's familiar tones.

"Hi, Charlie," she said in a loud, clear voice, leaving no doubt as to his identity for the benefit of the lounge crowd. She couldn't very well express annoyance, having been guilty of snooping on other dorm mates' conversations herself in the past. She also understood their curiosity. After four years of hearing her talk about nothing but Anton, and knowing about their on-again off-again relationship, people were naturally curious.

She was glad to hear Charlie's voice, in spite of her uncertain feelings for him, and happy to know he'd survived basic training. It was their first conversation since he began basic, which he was now, mercifully, about to finish. The call was to convey the invitation he promised her to join him as his guest at Fort Jackson for his graduation ceremony. She was happy to accept; anything to escape the loneliness and boredom. She packed a small bag, let the dorm director know of her destination for the weekend, and left campus, taking the bus directly to the army post. It felt good to have this senior privilege.

This was her second visit to a military instillation, so she was the professional this time undergoing security procedures. Unlike the amateurs, she was able to zip in and out with ease; a big difference from her first time on a military base for Anton's graduation from Officer Basic. She couldn't refrain from making comparisons and realized that the differences were stark. Jackson was one of the major east coast training centers for military recruits, and it was a beehive of activity. Two training battalions were holding graduation ceremonies that Friday, so there were visitors everywhere.

Charlie arranged lodging at a guesthouse on post. It was clean, but basic, a far cry from the hotel where she stayed in Georgia. His parents had already arrived, so Dorcus spent some time meeting and greeting. She had no problem identifying Charlie's dad, who was an older version of his son. Charlie clearly got his gentle personality and common sense from his mother, who was a roly-poly apple dumpling of a woman. They were a real life Jack Sprat and his wife. Dorcus knew she was on display, so she was on her best behavior, for she sensed that Charlie was seeking their approval of her. She smiled warmly, but her heart was still conflicted. Should she say yes to his proposal? Was it worth it to have that coveted ring for graduation, even if it wasn't from the man she desired for so long?

Visions of her future life swept the landscape of her mind. With Anton, she would enjoy lunch with other officers' wives in formal dining rooms at stately, dignified, well-preserved Officers Clubs. On every army post, there was an unwritten tradition that "O" Clubs be established in the oldest building standing. She saw herself enjoying tea with the general's wife and presiding over meetings of the Officers' Wives Club. She would do everything to help Anton on his way up the ranks, because as he advanced, so would she.

The reality of the hot Carolina sunshine reflecting off hard bleacher seats gave her a taste of life on the flip side. Charlie's company, ironically named Charlie Company, marched out onto the parade field looking sharp and crisp in their dress green uniforms, with polished brass reflecting the brilliant sun. Anton had been in dress blues. She followed the movements of the officers on the field, particularly the adjutant, with his snappy walk and sharp turns. She loved how they took charge, how they stood out from the sea of faces. She would have spotted Anton easily, but she had to stare intently to find Charlie, buried in the green mass.

After the ceremony, the company hosted a picnic for the graduates and their guests. Dorcus tolerated the festivities, rather than enjoying them. This was a beer and barbeque crowd, and black troops were well represented. As the crowd surged forward, lunging for the free food, she moved to one side. Many had never been exposed to so much bounty in their lives and walked away with plates of chicken and ribs piled higher than Mt. Kilimanjaro. Mothers and girlfriends swarmed their soldiers, touching their uniforms and whatever medals they'd earned, the men responding with pride. For many, this achievement represented their first step toward manhood. Most had never left their small towns before now, had never done anything on their own before now, and had never had to take responsibility for their own choices and decisions before now.

Dorcus noticed something disturbing, however; the racial divide still existed. Bonding and camaraderie was apparent, and there was no doubt that each man would have been willing to put his life on the line for the others, but the military could not force them to cross that divide and become friends. There was a lot of teasing and dapping, like fraternity brothers completing their initiations, but years of social isolation still forced them into white family groups in one corner and black families in another.

Basic training had treated Charlie very well. His beanpole figure gained some muscle, so he didn't look so puny and gangly anymore. He still wore glasses, but the military issue black-rimmed pair he now wore gave him a distinguished appearance, almost like a college professor. "Do you have to salute so much?" she asked, as he touched his eyebrow to what seemed like the hundredth person that day. Anton did his share of saluting, but she was enamored by the fact that, as an officer, people had to salute him first, so she didn't complain. As a Private First Class, Charlie was outranked by the entire world. "Your poor arm must be tired," she said coyly with a touch of cynicism.

"You get used to it. I've already earned one stripe. I'll move up in rank soon, and then there'll be others under me."

"Then they'll have to salute you?" she asked, already knowing the answer.

"I'm enlisted," he said, with pride, adding the old punch line, "I work for a living." He smiled as he repeated the insider's joke.

Dorcus didn't get it. Moreover, she became irritated at Charlie for his lack of ambition. The hints she threw at him like fireballs, suggesting that he improve his lot in life, were falling as flat as his joke. By the time she returned to campus, she decided she preferred the life of an officer's wife over that of an enlisted person's wife. She had to locate Anton. Something must have happened to him. She knew he wouldn't have just abandoned her. She dared not ask Charlie, but she needed to find out. She walked swiftly across the campus and entered the male domain of ROTC. "I need to locate someone," she demanded, to the surprise of the sergeant sitting behind the dilapidated gray metal desk who bounded to his feet with the precision and bearing customary for a trained noncommissioned officer.

"Yes, Ma'am," he replied. "Always happy to help."

XXVIII

Dorcus stopped talking. The sound of the ticking clock magnified as Dorcus interrupted her story. Sardis and Grace exchanged glances. "Why was it so important to find Anton?" Grace finally asked. "Charlie loved you. I told you that freshman year, sophomore year, junior year ..."

"I know, I *know*. I remember, but I gave Anton something I could never give another man," she responded, looking down at the card table. "That weekend in Georgia was magical. I had my first taste of sparkling wine, and my first taste of sparkling love," she chuckled. "We left his graduation party in the early morning hours. You both know I wasn't a night person, or a drinker, but I was with my man, and it was the best time of my life. I didn't want the magical evening to end."

"Want to see my new place?" Anton asked, matter-of-factly. Dorcus couldn't remember her answer, for she had already given herself over to the night. Soon, the car pulled up in front of his BOQ. As a junior officer, Anton had a single room with a connecting bath, which he shared with a fellow officer. The room came equipped with a small kitchenette, which consisted of a refrigerator and a four-burner stove. He pulled a bottle of Cold Duck from the half-empty refrigerator and filled two wine glasses, swaying a little as he gently set the glasses on the coffee table in front of her. She remembered getting the giggles as he pulled the convertible sofa out into a bed.

256

One minute she had been sitting on a narrow couch, and the next she was sprawling, laughing uncontrollably, on a queen-sized bed. Anton staggered over to a large cabinet and opened the double door to reveal a television set on a swivel base. Below it was a small stereo, which he switched on.

"To this day, whenever I hear James Brown singing 'It's a Man, Man, Man's World,' I see him shuffling across the room with that loopy smile." Her eyes turned inward, to something that was still unsettled within her soul. "I didn't want my first time with him to be like that," she whispered, choking back tears representing twenty years of regret.

Every warning from her mother, every sermon from her dad's pulpit, flooded into her boozy mind. From Mom: "I raised you right. You're a lady. Act like one. Don't let him have his way. A man respects that. You'll lose him forever if you weaken." Anton began to kiss her gently all over. From the pulpit: "Adam and Eve became one flesh only after God Almighty Himself said it was all right. Not before, young ladies and gentlemen, *not* before." His caresses enveloped her in a cocoon of desire from which she never wanted to emerge. From Mom again: "Why should a man buy the cow if he can get the milk for free?" From the pulpit: "Joseph didn't just walk out when Potiphar's wife asked him to lie with her; he fled. Flee, young people. Flee the temptations of lust." One bra strap fell away, quickly followed by the other, and then her panties were slipped off as he positioned himself expertly over her. Percy Sledge took over from James Brown with "When a Man Loves a Woman," as she surrendered.

She stopped her narrative again. Catching her breath she continued, "I was in such pain, physical, mental, and emotional, but I couldn't stop." Both of the others' heads bobbed up and down in acknowledgment as Dorcus recounted her experience, and both their minds traveled back in time to their own first time, and songs and places. "He took me back to the hotel the following morning. No good-bye kiss; I couldn't even look at him. I beat my roommate in by a half hour. I don't remember to this day how I looked, but I wanted to die. I spent half of the following day in the bathroom suffering the consequences of the night before. My roomy was far more experienced. She went full tilt the next day, but she paid for that weekend nine months later. At least she snagged her lieutenant. They got married when she was three months along and not showing yet. She sent me an invitation, with the prediction that I'd be next."

"Would you have married him if you'd gotten pregnant?" asked Sardis.

Dorcus thought for a minute. Foresight would have dictated one response, but hindsight dictated another. She didn't answer the question. "Before now, I never spoke about that experience to anyone—especially my mom—but I guess something in me had changed, because as a woman, she knew. She talked about that weekend later as if she knew what had gone down." She smiled. "Mom warned me, described what he had done like she'd been a fly on the wall peeping in. I figured that, since she knew so much, she must have gone through it herself. You don't imagine your folks doing that."

"Wonder if Cinderella knew what she was letting herself in for with that prince of hers," Grace added sarcastically, breaking the somber mood. "Those books always ended with 'and they lived happily ever after.'"

"Wonder if she would have even gone after the prince if she had any idea of what lay ahead? The first time is a killer. Do you think they would have gotten it together if she didn't have to leave the ball at midnight?" said Sardis, continuing to rewrite the fairy tale. They cracked up with laughter, and then the mood became somber once more.

"Times were changing. I knew that I'd lose him if I didn't give in," said Dorcus with a sigh. "I loved him, he told me to prove it, so I did," she reflected. "But we didn't get to live happily ever after. Neither did my roommate. Her husband died one month after stepping off a helicopter in Vietnam." Tears welled in her eyes again, and Sardis passed the box of tissue to her. The game continued in silence.

XXIX

Life on campus at State began to resume some sense of normalcy as slowly, some of the bid whist games returned, but it wasn't like before. The students sensed a great loss, and now some were demanding changes in many of the college's strict mandates. Anti-war activists also instigated demands to abolish the draft along with ROTC programs on campus. The campus-wide class boycotts began to lose their intensity, especially after officials threatened to close again. It was the seniors who led the way back to the books. In the meantime, the Henderson-Davis Players production schedule resumed, and Cyrus Bloom found a play that fit the mood of the campus. It was called *The Song of Bernadette* about a young girl who had visions of the Virgin Mary. The school needed some miraculous visions of its own at that time. Sardis had the lead in what was to be her final student production.

To help lighten the mood a little, Bloom decided to hold a campus award ceremony. Everyone knew he wanted to give Sardis special recognition, but just to make it "fair," he held a campus-wide ballot for best actor and best actress in lead roles, and for best actor and best actress in supporting roles. The voting for categories like best property master and best stage director was limited to the current speech class and drama club members. The awards proved to be the shot in the arm the campus needed to put some fun back into the corridors. It got the students' minds off the past, and on to the future, and a grateful faculty expressed their thanks to him during their annual banquet. Drama, as a study discipline, moved a notch closer to becoming a reality.

XXX

Grace stepped off the bus onto what to her was foreign soil, the North. Willie was waiting at the station in anticipation, and they leapt into each other's arms like two love-starved beings arriving at a long-awaited banquet. Willie had his Gracie at last. He whisked her off to the subway station, and as they passed a small florist shop, he stopped to buy her a rose. As the crowds pressed in on them, he held her hand tightly in his, like a mother who feared losing a child. Her excitement was mingled with fear, driven by paranoia, but the knots in her stomach kept the nausea in check. Everything was so big. There were so many people, and they moved so fast. She wondered if she'd done the right thing. The only certainty she possessed was the knowledge that she could not return to South Carolina. All those accusing eyes would not be able to find her now.

The train ride went on for what seemed like an eternity, while Willie continued to hold her close. Her eyes scanned the crowds, hoping to connect with a friendly face, but her attempts were met with suspicious scowls on the few faces that dared to look back. Blank and vacant stares were the norm, as people focused on their inner lives. Some read, while others caught up on the sleep they'd missed surrendering precious hours to connect their stretched-out lives between points A, B, C, and beyond. The speaker abruptly garbled something about the end of the line. They scrambled out of the train and emerged onto the streets of Harlem, the land of fables.

"I can't believe I'm here," she said in awe as they walked quickly from the train. The pace was so fast that she found herself half-walking and half-trotting to keep up, feeling like a three-year-old scampering along behind an impatient parent. She maintained a tight grasp on Willie's hand as they sped along the street. Twilight was setting in, and the weather was changing. To those around her, it was just a bit nippy, but to Grace, it was downright cold, and the sweater she was wearing was far from adequate. There was no snow on the ground, but the air was icy and prickly and seeped through to her bones like nothing she had ever experienced down South. She never owned a large wardrobe, and she junked the few pieces she had, along with all her books and other possessions, before she left State. Willie convinced her that she would have little use for them and promised to help her get new clothing. It was all a part of her new beginning.

"We'll have to get you some warm clothing," said Willie, as if reading her mind. With that, he unbuttoned his jacket and folded her inside it, slowing his pace to match hers. Suddenly, the cold vanished, taking with it her fears and anxieties. Everything was so different from what she'd heard and read about her new home. A lot of the streets didn't have names, just numbers. Harlem was a neighborhood of Manhattan, one of five boroughs of the city of New York. She heard about Harlem because, during the early part of the twentieth century, it had been a Mecca for many of the colored people who left South Carolina and other southern states seeking freedom from oppression. It was the new Promised Land for those who were looking for a better life. Harlem stretched from the East River to the Hudson River, between 155th Street, where it met Washington Heights, to an uneven border along the south side. There was also an area known as Spanish Harlem, which extended the boundaries even further. Even though the boundaries kept changing as the population changed, it was usually associated with the black migration.

The walk from the subway station seemed almost as long as the ride, but as they strode along, an interesting thought struck Grace. The place began to take on an air of familiarity. Alas, black neighborhoods had a way of mirroring each other. She exchanged the densely populated Alley, with its large wood-framed houses, for rows of densely populated brownstones.

The Alley houses had once been owned by wealthy people and maintained in grand style, and similarly, these brownstones represented some of the finest original townhouses in New York. They'd been designed and built by prominent architects of their day, like William Tuthill, Charles Buck, and James Renwick. Sadly, all were now in disrepair. She saw another alley parallel that she dreaded, too; rats. Lots of them, scurrying along streets filled with trash and wasted human beings. She recoiled in shock when a man suddenly stumbled out of a doorway and went sprawling a few feet in front of them. "You get used to that," Willie whispered. "It's a sad situation, but it's a reality around here. Remember what I told you about the drugs?" he said, as they stepped gingerly around the prone figure. "This neighborhood offers them a lot of choices, and many choose this. They hate the Liberation Front for trying to improve things. Tried to burn us out." He stopped abruptly, as if revealing information that wasn't meant for public knowledge. Grace pretended not to hear. Black churches were well represented. The neighborhood had its share of Baptists, and of course the AMEs, and other sects began to creep in as well. The Nation of Islam and a splinter group of Black Muslims had established mosques. There was also a proliferation of storefront churches and … "Here we are." Willie's announcement interrupted Grace's observations.

The small sign out front read Liberation Front. It, too, had once been a church, and had seen better days. It sat dwarfed between massive tenement complexes on either side, looming over it like overgrown redwood trees. He ushered her into the complex to the right. "This is where the women stay until they're paired up," he explained. The letters he had written to her while she was at school told her a lot about the group, but the visions she imagined did not match what she now faced. She imagined large, roomy apartments, with sunny balconies and beautiful city views. Instead, he walked her to the door of a single-room flat three flights up. It was sparsely furnished, with one bed, one lamp, a toilet, and a sink, and resembled a jail cell more than a room. Nevertheless, it was spotless, with gleaming hardwood floors and colorfully painted walls.

The group members didn't consider themselves to be a cult but modeled themselves on many of the social and economic principles espoused by the late Malcolm X. This included shedding their family names in favor of the X nomenclature. Their leader, who was known as Brother Martin, decided to form the cell, as it was called, after reading and becoming influenced by the works of Karl Marx, Albert Camus, and other architects of socialist society. He liked what they espoused about economic freedom and social independence, and thus he decided to recruit men as leaders who, in turn, could indoctrinate others in the philosophy. In a cold-war climate, espousing communist philosophy was like planting the red flag with hammer and sickle at your doorstep, and electronic eyes were always watching. He managed to find the empty property along 144th Street and acquired it through the latest federal entitlements designed for urban renewal. The area and the timing were just right. Harlem, once the Mecca of the great black migration, had fallen on hard times.

As she stood at the open door, Grace's eyes widened with fear. A thousand thoughts raced through her mind, and she reached back and grabbed Willie's hand again, seeking reassurance. Willie, sensing her apprehension, assured her that it was safe. Still not wanting to be left alone, she turned to him and was about to make a plea when suddenly, she became aware of another person's presence. A door had opened and closed very quietly, and now the dimly lit hallway took on a different texture as a figure bearing a candle moved toward them. Grace felt as though she could hear her heartbeat echoing off the walls, but Willie just stood calmly, finally turning to greet the white-clad woman who was approaching. He accepted the tray of food and drink she was carrying as if he had been expecting it all along, and passed it to Grace, kissing her gently on the forehead.

"As you're a single woman, it's against house rules for me to enter your inner sanctuary. Take this. It'll refresh you overnight." Grace smiled as she took the tray, which was loaded with fruit and milk. Inside, the building belied its unkempt exterior, and she sensed an atmosphere of warmth and caring. Before the mysterious woman made her silent exit, she turned on the room light, excising whatever ghosts the dark shadows may have been hiding. Now Grace was happy to walk inside the room.

"The men act as guards," said Willie. "This place is better maintained and more secure than over half the residential buildings in Harlem. You can sleep securely, my love. This will only be for a short time." His confidence gave her inner peace and strength. "You'll meet everyone tomorrow. Brother Martin was beside himself when he found out you would be joining us. I've been talking about you for four years and refused to be matched up with anyone else. He's prepared to welcome you into the organization, and we'll have the passage ceremony and jump the broom. Then we can have our own space in the family quarters. That's the building on the other side of the meeting hall."

"I wondered what I was in for," said Grace, creating another lull in the game.

"Sounds like a cult to me," said Dorcus. "And when you said jump the broom; does that mean what I think it means? He expected you to get married right away? No proposal, no engagement? No ring?"

"No warning?" added Sardis.

"Nothing," said Grace, picking up another card and picking up her story.

She didn't sleep that night. Now, the nightmares from State were replaced with different concerns. Her mind kept asking her if she'd made a good decision, and the strange street noises startled her every time she closed her eyes. Rattling trucks and screaming sirens wailed continually in a never-ending cacophony. Loud, fighting voices pierced the night, trying to be heard above the traffic. Now a baby's cry reverberated through all of it, like a soprano straining to reach the top of her range. Grace didn't like what she saw in the mirror the following morning after a bell pealed at 5:00 AM and the building came alive. Soon, she heard a gentle knock on the door, but was afraid to respond.

"Are you all right?" a female voice called. Cautiously, she opened the door, to be greeted by not one, but four smiling faces.

"They had a change of clothes for me. All the women wore this shapeless white garment that covered them from head to foot. The room I was in was called the isolation room. They put newcomers in there until they were properly attired, ready to meet the rest of the group. It was the job of the committee to see that I was presentable."

"It sounds like a cult," Dorcus chimed in again.

"Will you stop saying that? I had no clue at the time. I knew they were different, but the term cult was never used. All I know is, they stood for change, and they represented the structure that I needed at that time. You all had no idea what I was going through; no one did. The guilt I was carrying and the anguish I felt were eating me alive. None of them knew me. They couldn't accuse me of anything. They were kind and accepting and asked no questions. They brought more food and another glass of milk. Then one of them noticed that I hadn't drunk the glass from the night before. She kept pushing this stuff on me, but I didn't want to drink it, so when they weren't looking, I dumped it in the toilet.

"The group's philosophy was based on several basic tenets they believed they could attain through self-discipline and self-segregation. So here I am, fresh out of the South, where three students had died and a lot of people, including me, had been hurt trying to integrate things, and there they were practicing a form of self-segregation. But their segregation took on a different shape. Through segregation, they wanted to exercise the freedom to determine and guide their own destiny; they wanted to achieve full employment; they wanted to have decent housing; they wanted decent education for their children, good health care, an end to police interference and brutality; an end to an unjust war that sacrificed the lives of mostly black men; and they wanted land for independent use so all of these objectives could be achieved. I'd suddenly stepped into the middle of all this. I didn't know if I could adjust, especially since right from the beginning, I had a big problem in the form of Brother Martin."

The leader of the group was a big man. If a movie producer had gone to central casting to find someone to play a cult leader, he would have chosen Brother Martin hands down. He was in his mid-fifties, and his former lives included being a numbers runner for another colorful Harlemite by the name of Madame Stephanie St. Clair. His activities eventually brought him to the attention of the NYPD, leading to a short stint behind bars. After his release, he became a businessman, dabbling in everything from being a boxing promoter to owning a night club. None of these schemes worked until he began the Liberation Front, where his temperament and nature were perfect for the leadership role he assumed. "We welcome Grace to the fold," his booming baritone rang out as she entered the great hall for the first time. Then he wrapped his meaty arms around her, almost smothering her in his folds of belly fat.

"He smelled like a fat man, and I didn't like his gold teeth," Grace continued. "I looked around for Willie, but he was nowhere to be seen. That's when I began to feel just a little uneasy."

They had breakfast. The men ate first, with the women serving, and then the women ate, after the men finished. She realized immediately that this wasn't a true democracy; the emphasis was on male sovereignty.

"The entire thing was supposedly designed to counteract years of cultural indoctrination allegedly imposed by the white man upon slaves. Bottom line, I wasn't going to fit."

The women and the men were then given their work assignments for the day. The organization dabbled in many industries to provide an income. Some worked in the small restaurant that was located on the ground floor of the family building. People came from miles around to purchase the vegetarian cuisine and specialty pastries they sold. When Grace was given a tour, she saw Willie's influence immediately. They had adopted a modified version of the idea he'd shared with her years ago. The menu contained "suggested" prices for their entrées. "We've never had anyone pay less than the suggested price, and in most cases, our patrons pay more," Grace's guide told her. "That way, we can provide a limited number of free meals."

Grace smiled knowingly, wishing Hatta Mae could see Willie's idea at work.

Several floors up in the women's building, they operated a school. It ranged from preschool through elementary grades, with an emphasis on black culture and achievement. The school originally started for the children of group members, but other neighborhood children were eventually enrolled. Those parents who could afford it paid a small fee, while other funds were obtained through a government grant. Now, they accommodated over five hundred children on a daily basis, 150 of whom were members of the group.

Willie worked as the restaurant manager, which came as no surprise to Grace, but he was missing all day, and she was disappointed. She wanted to model her new wardrobe for him. His absence created no anxiety among the group, however, so Grace didn't ask any questions. She was put to work at the school in an entry-level position until she could become a trusted member. Then she would be allowed to move into a position with more responsibility. With her educational background, even though she didn't have her degree, it wouldn't take her long to work her way up into a teaching position. She could never become the principal, however. That position would always be occupied by one of the men.

Group members earned no salary and had to contribute any outside earnings to the general welfare fund. They lived in the housing complex and received sustenance, so all funds received were used to maintain the complexes and purchase food and other needs. The all-male council controlled spending. Women were not privy to their activities and received no accounting reports. Any who dared to ask were summarily rebuffed and told that as long as the hunter provided for his tribe, he didn't have to reveal anything.

"Brother Martin saw this as the perfect society. Everyone was equal with everyone else. He boasted about how we had achieved the ideal civilization; a utopian world, he called it. Not even the Soviet Union could sustain this concept," said Grace, her voice growing agitated.

"Suppose you wanted to go to a movie or do something else?" said Sardis, thinking of her own situation.

"That wasn't allowed. There was no such thing as individual desires," said Grace, her voice little more than a whisper. "That's what started the problems between Willie and me. I felt trapped."

By the end of her first long day, Grace was tired and desperately wanted to see Willie, but no one would tell her anything about his whereabouts. Everyone was pleasant and kind to her, but she felt desperately alone. Dinner time came, and once again the women went, zombie-like, through the same ritual of providing service to the men and then finally eating themselves. It was a large group. In addition to the children, there were at least two hundred and fifty men, and over twice as many women, nearly a thousand people in all.

The large dining hall on the ground floor of the women's building easily seated all of the men at the same time, but the women had to eat in shifts. After they'd eaten, the men would assemble next door in what was once the main church sanctuary, while the women would clean the dining area. Upon completing that task, everyone would then squeeze into the meeting hall, which had originally been designed to hold a thousand people. The children often sat on their parents' laps, allowing all the adults to be comfortably seated, which was welcome, because the meeting could last for hours, depending on Brother Martin's mood. On most evenings, he would report on the day's activities and only give them the news from outside sources he considered important for them to know. Television and radios were banned. It was the only time family groups could assemble together outside of their private quarters, and they occupied the front rows. The ratio of men to women meant there were very few unattached men, but the few they had sat in a row together right behind the family groups. Grace sat in the middle row of the sea of white-clad women who were consigned to the rear of the auditorium. Following the assembly, the women would return to the food service area and check whether they had any duties, which were allocated on a rotational basis, assigned for the evening. Some would be required to make preparations for the next day's meals, which were always simple dishes based on poultry, vegetables, or fish. Red meat was banned. Apart from the rotund Brother Martin, the strict diet agreed with the members. Grace suspected he didn't practice the messages he preached to his members. He ate privately in his quarters on the top floor of the family building, and his meals were prepared in his apartment kitchen by carefully selected cadre. Those duties were not rotated.

The other women dispersed down the hall into converted apartments that were now used as smaller meeting rooms, where they would tend to the children or sew, knit, and do other crafts. Some of their handiworks were sold, while others were used in-house to replace worn items. The thought of doing needlework rattled the maladroit Grace, whose lack of skills with her hands belied her name. Willie eased her fears by assuring her that the other women would teach her.

The men usually remained in the sanctuary, but this evening's activity deviated from the normal course. One of the brothers appeared at the dining room door and beckoned to one of the sisters to speak with him. When she returned, she stopped at the table where Grace was working with the group that was planning the coming week's menu. "It's time, Grace. You're to become one with us." The four women who served as her welcoming committee that morning now surrounded her, holding lit candles as they escorted her out of the dining room and down the long, dim hallway. This processional took Grace back to the Hell Week sorority initiations at State. She wanted nothing to do with sororities then, and she didn't want to undergo any strange rituals now. Before she could object, however, they ushered her into an apartment at the end of the hallway.

It was a larger, far more elaborately furnished room than the one she stayed in the previous night, and featured a majestic brass bed. They quickly removed her clothing and replaced her garments with a beautiful white satin nightgown. Then they led her to the bed, placed their candles at each of the four corners, and turned off the lights. No words passed between anyone, and their serene, expressionless faces provided no clues or answers. Once Grace was placed on the bed, the women departed, the last one blowing out three of the four candles as she left the room.

The remaining candle was at the foot of the bed, and of all the crazy things that might have crossed her mind, she now lay mesmerized by the solidly secured wax object, hoping it wouldn't start a fire. Her eyes scanned the room, while her mind tried to process what all of this meant. Her ears reverberated with the sound of her own breathing, her heartbeat drowned out the noises of the night, and her sweat glands went into overdrive, drenching the satin gown all the way down to her toes. She lay on the bed as stiff as a board, too afraid to tremble. Her ears picked up the sound of a door quietly opening and closing. It wasn't the door leading to the hallway, through which the women had disappeared, but one that was behind her. The thick shag carpet muffled approaching footsteps, but when she tilted her head slightly upward toward the sound, she recognized the massive frame that had entered the room, and saw the gold teeth glistening in the candlelight.

Brother Martin stood at the foot of the bed stark naked. Grace's eyes widened to the size of saucers, and the candlelight caught the shimmer of tears as they began to form. "Don't be afraid," he whispered. His voice was soothing, yet commanding.

So this is how the women become one with the group, she thought. She turned her head away, not wanting to witness the inevitable.

Brother Martin continued to speak in soothing, nonthreatening tones, but his words jabbed like a boxer's blows. "Don't turn away from me. If you want your precious Willie, you have to become one with me first." Then, he answered the question that had been on her mind all day. "Willie has been in isolation, preparing himself for his bride. You won't see each other again until the ceremony. He's cleansing himself internally, which is another ritual. Some of our men are staying with him. They have to watch him, because he has to fast. The only nourishment he's allowed is my secret elixir." He moved to the side of the bed and ran his hand slowly up and down her thigh. "I trust that you have also partaken of my elixir. It frees the mind, but binds the soul."

Elixir? she thought. That must be that milk-like stuff she tossed every chance she got. She determined right then and there she wouldn't drink it under any circumstance. Her eyes followed his movements around the small candlelit space.

Positioning himself at the foot of the bed once again, he continued with his diatribe. "Tomorrow, you will have Willie, but tonight, you will be my bride," he announced. He then took the candle and held it close to her face. She recoiled in fear as he smiled his golden smile. "Another thing. This little ritual will never be spoken of to anyone. Not another living soul. If it gets back to my ears, and it will, your husband-to-be will pay a dear price." He blew out the last candle, and the room was plunged into darkness, along with Grace's mind, her mood, and her spirit.

The next day, Brother Martin proudly announced that she had become one with the group. "Henceforth, she will be known as Sister Grace!" he boomed, like a conquering warrior. The crowd roared in celebration. She had to dig deep to fake a convincing expression of joy. She looked earnestly at the women's faces for the first time. They had no light in their eyes, and all wore the same serene, expressionless stare. They avoided eye contact with her because they all shared the same dark secret of which they dared not speak. Grace wondered if the men were aware of how the women became one with the group, if they even cared. She wanted to know how the men become one with the group but didn't want to risk finding out. Too many questions could lead to disciplinary action and would alert Brother Martin to her acts of rebellion by not drinking the elixir. All that day, regular activities proceeded as usual, but once the evening meal had concluded, the hall was quickly cleared, and a festive air replaced the normally somber mood. Once again, as they had done the previous evening, the four women surrounded Grace. *Now what?* she thought as they whisked her off to yet another room. This time, however, they helped her change into a beautiful white gown, topped with a veil, which covered her head and face.

In Sardis's den, the game stopped abruptly. "Wait a minute," said both Dorcus and Sardis simultaneously. "Don't tell me; you were getting married!" Dorcus continued, her voice revealing her incredulity.

Grace shook her head. "I was a bride. I never had a chance to say one thing about any of it," she said, taking another trick.

Once she was dressed, her four maidens walked her through another connecting door that led to the front of the sanctuary, which she entered to a chorus of oohs and ahs. Music was banned, being considered too European. Instead, the sound of an African drum could be heard in the distance, and the bride entered the hall to its rhythmic beat. As she stood in front of the sanctuary, facing a makeshift altar covered with Zebra-print cloth, the back door opened and the groom marched down the aisle to the same drumbeat. The warrior arrived to claim his bride. This was the first time Willie was seen in two days, and it looked like he was in a coma. His gait was shaky, and two of the brothers walked alongside him, ready to provide support if he needed it. Grace wanted to turn around and take in the spectacle, but her maidens would not allow it. "You will see your warrior prince when he arrives at your side," one admonished. However, she wasn't prepared for what she saw when he finally arrived. Willie was dressed in the traditional dark suit, but there was a fake leopard skin draped over the suit, and he was as unsteady on his feet as a man who'd rushed directly from a wild bachelor party. The four maidens and two warrior escorts, as they were called, stepped aside, leaving the bride and groom standing together before the high priest, Brother Martin.

Grace could see out through the veil, but the startled look on her face remained concealed. Suddenly, she wondered if she really wanted to marry this man. His eyes were dim and bloodshot, and his cheeks were sunken. He was clearly under the influence of something and looked like a man attending his own wake, not his wedding. When he reached over and took her hand, she could feel his hand was cold and clammy, but now her touch began to produce a noticeable change. Before her eyes, it was clear that he was drawing on her strength.

Brother Martin began the three-hour ceremony by reading from a ritual book, claiming that every sacrament was derived directly from the Motherland. At the end, he placed a homemade broom on the floor, which the couple jumped over. The ceremony itself was the only celebration. There was no reception afterward. The newly married couple was assigned an apartment in the family building, and the brothers helped move the groom out of his single place, while the bride's meager belongings were carried by the sisters. Their new life as husband and wife had begun.

XXXI

"I think that's horrible!" cried Sardis, before remembering her slumbering mother and lowering her voice. "And to think that you didn't even have the chance to give yourself to your husband first. Instead, you had to sleep with a complete stranger!"

Grace smiled slyly at her two friends. "Well, I wouldn't say that. Willie and I knew each other quite well by then. Mama couldn't watch us *every* hour of the day. I was just careful not to get pregnant, that's all. I told you, Michele Alley kept a lot of secrets. A *lot* of secrets."

"Well, at least I got a ring," Dorcus chimed in.

"We know, we know," the other two responded in unison.

Then, turning to Sardis, Grace asked, "Didn't you get one too? I wasn't around, but I seemed to recall hearing rumors on the proverbial grapevine."

"You guys are really digging deep tonight," said Sardis, pretending to concentrate on her card. She didn't want to yield to their curiosity, so she remained silent, hoping that someone else would chime in and create a distraction. None was forthcoming and so, with a deep sigh, she took up her narrative again.

XXXII

"Expelled for a year!" screeched Cyrus, jumping up out of his office chair, arms flailing theatrically. "How can they do that?"

A solemn, repentant J. B. sat slumped in the small office with his head bowed, his folded hands hanging down between his legs, looking for all the world like a wounded puppy. "I broke the rules and got caught," was all he could offer to his friend and mentor.

"Couldn't you *lie?* Tell them you were taking her to see her injured friend, or a sick relative or something? You're an actor! Why didn't you get into a character?"

"We were kissing, and I had my hand in a … how can I put this delicately … a compromising place. And I'd borrowed this guy's car, and as a junior, I didn't seek permission to go off campus. And …"

"Rules, smules! There are way too many! No wonder the students rebelled and boycotted." Cyrus rubbed the furrow that had replaced his forehead as he paced around and around in his tiny office, thinking hard. His head throbbed as he tried to figure out what to do next. He prepared himself to lose his female star, and had already begun grooming a freshman and a sophomore to step into her demanding roles, but he thought he would have his male star for at least one more year. The more critical task, however, was ensuring that J. B. wouldn't lose any of his skills by being inactive for an entire year. "Look," he said, calming down now after he assessed the situation and determined a solution. "Let me see if I can get you some real-world experience. A year is a long time. Maybe this was a good move. If not, we'll turn it into one." The more he spoke, the better his idea jelled. "I have a friend in England who's a theatrical agent. I already called him to see if he could take Sard on as a client. Maybe I can tag team the two of you as a couple." J. B. raised his head and smiled. "After all, marriage is what you had in mind, no?" Cyrus added, with a wink.

J. B. thanked his friend and raced out of the office and out of the building, making a beeline for Earle Hall. "She has to say yes, she just gotta say yes," he chanted, like a mantra, to keep his confidence up.

Sardis paused abruptly. Her faraway expression and lilting smile revealed she was reliving one of the most exciting and memorable days of her life. The two women waited anxiously for her to continue. She still had a flair for the dramatic. Finally, Grace, unable to contain her curiosity any longer blurted out, "Will you get on with it!"

Sardis motioned for her to keep her voice down and listened carefully, anticipating her mother's intervention at any minute, but all remained silent. "I said yes," she said, grinning from ear to ear. "I told him yes."

XXXIII

There, I can move my arm a little, Taletha thought, feeling a sense of accomplishment.

They can't see it yet, but that arm moved all the way from the edge of the bed to my side. My toes are cold. It's the first time I've felt cold. They tingle a little bit, too. Now, if only I could make them move and make my mouth talk to them. Taletha continued to struggle, but all her efforts proved useless. As a result of the stroke brought on by the beating, she suffered a severe loss of her motor functions.

"Who gonna pay fo' all dis?" her distraught parents continued to ask, over and over again. With no one assuming liability, they received answers from nowhere. Their pastor, along with the head of the local NAACP, was actively seeking assistance for the poverty-stricken family. They followed up rumor after rumor and attended hearing after hearing until eventually, they were exhausted.

"I still think they're planning to provide some money to the injured and to those boys' families to bury the dead. The civil rights groups are trying to get it to Washington," they said, but they soon discovered Washington began to distance itself from all knowledge of the incident. Southern politicians were very powerful men. At one point, the state legislature had, in order to restore racial harmony, proposed a small monetary stipend, but then had second thoughts; thus, the proposal died.

"The only hope we have now is to get someone to accept the blame," civil rights officials told them. "If that happens, then maybe we can get somebody to act on behalf of the students and make them pay."

Taletha, who was lying in the outer bedroom, heard the conversation, and tried to guess the identities of everyone in the living room. They were all talking about her, but none of them realized she could hear and understand every single word. She wanted to respond but couldn't, so now an overwhelming sense of grief enveloped her, but tears of comfort wouldn't fall. She felt like a grenade with a stuck firing pin. Oh, if only someone would just release the pressure.

XXXIV

"He's in Vietnam," a weeping Dorcus told a beaming Sardis when she entered their dorm room. She stopped abruptly, glanced at the ring Sardis sported on her left hand, and gasped. Sardis, feeling total guilt at her own good fortune, reacted with despair at the news Dorcus just relayed. This posed a major dilemma for the two friends; one had gotten the man of her dreams, while the other, now shrouded in a mixture of disappointment and anger, wept at the possibility of losing hers permanently. They hugged each other, and soon the room was awash in tears of gladness, joy, sadness, and anger, all intermingled. Neither knew which emotion dominated.

"When did this happen?" said Dorcus, grabbing Sardis's hand to get a better look at the sparkler that sat gleaming on her long, slender, light-skinned finger.

"He asked while you were at Ft. Jackson, but I just got the ring," said Sardis. "When did Anton contact you about his assignment?"

Dorcus fell silent before responding. "He didn't," she replied, releasing Sardis's hand. The ring flashed for an instant in the sunlight, teasing her, taunting her. His lack of concern churned her stomach. "He should have told me, but he didn't." She quaked at the thought. "You would think it would have been important enough … unless he didn't want me to worry." Before she could embarrass herself with the explanation of how she learned about Anton's assignment, the room

280

filled with well-wishers who greeted Sardis with hugs. This same outcast freshman girl had now become the toast of the senior class.

"Welcome to the ring club," several chanted, displaying and comparing newly acquired ornaments of their own. Meanwhile, Dorcus slipped unnoticed out of the room and down the hall. Picking up the telephone, she dialed a familiar number. *I will have my ring, too,* she vowed, as she waited for Charlie to pick up.

XXXV

State was settling into a new normalcy when the restoration process was disrupted on April 4, 1968. News reached the campus that Nobel Prize winner, Dr. Martin Luther King Jr., the architect of and principal advocate for the civil rights nonviolence movement, was assassinated. The irony was not lost on anyone that the man of peace was taken by violence.

State remained calm and peaceful as students mourned his death, along with the rest of the nation. The passing of such an icon of the civil rights movement overshadowed the deaths of the three State students. Alas, while Martin Luther King's place in history became secure, the place of three others in that same linear history faded into oblivion. At the news of Dr. King's death, most people decided to honor his legacy by holding prayer vigils and peaceful candlelight marches. However, riots broke out in some of the major cities. Chicago, Detroit, and Washington DC erupted, and so did New York's Harlem.

A month passed since Grace arrived in New York, and she had survived, if being confined to three buildings could be called survival. Fortunately, the systematic routine and relative stability provided by the Liberation Front helped her to slowly emerge from her psychosis. She loved Willie, and his emotional support helped to strengthen her, enabling her to overcome her guilt. He made her understand she hadn't injured her friends in any manner. According to his reasoning, her guilt was tied to a segregationist system that had enslaved her subconscious. It created victims by giving them a sense of inferiority, and then convinced those same victims that they perpetuated their own status. "Jim Crow laws held our people in bondage, yet when the shackles were removed through an act of insurrection, you were convinced you had done something wrong, especially when all that guilt was thrown back at the students," he told her. "Gracie, the only thing you and the other students were guilty of was taking a stand and making the establishment listen. You all forced them to the point where they had to release you from bondage. Blood, innocent blood, had to be spilled for that to happen, but you were not the responsible one."

Day by day, his ideology seeped through to Grace. She admired his strength, his leadership, and his knowledge, but she didn't like the culture of male dominance espoused by the Liberation Front. She was growing increasingly unhappy, a sure sign that the old Grace was returning. Her fragile state of mind had led her into this, and now her increased sense of herself began to tell her she needed to get out. That, however, was far easier said than done. As the newest convert, she was at the bottom of the hierarchy. Socialism may have aspired to a classless society, but there were still dues to pay. She wanted to work in the restaurant, and team up with Willie, but she was assigned to kitchen duties for the compound, serving the men at every meal, cleaning the dining hall, and washing hundreds of dishes, all performed without modern conveniences like automatic dishwashers.

Since she had almost completed her college degree, she was placed in a classroom as a teacher's helper, in preparation for taking on a class of her own. She found this task pleasant, but she had to read extensively to catch up on her knowledge of black history and achievements. Even the fourth-grade class where she worked knew more than she did. Between her daytime activity in the classroom, studying, and her duties in the compound, the Liberation Front became her whole life, but eventually she healed to the point where she now became homesick. She wanted desperately to contact her mother, and also her bid whist buddies, to let them know she was well. Communication with the outside, however, was only allowed by a very few. The only available telephone was in Brother Martin's apartment, a discovery Grace made by accident. Her curiosity led her to the "forbidden floor" where he lived, and she heard it ringing before the guards saw her and banished her with a warning. New members were allowed one infraction without punishment. Another rule stated that women had to obtain permission to contact outsiders. Married women had to obtain the permission of their husbands, who in turn had to seek Brother Martin's approval, while the host of single women had to apply directly to the leader himself.

Brother Martin ruled with absolute authority, and no one dared attempt anything without his authorization. He built the organization based upon the rules of socialism espoused by many emerging African nations, and while some viewed it as dictatorship, he insisted it was a new type of democracy. As those nations emerged from colonial rule, they decided to extricate themselves from any semblance of prior authority, and since most had been made to adhere to capitalist philosophy, they decided to sever all ties with capitalism. In their haste to replace old structures, many failed to put in place structurally sound governments, and thus by default many adopted a hybrid of socialism mixed with hefty doses of communism. A ruling body was quickly thrown into place with one man as either the head or figurehead, and a new government model was born. Brother Martin liked their ideas. If it was good enough for Africa, it was good enough for him.

He was well read and began to mold his utopian world after becoming familiar with some of the philosophies espoused by Karl Marx and Friedrich Engels. Their widely read books, *Das Kapital* and *The Communist Manifesto,* served as the foundation for most of the Soviet Socialist bloc. They argued that a medieval feudal system continued to produce social class levels that impacted the status of modern man. Brother Martin saw the credibility of their beliefs and applied their philosophy to the black man's struggle in America, claiming that it went beyond race. In hammering his propositions to potential followers, he would conclude his booming oratory with a final selling point reflecting this premise.

"The United States has more than three classes of people. There is the upper class, the middle class, the lower class, and the Afro class. We got no class, and that is what keeps the black man in his place. We had no voice in how to build our society. We were kicked off the plantations once the white man had no further use for us, and we have been on the outside looking in ever since, trying to figure out where we fit or if we fit. Join with me, and we will *all* have a place. We will build a new society, a black society based on our own principles."

At this point, he would unfurl the flag he designed and wave it boldly above the heads of onlookers, who were generally on their feet by now offering thunderous applause, and thus more converts entered the fold. He also believed in the teachings espoused by the existentialist philosophies of Jean-Paul Sartre and Albert Camus. They considered themselves the center of their own universe and thus declared that God was dead. This enabled Brother Martin to fashion his new world around himself and to make a complete break with the established religions of the day. He also dismissed the institution of conventional marriage as being an unnatural state, following the teachings of his adopted mentor, Sartre.

In the short time that Grace had been with the group, she discovered that Brother Martin practiced this last philosophical dictate with reckless abandon. The Front, in spite of their male-dominated views, gave its female followers a sense of belonging. At the same time, it gave Brother Martin and many of the other brothers a sense of entitlement. Following the indoctrination ceremony, Grace kept her distance from Brother Martin, but she couldn't distance herself from the other men and found herself turning down whispered propositions at every meal. The white garments were supposed to symbolize female purity, but wandering hands continually found their way up her thighs and across her butt and belly. She also heard rumors about underground caverns connecting each building, the location of the entrances to which only the men were privy. She suspected that one was behind the door leading from the massive room where her initiation ceremony had taken place. This was the means by which Brother Martin had entered, and it was the way he departed. Other entrances were hidden within the family building, all leading directly to the floors in the building occupied by the single women. Any man had access. Grace wondered if Willie had ever taken advantage of this "perk," although she was sure that, since their ceremony, he had been faithful to her.

As the architect and supreme ruler of the Liberation Front, Brother Martin dictated everything, at times making up new rules on a whim. If a member could not accept his dominance, he or she would be subjected to punishment, the form of which was never disclosed. Fortunately, discipline was never necessary. The men were satisfied; why shouldn't they be? As for the women, they had chosen to be there, or had they? Grace was formulating a theory. She hoped she was wrong, but first-hand observations seldom lie.

Grace faced a dilemma, and she feared the other women faced the same problem. She was there because the man she loved was happy there. She suspected, however, that other women were there against their will. They could never confide in one another, especially about their shared initiation secret, because no one knew who they could trust. Her suspicious mind became a massive thorn in Brother Martin's side. She lived with the fear of his possible awareness that she was not under the mind-numbing control induced by his concoction. Her clear-eyed stare at the evening meetings was sometimes met with a look of derision, or so she thought. She was also an outsider, the only woman in the compound with southern roots and a college education. It made her different, hard to fit in. She could bolt at any time and run to the authorities. She sensed that Brother Martin was keenly aware of her thoughts and suspicions. She wondered what secrets Willie withheld, but with Brother Martin's threats still ringing in her ears, she didn't want to take any chances by asking him.

The group believed in family, just not the white man's confining concept of marriage. Brother Martin's redefinition of this institution was another major selling point that touched the souls of reluctant men. "Slavery stripped us of the dignity of family bonding, so every man will have a woman, or maybe more, with whom he can create his nest."

He never called his philosophy polygamy. "It's community bonding. If a man is satisfied with one woman, he can keep her. If he wants more than one, he can arrange it. If he gets tired of the first one and wants to exchange, he has complete freedom to do so." And he meant just that. This concept of marriage also proved to be an attractive feature for some of the women. The raging Vietnam conflict siphoned off thousands of black men. Cultural changes and growing drug abuse claimed many more. A biased judicial system subjected still more to a life among the prison under-class. All these factors forced black women into accepting new realities, and more and more faced a life without even a prayer of ever obtaining a spouse. Brother Martin and his followers preyed on those fears. Thus, whenever a new, unattached man joined the group, he was immediately paired up with one of the single women. The man could choose; however, the woman could not. They also made sure that the rest of the sisterhood wasn't lonely, as evidenced by a rising pregnancy rate. Producing children was encouraged, and children borne by these women were raised by the entire group with the goal of them becoming future soldiers and leaders for the revolution that was sure to come.

Grace listened to the daily lectures, which in essence were mind control, but she couldn't buy into the concepts. She began to question whether women remained there out of loyalty or whether there was something more sinister binding them to the group. That was only one of many questions she bombarded Willie with every evening during their time alone in their apartment. She began by questioning the legality of their marriage. "Does Brother Martin have the authority to conduct weddings?" she asked. They had no license, no ring, nothing that said they were husband and wife, and she wasn't even allowed to mention it for fear of being reprimanded. "I don't want this. This is the same common-law relationship my sister has. We're no different from them, as far as the law is concerned," she said to Willie shortly after their ceremony.

"Grace, I love you. I love you with all my being," he replied. "I don't need the law to tell me to love you. Brother Martin said that marriage is just a piece of paper to prove that a man loves a woman. Who needs that piece of paper?"

"We do!" she replied. "We do!" She had no freedom, not even to come and go as she pleased, and now she wondered how they would manage to leave the group if they ever wanted to go. "We don't have any assurances that this thing is going to last; how are we going to get hold of our earnings if we leave?" Willie had no answers that would satisfy her. "I'm not happy here," she wailed, beginning to cry. "We live in a commune with little or no privacy. We have no say over our destiny. Brother Martin is a bully, no better than a despot. He needs us, we don't need him, but he makes us believe that we can't exist without him." Her tears usually persuaded Willie to do her bidding, but this time he was reluctant to cave in to her demands.

"Give it a chance," he responded, a tone of authority in his voice. "I was skeptical and had a lot of questions when I came here, but I've been a part of building this society and making it work. Now, we're so far advanced in our inner world that society is trying to catch up with us. We provide free meals to the neighborhood children, we have a medical facility that provides free care, and now the government is thinking about doing the same thing. We're above the law. This is our home, and this is where we're staying," he said, stabbing at the air while walking back and forth to accentuate his points. He stopped directly in front of Grace, who was slumped on the sofa, her head hanging in defeat.

Dropping to his knees, he gazed into her eyes, and after gently cupping her face in his hands, he began to kiss her tears away. She knew she'd lost this battle. The first time he did that, she gave herself to him. The second time he did it, he convinced her to join him in New York. Now, she closed her eyes in surrender to his decision. She loved this man, and he loved this make-believe world that they surrounded themselves with. Her resolve melted, but questions remained. In time, she knew she would receive answers, one way or another.

XXXVI

Taletha stared at the images flickering across the screen of the small black–and-white television set. Television was a denied luxury, because her mother thought it would be too upsetting, but now it appeared to be having the opposite effect.

The family gathered to receive all of the news surrounding Dr. King's assassination, and as riots began to unfold around the nation, it filtered into living rooms across the country, including Edisto Island. Enraged faces appeared, and police batons delivered crushing blows. Taletha watched with growing familiarity as internal images entered her mind; uniforms, helmets, snarling, hateful faces, and batons administering blow after blow. At this point, everything usually faded to black, as selective amnesia intervened. This time, however, the picture became clearer and clearer. As she sat propped up on mounds of pillows, Taletha's mind finally awoke to her fate on that dreadful night in Orangeburg. Her awakened mind transported her back to the scene, and the memories came flooding back. She now knew and was fully conscious about everything; her mind carefully processed the beating she took. The picture did not fade out this time, and it gave her a clear vision. She felt trapped in an emaciated body she barely recognized. As reality dawned, she discovered that her legs and arms no longer did her bidding. All of the accolades from family and friends about her education rang hollow in her ears. Wild eyes searched the room, hoping to pull someone's attention away from the mesmerizing blue/black screen. She tried with all of her being to call out, make a sound, a cry, anything, but what resounded in her ears could only be described as a gurgle at best. She had finally awoken from her internal slumber, but no one would ever know.

XXXVII

The walls had ears, and Brother Martin soon knew he would have to deal with Grace and her cancerous suspicions. From the very beginning, he knew he would need insurance to keep the flock devoted to the cause. Blistering rhetoric and youthful idealism were never enough to induce unwavering long-term loyalty to any cause, especially one mandating major lifestyle changes. Thus, the magic elixir was born. Only Brother Martin knew its formula, its purpose, and its effects. The members never knew or even suspected they were being sedated three times a day, every day. Like the snake oil salesman of the old West, he touted its properties, claiming that it cured everything. For their part, it gave them a feeling of well-being, so they believed in it, even welcomed it.

One day during the week following their confrontation, Willie arrived back at their apartment later than usual. "They know you aren't drinking the formula," he said as he walked into the front room. In one hand he held a glass, and in the other, he carried a jar with the formula. He poured the formula into the glass and placed it on the table in front of Grace. She took a deep breath and stared at the glass but refused to drink it.

"That's what's keeping all of the followers in their place, isn't it?" she said, casting a steely glare at him. There was an awkward silence, and then Willie picked up the glass and placed it in her hand.

"It's a natural cleanser," he said, as she took a small sip. "I lived on it for two whole days leading up to our vows."

Grace studied the liquid carefully. It had a milk-like consistency similar to condensed milk and was slightly sweet, but had a faintly bitter aftertaste that most people got used to after a while. It reminded Grace of the time her mother tricked her into taking a dose of castor oil by mixing it into diluted condensed milk. "I can't drink milk," she lied, setting the glass down on the table.

"It's designed especially for black people," said Willie. "Most of us can't digest milk. According to Brother Martin, none of us should drink milk. That's why he came up with this formula." Willie was trying his best to sell her on the idea. He picked up the glass again and handed it back to her. "It's designed to add years to your life; make you the strong, African, free-born person you were meant to be, keep you from catching any disease that is spewing out the gutters and being spread by city rats. Ask any of the sisters and brothers here. They'll attest that no one has even had the sniffles."

Grace knew from Willie's pleading tone he was being pressured. She knew if she didn't cooperate, he might be harmed. With a deep sigh, she took the glass and took a sip, smiled at him seductively, and raised the glass to her pursed lips once more. As she pretended to drink, he walked into the bedroom, satisfied he had done his job. As soon as he was gone, Grace raced into the bathroom and poured the accursed drink down the sink, being careful to leave no traces. "Not bad," she said, placing the empty glass on the table with a flourish as he rejoined her. Thus began a new ritual. She knew someone would always be watching to make sure she drank the stuff. Before, she simply poured it down the drain, or into the glasses of those around her, but now, she had to devise new ways to disguise her refusal to drink the vile liquid. In addition, she had to remember to maintain the vacant-eyed look and contented stare shared by the other members.

Grace's refusal to drink the substance kept her mind sharp. Another by-product of Brother Martin's elixir that made it magical was it contained properties that made them not only compliant but addicted. The more they drank, the more they craved it daily, and the less likely they were to object to Brother Martin's authority. He could have declared the sky was orange and they would accept it unequivocally as fact.

Grace saw right through him, because she was the only member with any knowledge of his philosophy. Existentialist theories were part of the English curriculum during her freshman year at State. These strange new concepts caused no end of internal conflict and turmoil and had greatly confused her, because in the black church, preachers hammered home a theology telling her she wasn't the center of her own universe; God was. She hadn't been prepared to kill God or strip Him from her life. Eventually, however, she began to examine the existentialist philosophy and adopt tenets of it that suited her purpose. In reality, a serious lack of discipline proved to be her undoing.

She simply did not want to get out of her warm bed early one Sunday morning. Dorcus, who was her alarm clock on Sundays when she didn't have cafeteria duty, would knock on Grace's door before her regular breakfast rendezvous with Charlie. Following breakfast, she would routinely return to the dorm to collect a now fully dressed but still half-asleep Grace and walk to the nearest congregation, sometimes with Charlie in tow. One morning, however, Dorcus's attempts to rouse Grace were met with a harsh, "Go away! I don't need that stuff anymore! I am my own person!"

She never made another visit inside a church. She missed it, but pride kept her from returning. Now, here she was being confronted once again by all those theories and ideas. This time, they didn't look anywhere near as inviting, especially since it was against her will. She invented clever and creative ways to avoid drinking the magic formula. Her refusal was putting her at risk, because she found it increasingly difficult to hide her displeasure with the group. She began to wonder whether or not it would be beneficial for her to dope herself with the stuff just so she wouldn't have to deal with the reality of her unhappiness. She never got the chance to test her theory, however, because the news of Dr. King's assassination reached the compound, and their previously controlled world was suddenly thrown into utter chaos. Everyone was called into the large meeting hall to give them the information. Brother Martin wore a grave look of concern that he normally kept hidden whenever women were present.

"I heard rioting is breaking out in some major cities," he told them grimly. "If it happens here, brothers, you know what we have to do." Grace surveyed the room as he spoke. All the brothers' heads nodded in unison, while the women sat frozen. In the few moments it took Grace to complete her observations, Brother Martin disappeared. As on the night of their tryst, she hadn't seen him leave. Two of the temple guards now stood on either side of the platform. They gave a signal, and the men sprang into action. Willie took Grace by the arm, and they, along with the other married couples, practically sprinted back to their apartments, while the single men escorted all the single women back to their building.

The reactions of the men versus those of the women confirmed Grace's theory. She was determined to get answers, and the moment she and Willie closed their apartment door, she flew into a rage. "The stuff the women drink is different from what the men are given, isn't it!" Willie did not reply. "Did you know about this?" she demanded. Still, Willie made no comment. "Why? The women were drugged in order to force them to stay, weren't they?" He tried to ignore her questions, and went about boarding up windows in preparation for what might become a very long night, but she was relentless. "That's how the men managed to take liberties with whomever they desired, isn't it? That's the only reason the women remained complacent and compliant, isn't it? Well?" Suddenly, Willie reached down and grabbed a shotgun from its well concealed hiding place beneath the floorboards. Grace recoiled in shock as he momentarily pointed the barrel in her direction. For a split second, she thought she might have pushed him over the edge.

"Please, Grace," he pleaded with surprising calm, as he moved toward the door. "We may have to defend our way of life, our very existence, against who knows what? The police, who are supposed to be protecting us; rioting hordes of brothers and sisters, who we don't want to hurt. I need you on my side tonight. Tomorrow, we'll talk."

Then it began. Breaking glass, screaming women, and yelling men confirmed their worst fears. Buildings were torched all around them, even black-owned businesses. The violence spared nothing. Wailing sirens and gunshots filled the air. For Grace, February 8 returned, and she retreated wide-eyed to the farthest corner of the bedroom. She assumed a defensive tactic she used ever since she was a little girl. She slid down the wall onto the floor, hugged her knees, and began rocking back and forth. Terror held her firmly in its grasp. The hallway filled with men running everywhere. "Get the women to safety," a voice ordered. She didn't know who gave the order, but it wasn't Brother Martin's voice. No one had seen or heard from him since the assembly. She expected Willie to reappear at any minute to rescue her, but when he didn't, she began to cry. Suddenly, the building plunged into darkness, and heavy, black smoke drifted upward. Grace's eyes began to sting, and she coughed violently as her lungs filled with the pungent fumes, but she was unable to overcome her panic and dash to safety.

Their apartment was located on the third floor, directly above the restaurant, and she heard frantic activity beneath her as Willie and the rest of the men tried to protect their property, and enterprises, from attack. She heard voices trying to appeal to the marauders, but how do you appeal to mindless masses hell-bent on destruction? How do you reason with failures wanting to retaliate against the world that dealt them a losing hand? The Brotherhood of the Liberation Front tried to stand their ground in front of their building, where it should have been clear to any of the rioters that they were hurting their own people, but one street hooligan yelled, "This is nothing personal, brother! I'm sad and I'm mad. This is my revolution! I intend to burn, baby, burn. Then maybe somebody will do something for us!" With that, he tossed a flaming torch at the Liberation Front's building.

That philosophy might have made sense in his street world, but to the rest of the world, it was pure folly. Those who own nothing have nothing to lose, and those owning nothing at the beginning of the day invariably have pretty much most of that nothing left at the end of each day, and it makes them mad, but to make sure their poverty is shared equally makes no sense. "I got plenty of nothin', and nothin's plenty for me," proclaimed the lyrics from Porgy and Bess, but they were wrong. This mob, now painting their neighborhood in ashes and soot, had nothing, and now, sadly, they were accomplishing nothing.

An explosive device crashed into the living quarters on the second floor, and the fire spread rapidly. As hallways filled with smoke, Willie grabbed a flashlight and made his way back into the building, searching for Grace. He found her still curled up in the corner, immobilized by fear. After gently picking her up, he wrapped her in a blanket and carried her to the stairway that, moments ago, provided his entry. Now it was a raging inferno. Some of the men made valiant efforts to fight the flames, but were forced to give up as the fire spread rapidly from floor to floor. The only thing they could do was to clear a path to the fire escape at the end of the hallway.

Willie knew he had to persuade Grace to conquer her fears if they were going to survive this ordeal. He set her on her feet, and to his amazement, she began to respond to his instructions. He pushed her toward the window and told her to follow the other women as they grabbed onto the outside fire escape. Beneath them, crowds were growing larger, noisier, and angrier, and the street was in utter chaos. The scene of destruction was devastating. Building after building was set afire and people ran amok, their arms full of clothing and televisions. Every time a window shattered, new items hit the streets, borne by mobs of jeering, laughing men and women.

Fires raged all around them, but there were no signs of either law enforcement or firefighters. This attempted escape was threatening to place them in as much danger as the fires they fled. As Willie tried to coax her onto the iron structure, Grace grabbed him in a vice-like grip and refused to let go. He drew her back inside, while another couple raced past to take advantage of the open window. Willie thought for a moment and decided to put another plan into action. The fire had not yet reached the back of the building, so he grabbed Grace's hand and felt his way along the long hallway until he found the door he was looking for. When he opened it, they found themselves confronted by a maze. Grace's eyes widened as her hazy mind realized her suspicions of a hidden passageway were being confirmed. She was probably the first and last woman to have the privilege of seeing this place. It was a roughly hewn cave that gave the appearance it could have been dug by prisoners on an escape mission. As Willie's flashlight illuminated the tunnel, she saw branches leading everywhere.

She had no doubt Brother Martin made extensive use of this labyrinth, with its numerous exits. Carved arrows identified some of the paths, such as those leading to the women's quarters, and to the restaurant and the chapel, but many had no delineation. No doubt those were the ones leading to the initiation chamber, or to Brother Martin's quarters. "This way," said Willie urgently, grabbing Grace's hand. He chose the path marked women's quarters, and as they headed toward the single women's building, Grace wondered how many times Willie had trod this path on his own personal missions.

"Brother Martin told the men to meet in the cafeteria if anything happened to threaten the group. He'll give us further instructions when we get there." Just as Willie was speaking, a massive explosion rocked the cave, stopping them in their tracks. To Willie's dismay, debris now blocked their path.

"We have to find another route. I hope these walls hold up," he said, now quickening their pace. After several wrong turns, they finally reached their destination. Willie motioned for Grace to fall in behind him. He would exit first, and then she would emerge stealthily because, as she suspected, the tunnels were off limits to women.

As he opened the door to the cafeteria, however, Willie was struck by an eerie silence. He could hear the noise from the street, but the cafeteria, which should have been bustling with people preparing to receive instructions from their leader, was silent. Willie looked out into the room, and then immediately closed the door again in an effort to shield Grace from what he had just seen. In his haste, he dropped the flashlight, which Grace instantly retrieved. When she turned it on him, the beam of light revealed a man stricken by horror. "They're all dead," he murmured when he was finally able to speak. Holding his stomach, he stared at Grace with a look of utter terror before turning away from her and vomiting.

Grace, not believing what he said or what she just witnessed, had to see for herself, so before Willie could gather his wits and stop her, she lunged toward the half-open door and peered into the cafeteria, where a mass of bodies lay piled on top of one another. The women, in their angelic white garments, looked like foam skimming the ocean. Family groups, including children, lay with their arms around each other in a final embrace. She, too, was sickened by the sight, but had no time to react, because another powerful explosion sent loose stones and gravel raining down on her head.

With her husband immobilized, it was Grace who now took the lead, wrapping her arm around his waist and leading him down an unmarked path. Smoke found its way into the tunnels, and she knew time was running out. She had to find a way out. When she heard the walls creak, like a mine that was about to collapse, she prayed for the first time in a long time. Willie was staggering, gasping for air as an asthmatic attack seized his lungs. *It's been so long, I guess God didn't hear me,* Grace mused as she turned down one meandering path after another until, just as her resolve was about to give out, she saw the proverbial light literally illuminating a strip under an exit door at the end of a tunnel. She raced toward the door, half-dragging a limp Willie along with her, but when she opened the door, they came face-to-face with their leader. "You!" he shouted as they stumbled through the doorway. He stood petrified, like a man who'd been caught with his pants down. Before the shocked couple had a chance to react, they were seized by two men, who they immediately recognized as one half of Brother Martin's personal team of temple guards. The other two soon appeared from another tunnel, carrying boxes and suitcases, which quickly disappeared into the trunk and back seats of two very large, very black Cadillacs. The fresh air in the open garage soon revived Willie, and now both of them stared accusingly as Brother Martin gave his men last-minute orders. Then he addressed the couple. "The others should be well on their journey by now," he said, trying to recapture some of the reverential tones and mystique that made him the formidable leader the Front revered. Willie attempted to free himself from the guard's hold, but was unsuccessful. "Is that what you call mass suicide?" he said, through clenched teeth. "A journey? Was that the ultimate plan to save all of us?"

Brother Martin glanced at his watch, a very expensive timepiece that, up until now, remained hidden. The opulent suit and shoes he sported were also a far cry from the threadbare uniform dark suit, white shirt, and dark tie he and his followers usually wore. "So now you know," he said, dropping his act. "I don't have much time," he said, before adding sarcastically, "and neither do you." In response to his nod, one of the guards eased in behind the wheel of one of the cars.

"This night was perfect. I just didn't expect it to come so soon. Harlem was ripe for another riot, and Dr. King's murder was just the thing I needed to escape from this ..." He finished his sentence with a flourish of his meaty, bejeweled hand. "The final batch of the elixir gave them the peace they said they wanted. This time, instead of the regular sedative, I simply added a sedating element ..."

"Poison!" spat Grace.

Ignoring her outburst, he continued. "That would give them the eternal peace they sought. But then, you never drank the formula. Don't think I didn't know." He lumbered over to where they stood and came toe to toe with a sullen, regretful Willie like a drill sergeant conducting a final inspection. "Couldn't get your woman to obey, could you, Willie? It would have been so painless." He turned and walked to the passenger side of the second vehicle, where guard number two was stationed behind the wheel. Before easing himself into the seat, he half turned and made a farewell announcement. "The final explosion will go off at any time now. Fire will destroy the evidence, and the rioters will get the blame. A perfect plan to end this perfect world."

He issued final instructions to the two uneasy guards who were still holding the mortified couple tightly, and then lowered his massive frame into the passenger seat. Suddenly, the ground rumbled again, but this explosion was slightly different from the other two. It felt more like an earthquake pushing up from beneath the surface. At the same time, the two vehicles roared to life, the garage doors swung open and both cars exited into an alleyway and disappeared into the night.

Police reinforcements, including elements of the riot-trained tactical patrol force, finally arrived, and now Grace and Willie heard someone shouting orders to the unruly mob as riot police tried to regain order. Fire units tried to enter the area earlier but were held at bay by the mobs. Their noisy sirens signaled their belated arrival on the scene. They began working on the now totally engulfed Liberation Front Buildings when suddenly something went terribly wrong. A secret store of ammunition and gunpowder ignited. "Get back!" one of the policemen yelled. "They're shooting at us!" shouted another as they took up firing positions behind makeshift shelters.

The deafening noise served as a perfect foil. The gunfire outside the garage couldn't be distinguished from the gunfire taking place within. Suddenly, Grace felt Willie's hand go limp and watched in horror as he slumped to the ground. His spotless white shirt, the proud symbol representing a dream he wanted to share forever with his woman, his life, his love, turned red. As she knelt beside him, his face looked calm and worry free as he mouthed, "I love you," before slipping off on his journey.

Grace, knowing and now wanting to share his fate, braced herself. The guard raised his weapon and took aim, but just as he fired, there was another powerful quake beneath them. Realizing the peril they were in, the two guards bolted toward the still-open garage door just as the building collapsed around them, entombing the Liberation Front forever.

XXXVIII

"It was a good thing I was in the garage. When the building fell, the garage crumbled, but I wasn't crushed. I still have some souvenirs from that night." Grace said holding up her hair to reveal a permanent knot at the base of her scalp where a part of the structure fell on her. Then she hiked up her shirt and showed them the place where a bullet caught her in the abdomen. "A few more inches to the right, and it would have killed my baby."

Sardis passed the tissue box again, and Grace dabbed at her eyes, then gathering her senses, she continued. "The two security guards perished in a gun battle with the police. They found the bodies of the other two in the cars, which were left at the airport. Our great leader didn't want to share the group's wealth with anyone.

"He turned up in Africa, thinking he could live like a king, but the FBI was watching him for some time. They blocked all the funds he tried to transfer. His African benefactors had no further use for him once his cash reserves ran out, so he vanished. I hope he's enjoying his journey, wherever he is."

"And you had the baby?" asked Dorcus.

Grace's face brightened. "He looks just like his daddy." Sardis and Dorcus's minds filled with all sorts of scenarios. Grace read their thoughts and chuckled. "Don't worry, he's Willie Jr., and yes, he has his daddy's dark eyes and golden skin."

XXXIX

The power of the magic box called television brought every event directly into viewers' living rooms, and images of the jungles of Vietnam filled with sniper fire flickered across the screens on a nightly basis, but this evening they were displaced by jeering faces of unruly hoards occupying a place called Harlem. "Grace," was all Hatta Mae managed to say before she struggled to her feet and hobbled across the neat, narrow housing complex pathway to her elder daughter's townhouse. With government assistance, both relocated to a fairly new subdivision in the growing North Charleston area. Some of the downtown businesses also relocated into the area, and shopping malls arrived, bringing with them large chain stores and jobs.

Her daughter found work as a sales clerk for a large merchant, so she and her common-law husband finally made their relationship legal, just before he was whisked off to Vietnam. Their complex was located close to the Navy Yard, so Hatta Mae's husband found work at last as a cook at the base hospital. Her quality of life improved tremendously, but Grace caused her heart to ache greatly. "I don' kno' what is a goin' on wid ma baby," she cried as she entered her daughter's house.

They held each other tightly staring at the box. Michele Alley was gone, and so was the Judge. Urban renewal, or black displacement, swept through Duncan Street and scattered most of its residents to the winds. Mother and daughter heard that the Judge and his grateful wife left for North Carolina, leaving them with no way to contact Willie. All she could do was watch through tearful eyes as events unfolded.

XL

"Sardis!"

The sudden interjection from the room above startled the players and changed their mood. Sardis motioned for everyone to remain silent. Play suspended. Eartha was awake, and Sardis sprinted up the stairs to placate her fears. As demanding as ever, she wanted to know who was in her house, especially at such a late hour. "Get rid of them!" she ordered. Dorcus and Grace heard the exchange and waited patiently in silence for Sardis to return. They knew she needed support, and more importantly, she needed friends. They weren't leaving. With Eartha asleep again, Sardis returned to her friends, and their game continued for a few moments in silence. Then Sardis took them back to State's activities as their card game went on.

Graduation day, May 26, 1968, was rapidly approaching. The seniors thought they'd never see the day, and the two weeks leading up to the big event were filled with joyful anticipation. Campus was abuzz with excitement, tinged with lingering sadness. None of the three men who died would have been in the graduating class, but nonetheless, their untimely deaths continued to overshadow every activity. State's yearbook, *The Bulldog*, contained a remembrance, and the newly completed athletic facility was christened the Smith-Hammond-Middleton Gymnasium in their honor. The vacant field where state police detained students at gunpoint, shooting many as

304

they sat, became a makeshift memorial. Fresh flowers appeared on a regular basis, and everyone vowed to keep the memory alive.

J. B. completed his finals and now had to make critical decisions. He filled the long, empty days leading up to Sardis's graduation ceremony plotting out his future. Should he return to State after completing his one-year suspension? He was already older than most of the students, and once he returned, he would be even more mature and have more acting experience. But an acting career took energy and connections. Should he disrupt his new life by returning to academia? His biggest concern was that Sardis would no longer be on campus with him. Life without her would be no life at all. Thinking about Sardis reminded him of another more immediate, and daunting, problem. What would he say upon meeting his mother-in-law for the first time?

Both Grace and Dorcus dropped their cards and stared at each other, their mouths gaping. They turned suspicious gazes at Sardis. "Don't you mean *future* mother-in-law?" asked Dorcus.

"Nope. We eloped shortly after he gave me the ring," said Sardis, smiling broadly at the memory. "I'd been Mrs. Story for about a month. The one-night honeymoon was heavenly." Grace and Dorcus gave each other high fives, and the game resumed.

"No wonder I never saw much of you," said Dorcus.

Of all the future events J. B. dreaded, meeting his new bride's mother and friends terrified him the most. "Did you tell her?" he asked Sardis following the brief civil ceremony.

Sardis shook her head. "I thought it would be best if we told her together. We'll do it at graduation. She'll be in a great mood then," Sardis assured him. "She's riding with some of my friends from high school and our priest. It's a good crowd, and everyone knows everyone else. She's comfortable with them, and they'll get her spirits up. We'll let everyone know at the same time. That way, she won't have any choice but to be happy for us."

The plan did not sit well with J. B., especially the part about making sure her mother was in a good mood. Sardis had said very little about her mother to anyone. The academic and nurturing environment she finally found at State allowed her to bury all of the bad memories. J. B., though curious, never pressed her for information. However, the few snippets she let slip in conversation was somewhat disturbing and shook his confidence. So to avoid conflict so early in their union, he conceded to her judgment.

To ease the transition to their new life, he decided to make one major purchase, and he sprang the news on her two days before the festive event. "I got a car. We can leave for New York right away after the ceremony. We can drive overnight, and then relax a little before auditioning for Cyrus's friend. You can send your stuff home with your mom."

Sardis was thrilled at the idea, and her face lit up like a roman candle. She could hardly contain her glee. The dream still seemed unreal. She'd never imagined herself on an international stage, or on any stage, for that matter. If they passed the New York auditions, they would be off to London for the production. Cyrus was proving to be a friend to the end. He believed in them; now they had to believe in themselves.

Meanwhile, Dorcus began to pack her worldly goods with great care, separating them into the "keep" pile, the "donate to the freshman dorm" pile and the "just toss it" pile. One decision was easy. Laundry items, such as detergent and drying racks, were carted over to the girls' and more particularly, the boys' dorms. There was always someone arriving unprepared, having forgotten that Mom was not doing his laundry any more.

It was tradition for drying racks to be marked with the senior class year when they were left. Since most were made out of wood, they tended to wear out within five or six years. So she took her pen and scratched a welcome message to the freshmen from the class of 1968. The last item she pulled out of the drawer was the one that produced tears she swore she wouldn't shed. "Mother Sadie's scarf," she said out loud, holding the garish item aloft. "Who would have thought red, green, and black would become a fashion statement with social commentary. Maybe she truly was a visionary." As she did in her freshman year, she placed it on the "just toss it" pile, but then sentimentality forced her to retrieve it. The old woman was still alive, but ailing, so as a tribute to her, she absentmindedly hung the scarf around her neck as she continued to pack.

"You won't need that scarf to keep you warm in Charleston, but I might need it in New York," said Sardis as she entered the room. In her usual efficient manner, her packing was done, but with the news of J. B.'s car, she had to do some rearranging. Now she had two piles; a "stuff to take to New York" pile and a "stuff to send to Charleston" pile.

The two women chattered incessantly, full of good cheer as they completed the task of clearing out the room, until Sardis reached under her bed and pulled out the bid whist board. The chatter ceased. They exchanged glances, looked at the board, which Sardis had spread across her lap, and suddenly, they were swept into a vortex of memories. Dry eyes gave way to a torrent of tears. Alas, reality crept upon them. They hugged knowing that in spite of sincere promises to keep in touch, this might be their last time together. Their hearts ached, for memories they were about to leave behind, for their uncertain futures, for their two missing friends, and for their friends' lost dreams and lost hopes. They slowly regained their composure as assorted parents and relatives began to arrive.

Just as Sardis had predicted, Eartha was in a somewhat jovial mood. She refused to join in the preliminary festivities, however, preferring to remain in Sardis's now-empty dorm room until it was almost time for the ceremony to begin. Her self-imposed entombment made her extremely sensitive to sunlight, and she also detested the darkening effect the sun had on her skin.

The ceremony was held in the open stadium, beneath a massive tent. Seating was limited, so each candidate received two tickets allowing selected guests to sit in the tented area. Tickets became as valuable as gold as the date drew closer, and students could be heard all over campus bartering in an attempt to purchase additional tickets from other students who anticipated having only one guest or none at all. In some instances, strife arose in large families when tickets went to a favorite aunt or uncle, banishing other relatives and friends to surrounding bleacher seats. Fortunately, the weather cooperated, and the day was bathed in sunshine, just perfect for the outdoor event.

Sardis greeted old high school friends, who barely recognized her now. The women envied her radiant glow and sophisticated manner, and their husbands felt stirrings and longings in suddenly reawakened loins that were dead for decades. J. B. helped her select a wintry white dress that complemented her complexion and accentuated her sleek figure, and she oozed sensuality. She usually shied away from wearing white because, against her fair skin, it tended to give her a washed-out appearance, but white dresses were mandated for women, with dark suits and ties the order of the day for men, even though they would be hidden under their dark rented academic robes. With her hair pulled back and anchored in a stylish bun, Sardis sparkled like the star she knew she would one day become.

After failing to cajole her mother into joining in the mirth, she squired the five couples around campus, making sure they met her mentor, Cyrus Bloom, the only person who knew the secret she and J. B. shared. They needed one witness, and J. B. wanted him as his best man. Today, though, J. B. had not yet made an appearance, and she was becoming concerned. Just as she was escorting her mother to the tented area, however, he pushed his way through the crowd, and with the grand gesture of a knight in shining armor, he presented his beloved with a bouquet of pink carnations, her favorite flowers. He couldn't contain the actor within, having received the school's first "Academy Award" proclaiming him the best actor of the year, and he needed to live up to his reputation. Living each moment as if on stage, every gesture he made was exaggerated, right over the top. Sardis's smile could have lit up the Eastern seaboard. In response to his presentation, and not to be outdone, she curtsied low. The princess accepted her prince. Still giggling at their silliness, she turned to her mother, while J. B. stood proudly, in great anticipation, holding a single red rose. His thick, dark, wavy hair was slicked back, and the tan suit he bought just for the occasion enhanced his smooth, dark features and covered his muscular frame to perfection. He had major stage presence.

Old prejudices continued to keep the doors of the theater world closed, but not much longer. J. B. Story oozed charm and charisma and was about to challenge the old school that dared keep those doors locked. Women looked on, drooling with envy. They all wanted to touch him, to embrace him, and their flirtatious looks beckoned, but he ignored their stares completely. Right now, all he wanted to do was to impress one woman.

He stood shifting uneasily from one foot to the other, looking from mother to daughter. Eartha showed no acknowledgment of what was taking place. Her focus was elsewhere, and she completely ignored the playful exchange happening between her daughter and someone she obviously loved. Sardis took J. B. by the arm and began to make her introduction. "Mother ..."

"Where is Father Mackey, dear?" said Eartha, agitated and totally oblivious to everything. "He promised to sit beside me," she said. Her gaze passed right through the lovers as her unsmiling eyes searched the crowd for the wayward priest who was last seen venturing off to find an elusive parking spot on or near the overly crowded campus.

Sardis, not sure how to react, began her introduction again. "Mother, I want you to meet my..." She stopped abruptly, searching for the right word. Her sudden pause caught J. B. by surprise, and he noticed she wasn't wearing her rings; his rings. Sardis, sensing his discomfort, mouthed silently to him, "She still doesn't know." J. B. nodded, letting her know he understood, but he became annoyed at how this was playing out.

Sardis knew her mother was hard-headed and stubborn, but she was neither deaf nor blind. The tent was filling up as time for the ceremony approached and she had to get them seated quickly. She felt uneasy leaving them alone together in the confined space of the tightly grouped chairs, but she had to join the marching line. "Mother, my friend Jeb will be sitting with you," she said. Then leaning close she whispered to her mother, "Get to know him." She gave J. B.

her bouquet just as he handed Eartha the rose, and then dashed out of the tented area, chiding herself for the clumsy way she handled things. *I should have told her, I should have told her,* she repeated, castigating herself. Before she could reach the end of the field where the candidates were waiting, however, she heard a familiar voice shouting her name, and turned to see their priest jogging in her direction.

"Your mother had a slight fainting spell," he said, struggling to catch his breath. He wasn't an old man, but the sprint across the field left him winded. "She appears to be doing better now. Your friend and I decided to exchange places. He gave me his ticket. He thought it would be better for her to have someone familiar beside her." Sardis sighed heavily, gave her approval, then turned on her heels and hurried to join the line, continuing to mentally thrash herself as she went.

XLI

Graduation ceremonies at State, as at many black schools, took on a serious tone. Families invested their life savings in reaching this day, choosing to leave bills unpaid while scrimping and saving meager earnings to make this day possible. Education, next to God, was the greatest legacy one could give to a black child. In this hundredth or so year since the abolition of slavery, many families were celebrating with their first ever college graduate. This was indeed a day of jubilation.

Edward Elgar's dignified march, "Pomp and Circumstance," defined the day. The pageantry was not taken lightly. Uniformity and precision were the orders of the day. The week leading up to this occasion was filled with rehearsals to ensure that everything went off without a hitch, and the greatest emphasis was placed on the Grand March.

"Start out on the right foot," the coordinators instructed everyone. "When the two individuals in front of you reach this mark," they said, pointing to a prominently painted X, "start out with the right foot. Right foot! Right foot!" If they had branding irons, "Right foot" would be seared onto each forehead as a reminder. It was worth the effort, however, for the result was a pageantry of rare beauty and elegance. Those sitting in the stands actually got a better view than those scrunched together in the tent, marveling at the magnificence of mortarboards and tassels all swinging from left to right at the same time as the long line stretched from the back of the field all the way through the tent. Often, the swaying began before the marchers began to walk. Anxiety, coupled with the grandeur of the music provided by the band, got into their souls like a shout in church. Nobody dared to mess it up by being that one person out of step.

School administrators, including the president, led the march. They, too, had to keep in step and in time with the music. Other dignitaries, speakers, and professors followed. The candidates entered last. The school did not offer doctoral degrees, so the masters candidates marched in first, followed by the majority, who were receiving bachelor's degrees. Each group was arranged alphabetically by last name.

"It was a thrilling moment," Dorcus's brothers confirmed after the event. "You done good," they chided, pulling her cap down over her eyes, reverting to childhood slang and teasing. Dorcus's family, as always, supported their "baby" sister full tilt. She was particularly happy to see two of her brothers. They had finally left the nest for Georgia and added two more women to the clan, even though one was still unofficial. Both women came along, however, to give their support and to earn brownie points on the side. Their family was displaced by urban renewal, just as the people from the Alley were, but it was a blessing, because they were able to move out of the church-owned dwelling in the city. A government-backed entitlement program, plus a generous relocation bonus from the city of Charleston, helped the family to buy a house. "It's a mansion!" Dorcus squealed on moving day when she took a quick pre-graduation run home. "I have to make sure my things make it in one piece. And I don't want people putting their hands all over my personal stuff." She also wanted to arrange her room, because her post-graduation plans were still uncertain, even though she was wearing Charlie's ring.

The family found a beautiful two-story brick house in a predominantly white suburban track and moved in a heartbeat. A few neighboring houses immediately sprouted "For sale" signs. However, the majority were tired of running from the prospects of a mixed neighborhood and were ready to accept the inevitable, so they stayed and welcomed them to the subdivision.

The preacher's church members formed a moving-day caravan. Trucks, cars, and anything else on wheels that moved independently was pressed into service to "get the preacher in his house." It turned into a house warming and a house blessing on the same day. People furnished tons of food and sang and ate and got to know the neighbors. Dorcus's two younger brothers made the move to suburbia with the family. They still had no motivation to set up their own households, even though the preacher often gave them hints about moving on. Under normal circumstances, that moving on process might have included a stint in the military, but the men of the family shared a trait that kept them out of military service; they all had horribly flat feet. Her oldest brother summed it up when he returned from his draft call. "Not even an ant could survive under the arches of these dogs." So all four strapping young men wound up 4F, and like their father before them, couldn't be pressed into service. "Has something to do with my ability, or inability, to march," her big brother explained to Dorcus. "Told you I'd be back home before the end of the day. The doctor took one look at these puppies and said, 'See you later. Don't call us, and we darn sure won't call you.'"

Another thing her brothers all had in common was the bond they shared as Morehouse Men. Morehouse College, a private, all-male, historically black liberal arts college, was established by William Jefferson White in 1867. It was founded to educate black men in the fields of ministry and education and was considered to be among the premiere schools in the United States, claiming among its most prominent graduates Nobel Laureate Dr. Martin Luther King Jr. and Dorcus's graduation speaker and retired sixth Morehouse college president, Dr. Benjamin E. Mays.

Even with business degrees tucked under their belts, job opportunities for Southern black men like Dorcus's brothers were still tight, however. Career options were limited, and when openings existed, the pay was terrible. They were expected to do more work at half the salary of their white counterparts. With the passage of the Civil Rights Act, and the government's commitment to building a new, inclusive society, Affirmative Action became the byword. It was launched as a means of finding and recruiting black and female candidates to entry-level positions within corporate America. Even the government opened up more entry level jobs, which eventually led to higher pay grade positions.

Once Affirmative Action became the order of the day, it opened doors for men like Dorcus's brothers, but change was a difficult row to hoe. Years of pent-up anger on both sides had to be assuaged, and orders to stop discriminatory practices could not melt employers' hearts to the point where they would either play fairly or by the rules.

Companies frequently paid lip service by opening dead-end positions with fabricated job titles. Unqualified individuals who were hired to meet quotas were frequently released as soon as the quotas were met. Black women flourished under the quota system by serving as a "two fer." In essence, it meant they were hired over black men because they were counted under both black and women hired categories. This practice raised the ire of black men and began driving a wedge between the sexes that had far-reaching and long-lasting social implications. Some companies made minimal efforts, letting one dark face grace their door and then saying "We're done. We can't find any more qualified candidates." The term "token hire" was coined to characterize this type of activity.

Dorcus's big brother was subjected to a lot of token hiring in Charleston, so she suggested he try another state. Even though he was older, she often displayed greater maturity and level headedness. "It worked," he shouted one day, practically leaping through the phone with excitement. "I got a position," he said, emphasizing the word position after she congratulated him on finding a job. "Laborers, like all of us used to be, find jobs. Executives find positions!"

"Oh, great! Now I got to learn a whole new terminology," Dorcus said and laughed. It was the highlight of her sophomore year at State.

Her brother's position gave him a new life, and enough income to fly from the nest, so he flew back to the fast-growing metropolis of Atlanta, Georgia, home of his alma mater, which was quickly becoming a Mecca for black professionals. This was the modern-day New York, signaling the beginning of a new reverse migration. Atlanta was ripe to benefit from the growing black middle class.

Harbored within this vast metropolis were five historically black institutions of higher learning. Right next door to Morehouse was Spellman College, a four-year liberal arts women's college. The Atlanta Baptist Female Seminary was founded in 1881 by two teachers, Harriet E. Giles and Sophie B. Packard, and in 1924 it became Spellman College. This was considered to be the top black college for females in the United States and numbered Dr. King's mother among its graduates. Graduates from both institutions benefited greatly over the years from the social climate generated by being next-door neighbors. College-educated women were still at a slight disadvantage, however, for Spellman's annual enrollment of approximately two thousand three hundred students exceeded Morehouse's numbers by at least three hundred.

Atlanta was also home to Atlanta University, which was founded in 1865 by the American Missionary Association with the assistance of the Freedmen's Bureau, whose goal was to train teachers and librarians, and Clark College, which was founded in 1869 by the Freedmen's Aid Society of the Methodist Episcopal Church. Their curriculum was theology based.

The fifth school was a struggling private, co-ed, liberal arts institution named Morris Brown College. This was founded in 1881 by former slaves affiliated with the AME Church. Its goal was to take students from poor backgrounds and return them to their respective communities as teachers.

These schools, along with the International Theological Center, formed in 1958, gave Atlanta a solid base from which an educated black middle class could evolve, and so the city became a magnet for upwardly mobile black citizens from all over the United States. It had a major impact on the city's racial balance. If their industrial base wanted to survive and thrive, they could not ignore or dismiss Affirmative Action, and doors had to open very quickly.

The preacher was proud and happy for his son, but his mother had mixed emotions. There was a special, unexplainable bond between a black mama and her sons. Going to Atlanta for school was one thing, but moving there permanently was another. She didn't want to hold on to him, but she didn't want to let him go, either; such maternal paradoxes cannot be explained. Release him, she did, however, for her keen intuition told her his move would have a positive influence on his siblings, which proved correct. His pioneering efforts served as a catalyst for brother number two, and she found herself having to say good-bye once again. Having acquired some knowledge of the growing area, big brother was able to secure a position for second brother very quickly. He was glad to have the company of his brother in the large city.

Successful black men with job security are marvels to behold, and when Dorcus first saw her older brother after he had spent a year in his new position, she was in total awe at the change in his appearance. His tall, portly frame was sculpted into a taut, more masculine build. He was self-assured, thus radiating self-confidence. He was smartly attired and ... "You have a girlfriend?" she exclaimed in mock surprise. "Who would want a big-headed numbskull like you?" she chided. They always articulated their pleasure and pride through teasing and playful banter, and so he knew she was very happy for him.

He did very little dating. As the preacher's son, he was considered a fine catch for members of his father's congregation, but knowing this made him shy away from the many girls and their pushy mamas who wanted the preacher for a father-in-law. His first date was for his high school senior prom. He took a very introverted girl who turned out to be a possessive, jealous vixen with a vicious temper. That relationship and one other, with an over-sexed college co-ed he met during his freshman year through a friend, set the scene for his wariness with women throughout his school years. Now, in Atlanta, working for a prestigious company, he was like refined gold. He had new choices, and his eventual selection opened a defining chapter in the family's life.

XLII

Dorcus's parents were sat comfortably beneath the tent along with Charlie, whom she parked next to after bartering a last-minute ticket. As she marched by, she saw their beaming faces and winked. From where she sat during the ceremony, she could see her brothers, and seated next to her oldest brother was a petite, striking, pale-skinned blonde; his wife. Brother number two sat directly to his right with his new love interest of one month, a leggy brunette with equally pale skin. His date's discomfort, as opposed to the confidence displayed by his brother's wife, was evident. She sat very close to him as both pretended to ignore the frosty, dagger-like stares aimed in their direction. Dorcus applauded her new in-law and prospective in-law's tenacity for stepping into the lion's den, so to speak. Many black people still held mixed feelings, reflecting deep-seated and still-raw emotions, about crossing racial dating lines, but black women, in particular, were not subtle in revealing their displeasure with the way this thing was playing itself out. Dorcus, however, accepted and even applauded her brothers' decisions. When they asked if they could bring their partners along, she issued fair warning. "Be prepared," she told them. "Black women, and a few men too, won't like what they see. You'll have to endure plenty of intense stares, and maybe even a few lewd comments." Her oldest brother and his wife, having already experienced such treatment, acknowledged her concerns. They alerted brother number two and his date about what they might experience, but they were willing to take their chances. "This is my day, and I don't want nobody hatin' on me," said Dorcus in her usual playful tone.

Hate was a term that barely began to describe the bottled-up anger and viper-tongued rhetoric displayed by her dorm mates. Dorcus didn't want to discourage her brothers, but interracial dating stirred up a hornet's nest. The mere thought of a black man dating and marrying a white woman was enough to give southern white men cardiac arrests, but their paranoia paled in comparison to the emotional distress and psychological meltdown experienced by black women.

Dorcus just wanted to get through her big day with peace and harmony, and yet she already knew that her brothers and their partners were going to draw animosity and unwanted attention to themselves and by extension, to her and the rest of her family. She'd chosen to remain silent for a long time, and stayed away from the gripe sessions about interracial dating, but it was virtually impossible to remain neutral. She and everyone else on campus were subjected to daily haranguing by a few vocal dorm mates. Their feelings, frequently expressed at high volume, were constantly on blatant display. They played on the insecurities of the crowd, who backed up their remarks with supporting choruses of "Preach, sister, preach," and "Amen."

As Dorcus passed by one room one day, she heard someone saying, "Ever since we been slaves together, who supported them? Who had their children while working in the fields alongside them? Who kept their houses in order? The black woman, that's who! So now look where they runnin' to!" The soapbox speaker in another room espoused a similar theme: "We supported the brothers in the liberation battle. Helped them rise out of poverty so they could get good jobs to support *us*. We kept our part of the bargain, but look at what they're doing. Stabbing us in the back by deserting to the enemy. The ultimate betrayal!"

"Amen. Preach, sister!"

All across campus, co-ed gatherings turned into heated debates about interracial dating, that is, if "debate" was the proper term for these informal forums that were sharply divided by gender; women shouting loudly on one side, and men listening passively on the other. Dorcus had never been a great activist but she, for one, began to tire of hearing only one side of the argument. She also decided, for her siblings' sake, she had to speak up on their behalf and let the chips fall where they may. She didn't want unrestrained anger directed at her family.

One evening, as graduation neared, she walked in on a lounge session in full progress. She waited patiently at the back of the room for a lull in the diatribe before speaking up. With a slight tremor in her voice, she gently asked the group of about twenty women a provocative question. She needed to hold their attention long enough to present the rest of her argument. "Isn't this what the marching and praying and fighting was all about?" she said. Everyone's head swerved in her direction. She took a deep breath to still her racing heartbeat, and continued in a calm and rational tone. She lined up her arguments, and she hoped the firebrands wouldn't disrupt her or shout her down. Deep down, her intuition told her there had to be other women in the room who shared her views. She knew they would be too intimidated to punctuate her comments with "amens," but they might keep some of the loudmouths from being rude and disrespectful.

"We wanted the laws to change. The fight was successful, the laws were changed, and now we can't put the genie back into the bottle." A low murmur rumbled through the room, especially when she mentioned success. She was getting to them. She presented another point with which no one could argue. "Just think, my sisters; until June 1967, less than one year ago, interracial marriage was still illegal in seventeen southern states. Black men died as a result of that law. Now it's gone. They—we—have choices."

The room grew still. The women had been draped lazily on chairs and couches, but now they sat up to listen. Emboldened, she stepped gingerly over outstretched legs and moved to the center of the crowd. "We can't simply pick and choose the results of those choices. We can't go back and erase all of the gain, to get rid of the outcome just because it impacts us in adverse and unexpected ways." She then hammered her final point home by providing a subtle reminder of recent events. "The fight continues, and we can't afford to be divided. We, men and women, are still fighting for our civil rights, and to have choices. Three brothers just died for their right to make choices, including other brothers' rights to choose whom they want to love." Invoking the memory of the three recently departed students cleared the room. Dorcus inhaled deeply. She knew the preacher would have been proud of his daughter's sermon. Dorcus became the peacemaker, even if the truce was only to last for one day, but she hadn't jumped into the fray just to keep the peace. She remembered the joy her brother experienced upon finally finding his life's mate. She didn't want anyone laying a guilt trip on him, or on the woman he had chosen to stand by his side.

XLIII

The graduating class of 1968 was like no other, and as the speaker stepped up to the podium, history was setting his remarks into motion. These men and women had survived a turbulent year, and were about to enter a turbulent society. Their oppressed parents fought the battles, and this class represented the generation that would begin to reap the benefits. Along with the benefits, however, came unexpected and hefty dues they had to pay.

As the graduation speaker admonished the often-dozing graduates to tread new ground, to explore new opportunities, and to change history, society was doing that for them. It was easier for earlier graduates to take that advice and run with it, for following their grand march, most returned to segregated communities where they contributed to society by becoming teachers or preachers. A handful became lawyers and doctors, but they didn't have to carve out new paths, kick open closed doors, or sail into uncharted waters.

For the sixty-eighters, however, it was an entirely new ball game. They were forced to take action, forced to find new ways, because the old ways were being retired. Like an unsighted person, they had to feel their way because, alas, they had no precedents to guide them. They faced lots of trials and committed lots of errors, and while the prior generations offered plenty of advice, they could offer very little by way of edification. They were left to fail or succeed on their own.

They were forced to adopt new thinking, because up until now, their highly regimented lives were dominated by segregation, Jim Crow laws, and "colored" and "white" signs. In this stifling environment, they knew what to expect and how to act or react to life's forces, but while they yawned as the lengthy ceremony progressed, that life was fading, and giving way to rules yet to be written. What could families expect, and what would the family resemble? How would the dating scene change? How do you go from being underprivileged to privileged, from hopelessness to having hope? How do you suddenly change dreams from black and white to Technicolor?

The sixty-eighters' lives were about to become social experiments. They would have to make choices with little or no foresight as to how their decisions would impact generations to come. Ironically, each decision, good, bad, or indifferent, greatly impacted many dimensions of black life. Now, as they flipped their tassels from one side to the other, little did they know they were assuming responsibilities of a new and untried world.

Dorcus shifted in her seat, trying to give her weary bottom some relief from the hard wooden chair. She and the other women of the class of '68 would have to do much more shifting in the future as the burden of change fell increasingly upon them. The dating debates were only the tip of a gigantic iceberg. Other changes were happening so fast, they had little or no time to process them. Many wished they had more time to sit and examine the implications, because far too many changes took them unwillingly in directions that unraveled the fabric of their lives, producing unforeseen and negative results.

As Affirmative Action began to spread its tentacles and enfold other disadvantaged segments of society, the women's movement become as vocal in their demands for parity as the black movement. Black women found themselves in the middle of two dynamic forces, each of which had the potential to benefit them equally but which tested their loyalties. Should their fight for equality be race-based or gender-based?

Black women were on the front line during civil rights marches from Selma to Birmingham to Montgomery and beyond. They knew and understood the price of freedom from racial oppression, and yet they also understood the importance of gaining equal rights for women. Equal pay for equal work and advancement opportunities based upon education combined with skills and knowledge were also worth fighting for. And in many households, like Grace's, survival depended upon the woman's income. Black women's fight for equality could not be taken lightly.

Eventually, black women began to win entry into boardrooms, but guilt, like walls moving in from two sides, served to envelop them. On one wall, it read "black rights," and on the other it read "women's rights." Rather than make a choice, many decided that once those two structures got close enough, they'd use both walls and climb to the top. This made enemies of every other group who considered themselves to be disadvantaged, but in particular, it angered black men.

This produced a schism that began to fray the nerves of sistas and brothas alike. A silent war was brewing that would result in intra-racial disharmony and disunity. The brothas began to see the sistas as a threat to their well-being until eventually, they considered them to be just as much of an enemy as white men had been. As sistas won more ground in the boardrooms, they lost major ground in the bedrooms, thus signaling the beginning of a new look for the black family structure.

Integration threw Dorcus's brother and his wife together. Both were hired at the same time as account executives for their company. They were the first of a new breed, and as token hires, both of them knew a lot was riding on their success. Hence they became extremely competitive with one another during their training and probationary periods. Neither trusted the other. "I'm not going to let this bossy white woman get the best of me," Dorcus's brother griped to her during one of their longer telephone sessions. His determination and drive impressed his little sister, but by the time they had their next conversation, he was singing a different tune. "You know, she's not too bad," he cooed. "I came out ahead in the training class, but she proved to be a big help. We formed an uneasy alliance and then realized we both had the same goals and dreams."

As he described his new situation, Dorcus detected a softness and tenderness in his voice she never heard before. It was evident whenever he referred to the "pushy white woman" who used to get under his skin. Dorcus and her new sister-in-law got along immediately. Her parents never commented or shared their thoughts with their children but simply accepted their new daughter-in-law just as she accepted them. Cultural differences posed no end of challenges, however, and for an entire month, the preacher had to deliver sermons on love and acceptance in order to keep tempers in check. He was glad when the couple returned to Atlanta after he married them.

Popular culture had already begun to pick up on the trend, and exploited it through a new movie called *Guess Who's Coming To Dinner*, which showcased the talents of Sidney Poitier, the first black man to be considered a genuine movie star.

Cyrus Bloom was happy for Poitier's success, although he still harbored the belief that if it hadn't been for Poitier, his own acting career might have taken off. However, he now accepted his role as a mentor and trainer for the next generation. He had the personal satisfaction of knowing that his predictions were beginning to materialize as the movie industry, theatrical world, and entertainment industry in general began to recognize black influences and talent. He held great hope that one member of the class of 1968 would take the theater by storm, and that her husband would be right there alongside her, and it strengthened his resolve to continue to promote theater as a legitimate major. It was time for the past generation's ideas about theater careers to be put to rest.

XLIV

J. B. was experiencing a jumble of emotions. First, he had to endure total rejection from his mother-in-law. When he gave her the rose, she reacted as if she saw him for the first time. She became hysterical, like a child having a tantrum, threw the flower to the ground, and began to hyperventilate. He was greatly relieved when the elusive Father Mackey suddenly appeared out of nowhere and calmed her down. Fortunately, once he found a seat on the bleachers, he could see Sardis the entire time, and they exchanged warm, loving glances throughout the ceremony, which made up for him having to give his ticket away. He sat in the car parked at the outer edge of the campus. They agreed to meet there, but it had been over an hour since the ceremony ended and he hadn't seen Sardis since the recessional march. The car was packed for their escape, and he was looking forward to a real honeymoon with his gorgeous wife. He fidgeted with the radio dial, trying to get something other than country music, when he saw her approaching, and could tell by her demeanor his day was not about to improve.

"I love you so much," she said, embracing him as she slid into the passenger seat alongside him. He waited in anticipation, because her tone suggested that another comment was about to follow. He was right. "I can't leave right now. The day's events have taken their toll on Mother. I wish you could have met the group. You would have loved them, and they you." He remained silent, rather than telling her he had met the group when he took the priest's seat in the bleachers. They treated him with the same disdain and indifference as her mother, with one exception. They were more civil, in that they acknowledged his presence by parting like the Biblical Red Sea when he sat in their midst. The rest of the time they dismissed him from their consciousness with a cold impassiveness. Their reactions told him he would never fit in, and he knew he had an uphill battle ahead of him.

"Sard, you're here now. What would stop you from riding off with me, right this minute?" he said.

She looked at his pleading, passionate face and beckoning, puppy-dog eyes; looked at the car piled high with the promise of a new life and smiled. "Let's go," she said.

They embraced once more, and shared a lingering kiss, which lasted long enough for the piercing wail of a siren to reach her ears. The ambulance appeared on the horizon, and she knew instinctively where it was headed. They both watched the vehicle until it entered the campus. Scenes from earlier times flashed before her. She had to make sure the vehicle was not for another relative. She jumped out of the car and ran toward the campus, quickening her pace when she saw that the emergency vehicle stopped in front of her dorm. Her suspicions were confirmed. She entered the building; stretched and before her on the lobby couch was her mother, panting heavily. J. B. appeared at the door. After a brief conversation with his beloved, he left and returned with her luggage, which he set down in the lobby before slipping silently away.

An hour later, Eartha was back to what was normal for her, sitting beside the priest, chirping away about the graduation ceremony. He was at the wheel of the parish station wagon, heading back to Charleston, with a three-vehicle caravan following behind them. Scrunched in the back seat was a silent, sullen Sardis.

XLV

The date, May 26, 1968, was not lost on Grace as she sat alone in the only shelter she was able to find with the meager assistance she managed to get from the state of New York, a Harlem flat that had seen far better days. It consisted of one room, and she was being fleeced fifty dollars a month for the privilege of staying there. If it was a white slum, it would only cost about thirty dollars. She thought things were different in the North, that there wasn't any segregation or racial discrimination. Wrong, wrong, and wrong. Other people's dreams and her reality suffered a terrible collision.

This place makes Michele Alley look like a palace, she thought. *At least we had space there, and could go outside and swing in the cool breeze, or sit on the stoop.* The high cost forced people to live in close quarters, and the same forces that allowed landlords to charge more rent also allowed them to perform less maintenance on their buildings. In Charleston, she had to deal with cicadas and other bugs, but the rat population was not as big a challenge as the one she now faced. *Rats, both the two-legged and four-legged kinds, hate humidity in the summer,* she recalled as she heard the familiar scurrying while preparing for another sleepless night. She lost a lot of sleep out of fear that the beasts would invade her space and begin to nibble on body parts if she didn't keep moving around or shooing them away. Fortunately for her, summer was approaching. The sweltering heat would make them lethargic and less active.

The building had no heat, no running hot water, and barely had lighting. Previous tenants stripped the wiring, which sold well on the black market. The cheap remaining wires were exposed to the elements, because the walls were stripped bare of plaster. She dreaded going into the hallway, where the walls were damp and smelly due to sewage from damaged plumbing, which only worked intermittently. There was evidence that the crumbling plaster had once been painted a pretty pastel color. As if the conditions weren't bad enough, there was no sense of community or pride. People were mean and rude, and they tossed garbage out of windows and into hallways and air shafts.

She longed for her Willie, her lover, protector, and friend. Although she didn't miss Brother Martin, and what he represented, she understood why Willie chose to live with the Liberation Front. She tried to block his name from her mind, because every time she thought about him, which was often, tears, unrestrained tears, began to flow.

Graduation day. Mama sure would have been proud. A smile let the sunshine in for a few moments when she thought about Hatta Mae. *Wonder what kind of dress she bought for the affair? The woman began saving for a brand new outfit the day I stepped onto the campus. Put it, along with a new pair of shoes, on lay-away at the beginning of my senior year.* Looking around the room she asked herself, *How could it all have gone so wrong?*

She was out of hospital for a month. The bullet did quite a bit of damage, and when her pregnancy was discovered, doctors at the emergency hospital were not able to perform all the repairs needed, or to give her as much pain medication as required. She moved to a recovery center for indigent women to complete her convalescence, and it was there that a case worker helped her to apply for welfare.

Even though she was still rather weak after her ordeal, she gathered her courage and returned to the pile of rubble that had once been her home. The bodies were removed after firefighters completed their work. The biggest press coverage ran while she was still isolated in the hospital, but rumors reached her ears. Some reports were accurate in calling it mass suicide, while others thought the group perished defending the organization against looters and police. A third version said the group instigated the riots to cover up illegal activity like gun running and drug sales. Grace, of course, knew the truth. She wished she could tell the real story of how they were betrayed, but recalling the Orangeburg massacre, and how the media treated the students, she knew this secret, along with the truth, would probably go with her to her grave. A haunting sense of loss overtook her as she wandered aimlessly by. Police barriers were still in place warning everyone to keep their distance; as if anyone wanted to venture into the rubble. The restaurant and store were gone, stripped of everything worth salvaging, and the living quarters, the school with its precious library, and the medical wing had all burned to the ground.

Her greatest loss, of course, was that of her husband. A lump arose in her throat when she realized she didn't even have a picture of him. Her child would never know its father. It was as if neither he nor their marriage ever existed. If it weren't for the child growing inside her, she would have completed the gunman's botched murder attempt.

As she sat lost in thought, there came a soft tapping on the door. Since moving to this hellhole, she learned to guard her privacy and protect herself. Charleston was open and friendly, but she was no longer in Charleston. She sat motionless, wishing she had x-ray vision to provide a clue, any clue, as to who or what awaited her on the other side of the door. Again, the knock came, a little more forceful this time. "Sister Grace?" a voice finally called. She was surprised that anyone would know or refer to her as "Sister Grace." Who could it be? Then a hint of recognition hit her, and she rose quickly to unlock the multiple locks, which were more for show than anything else. If someone really wanted to enter, all he or she had to do was kick through the rusted hinges and cheap plywood.

She opened the door to the sight of familiar, friendly faces, whom she welcomed with hugs and a torrent of tears. Some of the members survived. The two couples who made their escape through the open window that Willie tried to use never went to the cafeteria. "We returned to the site every day to search for other survivors. My man saw you from a distance and followed you. We came as soon as we were able to confirm that it was in fact you," one woman explained.

They traded one separatist group for another and decided to join forces with the Nation of Islam. They implored Grace to come with them. It didn't take a huge stretch of the imagination to understand the instant attraction. Brother Martin and the Liberation Front shared many of the same principles that were taught by the Nation of Islam. Brother Martin's biggest mistake, however, began when he and the organization merged into one entity. What began as a model for people of color to build a better life, based upon a classless society, where the group, not just an individual, could flourish as a whole, became a parody of a Utopia based upon the will of one man. He embellished his organization with a great infusion of himself and in the end, greed caused him to lose sight of his vision.

XLVI

Grace paused and stretched as she explained to her enraptured card partners, "I had to get out of that slum, so I went with them, but I couldn't join them in another self-made, regimented metropolis." Her face reflected inner turmoil still gripping her, even after twenty years. "I still have too much to work through. I was angry at everything. My world had crumbled, and everything I'd believed in was suddenly no longer valid. I broke promises I made to myself … and to my mother," she choked, throwing her cards on the table in disgust.

Dorcus and Sardis sat quietly as the wall clock announced the hour. "Four AM," said Sardis, rising to put on a pot of coffee. "We need to leave around eight o'clock in order to make it on time, so don't stop now. I want to hear the rest of this story."

"In 1966, the Black Panther Party established a group in Harlem, which still had major presence. This was the ultimate revolutionary group, the obvious place through which I could channel my anger so, I hooked up with them," said Grace.

Sardis popped her head in from the kitchen and with a tone of amazement, said, "You joined the Black Panther Party? I never knew you had it in you!"

"I'm not surprised," Dorcus chimed in. "You know what an agitator and aggravator Grace was. Who was it that dashed headlong out of the room yelling 'Power to the People' on the night of the massacre?"

Grace smiled as the two exchanged comments about her as if she wasn't in the room, and then added, "I don't remember saying that. Actually, my motives for joining the party were far more selfish. They were very successful in organizing nutrition programs for people in need. They ran free clinics and had free lunch and breakfast programs. I needed sustenance and medical care during my pregnancy. I think we as a race could have solved many of our own problems if the government had just left us alone. They were so paranoid about the socialistic nature of the group they had to destroy everything we built."

"You have to admit, the posters of Huey Newton in a wicker chair holding a spear and a big ole gun weren't exactly great marketing tools," said Dorcus. "That was a *big* turn off for a lot of people. I bought one of those posters as a joke, and my dad hit the ceiling," she said, laughing out loud at the memory. "He was still in the colored/black time warp. I can still hear his booming voice yelling, 'I'm trying to preach integration and all they're doing is teaching re-segregation. And another thing, they're too darn violent! Now get that thing out of this house!' He was still following the King tradition and trying to motivate a changing congregation to support time-honored traditions. He and a whole lotta folks didn't want to hear a thing about the Black Panthers, which is why I don't think they ever gained any strongholds in Charleston."

Sardis returned with the steaming brew, disrupting Dorcus' musings. She poured a cup for each of them and resumed her place opposite the dummy hand as Grace resumed her narrative.

"I managed to get my life somewhat in order, but when my son was born a few months later, I wanted him to be raised around family. I never met any of Willie's relatives in New York, so I decided to leave. I had enough bus fare to get me to Washington DC, and I figured once I made it that far, I could somehow get the rest to come all the way to Charleston. What I didn't know was, it would take me another nine years to do it."

XLVII

The day of May 26, 1968, was just another day in Taletha's life. Without medical attention or therapy, her physical condition deteriorated. Her mind, however, became sharper and sharper, but she still couldn't communicate with anyone. Each day was just like the one before.

Her parents received a letter during the week of final exams inviting them to attend the graduation ceremony. It informed them that the three dead students were going to be honored, and the administration also planned to recognize many others who had suffered. Taletha, however, could not graduate with her class, and her mother wept bitterly. She planned to teach home economics, but in order to do that, she needed to complete a mandatory six-week period of directed teaching. She had a choice of doing her stint out in the real world at the beginning of the semester, but she chose the end. Such a simple decision; such a world of difference. She wouldn't have been anywhere near the campus when the incident took place and would have been able to complete her senior year requirements and graduate with a teaching degree, and her present world would have been a pleasant place.

Taletha was propped up by the large picture window that gave their trailer house the appearance of a conventional structure when a dust cloud signaled the arrival of an automobile. The car came to rest in front of the house, and she recoiled when she saw Uncle Day alighting. "Looka here!" her mother chirped in the high, whiny voice she used whenever she feigned happiness. "She no you, Unk Day. She even seem ta git som life in 'em when you here."

"I have a surprise for ya," he said, moving closer. He reeked of old cooking oil, either the used fat women drained back into a jar to use again, or it might have been his cheap hair tonic. Either way, it wasn't a pleasant smell. "We woulda all been at yo' gratu-ashun today, but I got a present." He stepped aside to reveal a folded up used wheelchair. "Now when I come, we kin go fo' walks in the cornfield like befo'. Get ya some sunlight. Help ya feel good." This last statement he whispered close to her ear. The family was so pleased by the gift they helped move her to the chair and into the loving care of Uncle Day. "Take good kar, now. Ya'll have a good ride."

Taletha closed her eyes, and "Pomp and Circumstance" rang in her ear. She saw the caps moving back and forth in unison, saw her fellow grads moving their tassels from one side to the other, signifying passage from their artificial college environment to the real world. As she felt herself being lifted from the chair onto the soft, dry earth surrounded by high corn stalks, her awakened mind knew what was coming. She wasn't that frightened little girl any more, but she still couldn't tell anybody his dark secret, and he knew it. Somehow or another, she determined, she had to learn how to awaken the rest of her body.

Book III—THE REAL WORLD

I

By the time Sardis's caravan reached Charleston county, Eartha had made a complete recovery, and was actually quite cheerful, although not once did she bother to gauge her daughter's mood or inquire about the reasons for her silence. They made the familiar turn into Cummings Street, near her old high school, but then Father Mackey turned unexpectedly into the dirt yard behind the school, producing the first reaction from Sardis since they left State's campus. Her curiosity peaked. Since she never drove during her tenure at ICS, and since the gate was usually closed and locked, she never realized there was a parking lot on the school property. "I have to pick up some very urgent documents," the priest explained. "Rather than sitting here in this heat, why don't both of you come with me? It's been four years since you graced these halls, Sardis. Things may have changed since then." Sardis was morose and continued to sit sullenly. She felt like a kidnapping victim and wasn't going anywhere. *Let the heat multiply my misery,* she thought, crossing her arms as she sat slumped in the seat.

Her life had been hijacked, but her mother, who bounded out of the front seat, coaxed her into moving. If she was alert, she would have noticed the other cars pulled into the yard right behind them and had already dislodged their occupants. Located at the very rear of the schoolyard was a separate building named Father Cleary Hall for some long-forgotten priest. This building was used for fellowship and fun when Sardis attended the school, and Sardis blindly followed the priest as he headed toward it. Her mind and heart were traveling north in a large, used vehicle that swept into and out of her life so fast she couldn't remember the make and model. Entering the building, she didn't regain a sense of where she was until she heard a crowd of people shout *"Surprise!"*

She saw a congratulatory banner stretched out across the hall, shouting joyous exaltations for her achievement, but all she felt were empty expectations about her future. She inhaled deeply to keep tears from welling up and clasped her hands together tightly, almost prayerfully, trying to control her inner rage and utter emptiness. Always the actress, she managed to put herself into the part of a gracious and grateful hostess with a convincing smile and kind words. She was truly touched by their thoughtfulness, but her heart bled.

The party ran late into the evening, and Sardis managed to hold it all together. The day had been a long one, with the morning graduation, the two-hour drive, and now these unexpected festivities, and Sardis was feeling the strain. She hoped it would all end soon, until she remembered what awaited her outside; her old room, and her mother. She sat slumped in a chair, emotionally detached from the event, her sharp mind planning and plotting her escape. Her eyes swept the room, searching for someone, anyone, who might prove to be her ally.

"You haven't changed a bit," said a tenor voice, disrupting her musings. "It's been a long time. May I have this dance?" Sardis turned toward the voice, and her mind raced, trying to put a name to the face. "Clancy?" she half-spoke, half-asked, hoping it wasn't him, but realizing it was.

Clancy was a heavy-set man. He was always large, even as a child, and as he grew, his parents hoped their only child would inherit his father's height, but he hadn't. Instead, he took on the appearance of a large beach ball. His complexion was so pale it almost washed out his features. His acne cleared, leaving pockmarks here and there. The most distinguishing thing about his face was the constant presence of the wire-rimmed glasses framing pale-brown eyes. If anyone were to describe Clancy in one word, it would be "beige," from the color of his coarse hair and eyebrows, to the clothes he seemed to favor. Clancy was the type of boy girls thought of as their brother, not their sweetheart, and he was smart. Throughout school, he maintained a straight-A average. He always won the science fair and even won a full scholarship as a national merit scholar. It wasn't as if his folks couldn't afford to send him to college. His father was a practicing attorney, one of the first black lawyers to hang his shingle in Charleston and not have it torn down, and his mother was a teacher until Clancy was born, at which time she became a full-time housewife.

Ever since Sardis first became conscious of time, there was Clancy. He counted himself as one of her brother's friends and had the annoying habit of calling her "Li'l Sis." All through school, and at church, there was Clancy. Some people thought they looked so cute together they might have been childhood sweethearts. For his part, Clancy had a major crush on her, but for whatever reason, she hadn't been able to bring herself to return his attention and affections. He liked to bring her little gifts, a flower he picked, a box of candy he bought with his allowance, even a stink bug he took from his science collection. "He's in love, Sard," her friends teased when they saw the stink bug. "If a guy gives you a bug, he's serious." *Right. Serious in the fourth grade.* She smiled at the memory. Now, here he was again, holding out an inviting hand, waiting for her to respond. Before she could think of an excuse to turn him down, he took her hand and practically yanked her to her feet.

"I'm surprised to see you here," she said as he lumbered around the floor, half-dancing, half-walking. The music was soft and easy, for only Cotillion-style dancing was allowed in Father Cleary Hall, none of the modern rock and roll stuff, but it didn't matter either way. Clancy would have been just as awkward whether he was holding a partner or dancing by himself. "Rumor had it you left Charleston," she continued, as the dancing started to ease her mood. As usual, Clancy was living up to his other well-known trait; he was the personification of dull and boring. As they moved back and forth across the dance floor, a quasi-smile crossed her face as she recalled a sort of date she had with him in high school. She needed an escort for her debutante ball, and her mother insisted he would make an excellent candidate.

At Eartha's encouragement, make that persistence, Sardis reluctantly agreed to a "get acquainted" dinner with him. She already knew him, but then, she didn't, really. She hoped the dinner would change her opinion about him, but it didn't. The evening was punctuated by periods of awkward silence, when he would stare at her in a strangely intent way and then look away abruptly. She was puzzled but said nothing, just wanting the entire ordeal to end. When the thankfully short evening came to a close, and he deposited her safely back to her door, he took her hands in his sweaty palms, looked intently into her eyes and said, "You probably caught me staring at you several times this evening ..." The rest of his comments were lost to history, for Sardis had to bite her lip and cough loudly to keep from laughing in his face. *So, that's what those jerky glances were all about,* she thought, stifling a guffaw welling up from deep within. *From what movie or TV show did he steal that line? He waited all evening to impress me with this rubbish?*

Bolstered by her invitation to the ball, which, unbeknownst to him, she was coerced into issuing, he made an attempt to win her exclusive loyalty before he left for college. He asked her to go steady with him. As she sought a tactful way to refuse, along with a forceful way to discourage him from asking again, he drew upon his vast media knowledge once more and demanded an answer immediately, because he didn't want to play a waiting game. Tossing tact aside, she gave him a quick and resounding no. He went to Harvard, and that was their last contact.

"A little bird told me you were engaged to get married," she said nonchalantly, still trying to draw him into the conversation. *Just say something,* she thought, exuding a long sigh, but to her surprise, he suddenly stopped dead in the middle of the floor, released her from his arms, dropped his head to his chest, and began to sniffle, leaving her standing alone in the middle of the room. In a sense, his behavior didn't surprise her, given their history, but when his mother suddenly appeared at his side and led him away to a secluded corner, Sardis's curiosity was piqued. For the first time all day, her attention shifted to another person besides Jeb. She stood transfixed, gawking at the strange scene unfolding before her, but before she could make a move, he returned onto the floor, took her in his arms, and resumed their waltz as if nothing had happened. When the dance ended, he walked her to her seat, bowed courteously, and left the party. Now that the exciting, if somewhat unusual, interlude was over, the party returned to normal, and Sardis returned to her brooding and pining.

The following morning, she awakened to the telephone ringing. At first, her foggy brain told her she shouldn't have set her alarm, and she looked at the clock without registering the time. It felt strange, scary even, not having anything to do or anywhere to go. The phone rang a second time, jolting her out of bed. She raced down the back stairs to answer it, deciding she would have to get an extension or a separate line for her room. Having only one phone was a pain in the butt, she thought, as she picked up the receiver.

"Jeb?" she said, her heart skipping a beat at the sound of his voice. Their mutual excitement reignited a smoldering flame. Jeb's voice caught in his throat and cracked at his first hello. For Sardis's part, merely uttering his name brought all of her despair and anguish to the surface and she began to cry. Jeb longed to hold her and soothe away her pain, while she wanted to reach through the wires and caress him. He ached to rub her back, letting his fingers glide gently up and down her spine like he used to do until all her nerve endings tingled. He did his best to remain strong for both of them, but as they talked, his quivering, unsteady voice betrayed his hurting heart. She told him about the party, and he shared the story of his adventurous drive to New York, wishing she were with him. Suddenly he remembered the secondary purpose for his call.

"You'll never guess who's here. I drove like a maniac all night to get here, walked into the rehearsal hall for the audition, and found myself looking into Cyrus Bloom's face. He caught a late flight and beat me here by a couple of hours." Then, measuring his words carefully in an effort to refrain from adding to her anguish, he added, "He was greatly saddened and really disappointed to discover that you couldn't make the trip yet."

Sardis had to gather all the strength she possessed to keep from crumbling, given the torment eating at her. If only there was a way. Cyrus took the phone, having heard J. B. mention his name, and the three of them tried to find a workable solution to Sardis's situation. She lost track of time as the three-way conversation again became a two-way conversation. Then came the long good-bye and the hang up. Sardis closed her eyes and leaned wearily against the wall, deep in thought.

"Hope you weren't talking to that boy you tried to stick me with." Sardis didn't move as Eartha's frigid tone interrupted her thoughts. She hoped to have a few more hours of peace and tranquility to herself before having to deal with her mother. The telephone must have awakened her. Her pleasantness, vim, and vigor from the previous day disappeared and was replaced by a haggard, drawn, depressed, paranoid shell of a woman. She threw a change purse at Sardis. "Go to Amar's and get me some BC Powder. I have a fierce headache." Sardis turned and tottered out of the kitchen. "While you're there, pick up a pack for yourself. You look as if you could use it."

Sardis took a slow, deliberate stroll through downtown, making note of the positive changes and influences integration produced. As she meandered through the city, she strolled by the old Dock Street Theater, which brought back a lot of memories. Downtown had seen the first influx of the national chain stores that were pushing many of the Jewish merchants into suburbia or out of business all together. Some things changed very little, however. When she reached Calhoun Street, the old city division remained in sharp focus, but right across the street from her old drug store, she was surprised to see a new central library. *I have to find a job and earn some money if I'm ever going to have a prayer of getting out of this city,* she thought, her pace quickening as she neared the pink-tinted library building, which was a far cry from the old segregated Hampton Library.

Sardis never thought about finding a job upon graduation. Her goals were to hone her craft and become a good actress and be a great wife, but now she found herself entering the building with great anticipation and determination. She returned home with a much lighter heart and a job application in hand. As she rounded the corner of Logan Street, she walked head-on into a rather cheerful Clancy. The encounter created an instant flashback of a momentous collision with another guy. The contrast was stark, however; the first one swept her off her feet. This one just stepped on her feet and knocked her backward, leaving her feeling total disgust. "So I guess we'll be seeing a lot more of each other," he said, smiling broadly as he readjusted his glasses, which were knocked slightly askew. Before he could finish his clichéd sentence, Sardis rolled her eyes in despair, and then looked at him intently, as if to say, "What is this fool talking about?"

Clancy picked up on her quizzical look. "Your mother said you were a really good cook, so she invited me and my folks to dinner tonight." His broad grin exposed a set of even white teeth. As the first kid at ICS to get braces, he was subjected to a lot of teasing, which he endured rather well, managing to convince his tormentors that the braces were a scientific experiment, and he was the test subject. "Then, my mom wants you to come over tomorrow," he continued proudly. Assuming a conspiratorial pose, he leaned close to her ear, as if whispering a trade secret. "Between you and me, I think they're trying to play matchmakers." Then, sticking his chest out, he added with a smirk, "Not a bad idea, huh?"

As Sardis learned as an actress, it takes very little effort to switch into and out of various emotions. You can go all the way from love to hate in a heartbeat; from calm to outrage took a little more effort, but with the right catalytic agent, a flame could be started instantaneously, and right now, a flaming rage was building. Sardis feared she didn't have the ability to contain or even to mask her outrage. "I wonder how long she's been planning this?" she muttered through clenched teeth as Clancy strained to hear what she said.

"See you later," he called, cheerfully waddling away, waving his chubby hand in a little-boy manner he never outgrew. She heard him humming merrily as he went.

When Sardis got home and walked into the kitchen, she saw a different Eartha from the one she left earlier. She was full of cheer as she worked happily away at the stove. "We're having company for dinner tonight, so we better fix something special," she said, studying her cooking encyclopedia. "I knew things would get so much better with you back home," she chirped, not even bothering to glance in Sardis's direction. Sardis slammed the headache medicine down on the table, went straight to the bathroom, and threw up. When she emerged, she sat down at the table and filled out the job application.

II

Dorcus and her family arrived at their new palatial home, which was so different from the cramped quarters they lived in on Duncan Street. "This is like living in the country," she enthused, running from front to back, and then from tree to tree.

"Don't get to used it," said her mother. "Charlie told us you two have an important date to set very soon." Dorcus stopped dead in her tracks, wishing her mother hadn't poured cold water on her sunshine day. It had gone perfectly. Her church family held a huge banquet in the fellowship hall, and she received gifts, gifts, and more gifts.

A uniform-clad Charlie was by her side all day. She had to admit, he cut a dashing figure. Some of the many single women made passes, and although she was willing to hand him off, she felt a twinge of jealousy whenever someone flirted with him or pinned him into a corner. Even Miss Julie licked her lips as she passed by him carrying her tray of cookies. As she displayed the ring for all to see, she still imagined the pandemonium that would have ensued if she had Anton by her side, his broad shoulders decorated with officer's bars. Right now, Charlie, with his newly earned sergeant's stripes, was a good substitute. It was better than having no one at all, she reasoned. Now that the celebrations were over, however, reality set in, meaning she had to make some difficult decisions, including about a job.

III

Sardis was up very early, whereupon she dressed quickly, fixed something to eat, and left the house before her mother arose. This became her routine for several months ever since her first day at work for the library. Getting the job was easier than she ever imagined. She sailed through the interview process since the library was ecstatic at finding someone so qualified to work alongside the mostly volunteer staff. As usual, things didn't go smoothly when she told her mother about her new job. "Why not just get married?" she said. "You don't have to work. I never did. Clancy is a good match for you. I know he likes you very much, and his mother and father are crazy about you. He's single, has a good education, is in a respectable profession, and is well established in our community. I don't know why his fiancée called off their wedding, but it happened just in time. Things worked out just right."

A weary Sardis wanted to shout, "But I'm already married. I just can't be with my husband yet." Her rings were carefully secured in a jeweled case, and hidden away at the back of a chest of drawers, where she was sure her mother wouldn't snoop. Neither Clancy nor his domineering mother held any appeal for her. His fiancée made a smart move by breaking off what had drifted into a five-year engagement. Both sets of mothers took the fact that she dumped him on the same day Sardis graduated as a good omen.

Sardis cringed when she recalled Clancy's odd reaction after she asked him about his engagement. His mother's over-the-top response should have removed any doubt about why he was still unattached. The girl grew tired of waiting for Clancy to cut the apron strings. "They're a good family. His father is a good lawyer. Clancy can support you, and you can start a family. It is important that you keep our bloodline going." Sardis dropped into her chair. Her head sank wearily into her hands as she prepared herself for what was becoming a nightly ritual. With her elbows propped on the cluttered dinner table, she braced herself for another Clancy marketing session. She tried her best to replace her mother's chatter with a picture of Jeb in her mind, but the nightly propaganda campaign was causing his image to slip away from her, and it frightened her. The harder Sardis tried to keep Clancy out of her life, the more he intervened. He began a ritual of popping in once a week, just to visit; then it became two or three times a week. Then, at Eartha's insistence and behest, his presence grew to weekends. He began to refer to his visits as date nights, while she called them intrusions. Through the hot summer days and into the fall, Clancy became a fixture, much like a lamp with a very dim bulb, which Sardis wished she could extinguish. How her heart ached for Jeb. How she longed to join him in New York, but things were not going as planned.

Nine months slipped past before she knew it. Working at the library was the only soothing balm of relief in her otherwise festering wound of existence, but after spending long hours each day lifting, shelving, and checking books out and in, Sardis was no closer to her goal. At first, her meager salary began to accumulate into a healthy savings account, but then household expenses intervened. Her mother's miniscule income was unable to keep pace with the high cost of urban renewal, forcing Sardis to make a choice between either hoarding her finances or ensuring that they didn't lose their house because of previous unpaid assessments and increased taxation. With her bank balance now shrinking rapidly, Sardis could only watch helplessly as the stage door slowly closed on a promising career. Her financial status helped to fortify her mother's case for marriage, however. Jeb and Cyrus remained faithful supporters and exceptional cheerleaders, but they couldn't provide the financial assistance she needed to get an acting career off the ground. Jeb was living that reality daily in New York City.

His initial audition went well, but the production never got off the ground, so, in the tradition of countless actors before him, he found temporary day jobs as a waiter, then a bartender, and sometimes a physical trainer while making the rounds for audition after audition. Auditioning was an art in itself, and although he made a favorable impression at each one, those doors still refused to open. Preparing for each audition was like a salve serving to ease the loneliness he faced in a big, cold, uncaring city. One part of him longed to have Sardis by his side, but each night, as he gradually lulled himself to sleep in his small, poorly heated flat, he was happy she had the warmth of her home to provide security.

Meanwhile, Sardis stared mindlessly at the television each night, unable to hear much of what was being said due to her mother droning on and on in the background like a swarm of bees. She learned a long time ago that silence was the only way she could maintain some semblance of sanity, and so she listened without hearing a word, while her mother's monologue became part of the background noise, like a laugh track on the sitcom flickering on the screen. As her mother muttered on endlessly, Sardis anesthetized her loneliness by recalling her last conversation with J. B.

"The first production company finally came through," he told her, almost shouting with joy. "It took a year, but I'm finally on my way to England to star in a Shakespearean production. I'll be gone for six months, and if it's successful, I may be there even longer." As he spoke, his excitement reached the point where his words tumbled out on top of each other. "I'll get real-world experience, and when I return to the States, I might be able to get a part in a Broadway production. Cyrus is working on his doctorate. Once he completes his studies, he plans to move into theater production and open his own company here in New York, so even if I can't get to Broadway right away, he promised that he'd get something going for me when I return." He was speaking so quickly she nearly missed his last comment. "My love, if this works out, I'll send for you. Our dreams and our plans can finally come true. A talent like yours can't languish. You'll always be my leading lady. I can't wait until you can share the stage, my world, and my life." His words were like a banquet in her love-starved world, and provided the nourishment she needed every evening as Clancy, and constant reminders of Clancy, repeatedly invaded her universe.

While she was reminiscing, Sardis continued to half-focus on the images flickering across the television screen. Suddenly, something hit her squarely between the eyes. She grabbed the remote control and turned the volume up to the point where even the neighbors could hear. She leapt up and dropped to her knees directly in front of the console; her mouth fell open and her face burst into a gigantic smile. Eartha was dumbfounded. She couldn't understand what prompted this sudden fascination for her daughter, who remained planted directly in front of the screen. "I'd know that grape anywhere!" she gasped, as the Fruit of the Loom commercial faded from the screen.

"He didn't tell me about this job," she lamented. "He really is a working actor now," she said out loud, the tears beginning to form while she remained rooted to the spot in front of the screen, willing his image to reappear.

"Actor?" scoffed Eartha, recovering her senses. "No security in that. Anyway, how do you know him?" Then her memory flashed back to graduation day. "Is he that colored boy Father Mackey kicked out of the tent?"

"Colored boy?" stammered Sardis, not daring to look back at her mother. The cold February wind blowing outside was no match for the blizzard now forming in Sardis's heart.

"I hope you weren't serious about him," Eartha continued nonchalantly. In her world, where anyone darker than the color of a faded burlap sack didn't exist, she literally could not see certain colors. Her memory of a little girl who'd once been too dark for ICS was repressed out of existence. "How you could ever even think to let the good Father sit exposed to the sun and let that ... that ... act-tor ... sit beside me ..." she scoffed, scolding Sardis for her faux pas.

So she did notice him, thought Sardis, her mind also racing back almost a year to graduation day and how her mother never said one word to J. B., or even about him. "Did you fake your fainting spell so that Father Mackey could sit next to you?" Sardis demanded, confronting her. Eartha shifted restlessly, like a cornered animal facing a hunter's gun. "What else did you fake? Did you feign the attack in the dorm? Did you fake being happy for me? Were you ever real with me?" Sardis continued. For the first time all evening, indeed the first time in months, there was silence. Sardis rose slowly to her feet. "What a fool I was," she whispered dejectedly to herself, not looking at her shame-faced mother.

Eartha, the master of manipulation, knew when to push and when to back off, and knew she already said too much. She felt mired in guilt. The last time she felt this vulnerable was the day her son died. Tough questions still plagued her in that regard. Should she have argued with him about his decision not to enter the medical field? She recalled words like "failure" and "family disgrace" slipping out in anger. Had she pushed him too far about the choices he made? When he said Jessie was more than just a friend? Had he actually committed suicide, disguised as a stupid game?

Trying to repair the damage she did without losing more ground, she said reassuringly, "You were not foolish, my dear. He was, as you said, acting. He turned your head with flowers, and all that false bravado and charm. Now, he's on to bigger and better things. He's probably forgotten you even exist. He would never fit into our ... your world." Like a broken record, she continued, "Now Clancy on the other hand, will make an excellent husband."

"I don't love Clancy!" said Sardis flipping channels looking for the elusive grape. "I can't stand Clancy!"

"Love?" Eartha sneered. "Love is a myth. It doesn't exist. There's only respect and duty." She reached out and grabbed the remote control from her dejected daughter's hand and, having regained her confidence, continued. "My high school graduation day was almost my wedding day. I had no choice. My mother found the ideal solution to get her darkest child out of the house."

Long-forgotten memories began to produce long-suppressed tears, and she swallowed hard to regain her composure before continuing. "In this society, a woman does as she is told. And," Eartha added emphatically pointing the remote like a weapon, "you will marry Clancy." Sardis toyed briefly with the idea of revealing her secret, but felt the time still wasn't right. Besides, what would it accomplish now? "You'll grow to love him over time," Eartha continued. "Or speaking from experience, grow to tolerate him. It's something that women like us have to face. We don't marry for love, we marry for security. We marry to preserve the pure bloodline. I told you all along, any man who was interested in you had to fit into our community. That dark man for a husband? ICS would reject your children outright. I went through that type of rejection once, and I'm not going through it again." She sat back in her comfortable chair and flipped the channel again. As if the gods were teasing her, J. B.'s face suddenly appeared. "Popular commercial," she sniffed, quickly changing the channel again and again.

IV

Dorcus had a fun summer following graduation. She spent half of her time avoiding Charlie's attempts to set a wedding date without letting him off the hook. Her second brother in Atlanta got married that summer, providing the perfect excuse to put off their own wedding plans. Meanwhile she managed to obtain a teaching position at Lamb's Elementary School in North Charleston, where her mother worked for years, but she soon discovered how difficult it was to live in her mother's shadow and up to her good reputation. She knew if she wanted to establish a name for herself, she would have to move to a different school or to a different state.

The greatest joy she had that summer, however, was receiving a letter, at long last, from Anton. He congratulated her and apologized for not being able to attend her graduation ceremony. He told her about the problems he faced while the Orangeburg Massacre took place, and about the court-martial. Now she was overcome with guilt, having harbored resentment against him for not inquiring about her safety during that horrible week. She gladly forgave him. The judicial hearing cleared him of culpability in the fragging incident. However, since his records were flagged during the investigation, he was promoted to captain later than the rest of his class. "My date of rank should have been retroactive, but no one cuts black officers any slack," he complained. She was encouraged by his disclosures, and his courage in revealing his hurt.

He trusts me with his heart, she sighed, holding the letter to her breast. She carefully folded the two-page document and returned it to its envelope for safekeeping.

Anton looked forward to completing his tour of duty in Vietnam by the middle of 1969 but didn't know where he would be stationed after that. With the adversities he faced, he wondered if he wanted to continue with a military career. Dorcus held out hope he would return to South Carolina, and she closed her eyes, as if wishing on a star, like she used to do as a little girl. *I hope he'll be assigned to Ft. Jackson,* she thought. *Then, we can to get to know each other again. If not, I'll be there for him, wherever he is,* she vowed, carefully placing the precious envelope in her jewelry box, where she also kept her engagement ring most of the time.

She never told Charlie about the letter and didn't know if Charlie ever said anything to Anton about their engagement, although Anton gave no indications in his letter. Her high-wire act became more precarious with every passing day, and she longed for a safety net. It was a lonesome burden to bear, and at times she thought about calling her old roommate Sardis, but once they returned to Charleston, that old color schism stood in the way. She was amazed she could now have white neighbors and white sisters-in-law and yet still be so far removed from black people of a lighter hue. Charlie kept pressing her to set a date, and she managed to put him off, until one day a fateful telephone call forced her into a decision. She could no longer ignore his pleas. "I'm on orders to go overseas," he told her.

Dorcus breathed a sigh of relief. She secretly hoped that he, too, would be sent to Vietnam. That way, she could be free of him for at least a year. Meanwhile, Anton would return, which might give her a chance to rekindle what they once had, for a weekend at least. Everything would work out neatly. Dorcus loved neat endings. That bubble, however, soon burst, and calamity ensued. "Dear Uncle Sam is sending me to Germany for a three-year tour, and since I'm allowed to be accompanied by my family, I want my wife to join me. So it's now, Dorcus." Her heart caught in her throat, especially at his reference to her as his wife, as if it were a done deed, and a wave of panic engulfed her.

Despite her shock, she had the presence of mind to ask him more questions, like how soon and where. As Charlie answered each one, she tried to raise objections. She didn't want to let a sure thing go just yet. She wanted to buy time to work things out with the man who was still her first love. She couldn't remember what conclusion she finally reached, but when the call ended, she slumped to the floor, her body drenched in sweat and her head numb from frantically drumming up questions and excuses. "Next week. In Columbia. At a Justice of the Peace," Charlie concluded emphatically. He was just as emotionally drained as she was, and he was tired of excuses. "We won't have time to plan a big wedding. When we return stateside, we can have a real ceremony, with all of the relatives. That should please everybody," he decreed.

Dorcus knew this solution was like stepping into a minefield. It would please no one. What would she tell her family? How could she inform her church members that the preacher's daughter would not be married by her father, or that the union would not be blessed by clergy? "I'm the only daughter," she pleaded. "My dad has dreamt of the day when he could not only give me away, but bless the union. And oh dear me; Mom. She would never, ever forgive me." Reverting to a childhood habit, she slipped into the solitude of a closet, which always served to shield her from trouble when she didn't want anyone, not even God, to find her. Lying on the floor, her legs drawn tightly to her chest, she wept silently.

V

The first day of August 1969 was to live in Sardis's memory forever. It was dominated by one phrase: "If only ..."

"If only I'd had more time. If only I could have flown to be with him. Oh, if only I'd had a chance to speak to him just one more time. If only I'd gotten his call before my mother did." Sardis mumbled, head bowed in prayer, as she waited for the wedding march to begin. Her tears were staining the satin fabric, but she didn't care. *I was so close,* she thought, thinking of her bank balance. *So close.*

Following his highly acclaimed performance during a six-week run of *The Two Gentlemen of Verona,* J. B. returned to the United States long enough to film some television productions, including the commercial Sardis and her mother saw, before returning to Europe to star in another long-running play. Given his vagabond existence, it was very difficult for Sardis to either call or write, so Cyrus Bloom played intermediary. He still wanted to see both of his star performers flourish. "I know there are future productions with good roles for black actresses in the works," Bloom relayed to her. "And Sard, if you can get to Europe, performance opportunities abound. With your looks and talent, you can have your pick of a thousand parts. Did you catch our boy in a national commercial?" He had begun referring to J. B. as "our boy," a term of endearment, since he felt a kinship and fatherly bond with both of them. He witnessed the beginning of their relationship, kept their secret, and was now witnessing the sad end he knew would be inevitable, even though he still hoped for a happily ever after.

Marriage is difficult enough when two people are sharing the same space, but if it has to exist in theory, and not in reality, it has no chance, so Cyrus appointed himself as their liaison. What he couldn't do, however, was sustain their feelings for one another. His acting skills could never convey their emotions by means of relayed messages. He helped them to celebrate their one-year anniversary, but he knew in his heart there would likely be no more.

When the letter arrived on that summer day in June, Sardis's world imploded in an instant. The fact that she was even able to receive his letters at all was miraculous. She rented a private mail box after discovering that Eartha read and dumped Jeb's first correspondences and after continuous protests were ignored. "I have a right to receive and read every document that is delivered to this house," her mother said. "Why would you want to hide anything from me? Letters from that boy won't change anything. In fact, go ahead and read them, and when you get the one saying he is moving on, I want to be the first to know about that."

That fateful letter arrived postmarked in England. She sensed a different tone as soon as she ripped the envelope open. He addressed it "Dear Sard." His others were addressed to "My Dear, Sweet Love," followed immediately by "I miss you so much." As she read further, her suspicions were confirmed. Enclosed with the letter was an application for divorce. Her immediate response would have been to cry out, but not wanting to create chaos in the post office lobby, she quickly walked out into the street, where she read the letter again. She sensed a tender passion from the comments he made, and his awkward phrasing revealed the struggle he had in coming to his decision. One paragraph caught her eye, however, revealing he had help in making his decision. "I understand that your childhood sweetheart has reentered your life and wishes to marry you." A murderous rage stirred within her, and her thoughts frightened her as she contemplated everything from suicide to murder.

She thought of going home but feared what she might say, or do, if she saw her mother, and she refused to retreat to her room and lock herself away. That sounded too much like mother like daughter, so she forced herself to hold her head high and continue in the opposite direction, boldly placing one foot in front of the other. It was only by sheer force of will that she was able to enter the library that day. She greeted her fellow workers as always, never letting on to the turmoil she experienced within. Her stomach was tied in knots and her head throbbed, as if cannons were being fired at regular intervals. She spent most of the day hidden away in a remote corner with obsolete, unread, and out-of-date books, where she could work and cry in peace. At noon, she left the cool surrounds of the library and walked out into the blazing summer heat, but the temperature change was irrelevant. Her body was numb to her surroundings. She took the crumpled envelope from her purse and walked on to Marion Square, where she snatched a morsel of shade so she could read his words again.

"You will always be my first love, but I, too, have to move on with my life. I met a delightful girl, and have asked her to be my wife. She, like you, is an actress. We met when I returned to Britain to star in the second Shakespearean production. I never expected to love anyone else but ... you will also be free to pursue other interests."

She couldn't read any more. How could her heart ache so much and yet sustain its living soul? After signing and mailing the documents, she managed to pick herself up and complete her work, but by the end of the day, she felt as though her head was about to split from tension and lack of food. After crossing King Street, she stepped into the cool Amar Drug Store and got the surprise of her life when a very elderly black pharmacist suddenly appeared, as if by magic, from out of the shadows. "BC Powder, please," she said.

He stared at her for a minute, and then, in a warm, friendly voice, said, "Wouldn't you rather have the tablets? I know the powder is an old remedy, but in spite of the store's appearance, we do have modern medicine."

This drew a smile from her. "It was an automatic request. My mother insists on using it. Claims it's so much better than tablets. Tell you what, let me have both. Sooner or later, she'll probably need the tablets." Peering curiously at the kindly old druggist, she finally asked, "Who are you? I've never seen you here before." In one way, she was happy to see him, because the starchy, regular druggist was not whom she needed to see today. He might have been the owner of the store, but he was definitely in dire need of a personality transplant. She often wondered how he kept his customers. He was always gruff and in a hurry, as if to say, "Don't bother me, I'm busy. I haven't got time for you."

"I've been here a long time, on and off. In fact, I've been everywhere, on and off. Once, I was the only colored druggist around. I'd pick up prescriptions for all of the colored patients, fill them through Roper Hospital, and then bring them back for the druggist to give to the patients, but now things are opening up, I don't have to work in the shadows any more. I work part-time at several different places, and like today, when the regular druggist is ill, they call me in."

"My dad worked at Roper," Sardis said absentmindedly.

He smiled a bright, gleaming smile. "I know, Miss Fontain. He was a fine man."

Sardis's mouth dropped and her eyes opened wide in surprise at his recognition. He smiled slyly, winked, and then disappeared to get her medicine. She forgot her pain for a few minutes as she looked around the shelves, packed with bottles, silently wishing for one containing a magic formula that could transform her misery into instant happiness. *If only there was* ... She paused, as a purple-hued vial, etched with skull and crossbones, came into view. Her imagination took flight. *Oh how easy it would be to* ... Again, she paused. *That would solve so much,* she mused. She found herself unable to complete any of her thoughts. Completing thoughts meant completing acts, and she dared not think about the act.

"It's a decoy," a soft voice murmured behind her. She turned and stared blankly at the druggist, then shuddered, not so much at what she was thinking, but at the realization that he could see right through her. His longish, graying hair half-covered his face. It was soft and wavy, as if it had been processed, typical of light-skinned black men. Brushing it back, he spoke again. "That bottle is a decoy. People come in and like you, ask for medicine for their headaches, but then they spot that little bottle and they think, 'Ah, it contains poison. What if …' And then their real aches surface. They believe that little bottle will solve all of their problems. 'If I can only get rid of ….' Who? Parent? Spouse? Child? Lover? That last one is usually the most popular." Sardis couldn't help but smile again. He set her package on the counter and rang the sale up on what must have been one of the first cash registers ever made. As he did so, he continued to talk. "When Mr. Bernard and Mr. Council invented this powder, they didn't intend for it to be mixed with anything other than soda water, and certainly didn't mean it to be poison powder in disguise. Now, would you like to tell me what kind of aches you might be hiding?"

There was something about the way he looked at her, with his soulful blue-gray eyes and his willingness to listen, that broke through her defenses, and she broke down and cried her eyes dry again. Sardis eventually walked into her house very late that evening. She had with her a bag containing her mother's BC Powder and a bottle of tablets. She also had a sense of calm, and of peace.

VI

Dorcus felt surprisingly calm as the plane soared above the cloud cover, the knots in her stomach easing as she began to recover from the turbulence of her first flight, and from the squalls she created at ground level before she left South Carolina. As she marveled at the heavenly splendor of the sun radiating off the puffy white cumulus beneath her, she was consumed with guilt about how poorly she handled the situation. But what else could she do?

A week after Charlie called, she slipped out of her house very early on Saturday morning and drove to Columbia to keep her date with him. Because of his accounting skills, and his degree, he moved up the ranks rather quickly. He entered a career path that made him a specialist in his field, and as a result, he wasn't required to participate in field exercises or combat training. Instead, he worked in an office, and following his advanced training, he was assigned at his training base at Ft. Jackson, South Carolina The assignment thrilled him, but not Dorcus, who wished things were reversed; Charlie in Vietnam and Anton close by. When Dorcus asked him about his chances of getting an assignment in "Nam," he teased her by responding with an amusing rhyme. "Twinkle twinkle little shield, keep me off the battlefield." Then, pointing to a symbol on his uniform lapel he added, "See these shields? They help me to stay in the office. I push papers and pencils, not bullets."

Dorcus didn't comprehend any of it, but she indulged his witticisms with a smile and a consenting nod; however, the time came for him to rotate to another assignment. Germany sounded like an exciting place. Her travel experience was limited to one out-of-state trip to North Carolina for a Sunday school convention and a few to Atlanta for sibling celebrations: graduations, weddings, and births. She longed for exotic travel, but this was Charlie. She wasn't even sure she loved him. His love for her, however, was constantly on display for all to see. On weekends when he wasn't on duty, he could be found sitting at her side in the first family pew. The preacher even made him a member of the Deacons Board, the congregation having accepted him as one of their own. A smile crossed Dorcus's face when she remembered some advice frail old Mother Sadie gave her as she noted a year had passed without a wedding date being set. "Bag him while you still can, baby. A good man is hard to come by."

"But I'm not sure I really love him," she recalled protesting.

Sadie scoffed at the idea. "A man loves you, but you respect him. If you waitin' to love him, you'll end up like that other gal with them terrible cookies." This from a woman entering her second century. As she burnt rubber down the highway, her mind tried to process a jumble of thoughts, but it only caused more confusion.

Charlie met her at his house. He had everything all arranged. "I thought you said a friend would be coming with you?" he said, surprised when she arrived alone. It should have tipped him off that something was amiss. Dorcus stammered an explanation as she got into his vehicle, and they drove all the way through Columbia to a small white chapel.

Unlike the excitement that surrounds most couples who are about to elope, they were unusually silent during the drive. As they entered the gravel parking lot, Charlie saw some of his base buddies had already arrived. During one of his brief jaunts back to Charleston, they secretly obtained a marriage license, and Dorcus stored it with her ring for safekeeping, until they could set a date; at least that's what she told herself. Just as they were about to enter into the chapel, Dorcus stopped abruptly. "Oh, I forgot to bring the license." Then, smiling sweetly at Charlie, she chirped, "Maybe we can postpone this for another time."

Dorcus, never an actress, now prayed her charm and sweet innocent smile would not betray the guilt she suppressed. Charlie deserved better and she knew it. Why couldn't she surrender? Why couldn't she accept him, care for him as much as he obviously cared for her—love him?

Charlie's usually mild-mannered demeanor disappeared. His face darkened, and his eyes flashed with fury. Then he noticed she wasn't even wearing his ring. Charlie looked at Dorcus as if he was seeing her for the first time, and she shrank under the intensity of his gaze. Finally, he was seeing someone he thought he knew, but didn't; someone whose love he thought he had won, but couldn't; someone he never wanted to lose, but whom, he now realized, was never his in the first place. William Shakespeare wrote many plays that captured moments such as this. They were called tragedies. Tragedies often revolved around a series of events such as this, the loss of hope, the loss of love, or the loss of a promising future. Most tragedies eventually resulted in the loss of someone's life, after the human mind finally snaps and emotions dictate regrettable actions, as this scene was close to fulfilling. Charlie thought how easy it would be to simply reach out and, with one quick twist, snap her neck and put an end to his nightmare. His slight body was tense and rigid to the point where veins were bulging out everywhere. His heart raced and then broke into a million pieces, and his thoughts frightened him as murderous fury overtook him.

One of his friends, sensing his distress, approached from behind and placed a comforting hand on his shoulder. Charlie turned to him and said, "Take her back to my house so she can pick up her car and go home." He then executed a razor-sharp about face and headed straight for his vehicle. Dorcus stood in stunned silence, still greatly alarmed, but hopeful all the same. From prior experience, she didn't think Charlie would remain angry with her for very long and anticipated that, any second now, he'd forgive her, turn around, come back, and embrace her and tell her that he understood. She expected he would find the entire thing amusing, and he would then tell her to wait for him until he returned from Germany, for by then she would know for sure if he was the right man, but he kept walking. This was not going according to her expectations. As he reached his car, Charlie stopped and looked back at her standing, waiting in expectation. His demeanor had already softened, and her face lit up, hoping that she'd been right.

"He's at Ft. Ord in California," said Charlie. Then, noticing her puzzled expression, he said, "Anton." The sound of his name made Dorcus's heart skip a beat. "He's stationed at Ft. Ord. And I never told him about us. I always prayed you'd have a change of heart and change your mind about him, dreamt that you'd tell him about the man who really loved you. I wish happiness for the both of you." At that, he climbed into his car and spun out of the parking lot, and out of Dorcus's life.

The next week, as her flight landed in Monterey, California, the excitement she felt made her light-headed. Once again, she was about to come face-to-face with the love of her life, the man she fought so hard to win in what seemed like a lifetime ago on State's campus; her lover, her light, her world.

VII

There is much truth in the axiom that when you marry, you marry the man *and* his family. Clancy's family lived two blocks south and one block east on Legare Street. Sardis was a teen before she learned the street's name was pronounced "La-gree." What mattered to her now, however, was that it was within walking distance, a fact that her nondriving mother-in-law took advantage of almost daily. Clancy moved into the Fontain residence as a result of a pact the two mothers made without consulting either Sardis or Clancy. Of course, he readily agreed to the deal, since it meant he would inherit the property and wouldn't have to go to the trouble of finding a new house for himself and his bride of three months. "It just makes good sense," his mother stated. "Eartha would be alone and without the support she needs. Now, there will be a man in the house."

Sardis' attention turned briefly from the card game, and a sneer crossed her features. They took a brief rest from the game while Dorcus used the restroom. "We still had no man in the house," Sardis mumbled to Grace.

"Clancy was a college educated, light-skinned black man from a prime Charleston family, with a good profession and excellent future prospects. He shared a thriving practice with his father and was a good provider. As desegregation opened up more and more opportunities, they were able to find and rent a small office on Broad Street, in the heart of the downtown business district, not far from the prime intersection of Broad and Meeting, known traditionally as the four corners of law. Their business grew as more and more white clients sought out their services. But he was still his mother's little boy. A ton of guilt weighed me down. I lost the battle, lost the war, and surrendered. I wished I could love this man who claimed me as his wife. Somewhere in the world, there was a woman who would jump through hoops to have him, but I was not that woman. Now, however, I was stuck with him."

Dorcus rejoined the game, and Sardis continued.

"I took over where his Mommy left off. He allowed me to work as long as we didn't have children, but he made it clear his offspring would not have a working mother. Then he and my mom got together and tried to influence nature. They hoped to tire me out, so I'd give up the idea of working at the library, but I prevailed. I would have gone insane if I'd stayed in this house day in, day out. Mom refused to help with the housework, so it fell on me to have his dinner ready and on the table when he got home. He even expected the table to be formally set every day. We couldn't eat in the kitchen anymore; it was always the formal dining room. But I wouldn't let them get to me. We took over the bedroom that used to be my brother's room. That was another big fight. I suggested moving Mom out of the master bedroom, since the house was now ours. Ever tried pulling a locomotive with a small car? It would have been easier. A lot of time had passed since my brother's death, but I could still feel his presence. It made me sick to my stomach the first week or so that I slept in that room, and all the throwing up gave everyone false hope that I was pregnant. If anyone had known about his attempts at intimacy, though, they would have known that having children would be an unfulfilled dream for a long time." Her body stiffened at the mere thought of him touching her. "He may have had a basic knowledge of science, but conception and reproduction were not his forte." They all laughed at the picture she painted, and howled when she provided a more detailed description and then resorted to stifled snickers when Eartha stirred in her restless sleep.

Her mother hounded her about her duty to her husband day in, day out, but Sardis was starved for affection, and her skin hungered for a romantic caress. She yearned for an erotic sensation, recalling Jeb and that special gift; or perhaps it had been because she loved him dearly and actually wanted him to touch her. When two people who are right for each other find each other, even a simple act like holding hands becomes soulful and erotic. As much as she cared for Byron the four years they dated, nothing he did ever made her quiver the way Jeb could, the way he looked at her, the sound of his voice, just sitting together, shoulder to shoulder.

From time to time, just to escape the daily drudgery, she would steal away to the library basement and there, in the dark, imagine his touch. It wasn't sexual; if a relationship is right, it doesn't have to be sexual. Their hands would touch, with fingers intertwined, and they would hold each other tight, unable to take sufficient breaths. Her head would list from side to side as she imagined Jeb's hand inching slowly down her spine, vertebra by sweet vertebra, sending tingling, electric vibrations through each nerve ending in her body.

"That's how we got caught, and why Jeb got suspended. We were sitting at a drive-in theater scrunched way down in the backseat of his friend's car. Orangeburg still hadn't recovered from the massacre trauma, and someone thought we were an interracial couple making out on the floor, so the theater owners called the police."

Dorcus, irritated, looked up from her hand. "I remember I had to educate our dorm sisters about the expired laws on interracial dating. Even though it didn't apply in your case, the thought of it still rankles. Ignorance reigns supreme, I guess."

"People didn't care about laws," said Sardis. "And they never thought laws were passed to benefit both black and white people. They were still paralyzed by paranoia, fear, and insecurity, and it was obvious they didn't want to ignite any more racial fires. The police arrived, and they were very polite for a change. The misunderstanding was quickly cleared up, but not before a college staff member saw us. You would think with all the college had been through, and with all the complaints the students lodged about the stupid rules and regulations, they would have looked the other way, but no, they gave him up. Their loss, his gain. He never returned for the diploma; just got his degree in life."

Sardis's "mini-vacation" trips to the library basement increased as Jeb's appearances on television and in movies became increasingly frequent. Her spirits soared so much at the sight of him that Clancy banned his likeness from their house. This only heightened her yearnings, which in turn made her more creative in finding new ways to view his work.

"I wanted him so much, I started getting headaches. They were real on days when I saw him on screen and faked whenever my imagination took over. Before I knew it, I was suffering from a headache every day. They served their purpose, though, because they held the big oaf I'd married at bay for a while, but my idiot husband must have complained to his mother that I was denying him. So, as usual, she got involved, and began dropping more frequent hints about wanting grandchildren, hoping I would get her subtle and not-so-subtle messages. I was determined not to cooperate, but Clancy didn't dare refuse Mommy anything she wanted. He began to wait until I fell asleep. I would feel the bed beginning to shake as he hovered over me. Then, whether I was ready or not, or even wanted him or not, he'd move into action."

Her forlorn look drew her companions into the loveless bed with her. "Each time I refused, or pushed him away, he would whine about his rights. I asked him where *my* rights were, and he had the nerve to answer that I had no rights. It became a nightly struggle until I threatened to move back into my old room."

"And I used to think you had it made," Grace mumbled under her breath, playing a trump card.

"He didn't believe me, so we began to play a nightly game. After we closed the door to our living quarters, I retreated to my old room, locked the door, and stayed there, while he cried and begged and plead for me to return to our marriage bed. This happened every night for a month."

"Did you ever give in?" Dorcus asked gently.

Sardis nodded, but refrained from providing them with any further details. The den was enveloped in silence as Grace dealt the cards for another hand. She could never share the condition of her heart with another single soul. As their play continued, her memory swept back to a defeated Clancy, who dried his tears as she entered their room. She sat majestically on the bed next to him, and he looked at her as a whipped dog looks at its master.

"You can have my body but never my heart," she began slowly. "Call me your wife, but never your woman. My love belongs to another; always has, and always will." Then she turned out the light and went to sleep.

VIII

When her flight landed, Dorcus quickly grabbed her single piece of luggage and made a beeline for the bathroom, where she checked herself out in the mirror one last time, her excitement growing by the second. She was wearing the cute pixie haircut he would remember and sported a dress similar to the one she wore when they first met. *I want to make sure he recognizes me,* she thought. *It's been a long time; three years with no pictures, nothing.* She sent her flight details to Anton, so he was expecting her, but as she scanned the faces in the surrounding crowd, she couldn't see anyone even remotely resembling him. Then, she spotted a blond-haired, blue-eyed man standing to one side with a small, hand-printed sign reading, "Dorcus Dupree." *He couldn't have changed that much,* she thought, to her amusement. "I'm Dorcus Dupree," she said, extending her hand.

"I'm Milt. Big A couldn't get away in time to pick you up, so I'm subbing. Your limo awaits without." Dorcus smiled as he escorted her to the "limo," which turned out to be a yellow Porsche convertible roadster. When Milt put the top down, Dorcus felt like she just arrived in Paradise. *Now this is more like it,* she thought to herself as they sped away from the airport. As the mellow strains of Simon and Garfunkel's "The Sounds of Silence" drifted from the radio, she felt as if she were in a commercial. She didn't care what the product was, she was just enjoying the happiness it produced. Monterey, with its unique charm, was an old Mission city, full of grace and romance. Milt took her on a short sightseeing excursion as they sped through some of the most scenic real estate on planet Earth. He pointed out landmarks in Carmel Valley, Salinas, Pacific Grove, and Seaside. The Pacific Ocean was alongside her, and clear blue sky was overhead. Milt turned onto "Seventeen-Mile Drive," a scenic drive through Pacific Grove and Pebble Beach, home of one of the most famous golf courses in the world. After being waved through the guarded entry gate, they glided along meandering paths, each with phenomenal views.

"I'm taking the long way in so you can see the splendor of this place," he said as they drove past beaches and up hills with breathtaking views.

Dorcus sat back and drank in the warm sunshine, cooled by a light breeze that was coming from the ocean, admiring magnificent houses all boasting of opulence and well-being. Eventually, they turned into a road named Sunridge Drive, the street Anton mentioned in his brief letter. They rounded a bend, and Milt pulled up in front of a sprawling, single-story, L-shaped residence. It had a two-car garage attached to the house, but there were at least five more cars parked off the roadway in front. Dorcus's eyes widened with wonder as her active imagination took over. She saw herself waking up to the splendor of the ocean roar. She would get her husband off to work in the morning, then wake their two, no three, children and get them off to school. She couldn't recall having seen any schools on the way in, but there must be schools somewhere nearby. Maybe she could learn how to play golf, and join the other officers' wives in taking advantage of their famous local course. *This is even better than my brothers' houses in Atlanta,* she thought as she eased herself out of the car seat. *They're going to be blown away when they see what their little sister has.*

"Welcome to the Sunridge Inn," said Milt. Dorcus's mind slowly processed his comment as he closed the car door behind her, but thinking this was just another military reference she didn't comprehend, she let it pass without question. The home had a grand view of the Salinas Valley and was large and spacious. The front door was adorned with a large poster featuring a picture of a marijuana cigarette over large lettering stating, "Keep off the Grass."

"Hello, everyone. This is Dorcus," Milt called to a group of people who were sitting around a large Monopoly board. There were a few waves, and various forms of greetings, but most didn't even bother to look in her direction. "Now, I believe Big A said you were only here for the weekend, right?" said Milt, taking her bag to the entrance of a hallway. "I think we were going to let you use this room over here, unless you were planning to crib with Big A. He kind of hinted that you two were just friends."

Dorcus's mind became paralyzed with questions. In her astonishment, her mouth opened, but no sound emerged, and she stood frozen in her tracks. Milt guided her gently into a bedroom that obviously belonged to someone she would only temporarily displace. The closets were filled with fatigues and combat boots, and pictures on the dresser were of a smiling couple posed in front of some of the landmarks she had just seen.

"Big A's pad is right next door. This guy is gone for the weekend with his fiancée, so you can crash in here, but only until Sunday. By then, though you and Big A might have made other arrangements." He looked at his watch and added, "He should be here any time now. Come out and join the gang if you want. We welcome everybody here. We never know who'll show up over a given weekend." Milt left the room, closing the door as he went, leaving a perplexed Dorcus with the room, and her thoughts, to herself. *Who are these people, and why are they in Anton's house; our house?* she wondered over and over as she sat gingerly on the edge of the bed. Suddenly, she heard a rear door open. "Your guest is here," she heard a voice call out. "Check the room next door to yours." Next, she heard a gentle rapping, but she didn't move or answer right away, since she still hadn't found her voice.

"Dorc?" she heard a somewhat familiar voice call. He sounded the same, yet different. It was no longer the voice of a young twenty-year-old lieutenant, but a mature voice; an ageing voice; a weary voice. She rose, walked to the door, and opened it. She took two steps backward and emitted an audible gasp before she had a chance to stifle it. Anton smiled his familiar smile, pretending not to notice her reaction. "You look fantastic," he said, giving her a warm, brotherly

371

embrace. Then, gently caressing her hands, his eyes scanned her up and down, like an x-ray machine before he added approvingly, "I'd know you anywhere, but guess I've changed quite a bit."

She wanted to lie, but before her stood a stranger, his once-smooth skin covered in tiny, and some not so tiny, boils and cysts. After storing his gear and fatigues in the room next to hers, he invited her for a stroll through the canyon so they could catch up. As they left the house, she noticed that the crowd in the front room had increased by two.

"I had a run in with a chemical called Agent Orange," he explained. "My squad was trying to clear out some Vietnamese nests hidden deep in the jungle, and they sprayed this stuff to get rid of a lot of the vegetation. It worked. We found those guys and rousted them out, but the stuff got all over me and I couldn't decontaminate in time. The hospital here at the base takes care of me. I have to get my skin treated with special chemical baths every week. It burns like fire, but it eases the constant pain."

The once clear green eyes were now bloodshot and smoky. "Lack of a lot of sleep," he told her. "Both in the Nam, and since I've been back. Constant nightmares. I relive scenes every night. When I'm in the field, I sometimes take my rifle and go to the range late at night and fire. Fire at anything. Anything that will get these ghosts out of my head. Every time some draft-dodging, card-burning, pinko hippie calls me baby killer, I feel like turning one of those rounds on him." His hair really took her by surprise. She remembered he'd worn it slicked back and carefully groomed. She ran her fingers through it once and thought it was natural. Now, he sported a mini-Afro. "Oh that," he laughed, seeing her gaze. "Man, I stopped using that processing junk years ago. Couldn't find any in the jungle anyhow. The troops liked it this way too. Still can't grow it out the way I want, but once I leave this man's army, I plan to do it right. Like the Panther brothers. They got the right idea." The nicotine-stained teeth and fingers needed no explanation, as he grabbed a cigarette from his shirt pocket and lit it as soon as he released her from their embrace. That one was followed by a second, and then a third, which he lit with the nubs of the ones he just finished.

Their walking route took them to a favorite lookout point, where they stopped briefly while Anton embraced her. She felt some slight stirrings, but the old flame failed to reignite. They returned to the house, and after he showered and changed his attire, he escorted her to a battered old Mustang and whisked her away to an evening of what he said would be fantastic entertainment. As they left, she noticed there was at least one more car in front of the place. The house was filling up. "It's a good thing I knew you were coming," he laughed, "so I was able to secure you a bed. You never know what or who will pop up at that place over the weekend." Dorcus sat looking straight ahead. He reached over and grabbed her hand and added, "Of course, we can free up that bed if you want to stay with me. Take up where we left off on OB grad night." She turned to him and smiled, but politely refused his proposal. *Can't lose it tonight, girl,* she told herself. *Nothing stronger than soda.*

They began their night at the Officers Club at Ft. Ord. Like most "O" clubs, as they were known, this one was located in what had once been a large mansion. The building was built in the Spanish tradition that characterized much of the area surrounding the old post. It was Friday evening, so the popular all-you-can-eat seafood buffet was on offer, and the dining room was packed.

"Now I'll take you to the *real* 'O' club," said Anton as they pulled out of the parking lot. "This place is in Carmel. It's called the Mission Inn. A lot of the junior officers go there on weekends and dance their cares away."

Nighttime Monterey was different from daytime Monterey. The winding roads she enjoyed upon her arrival became dark, haunting places at night. A slightly inebriated Anton heightened the tension as the poorly maintained vehicle sputtered up and down treacherous paths. A part of her wished for this night to end, yet another part pined to recreate that special graduation night. Nighttime noises intruded, punctuating their lack of conversation. She was happy to see the bright lights pointing the way to the Mission San Carlos Borromeo de Carmelo, one of the many religious outposts built by the Spanish, which figured prominently in California's history. The club was a more modern structure adjacent to the ancient mission.

The crowd was clearly a mixture of military and civilians, each distinguished by their attire. Even out of uniform, military men looked like military men. Not only did their short hair give them away, but their attire of slacks with sport shirts, most of which were purchased at the Post Exchange, looked just as uniform as the battle attire they wore daily. Tie dyes, bell bottoms, long hair, granny dresses, hot pants, love beads, and the ever-present peace symbol adorned those determined to make a statement about the military and about the war in general. In the small space with its minuscule dance floor, however, they all came together for one purpose: to dance their woes, sorrows, and tribulations away, or to meet and connect, gaining new woes, sorrows, and tribulations in a frenzy of gyrations to the loud, endless beat. Dorcus discovered Anton was a regular customer when the house staff and the DJ spinning records all greeted Big A by name. They danced, he drank, they danced some more, he drank some more. She wondered what kind of pain he was trying to dull, or what he might be trying to forget. Moreover, she wondered if she could ever fit into this world of his.

Dorcus still had lots of questions to ask him, but as they left the Mission Inn, fatigue overtook both of them, so she knew the answers would not be forthcoming that evening. They returned to the house well after midnight and were greeted by yet another party. The house was wall-to-wall people, dancing and drinking a seemingly endless supply of BYO alcohol. The ever-present Monopoly game continued, and there were a few poker games in full swing.

"Well, doesn't look like we'll get much sleep tonight," shouted Anton over the noise as he was welcomed to cheers of "Big A is in the house" and "Hey, Baylor, over here. Bring your friend." Dorcus excused herself, however, citing jet lag and fatigue. When she reached the back room, she glanced over her shoulder just before entering and saw Anton grab a glass of some type of liquid before swaggering over to a poker table.

As it turned out, she might as well have joined the party after all, because she couldn't sleep. The party wasn't all that loud, but there was sufficient noise to remind her that it was going on. Regardless of the party, however, her head was spinning with thoughts and questions. Lying there in the dark room, she relived their last time together and how sweet it was in spite of her ambivalence. She envisioned Anton in the ROTC parade, which now seemed a lifetime ago, and remembered the happy time at State's graduation, when he'd managed to score an extra ticket so she could sit with his parents. *I'll see if I can get some answers tomorrow,* she vowed, *and if not tomorrow, maybe the next day. Maybe he just needs a good woman by his side to give him stability,* she told herself between silent sobs. *I can do that. I'll be there for him.*

She didn't know how long she slept, but the smell of something cooking for breakfast roused her. After carefully dressing, she made her way through the slumbering bodies piled here and there throughout the living room and dining areas. For the first time, she noticed how sparsely furnished the rooms were. The living room was practically devoid of furniture, except for a large couch that appeared to be a sleeper. It had a television, but the only other furniture in the room was the card tables and chairs. The scenario was similar in the dining area. It was obvious that this house was structured for pleasure.

To gain entrance to the large kitchen, it was necessary to pass through a swinging door, and Dorcus opened the door cautiously, not knowing what she would find. To her surprise, it was a beautiful, warm, inviting room, full of morning sunshine. Given that the rest of the house was so modern, the kitchen was old-fashioned in its design, with lots of cabinet and counter space. It was her dream kitchen, but this morning, two other people were in it. As she walked into the room, Milt turned and greeted her joyfully. "I told you we'd have at least one other person join us if we cooked something up," he told his female companion. With their matching blue eyes and blond hair, they looked like Barbie and Ken dolls. It was obvious they were a serious couple.

"Join us, please," the girl chirped, producing another plate. She took a pie pan out of the oven and cut a slice, then reached into a toaster oven and took out some flat bread with holes in it. She placed both items on the plate and set it before Dorcus. After years of breakfast fare consisting of hominy grits and gravy, or pancakes with sausage and biscuits and eggs and ham, Dorcus didn't know how she was supposed to eat this. She was a quick study, however, and soon learned that quiche and English muffins with butter and jam were a satisfying treat.

Milt proceeded to explain the workings of the house. "It's only like this on the weekends, for the most part," he said. "I guess Big A didn't explain much to you before you arrived." Dorcus smiled to herself as she took another mouthful of food. *Big A,* she thought, picking up on his popular moniker, *didn't have much time to do much of anything.*

As soon as Charlie revealed his location to her on that dreadful day, she drove straight back to Charleston. *Orangeburg is on the way,* she told herself. *Perhaps the ROTC office can assist me again,* she wondered, and they did. She contacted him immediately and told him of her planned visit. She viewed the visit as the military views reconnaissance missions. If things went according to plan, she would return to Charleston just long enough to quit her job, pack her belongings, and drive west. He mentioned a house and she thought … she stopped her musings before tears had a chance to form.

"I don't want you to get the wrong impression," Milt continued. "Normally, there are only five guys actually living here. It's a five-bedroom house, and we share the rent."

He went on to explain how, over the three years since the first occupants moved in, it gradually evolved into a retreat from daily life. The original tenants had long since left, to be replaced by others. The vacant room was usually rented to a captain, although a major snuck in once, but since they had to be careful about fraternization, most of those who crashed and partied every weekend were captains.

Life was becoming more difficult for those serving on active duty. Dorcus had already heard the "commie pinko" tirade from Anton, and she knew about the growing unrest across the nation. People were no longer grateful for the sacrifices the military was making but instead, they'd begun to blame the military for the unpopular war in Vietnam. Experiencing the hatred firsthand gave her a new, chilling perspective. Maybe now she could help Anton to overcome his demons and his pain. As she sat across the table from this couple who were obviously very much in love, her dreams returned, and she looked forward to spending the next two days with Anton. It would give them a chance to talk and to plan their future. Suddenly, things were looking bright again. This new day held great promise and exceptional hope.

IX

The friendly old druggist soon became like a second father to Sardis. He began working more regular hours, and on Wednesday afternoons, Sardis could usually count on finding him behind the counter. She began taking her lunch break a half an hour later than normal, so she could sit and talk, while he became her private therapist and mentor. Her relationship with Clancy remained the same; no better, no worse. Pressure was closing in on all sides to do her womanly deed and begin a family, to quit her useless job and become a housewife. However, she didn't want to produce any children with a man she didn't love, and she enjoyed working, even though she no longer controlled all of her own salary.

With a man in the house, her duty as a submissive wife was to turn over everything she earned to her husband, but she never disclosed the full amount of her earnings, so what Clancy received every payday was only a small fraction of her check. As long as he didn't think to question why she always gave him cash, and never discovered the drawer where she stashed her bankbook, her secret remained well hidden. She hated keeping secrets, however, and her silent rebellion was taking its toll, but she still longed for the day when she could claim her independence.

The seeds of feminism had begun to plant themselves in the soil of southern womanhood, much to the chagrin of southern manhood, and had started to put a choke hold on tradition as women gradually began to free themselves from a different kind of slavery. Even the myth of the helpless, flighty, Southern Belle, which lived in theory, if not in reality, was dying. Southern men liked traditions, cherished them, in fact, and so they did their level best to discourage the growth of the women's rights movement. Irrespective of race, they all shared a love of gentility and dominance; they loved to exercise power and to have absolute control. Clancy was a living, breathing, walking, talking example of a man of the South.

Women, on the other hand, were married to the houses over which their husbands reigned, and so Sardis, in the role of dutiful wife, was expected to love, honor, cherish, and obey. In her own way, she began silently breaking those bonds, but what she didn't realize was that her personal revolution already had a name. She learned how to play games when the family was around, how to love without giving, how to honor without respect, how to cherish but not esteem, and how to obey—marginally. That was a tough act, even for such a talented actress. Her disobedience challenged her Catholic upbringing and beliefs, and she struggled with her role as a woman and particularly, as a wife.

One day, Sardis came upon a book in her basement sanctuary at work, *The Feminine Mystique*, by Betty Friedan. It was now old stock, having been published in 1963, and it was consigned to the next clearance sale to make room on the shelf for newer publications. The copy she held in her hands, however, was new, having never been opened. Indeed, Sardis questioned whether it had ever been shelved. It was possible that it had been hidden away ever since arriving at the library. Some of the older staff were in the habit of censoring any literature they either didn't like or thought might be harmful to impressionable readers. She would never know for sure how it ended in the dead-literature bin, but regardless, the title intrigued her. She'd heard of the title because, by 1969, both the book and its author had become widely known as dangerous elements for their contribution toward planting preposterous ideas in women's minds. The South was still trying to adjust to the black civil rights movement, and now, adding women's issues on top of that was testing the limits of Southern tolerance. The self-appointed censor must have felt that she was doing the South a favor. Sardis sat down and began to read the book, internalizing much of what she read. It validated her as a woman in control of her own life, especially in her decision not to reproduce.

"After I read that, I became resolute. The following day was a Wednesday, and I made my usual visit to the drugstore. I asked very cautiously if he could get me a supply of birth control pills without revealing anything about the patient. I knew this question would test the bonds of our friendship. Never in my life had I ever thought I'd want that item in my body," Sardis continued. "I can still remember Father Macky's warning to us Catholic women during the early '60s, when this thing was first introduced, that we would surely burn in hell if we disrupted the natural course of life by interfering with the beauty of reproduction."

"Beauty, sure," interjected Grace, chuckling to herself. "They didn't have to deal with the pain."

"I was grateful that my friend, who was just as Catholic as I was, didn't pass judgment or give me a lecture. The next thing I knew, there I was, clutching my first supply as if it were gold."

"Did Clancy ever find out?" asked Dorcus, sure she already knew the answer.

"Are you out of your mind? I think his mom may have suspected. She hinted and hinted, even wanted to take me, against my will, mind you, to be examined for fertility problems. She was so sure that her Clancy could reproduce. It was one of the few times my own mom came to my defense. 'What are you saying?' she said. 'That it's my family's fault they're not productive?' I can still hear that blow up." Sardis smiled at the memory. "Those pills never entered this house. I kept my supply locked securely in my office drawer. If they'd been discovered, I wouldn't have been the only one in big trouble. During those heady days, the pill was only prescribed to married women, and it had to be with the consent of their husbands. My friend put his license in jeopardy for my happiness. I've never forgotten him, even though he's been gone for over five years now. I still miss his kindness and care." Dorcus reached over and gently patted Sardis's hand when she saw the tears beginning to well.

X

The game continued in silence for awhile until Dorcus recovered enough to continue.

"Milt is going to take my car, and he said it would be all right if you pal around with him and Cindy all day. I have to tend to a company emergency," said Anton, kissing Dorcus on the forehead like her brothers used to do. Life was returning to the house as people began to rise and amble about, although their stiff gait, glazed eyes, and whispered tones spoke of massive hangovers. The odor of stale booze hung heavy in the air, causing some to retch while reaching for the gigantic, ever-present, PX-issued, generic aspirin bottle. "Things like this happen all the time. That's the life of a company commander in a training battalion. You never know what to expect." With that, he grabbed a cup of coffee, picked up his gear and uniform, and was out the door before she could utter a word. A false smile crept across her face as she stared at the lovebirds still cooing at each other across the table from her. *Just what I need,* she thought. *Spending a day with two people who would rather I was somewhere else,* but to her surprise, they seemed genuinely delighted with their fifth wheel. Milt didn't like crawling around antique shops with Cindy, so Dorcus, who loved roaming, provided good companionship, while Milt stepped happily into the role of chauffeur and guide.

Downtown Carmel was just right for their browsing. It was a quaint old city that reminded Dorcus of Charleston, with its artsy atmosphere and breezy climate. Leaving Carmel, they gradually drifted down the scenic coast to the outlet called Big Sur, then meandering their way back, they encountered Cannery Row, immortalized by native son John Steinbeck. The fishing industry had long since abandoned most of the cannery district, and the buildings now housed small restaurants and boutiques, providing a souvenir Mecca for tourists. Dorcus took great advantage, buying numerous whimsical gifts for the family.

Lunch was at a delightful Mexican restaurant in the middle of old Monterey, after which they made quick trips to several military facilities housed in the area, including the Defense Language Institute and the Naval Post Graduate School, on the beautiful Presidio of Monterey. "Being with a military man has its advantages. I just love to visit this beautiful area, although I'd never be able to afford it on my nursing salary, but with my Milty stationed here, I just visit with him," Cindy beamed cheerfully as they left the Presidio and headed toward Seaside.

"I would never have known it was a military facility," said Dorcus. She then added innocently, "No one was in uniform." Milt's hands noticeably tightened around the steering wheel, his face became drawn, and his jaw line tightened. Cindy reacted as well. Her head suddenly dropped and her smile disappeared. An uneasiness descended over the car, and Dorcus was gripped by anxiety. Her sensitivity told her she'd said something wrong, but she couldn't figure out what it was. It was Milt who broke the awkward silence.

"We were told not to," he said, in a very subdued tone of voice. "There was a time when I used to fly all around the world proudly wearing my uniform. Then this anti-war thing reared its ugly head, and some of us had to endure being spat on and insulted for serving our nation. Finally, for our safety, the command ordered military personnel to stop wearing uniforms off the post or while traveling. Our haircuts give us away a lot of the time, but we can't be openly identified with our nation anymore." Cindy placed a reassuring arm around Milt's shoulder as he spat out the words.

"So that's it," said Dorcus. "That explains why I haven't seen Anton …" She paused, smiled, and continued, "Big A in uniform. Vietnam certainly has changed our loyalties."

"It's no joke, especially for him. He hasn't had it easy since his wife got killed in Nam," Milt said nonchalantly, unaware of the firestorm he ignited. Dorcus pretended nothing was wrong, but suddenly she felt a hot flash, and her temple began to throb. She thought she heard correctly, but had Milt just said "wife"? She remained silent, hoping he would continue without her prompting. He did. "I understand he witnessed the entire thing. He managed to save their son, but then later, when he had to rotate out, he couldn't bring the kid out of the country with him." Milt shook his head and added, "He's a much stronger man than I am. I don't think I could have handled it. I do know one thing, though. If I had to leave my kid behind …" His narrative was suddenly interrupted by Cindy asking him to make another stop that might be of interest to Dorcus. Little did they know, however, Dorcus's day ended at the mention of Anton's wife and child.

His wife? her mind kept repeating, eyes glazing over. She pretended to gaze passionately at the sights, but it was all a blur. *His son? His kid?* Suddenly, all she wanted to do was return to the house at Sunridge.

"When did you intend to tell me about your other Vietnam experiences, or didn't you intend to?" she shouted angrily as she burst through the front door following their day out sightseeing. The house was eerily quiet. Anton sat on the lone couch, his ever-present cigarette in one hand and ever-present drink in the other, staring in the direction of the flickering television screen. Cindy and Milt immediately retired to Milt's room. They had been very gracious to Dorcus, but after having to share an entire day of their precious weekend with a total stranger, they craved time alone. Meanwhile, Dorcus dropped down beside Anton on the sofa.

There was a grave weariness about him. The blazing green eyes had long lost the luster she once found intriguing and now reflected the numbing visions of every man who has ever witnessed the ravages of war. His soul had become hardened by having to walk over detached limbs and disemboweled children, by having to face an unknown enemy and by having to terminate those who pretended to be friends. It had taken a heavy toll. Post-Traumatic Stress Disorder had yet to be recognized as a psychiatric malady, but Anton Baylor was well on his way to becoming its poster child. He offered her a drink, which she refused, but it didn't stop him from refreshing his own from among the many bottles that remained in the house. As he rejoined her on the couch, the front door flew open, admitting another group of revelers.

"Hey, no fair," someone yelled. "Getting a head start on the competition!" Then, addressing Dorcus as if she were a knowledgeable conspirator, "This guy still holds the record for drinking everybody under the table, but we have a new challenger for you tonight, Buddy Boy. Got a fresh supply right here," the newcomer said, tapping a brown paper bag. Anton smiled, signaled his acceptance, and ushered Dorcus out through the back door to the small, surprisingly well-kept yard overlooking the valley. Twilight was setting in, and stars twinkled brightly overhead, like bridesmaids anticipating the arrival of the shimmering maiden. A full moon, like the chaste, white bridal veil, began to rise, ushering in the kind of night that inspired generations of songwriters and poets to express romantic dreams of love. A soft, gentle wind added enough breath to push love-struck couples into a close embrace for warmth, comfort, and protection.

For four years, Dorcus waited for this defining moment. She knew the words she and Anton would say to each other, the tender glances they would exchange, the declarations of love they would express, and the lifetime commitment they would make to one another. Her scripted fantasy, right down to the cute bench upon which they sat, had finally come to life, but instead of rousing endearment, it now mocked her, weighed down by her sadness and her anger.

"She worked for the officers' club in Saigon," he began. "She was in a responsible position because she had an education, and spoke English very well, so she wasn't selling herself, like so many of the bargirls always hanging around. That's what I liked about her; her smarts and abilities. She had a small child, too. Her husband was killed in the war. She could have been bitter, but she wasn't." As Dorcus listened to the story unfold, she heard great admiration in his voice, and saw a calming light wash over his face. His weariness was replaced by warmth. She also saw something else she never saw in all their time together; she saw a man in love. She saw the way his head moved and tilted to one side with a sigh whenever he mentioned her name. His heart was glowing. Anton had never looked at her like that, but someone else had. Cousins tended to share similar character traits, and now, as she watched him, she made a big discovery, and realized she made a big mistake. "Charlie, on the other hand ..." The mention of his name drew her back into consciousness. "Good guy," she heard him say.

"What about Charlie?" she said, zoning back into the conversation. She hadn't thought about him at all.

"He kept things going between us. He wanted so much to see you happy, but I knew it could never work. You're a nice girl. A lot like my real son's mother from college."

Oh my, she thought, her head now beginning to throb fiercely. She remembered the rumors at State about his old girlfriend. Dorcus didn't think his relationship with her had been real. He never mentioned her or spoke her name. Dorcus's breathing became shallow, and she started to feel faint, but she shook it off and tuned back in when he addressed her by that detestable name. "Dorc. Dorky Dorc," he said teasingly, hammering a spike directly into her heart. "I've grown up a lot. I want to go back to Vietnam and find and raise my wife's son. Then, I need to marry the mother of my real son. We've kept in touch over the years, and I've been sending her an allowance to help raise him. She's forgiven me for a lot." He was standing with his back to her, and spoke as if he were still formulating his life's plan. She could sense his anguish. "War allows a man to face his own mortality. I had a chance to do a lot of thinking over there, and I was able to return to make things right." He faced her, but he looked right past her. "Go home, Dorcus. I can't love you." Then, turning away again, he added, "I can't even love myself anymore."

Dorcus ran back inside the house, racing past a room full of people getting ready for another carefree night of Monopoly, charades, dancing, and drinking. She repacked the few things she'd taken out of her bag and met Anton at the door. "Does this mean the room is open? I got dibs for tonight," a voice called.

"There's a scenic spot on Seventeen-Mile Drive called the Lone Cypress," she told the players. "I could have sworn that darn tree winked at me and waved when we passed on the way back to the airport. I decided to adopt it as my mascot. I felt so stupid and so alone."

"I kept trying to tell you to stick with Charlie. Didn't I tell you that?" declared Grace. Her righteous rebuke was quickly followed by a regretful, "Oh darn. Now, look what you made me do," after playing a card she shouldn't have. Dorcus smiled in vindication, hoping she would not hear that admonition again.

"Some things never change," said Sardis, chiding Grace for her usual candor, while taking advantage of her misplay. Then, turning to Dorcus, she said, "Did you ever make amends to Charlie?"

"Tried to. Did you know there was such a thing as a world-wide military locator that helps you to find people? I looked him up and sent letters. He didn't respond at first, but finally a letter came. I had to work for two more months to earn enough money to pay for my trip. Charlie was assigned to the Berlin Brigade, in Germany. It wasn't easy getting into the city because of its East-West division. I knew he was just being stubborn, trying to make me pay for what I'd done, so I simply sent him a wire telling him I was coming. He met me at Templehoff Airport when I arrived, and escorted me to his car, where I met his new bride of two days."

"Oh no," muttered both Sardis and Grace.

"Oh yes. And girls, she was a duplicate of me. Everybody who saw us together during those brief two days said so. We would have been twins if she wasn't German with bright red hair." The group broke up in laughter.

"When I returned to Charleston following my great adventure to California and my freewheeling trip to Germany, I felt sort of lost, even embarrassed to talk about it, especially to my folks. I felt they would never understand and they were always wise enough to know when and when not to butt into their children's lives, so they asked no questions."

"You could have called me." Sardis sighed, still wondering why a division existed between friends.

"You know, Sard, it never crossed my mind. So, I began splitting my time between Charleston and Atlanta and decided to make a fresh start. I found out about a private school with a heart for shaping young minds and a desire to bring in black teachers. I applied for the job, and the rest, as they say, is history. I packed up my worldly goods and sponged off my two brothers, hoping for the white knight to ride to my rescue. But since he never showed up, I saved enough for a place for myself. On weekends, I play aunt to nieces and nephews and sometimes still put on my damsel in distress attire and hope for that knight to ride past."

"Do you wish you had married Charlie after all?" asked Sardis.

Dorcus put down her cards and thought for a while. "I don't know. I honestly don't know. I still can't say I really loved him. In spite of the advice your mom gave you, and Mother Sadie gave me about marrying out of duty, I'm not sure it's the wisest thing to do. Choices and opportunities were opening to us like never before. It made decisions far more complex for us than for their generation. But it does make you wonder if anybody's parents really loved each other, or whether they got married for other reasons. Scary!"

XI

The ticking clock approached 3:00 AM, signaling another hour was overtaking the players since they became captive within the time capsule like prisoners trapped in memories of their pasts. An uneasy silence engulfed them as the long hand crept to twelve. It was just as uneasy as the paradigm shift created when the '60s melded into the '70s.

Time has a way of moving either too slowly or too quickly but never at the right pace. The year 1970 made its grand entrance, ushering in not just a new year, but a new decade. Gone, alas, were the turbulent '60s, with its assassinations and civil upheaval. Many longed for new beginnings, for old slates to be clean again. They looked forward with great hope and anticipation. What they got instead was more of the same; mounting unrest and discontentment carried over from past, unwise decisions and a lingering war. A year of hope and promise quickly deteriorated further into a year of disappointment and broken dreams. By the month of May, civil unrest took a definite turn for the worse.

The original U. S. Civil War pitted the North against the South in what was defined as a battle for states' rights. However, one incident declared a new Civil War, with no clearly defined boundaries, just like the non-war in Asia. It pitted one generation against another; it pitted those with a desire to serve and protect their nation against those who did not. And in a subtle way, it pitted those who were considered to be of worth against those of little substance.

On May 4, on the campus of Kent State University in the city of Kent, Ohio, a massacre took place that left four students dead and many others wounded. Kent became the second college in the United States to experience an uprising so grave as to earn a place in history books. It caused a sense of déjà vu to sweep through those who experienced the Orangeburg massacre, but for the rest of the nation, it was a new, defining moment in history. And as if two tragedies weren't enough, history repeated itself again on May 14 and May 15 at Jackson State College, in Jackson, Mississippi.

The three episodes devastated their respective local communities, but at Kent State, where white students were on the receiving end of a marksman's volley, the public outcry was heard around the world. Each of the three episodes shared great similarities, and yet it was Kent State that received the lion's share of the attention, the outrage, the sympathy, and the justice. As for the black students; well, there was a sense of they got what they deserved.

In each case, armed representatives of a duly recognized United States resident law enforcement unit turned their weapons on the unarmed sons and daughters of its own citizens in an undeclared skirmish. In each case, disfranchised young adults were voting with their passion, proclaiming their right to free speech as provided by the Constitution, and they paid for those rights by being either slaughtered or wounded without due process of the law. Three paid the ultimate price at South Carolina State, four at Kent State, and two at Jackson State, and bullets also ripped into the flesh and blood of twenty-nine innocent idealists in the state of South Carolina, eleven in the state of Ohio, and twelve in Mississippi. Each wounded person, along with their families, suffered while asking if they still lived in America, and even though their causes differed slightly, constitutional guarantees united their spirits and bound their flesh. They despaired at being denied their constitutional right to the pursuit of happiness. In South Carolina, students were unhappy with their status as second-class citizens. At Kent State, they were unhappy with an undeclared war in which they would eventually be forced to participate, and at Jackson State, they were unhappy about both. Each event was an unspeakable massacre, which traumatized students and teachers alike, disrupted the education process, and forced changes that should have taken place in a less stressful, less volatile, more peaceful environment.

The differences, on the other hand, revealed the heart and soul of a still-divided nation. The Civil Rights Act was the law, but black life and efforts were still not seen as equal in the eyes of its citizens, especially those entrusted with running the government. State students were outraged by Kent State headlines, proclaiming these killings as the first of their kind to occur on a college campus. As if survivors of the Orangeburg Massacre had not endured enough, Kent State shootings not only eclipsed those at South Carolina State, but written accounts now robbed them of their, albeit regrettable, place in history.

"I can't believe this!" cried Grace in exasperation reading the account in the Washington, DC paper.

"That's a bunch of hogwash!" stammered Dorcus to her brother as she threw his *Atlanta Constitution* on the floor, while Sardis just cried as she watched reports on television in Charleston. In addition to receiving major countrywide and worldwide headlines, a photographer, in capturing a defining moment on Kent State's campus, took a photograph of a female student, half-kneeling, crying in anguish over the body of her slain comrade, and won numerous major awards. This one picture kept the episode alive for years to follow. Reporters and other observers swarmed the campus, freezing significant movements and actions in time. Those perpetrating the mayhem were documented, and those on the receiving end had their stories preserved for all of history.

In South Carolina, reporters were barred from the campus, and a true and complete picture depicting the nature of the upheaval never emerged. Students were practically ignored, and accounts were filtered through self-serving government officials bent on blaming the victims for their own demise; thus the true nature of events remained cloaked in darkness. And at Jackson State, no one seemed to care.

Kent State inspired artistic tributes in almost every creative genre. It aroused creativity in poets who had never rhymed words on paper before, and it got the creative juices of songwriters flowing with mass tributes, while writers were inspired to create plays and books and films. It also reinvigorated anti-war protesters, kicking their activities into high gear. By contrast, artistic endeavors inspired by the events at South Carolina State were few and far between. A single book, chronicling events from that horrible night, fought for shelf space in local bookstores. Following its publication, it came under scrutiny of a suspicious, skeptical government that was still in denial, and who tried to bury it, along with the deceased students, while a film project about it struggled for financial resources and backing and had yet to see the light of day.

But the biggest insults were yet to come. Kent State families were eventually awarded $63,000 per victim, which came with an apology. South Carolina State families waited and waited, but received nothing. The Jackson State victims, Phillip Gibbs, James Green, and the twelve wounded, became ditto marks to the South Carolina State account, and they too faded into a historical abyss.

XII

Taletha was sitting in the warm sun outside the trailer when she saw the dust cloud. She had recovered a little feeling in her hands and legs, but for the most part, her body, which was now half the size it was when she was at State, still wouldn't do her bidding. Her mind told her this car held no threat to her. Still, she was anxious to see who would alight and was happy to discover it was the rev. By the look on his face, however, she could sense he was here for serious business.

As he usually did whenever he saw her, he knelt beside her, placed his hand on her head, and uttered a prayer. Then he hugged her and went inside to talk with her parents. She was close enough to the door to hear the conversation, and since they didn't know she could comprehend speech, or was aware of her surroundings, they made no effort to disguise their dialogue or to talk in secret.

"Our last hope is gone, for the time being," the rev was saying. "The federal court dismissed the charges against the nine troops we thought would be held responsible for shooting up our kids. No punishment; no blame. No chance to sue, to make them pay." She heard her mother sobbing softly. "That's not all. On top of that, they plan to prosecute one of our own folks for instigating a riot. Now, they know good and well we can't go after him. These people are still trifling after all these years." They thanked the Rev, and he left, patting Taletha on the head as he departed.

Her parents continued their lament. "Guess we hav' ta continya ta let yo' brotha take charge. I don' lik him, but he seem ta hep," her father was saying. Taletha closed her eyes in agony as she heard their decision. Everything in her being was trying to cry out, "No! No! No!"

"I's callin' Dudley en see if'n he kin come mo' times then one time a mont'. He 'n Tee always had a connekshin, ev'n when she's li'l. She da one done calls him Unka Day 'cause she can't say Dudley," her mother agreed. Then she hugged her distressed daughter from behind and whispered hopefully, "He's gon' hep ya git betta, Tee."

I have to get better! I'm going to get better! she resolved, crying within. *Have to!*

XIII

Apart from her outburst about Charlie, Grace became very subdued after telling of her near-death experience. She didn't want to encourage questions about where the new decade found her. Shortly after stepping off the bus in Washington DC, penniless and with a young baby, her first instinct told her to locate the nearest welfare office and apply for benefits. She learned the system for obtaining financial aid while in New York, so she knew her way around the regulations; what to do, what to say, how to act. The pride Hatta Mae took so long to instill, and the lessons about not living on the dole, soon disappeared with the pressing urgency of the need to eat, and to feed and house her son. With new housing vouchers and food stamps in hand, she headed out of the office door, only to be stopped just outside on the street by a well-dressed young man. "I heard you tell the caseworker you were new in town," he said, smiling from ear to ear. Grace eyed him suspiciously, wondering what this white boy wanted. Years of history in the South made it hard to erase distrust, and even harder to forget mistreatment. "I just wondered if you had a place to stay. It's hard to find housing, especially with children, and that voucher won't go far," he told her, as if presenting an argument before a jury.

He was not what you would call great-looking, on the shortish side with an average build. His most distinguishing features were his head of thick, black, curly hair and his matching bushy mustache. With his olive-toned skin, which he often tanned to a golden brown under the Afro-like hair, he was frequently mistaken for a light-skinned black. He even tried to copy the strut that many black men had adopted with their new-found black pride. Blaxploitation movies, as they were called, were the rage giving black men a different type of role model. Denny fancied himself a black movie character and embraced black movies, *Putney Swope* and *The Lost Man* being particular favorites, so he introduced himself to Grace as a blue-eyed soul brother. His eyes, which were hidden behind coke-bottle glasses, were actually brown, but it was a term of endearment applied to white men who empathized with the black power movement and wanted to do something more than just pay lip service.

"I live very close, in a duplex I own, by the way. Why don't you and the baby stay there? We can make arrangements about the rent." Grace's suspicious stares must have made him nervous. He kept fidgeting with his jacket pockets as he spoke and stared at the ground, never quite making eye contact. She thanked him kindly but told him she needed to move on. Denny gave her a slip of paper with his address if she changed her mind.

Following Dr. King's assassination in 1968, DC, like Harlem, had exploded in riots. Grace discovered how devastating they were when she arrived in the neighborhood of Columbia Heights. Many of the places where she might have found shelter for herself and the baby were burnt out, and shops that might have hired her were gone, many of them not to return for decades, if ever. Her next attempt was in the Shaw district, where she encountered the same situation. The burnt-out buildings were beginning to have a grave psychological impact on Grace. Passing by row after row of destroyed houses and businesses felt like camera shots superimposed on the carnage she'd experienced in Harlem. During her housing search, she made two other discoveries. The first was that children, no matter how young, were not welcomed by landlords. The second was that single women weren't exactly welcomed with open arms either, and here she was, a single black woman with a baby. By the time she located an affordable place that accepted her, the baby, and her vouchers, she longed for the ramshackle buildings of Michele Alley.

"Ghetto housing is ghetto housing, no matter what city it's in. The rats are all the same color, the roaches bite the same way, and the litter-lined streets carry the same diseases and hopelessness," she said to her card partners after much hesitation before recounting those dark days.

After two days of discouragement and defeat, she returned to the temporary shelter each night that the welfare office had arranged. It was a motel that had seen better days, but she didn't care, because it was clean, bright, warm, and inviting. All the same, she had to find permanent housing quickly. The temporary shelter was only available for two weeks, and then it was on her to either pay or move. She still hated snow, and after she pulled off her well-worn, donated boots with numb, uncovered hands, she instinctively jammed them into the pockets of her jeans to warm them up, whereupon she discovered the address Denny had given her.

Soon, she was looking for the address in Le Droit Park. "Even the name sounds romantic. Le Droit Park," she repeated, as she walked along the narrow, tree-lined streets in her threadbare cloth coat. More than just the cold night air was making her feel uncomfortable, however. She had a strange feeling that unseen eyes were following her every movement. The neighborhood was formerly protected by gates and guards to keep people like her out. When Jim Crow ruled, many of its current residents would have been denied entrance, but during a fit of protest by students at the nearby black Howard University, the racially divisive walls, like those of Jericho in the Bible, came tumbling down. It was then converted from its previous all-white status to an area known for its elite black population. Denny moved in to make a point, and to prove how open-minded he was and how accepting he was of change. Before the night was old, she found herself knocking on the door of a well-maintained duplex on a clean, well-lit street. "Now, this is more like it," she whispered to the sleeping infant. She didn't know what this was going to cost her, but she was ready to deal and to make any arrangements Denny demanded.

XIV

Nature's call temporarily disrupted both Grace's narrative and the game as she headed for the restroom. "So, Sardis," said Dorcus gently as she stood to stretch her legs. "Where's Clancy? Did you finally dump him after your enlightenment?"

"I guess I was getting pretty angry," said Sardis.

Another book, *The Female Eunuch*, by Germaine Greer, hit the literary circuit, picking up where Freidan left off. Whereas *The Feminine Mystique* whetted her appetite for freedom, Greer's book galvanized many women, including Sardis, into taking action, and fed Sardis's growing contempt and discontent. Greer spoke directly to her very being when she surmised that women didn't realize how much men hated them, and how much they hated themselves. She grabbed the only copy the moment it arrived in the library, hid the book under wraps, and sought out lonely corners during her breaks, where she sat reading and absorbing every word. *I'm guessing this is how* The Feminine Mystique *must have ended up in the basement,* she surmised as she fed hungrily on the words of this new work. "My fellow librarian kindred spirit of a sister also had to hide her passion in the basement reading room in the early years," said Sardis.

Her ability to permanently escape from her house of horrors eluded her as long as Clancy controlled their bank accounts, but every once in a while she got the chance to flee by means of a welcome call at work from Cyrus Bloom, PhD, who now had his own theatrical production and management company. Jeb was thriving, just as everyone predicted, and under Cyrus's management, he hooked up with some major studios like Disney for voiceover work and live features. "He even performed as an animated character using that dreaded native Jamaican accent I worked so hard to get rid of. I think he did it to get back at me," Cyrus relayed, chuckling. Cyrus's mentorship, combined with Jeb's hard work, led to more television screen time, which in turn led to a motion picture appearance. He was now poised to hit the stage on Broadway, his original goal.

Cyrus's calls provided a ray of sunshine, a gigantic boost Sardis's soul needed, and joy and pride overwhelmed her whenever she heard about Jeb's successes or saw his work. He never seemed to age or change in any way, maintaining his same rugged good looks and firm, trim physique. She still yearned for the theater, but the closest she got was in the audience of the old Dock Street Theater. She no longer had to fear attending performances undisguised, though many still mistook her for white. It provided a great release for her on weekends. Clancy was usually away, much to her relief, for he and his father shared a passion for fishing. They owned a small river runner and every weekend during the spring and summer months, they would set out from Goose Creek to spend "men's" time on the water. Sardis was happy to be rid of him. Indeed, sometimes she secretly wished the river would claim him and he'd never come back. This was especially true whenever they returned with a catch of fish.

The streams and rivers surrounding the many small islands off the peninsula of Charleston were rich with seafood, and they invariably caught a swag of fish that were so small they couldn't be skinned and deboned to provide meaty fillets, but had to be scaled, beheaded, sliced open, and then gutted. It was a terrible job, and not surprisingly, it fell to women to do it.

"I'll never forget the very first time he walked into this house with those horrible, smelly things. They were hardly worth eating, but he'd caught them, so I guess it's a man thing to eat what you catch," she told the others, now that Grace had returned to the table. Her nose wrinkled up automatically as if the stench was still present.

"He tossed the mess on the counter and said 'Fix these for dinner, and if there are any left over, reheat them in the morning for breakfast before I go to work,'" she said, conveying the derision she felt by doing her best Clancy imitation. "I'd never dealt with fish before, but I recalled learning somewhere along the line that people would fry them, so I fried them, just as they were."

Dorcus and Grace doubled over with laughter. "You mean you didn't clean them?" said Grace.

"That's exactly what he said when he saw the head still attached and the burnt scales. He wasn't very happy having to throw away his weekend's labor. He ran home to his mother, who made sure that I was properly schooled in the fine art of cleaning and preparing fish for *my* man. Everything had to be done right for *my* man. If society had been under the control of Clancy and his mother, women's lives would never have evolved from the dark ages. That fish was what did him in, in the long run," she said calmly, making no effort to hide her relief. Dorcus and Grace, aware of Sardis's disdain for her husband, were nonetheless surprised by her demeanor, and lack of grief; however, where there is no love, there is no loss.

"We had a big blowout of an argument. I'd had it up to here with those horrible fish, with that horrible life," she said, placing her hand across her throat. "I told him if he brought those foul-smelling things home again, he'd have to scale them, clean them, and even cook them himself."

The explosion had been building for years, and she could tolerate no more. She wanted out of a marriage, which began sliding downhill from the second he tripped on her gown as they left the altar. Divorce was anathema in the Catholic church, and she risked being shunned by her community, but she was desperate enough to chance it. Then the memory of her outcast status during her freshman year at State intervened and made her re-examine her options carefully. She could attempt to get the marriage annulled if, somehow or other, she could get Clancy to cooperate. In spite of his constant pleading, she hadn't slept with him for months, hoping it would make him miserable enough to complain that she had abandoned her wifely duties, but if he complained at all, it was probably to his mother. Sardis had to find a way to push him far enough that he would go to Father Mackey. Little by little, she began dropping hints that she was preventing the possibility of a pregnancy. She knew she risked excommunication, not to mention her druggist friend's livelihood, but she was desperate.

A subtle smile crossed her face. "After all of my scheming, five little fish did the trick. He didn't believe me. He brought them things home and flopped them on the counter, as was his habit, but I didn't touch them. 'Baby, did you see the fish?' he said. I don't remember when he began to use the term 'baby' with me," Sardis bristled. "He must have picked it up from some TV show, because it wasn't something he would have thought of on his own. I detested being called 'baby,' especially by a juvenile, infantile, mollycoddled, spoiled brat like him. Men may think of it as an endearing term, but it denotes a lack of power. It says, woman, you're helpless, just like an infant child. It assigns the role of protector to the man. He becomes the dictator and parent. I was becoming empowered, and here was this Mommy's boy placing me in a subservient role, calling me 'baby.' I was having none of it. And to further prove my point, I let those cursed things stay right where he put them. Didn't go near them. They started to stink, then somewhere along the way both they and he disappeared. I knew exactly where he lugged his big butt off to, and I waited and waited to hear that shrill voice either entering the house or on the phone. The cursed thing finally rang, so I braced myself and answered the call, but the voice on the other end wasn't the one I'd expected. It was his father. I could tell from his somber tone and the manner in which he was stammering over his words something was terribly wrong." She paused, ever the actress, for dramatic effect. "'We just rushed your husband here to Roper,' he said. 'He got a fish bone lodged in his throat.' I recall my thoughts at the time, and I'm still ashamed to admit it, but I was wishing he would choke to death," she said, showing remorse for the first time. "But then, when he said Clancy was dead, I didn't believe him. I'd never prayed for his death. If I had, guilt would have consumed me and haunted me to my grave, and yet I was so relieved. I felt as if a prayer was answered. He was gone. Just like that. My five-year ordeal was over."

XV

Grace often thought about Charleston, and especially about Hatta Mae. She had not seen or contacted her in over three years. A part of Grace wanted to find her, but her guilt-ridden part reminded her what a big disappointment she turned out to be. *My mama would be furious if she knew about me and Denny,* she thought. *She warned me and warned me never get into a common-law relationship, and here I am, pregnant with his child. I hope the baby will convince him to make our relationship permanent,* she speculated as she sat staring out the window of their breakfast nook, daydreaming and mindlessly rubbing her expanding belly. Denny would never replace Willie in her heart, but he provided for her and loved her child.

She wondered how Hatta Mae would react to little Willie, who was playing nearby, and how she would view this nice neighborhood and how well things were going. "But you ain' got no secur-tee," her mother's words rang in her ears. Silently, she observed tiny buds forming on trees beyond her kitchen window and sighed with contentment. April showers brought May flowers, and also May sun.

After she got Denny off to work, she sat back with a second cup of coffee, reflecting. Her welfare check didn't go very far, but it was stretching a lot further since she moved in with Denny. She stopped paying him rent, and he took care of food and household expenses, while she took care of Little Willie and incidentals like clothing.

She didn't need to find work outside her home, so she became a homemaker. She loved these quiet early mornings, and domestic tranquility overcame her as she watched tiny dust motes dancing around and around in rays of sunlight before hitting the floor. She could have stayed like this forever, but life has a habit of sneaking back in at the most pleasant of times.

"What do you mean we have to move?" said Grace, with agitation in her voice.

Denny stared at the floor, as he always did when he didn't want to face an unpleasant situation. "My folks are selling this place, and they aren't going to provide me with as much subsidy anymore," he said softly, like a kid who'd been caught stealing candy. "My Dad has a big real estate firm in Philadelphia, and things are sort of slow right now." He glanced up slowly at her startled face, and then lowered his eyes to the floor again. "I should have told you sooner, but I thought you would have guessed I could never afford this place on my salary as a case worker. Dad wanted me to work in the family business, but I wanted to do things on my own terms; get out from under his thumb and out of the starchy Philadelphia society. Then Dad acquired this house as an investment. He made me manager, so I could get a taste of the business, and I was able to rent it from him at a major discount until he could eventually sell it. I couldn't turn it down. Then the riots happened, year before last. This area wasn't torched, but people got cold feet about investing in DC. We couldn't sell it, so he just wrote it off as a loss each year; until now. The housing market is slowly returning to its pre-riot days, and he wants out." Grace fumed as she considered her options, while Denny pleaded with her not to leave him. She felt so powerful that this "Master's son" wanted her, but she wondered what Hatta Mae would think about that. And so it was that they moved out and rented a small house in the quiet hamlet of Mount Pleasant. With its growing well-integrated, artsy population, they felt accepted there and quickly settled in for the long haul.

"We had two sons," said Grace proudly, "and Sardis, both of them have their father's light skin. Never thought I would have kids that pale. They could be your neighbors here in Browntown."

Dorcus was growing increasingly irritated by Grace's cavalier attitude and welfare mind-set. "In case you haven't noticed," she said, exasperation creeping into her voice, "anybody can live down here now. College of Charleston expanded and renovated a lot of the houses, so we're surrounded by fraternity and sorority houses and faculty residences with people of every shade and hue." Dorcus hoped Grace wouldn't get under her skin. She recalled her mother's warnings about the Alley people and their welfare mind-set. Those mind-sets were hard to overcome, since they shaped attitudes, and attitudes determined life's goals. She recalled how happy she was when she first encountered Grace at State, and felt sure that exposure to new experiences and to successful, productive people would reshape her thinking and help her to overcome her meager, humble beginnings. She believed and hoped Grace would be able to triumph over her circumstances, but now, twenty years later, it appeared to Dorcus that her mother may have been right. Not only had she fallen into the trap that ensnared her family, keeping them failure-bound, she couldn't see how the world had changed around her. "So," Dorcus got around to asking, now that the door was open. "Did you and Denny get married? Where are your sons now?" She had a suspicious feeling Grace was trying to dodge tough questions all night, and now she shifted uneasily in her seat. Dorcus smiled, satisfied her suspicions proved correct.

"His social experimentation ended in 1978. He decided he had enough of playing house, and he wanted the real deal." She then became quiet and introspective while trying to decide how to put a positive spin on her tale. "One day, he just left. Went to work and never came home. A week later, I went to the welfare office where he worked. I hadn't been there since we first met, but I learned that my records were conveniently transferred out. Guess it should have raised my suspicions about why he didn't wanted me to go back there. I thought it was for my protection, since my benefits could have been stopped if they found out about our living arrangements, but I saw it was for his benefit as much as mine. It seemed like he had his escape mapped out from the very beginning."

Grace noticed a banner still stretched across a back wall reading, "Congratulations, Denny." Not wishing to appear overly interested, she casually asked a clerk about it. "Oh that? Someone needs to take it down now," she laughed "One of our case workers left us a couple of weeks ago." Then, like a proud mother hen, she proceeded to inform Grace about this baby chick who'd flown the coop. "He was always so quiet and secretive about his life, so he shocked us all when he told us about his engagement to a girl from a very prominent Philly family. Tell you the truth, this guy was so shy, it must have been an arranged affair, but we're all so happy for him."

After hearing the complete story, Grace had to walk outside the office for some fresh air. In the weeks that followed, she made more discoveries than she cared to make. Society pages were filled with lines of type about the Philadelphia debutante who was marrying another scion of society. Denny's family roots went all the way back to the Revolutionary War era, and beyond. His family ties could be traced to one of the nation's founding fathers. The family had old money, but in addition to that, his father owned property in practically every state on the east coast.

"Big stuff. The family was rich for days. And he was bound, by tradition and duty, to take over the family business one day. He was betrothed, as a kid, to marry some girl from another prominent family to make sure the old money stayed in old hands," Grace confessed. "I was furious! I wanted to get my hands around his scrawny neck!"

"And your paws on his not so scrawny money," Dorcus interjected.

"It would have helped," Grace replied, unashamedly. "I tried to contact him any way I could, to get some money for our sons, but the family drew a curtain around him. I finally found a black lawyer, and wouldn't you know, the curtain suddenly parted. Families like them don't like scandals, so he sent me a check. Told me to buy the house where we were living, but instead I decided to buy bus fare for me and the kids and moved back to Charleston."

Sardis looked at her in complete surprise. "So you've been right here in town for ten years and didn't contact me even once?"

Grace smiled sheepishly. "Been busy. Had three boys to raise. With the help of ye ole phone book, I located my sister and mom, just like I found you. Dad passed on while I was in DC, but no one knew where I was. Mom thought I was killed in the Harlem riot. My sister's husband came back from Vietnam in a flag-draped box, so with the benefit money she received, she bought a house across the Ashley River, and my mom moved in with her. I got a place right down the street with the money Denny gave me, so we've been raising our kids and trying to keep them out of trouble." She paused for a moment to play the last card in her hand before continuing. "Had another baby, my last. She's now eight. And before you ask, her daddy is from Cuba. He moved in, and we were supposed to get married. I fell hard for him. Maybe it was the accent. He looked so much like that Ricky Ricardo on *Lucy*. But all he wanted was his green card. He forgot to tell me he already had a wife and five children back in Cuba. By the time I found out, my daughter was on the way. Mom never expressed any disappointment. She loved the kids, and showed them off to all the neighbors. She was a different person once she left Michelle Alley. She was warm and funny, and people loved her to pieces. She keeps trying to get me to complete my college degree. Do you know, she still has the dress she bought to wear at the graduation? Untouched, and in the original Mangles box."

"So why don't you finish?" asked Dorcus, ever the educator.

Grace took a deep breath. "I haven't been able to go back on the campus. I still remember how I left Tee that night. I can still see her slumped over on the floor." Tears welled up in her eyes, then those of Sardis, and then Dorcus. "If only I knew," Grace concluded, passing the tissue box around the table.

XVI

Clancy's untimely demise made Sardis a wealthy woman. He was a saver, on the verge of being a miser, who squeezed maximum value out of every dime he ever earned, and when he passed on, Sardis inherited his entire estate. His mother raised objections, because Sardis never produced any children, but Sardis prevailed. With her savings, combined with his, secure in a bank account in her name, along with a generous insurance settlement, she was finally in control of her life. During the six months it took for everything to be settled, Sardis made plans. Eartha was unusually silent, and her in-laws, harboring a boatload of guilt over their son's demise, practically severed all ties once the funeral was over. "Can you imagine what I would have faced if he had died of my cooking?" Clancy's father made one or two calls to ensure that some business transactions went smoothly, but he kept them brief, limiting their conversation to the business at hand.

Sardis could not yet display the explosive inner joy and serenity she now felt, so she kept her emotions subdued. Her instincts, however, told her that something was amiss. It was like waiting for lightning to strike, but not knowing quite where. She quit her job, which was heartbreaking, for the now well-integrated staff had grown to love and respect their senior librarian. Along with leaving her dear coworkers behind, quitting meant no more Wednesday lunch sessions at Amar's with her dear friend, her mentor, her rock. By this time, her psyche no longer needed healing, but out of sheer habit, she kept her unscheduled appointment until the week before her resignation. Unfortunately, her old friend was ill that week, so she didn't get a chance to say good-bye or to thank him properly.

I'll stop by before I leave for New York, she promised herself, even though she suspected that, with the time needed for all her preparations, she wouldn't get to fulfill that promise.

Cyrus was beside himself when she called. He had all sorts of projects in mind, including an off-Broadway musical he said would suit her talents. "And, you know, *The Wiz* has been doing rather well on Broadway. I have connections. I might be able to get you in," he said excitedly. "I've arranged for you to take singing and dancing lessons," he crowed. His enthusiasm filled her with hope, even though she harbored serious doubts that she could ever learn such skills.

"As a singer, I sound like a foghorn. Those things can awaken the dead with their long, low monotonous tone. And as a dancer ...?"

"I know the best people," he interrupted. "You'll be surprised what they can do."

Sardis's overflowing hope and optimism eclipsed Eartha's darkening mood. She began retreating to her room again, closing out the light and withdrawing into her darkened cell. She liked Clancy, liked having him around, her new son, her ally, her future hope, and mourned his loss, together with that of his parents, who used to pop in at regular intervals. For a brief while, she had a real family again, and then it was suddenly snatched away from her. She kept losing people; everyone left her except Sardis, and she was making plans—plotting. She heard the conversations, even though Sardis didn't know she heard. But she heard, all right.

Even with her heart now lightened and her soul dancing, Sardis's stomach ached and churned whenever she faced the realization that somewhere along the line she would have to face her mother. She feared the storm brewing in those dark clouds. Would Eartha become a tornado, a fierce hurricane, or would she accept the inevitable? Thoughts about the previous confrontation of this nature created a clammy, nauseous feeling in her gut. *I could just leave her a note,* she thought. *But why? I'm an adult. Why do I let her do this to me? I'll just say, Mother, it's time for me to live life on my own terms. Even if I make a mistake, I have to know if I could have survived out there.* She pretended she was in a play. The morning prior to her planned departure arrived, and she braced herself. *Tomorrow is opening night,* she thought. She emboldened and reassured herself by rehearsing her lines over and over, saying what she wanted to say, and trying to anticipate every response or objection. She had her lines down cold, but opening night never arrived.

Meandering lightheartedly down the back stairs, she was startled to see her mother roaming around in the kitchen so bright and early. It was her habit to stay in her room until past nine, but here it was seven o'clock and she was up and about and cooking. What surprised Sardis even more was the fact that her mother was neatly attired. She'd traded her usual sloppy chenille housecoat for a house dress, and her hair was combed and curler free.

"Roper called for you a while back," she said, matter-of-factly. The very mention of Roper Hospital made the hairs on the back of Sardis's neck bristle. Her hands began to sweat, and small beads of perspiration popped out of usually dry pores. Lightning was about to strike. "Your pharmacist forgot to pick up your new supply of birth control pills, so they needed instructions about how to get them to you." Sardis was silent. Eartha reached into her dress pocket, pulled out the circular pack and slapped them down on the table. Her eyes spit fire. They blazed hotter than the fire under the pan blackening on the stove. Perspiration beads on Sardis forehead said it all. She sat down at the kitchen table, waiting for the clap of thunder and the torrential rain. She could feel pressure building in the small room as the silence became deafening. Suddenly, her mother turned from the stove and charged to within an inch of Sardis. She was in a wild-eyed frenzy, both fists raised above her head. In one hand she held a spatula saturated with hot oil, which was suspended in mid-air almost directly over Sardis's head.

Instinctively, Sardis leapt out of her chair. Her mother lunged toward her, but her movements had been slowed by age and atrophy, and she tripped over the now-vacant chair and went flying headlong into the wall. The hot spatula caught her squarely on the forehead, producing a permanent brand. Sardis's shadow hovered over the crumpled frame lying on the floor as her mother slowly regained her senses and attempted to stand. Sardis extended a helping hand, which her mother brushed off. Recovering her dignity, she pulled herself up to full height like an inebriated woman on wobbly legs. Ever since Sardis reached her full growth at the age of thirteen, she towered over her mother. Her mother, smiting and hating herself for losing her temper, felt even smaller, however, because she knew she held a trump card in this game. Turning to face her startled daughter, she exploded. "You robbed me!" She hobbled to the frying pan and proceeded to take out her frustrations on whatever it was she had sizzling on the stove. Sardis sat down gingerly, watching intently, barely breathing, fearing that any movement would set her mother off again. She didn't have long to wait before she began to rant again. "And you weren't alone. You had help, and I know who did it. He robbed me! I wanted grandchildren! Just like the ones running around his house! Climbing on his lap! Delivering sweet, sugary, sticky kisses!" Her dentures, loosened in the fall, punctuated every sibilate sound with a snakelike hiss. "I wanted to have some life return to this dreary mausoleum of a house, and he robbed me! Killed mine! All gone, now. He stole my happiness!" Sardis stiffened as her mother turned to face her again, still absentmindedly waving the hot spatula to emphasize every sentence. A droplet of grease flew onto Sardis's arm and hot oil singed her skin, but she didn't flinch.

The room seemed to shrink as her mother paced, cried, and fumed, while Sardis sat stoically, watching as the veins in her mother's neck rose to the surface, but she revealed no emotion and offered no reaction. "So, you are free to do what you want, but hear this, he will pay; pay dearly. Pay every day for the rest of his life. I will make his life hell on Earth!"

"You can't hurt him," said Sardis at last, surprised at her calm demeanor. "Or me."

"Oh yes I can," replied her mother in a solemn tone. Turning back to her cooking and away from her suspicious daughter, she added, "But you can stay and make sure that doesn't happen." Sardis inhaled deeply as a knowing smirk began to spread across her tense features. That was it. The trump card was revealed. Eartha faced her daughter again. Her flare for the dramatic and her controlling demeanor told Sardis here was another actress in the family. Her mother was giving an award-winning performance.

"I'm sure the medical board won't take too kindly to a druggist writing a prescription. And to give pills like this to a married woman without her husband's consent! How did he get them? Did he forge a doctor's name? Ever thought about that? Your father's reputation still carries a lot of weight in the medical community. I'll have no problems being heard by the board." Then, hoping to drive the last nail into the coffin of Sardis's dream, she continued. "Clancy's parents would love to know about this. I believe there are grounds here for an annulment, even though Clancy is gone. If I'm not mistaken, that would then make his parents the legal heirs to his estate."

Sardis's heart sank. She took a deep breath and closed her eyes to think. Like a dying person whose life flashes before his eyes, she envisioned her future. One vision delighted her, and the other darkened her soul. Then she decided. Not this time. She would not let her mother control her life. She rose and adopted a defiant posture. "Do what you will. I know things will work themselves out for the best for everyone involved. I'm going to New York." With that, she raced out of the kitchen and up the stairs, determined to put all of this behind her. *Even if I have to spend the night in a motel until my flight leaves tomorrow, I have to get out of this house,* she thought.

Grabbing her half-packed luggage, she threw in a few more items and descended the front stairs. She reached the front door, but as her hand closed over the doorknob, she heard a sudden crash in the kitchen. Then, she heard a loud thump. Dropping her bags reluctantly, she headed toward noise.

Sardis paused abruptly, causing the other two to look up from their cards. "I found her on the floor, gasping for air. I was furious that she would pull that old stunt again, until I realized her medical problem was real this time. She'd faked heart problems for so long neither one of us believed this was actually happening. She was released from the hospital after two weeks, and placed directly into my care, where she's been ever since. And, *The Wiz* left Broadway. Jeb got his first Tony nomination in 1984, for his performance in *The Tap Dance Kid*. Mom and I were watching *The Cosby Show* one day and there he was, playing the part of a doctor. Do you know what she had the nerve to say? 'He's a nice-looking man. Maybe I should have let him have that seat at graduation.'"

"Have you talked to him in all these years?" said Dorcus, playing a trump card while Sardis was distracted.

"Never again," Sardis replied, taking the trick regardless. With that, they all stood, stretched, and then dealt another hand.

When Sardis uttered the words "Never again," Dorcus wished she had one of those, "Never again" experiences, but alas, she had one final encounter with the two men who had once been her whole life. On an early autumn morning in Atlanta, she responded to a call she received from a sick friend who needed blood. When she walked through the doors of the Veteran's Administration Hospital, she recognized his face immediately. The light in his eyes when he saw her told her instantly there was still tenderness in his heart.

"Charlie; what a surprise. And you're still in uniform," she said as he greeted her with a peck on the cheek. After catching up on their lives, they knew one question lingered. She didn't have to ask.

"He's here," said Charlie, on the brink of tears. He then led her to a ward at the rear of the facility. Doors to the unit were secured, and only relatives had access. Since Charlie was a cousin, and since he'd just left, the attendant recognized him, skipped the usual security check, and immediately reopened the heavy, padded door, admitting them to a surreal world, where pajama-clad men strode aimlessly about, while some sat silently in wheelchairs. Others were congregated in a large recreation and visitation room, while many were outside in the enclosed, gated grounds, reliving their respective wars and the heroic glory days only they could see.

"There he is," said Charlie, pointing to a solitary figure sitting in the corner, dozing. His head was bald and covered with scabs, as was most of his body, and he looked ancient. Agent Orange had claimed another victim. As they approached, Charlie warned Dorcus not to startle him. His nerves were shot, and there were times when his mind was back in the jungle. He was in the midst of firefights, holding off an unseen and unrecognizable enemy. Anyone entering his space could be annihilated. "Anton," said Charlie cautiously, hoping he would recognize his voice. The hazy green eyes opened, but there was no light in them. "I have a friend with me," he continued softly. White clad attendants sitting nearby stirred restlessly, ready to spring into action at a moment's notice, but there was no need. He looked from one face to the other, but there was no hint of recognition. Then, he lowered his head to his chest, and returned to the jungle once more.

"It wasn't only the Agent Orange. The alcohol and secret drug abuse on top of everything else fried his brain," said Dorcus, unable to hold back the tears. Yet again, play was temporarily suspended while they passed the tissue box. "Charlie was still playing his role as guardian. He stuck it out in the army, in spite of his early disdain for the military, and even became some sort of an officer—a warrant officer. That's it. I remember asking him if he wrote warrants, and he laughed and told me, no, it was a special rank." After a brief pause, she added, "So I could have had me an officer after all … and five children on top of that. Oy." This provided the bit of levity they needed after such a long night. The clock read 5:00 AM.

"We have time for at least one more hand. More coffee?" said Sardis, pouring another round.

XVII

Taletha's mother sat beside her bed, as she did on practically every morning, sewing and singing softly to her "baby." She waited for her brother to arrive to take over Taletha's care before leaving for church. Unbeknownst to her, though, he was less attentive lately. Taletha secretly made minute progress in her self-determined convalescence and gained strength and mobility in her arms and legs, not much, but sufficient enough to administer a well-aimed, well-timed kick in the groin during his last visit.

Her mother put down her sewing and quickly left the room when she heard her brother's car approaching, while Taletha, alert as usual, bristled. The roads were now covered with asphalt, making their community more accessible, and they moved into a completely rebuilt house on the spot where Taletha's grandmother's house once stood. The skeletal remains of the burnt-out shell stood for over a decade until a charitable builder, touched by Taletha's plight, mercifully built the new house in order to accommodate her physical challenges. Taletha noticed that, in her haste to leave, her mother left her sewing on the edge of the bed, along with a pair of scissors. Dragging herself to the edge, she reached out, and with a tremendous force of will, grasped the scissors. *If only I can gather enough strength,* she thought. *I can do it,* she resolved, propping them on the bed next to her, the pointed end facing upward. She gathered all her strength, closed her eyes, and then rolled her body over onto the scissors, hoping to pierce some vital organ. However, without adequate support, the scissors slid harmlessly beneath her. She heard familiar footsteps, saw the doorknob slowly turn, and wanted to cry. She was so tired and longed for peace; she longed to go "home," to be free of this world, and of being a burden on her family, but she didn't have enough time to try again.

"Uncle Day is back," he said, as he moved to the foot of the bed, partially removing the covers to expose the atrophied legs that did her bidding last time. "I know your tricks," he slurred, grabbing her legs and working them up and down in an attempt to tire out the muscles before letting them flop back down onto the bed. Little did he realize, however, that he was actually helping to strengthen them. "Now, try and move 'em," he teased. "Too tired, huh? Can't lift 'em now, can ya?" he taunted. She wished he'd get it over with, instead of teasing her like this. Having never regained her ability to speak, Taletha was unable to cry out, but her eyes spoke volumes as they followed his movements around the room. He'd been drinking before he arrived and reeked of cheap, foul-smelling corn liquor. He pulled a pint bottle from his back pocket. He couldn't tickle her any more, since the strokes left her numb, robbing her of much of her sensitivity.

Truth be told, he was afraid. Taletha had made far more progress than he ever imagined, and he was worried that soon she might be able to talk, to speak clearly enough to tell the family about their years and years of "adventures" together, as he liked to call them. They were adventures anywhere he managed to be alone with her, in the cornfield, in the back of his car, but most recently, right there in the house. He continued to pace the floor and drink from his bottle, while Taletha, her eyes ever alert and full of hate, followed his every move. He finished the liquor and let the bottle drop to the floor before staggering to the door and locking it, even though they were the only ones left in the house. Then, he stripped down to his shorts, as was his habit. For whatever reason, he never wanted her to see him completely naked. Perhaps he was hiding deficiencies or deformities of some kind. He approached the side of the bed. "You too smart now. Never likes smart women, but I gots to give you therapy one more time." Meanwhile, Taletha suddenly felt her previously numb fingers close firmly around the shaft of the scissors that were still hidden beneath her body and knew she was being granted miraculous powers for this one, last time.

Flinging back the covers, another habit, Uncle Day threw himself on top of her, at the same time wriggling out of his final piece of clothing. Suddenly he tensed. The pain was intense, like a boxer's jab to the heart. It consumed his entire body, making him think she had somehow managed to kick him again, just like the last time. "Not again," he seethed. "She couldn't possibly use them legs." He felt something warm and syrupy. Looking down, he was shocked to see the white sheets becoming crimson. He made a gurgling sound, and his astonished eyes told Taletha all she needed to know. The blade found its target. She managed to gather enough strength in her withered arms to push his body to one side, then closed her eyes and drifted peacefully off into a world where she no longer had any worries or cares. At long last, the nightmare ended.

XVIII

As the clock struck 6:00 AM, the players set their cards down on the table and looked at one another. The game was over, and a heavy pall hung over the room. Grace picked up the large bag she brought, while Dorcus quickly exited through the front door, racing to her car to grab the garment bag she left hanging inside.

Sardis opened the shutters, letting in the first of the morning sunlight. "You can change in the middle bedroom," she said, leading them quietly up the front stairs. She returned to the den and had just begun putting away the cards and card table, which would probably never be used again, when suddenly she heard a commotion. Racing up the back stairs, she found her disheveled mother standing in the connecting doorway ranting at her friends.

"Who are you? What are you doing here in my house?" she yelled. She held a lamp high above her head, and with wide-open eyes blazing, nostrils flaring, and matted hair framing her face, she was an imposing and threatening sight. Sardis wrapped a gentle arm around her frail and shrunken mother, trying to calm her. "Voices never lie," she kept repeating. "I knew I heard strangers all through the night." Finding strength that belied her frail appearance, her mother wrenched herself free and for a moment started back into the room where the two startled women were changing.

"It's all right, Mom," said Sardis firmly. Taking possession of the lamp, she half-carried a still-agitated Eartha back into her room before closing the connecting door.

"You! You brought them here! How many times do I have to tell you? No strangers in this house!" she yelled, pointing an accusatory finger at her daughter.

"They're not strangers, Mom. They're friends," Sardis whispered, cradling her mother, trying to calm her.

Friends who managed to find each other, over the miles and over time, when it mattered.

XIX

Neither Grace nor Sardis could ignore the sensational *Courier* headline:

"Comatose Woman Murders Abuser"

When Grace scanned the article and saw the name, scenes from the past immediately overtook her, haunting her and robbing her of sleep, much as they'd done during those horrible days immediately following the massacre. Hatta Mae noticed the change in her daughter but refused to intervene. She did not know why Grace was acting so strangely, so she didn't know what to do. For two days, Grace didn't even get out of bed, and her appearance became increasingly disheveled, while she neglected her house and three children who still shared her home. The kids were trained to call their older brother Willie Jr. to their aid when things went wrong. He and Grace shared a special bond, and over the years, he became both her protector and a father figure to his younger siblings. This time, however, he couldn't race home to help out. Driving from Parris Island when he was stationed in South Carolina wasn't a problem, but the marine corps needed him at Camp Pendleton in California, so he contacted Hatta Mae.

After twenty years, Grace was finally able to unload the guilt still weighing heavily on her. She cried and ranted and at last found the courage to let go of her anguish. Hatta Mae pushed her even further by encouraging her to find her bid whist friends and to confront her past. Since she left without so much as a good-bye, she was afraid of how they would react toward her, so she weighed the idea for a couple of days. At first, she balked because her rekindled memories continued to fester like an open wound, but Hatta Mae prevailed. At long last, a mother's wisdom finally brought closure to her daughter's angst.

Sardis reclaimed her maiden name after Clancy died, so it wasn't difficult for Grace to locate her through the telephone directory. When she picked up the phone, however, she stared at it for what seemed like an eternity before her trembling fingers began to dial the number. "I didn't know she survived all this time!" Grace wailed, the guilt still haunting her. "I just left her there. I should have stayed!" she sobbed, full of remorse. Sardis lent the sympathetic ear Grace needed, and she regretted not sharing her anguish with her old friend before, thinking about all the wasted years when their friendships could have thrived and flourished.

After Grace contacted Sardis, Sardis set about finding Dorcus, which was a little harder. Her dad retired from his old church, but her parents still resided in their well-maintained brick house. Their once-integrated neighborhood had re-segregated over the years as other black families sought to escape the city. They were happy to hear Sardis's voice and immediately put her in touch with Dorcus, living in Atlanta, not far from the three of her four brothers who made the city their home.

The call from Sardis with the news about Taletha was like a salve in a way. All three of them discovered they each harbored guilt for not tracking down their badly injured friend. It was at Dorcus's suggestion that they reunited to play the memorial game. Now it was time to say a final good-bye to their friend and bid whist fourth, whose life had effectively ended on the eighth day of February 1968, but who had taken twenty years to die.

XX

All was quiet in the house when Sardis returned from the funeral. Her mother became irate and inconsolable when she realized Sardis was going away with the strangers. She feared her daughter would never return. She berated them until they were down the stairs and out the front door. A mild sedative Sardis gave her had little effect. The stillness was promising. Maybe the pill finally worked, and her mother was sleeping. At least things were calm and peaceful now. Sardis heard faint sounds of the television in the den. She walked quietly toward the sound, praying that the medication hadn't worn off. The last thing she wanted to do was stir up her mother's wrath again. When she reached the doorway, she saw her mother sitting upright in her lounge chair with a faint smile pasted on her serene face. Sardis realized in an instant that her mother would never wake up again.

Sardis did not have to suffer through her grief alone. Grace and Dorcus came alongside and nursed her through the pain with another midnight game. Dorcus had extended her visit with her parents, and little could she have known it would be the last time she would see the beloved preacher, her father, alive. A heart attack took him suddenly, so within a week Sardis found herself in the role of comforter as she and Grace provided solace to a grieving Dorcus as she bade farewell to her beloved dad. There is an old wives tale that the Grim Reaper won't leave unless he has three souls to take with him. Hatta Mae became his last target. Three weeks of sorrow was soothed by bid whist. The game got them through it as they played and cried and reminisced, just as it had first bonded them through tests, boyfriends, and friendships.

Alas, with the final memorial game and service completed, Sardis returned to a quiet, now-empty house. *I hope that was the last funeral for a very long time,* she thought, as she cleaned the cards off the table. *Now what?* she wondered, sighing heavily. She picked up the card table and was putting it away when suddenly her face brightened. Picking up the telephone, she dialed an old, old number, praying silently that the voice on the other end would still be the same. "Sardini!" boomed Cyrus. He'd lost none of his famous, familiar flair. "Ready for the bright lights?"

"Oh, I can't act anymore. The real world has intervened and stolen my abilities, but I have an idea for a play. One that's long overdue."

"Talk to me," said Cyrus, interested. "And … I'll decide if the talent is gone."

"It begins on the night before a funeral for a dear old friend …"

THE END

About the Author

At Los Angeles Southwest College, I won a writing contest with the short story, "Miss Jessie's Tale." Other writing experiences include four years as a staff writer for *The Herald Dispatch* and the *Watts Star Review*. My latest work was in the January/February 2010 edition of *Good Old Days Magazine* titled, "Secrets." Vietnam era veteran and child of the untamed 60s generation.

Printed in the United States
by Baker & Taylor Publisher Services

Printed in the United States
by Baker & Taylor Publisher Services